MÁRCIO SOUZA was born in 1946 in Manaus, the Amazon region of Brazil. He began writing film criticism for newspapers when he was fourteen years old. He studied social sciences at the University of São Paulo. Souza is also a filmmaker and a dramatist. As a playwright, he works with Teatro Experimental do Sesc Amazonas, a group fighting for the preservation and defense of the Amazon. His first novel, *The Emperor of the Amazon*, was an extraordinary bestseller in Brazil, and is available from Avon Books.

THE EMPEROR OF THE AMAZON

"A comic delight and a set of improbable, half-true adventures, recounted with skill and economy. It is also brilliantly translated."

The New Yorker

"*The Emperor of the Amazon* is an intriguing fantasy of a frontier which, unlike our own, has yet to recede into myth... Márcio Souza deserves our applause."

The New York Times
Book Review

"The novel is a delight...a remarkable debut."

The New York Times

Other Avon Books by
Márcio Souza

THE EMPEROR OF THE AMAZON

MAD MARIA

MÁRCIO SOUZA

Translated by
Thomas Colchie

A BARD BOOK/PUBLISHED BY AVON BOOKS

Published in Brazil by Editora Marco Zero Ltda.

AVON BOOKS
A division of
The Hearst Corporation
1790 Broadway
New York, New York 10019

Cover illustration by Richard Bober

First Bard Printing, October 1985

Printed in the U.S.A.

OPM 10 9 8 7 6 5 4 3 2 1

For Jamacy
and América,
my parents.

Almost everything in this book could have happened the way it's told. Insofar as it details the building of the railroad, I have tried to be meticulous —likewise with the politics of the powers that be. And wherever the reader judges something to be familiar, he is probably not mistaken. Capitalism has seldom been ashamed to repeat itself:

"He may be a son of a bitch, but he's *our* son of a bitch!" Don't worry, though, it's only a novel. All that's required is that you pay some attention. . . .

BOOK I

Occident Express

1

Finnegan had no idea that scorpions would appear with the onset of summer. As a matter of fact, what in blazes did summer mean in a place like this anyway?

As far as Finnegan could gather, summer was when the rains came with a vengeance and the damnable scorpions suddenly turned up out of nowhere: on the floor of the hut, in the sheets and blankets of the field beds, or in whatever shoes or boots you were likely to put on. With claws and tails raised defiantly, they stood potently immobile like tiny mechanical excavators.

This would be the first summer Finnegan was to spend here and he quickly taught himself to make war on scorpions. Why had no one even bothered to warn him? But he could hardly complain about that, when a list of horrors too long to be taken seriously by any man had already been served up to him as introduction to the place.

Now Finnegan had always assumed that life's horrors had to be kept more or less palatable, in order to be taken at all seriously. In this part of the world, however, a man's imagination was expected to contemplate such a vast array of threats and dangers, tangible or otherwise, that Finnegan had first attempted to see in this some unaccountable mystery, camouflaged behind a subtle wall of exaggeration. Yet two weeks in the jungle—possibly one—were enough to prove to anyone's satisfaction that there were no mysteries and that the list, if anything, was incomplete.

You see, the real problem with our Finnegan was this sense of decorum that he had cultivated with respect to horrors and that, though proper for a young physician, could not be stretched to encompass the dimensions of savagery to which he was now a witness. What until then had been defined by Finnegan as horrendous, now and in such a place seemed little more than minor, pangless, almost petty calamity. Here, the persistence of horror upon horror proved endless, like the procession of

3

deadly scorpions. The tragedies exploded upon him and in those first few days acquired an almost inscrutable physiognomy. The good boy that in effect he was grew bewildered by the capacity of men to endure the vilest circumstances—and what was worse, they deliberately sought out such extremes, then pretended to themselves, looked the other way, only to die in turn amid screams of agony or remain doggedly sullen and indifferent in the face of another's misfortune.

Life's way, perhaps.

Finnegan did not know if someday he might find himself capable of such willful and sullen indifference, fruit of the very insolence of squalor, so different from the spirit of adventure that he had judged to be the principal motive of all those who would come to such a place. And the irony was that the said misfortunes were not even tragic: they were happenstance, accidents of the trade, contingencies locked into a web of the prosaic.

That particular morning Finnegan had already squashed a number of scorpions. Physically speaking, he felt no untoward complaints as far as could be medically ascertained. He had simply gotten out of bed and proceeded to shake his boots out vigorously before pulling them on—from which there inevitably fell one or two of those repellent visitors. The mashed carcasses still dotted the wooden floor of the hut but would soon be carted off by battalions of small, busy red ants playing their own part in the interminable chain of natural calamities that gravitated around the direst one of all: the calamity of man. To be honest Finnegan was still too uncertain to hazard any definitive judgment of it all. He was a clever young fellow but somewhat lacking in worldly experience. His thinking was still rudimentary, and he had yet to decide if in fact he had not been bamboozled into accepting employment in such an ungodly place.

The young physician peered out of the hut. The panes in the only window were so filthy that there was no possibility of glimpsing the to and fro of workers who—barely was the sun up—had already set noisily about their furious exertions. The panes nevertheless allowed the strong light to penetrate the interior of the hut. The heat had yet to install itself, today. Every morning the same heat was obliged to overpower the humidity that wholly permeated everything and that sometimes in the early morning hours pierced the very marrow, hammering the joints with the remorseless precision of a professional boxer as he pounds away at his artless contender. Despite the knowledge that the heat would ultimately prevail, Finnegan was totally covered. He looked to be completely impervious to the aura of sickly sauna that pervaded his daily routine—one that habitually ran from eleven in the morning to three in the afternoon. He wore his complete uniform, then, because it was his personal rule to do so. At least his professional competency lay beyond the reach of such horrors, he told himself, for this was the only weapon he had managed to muster thus far, to counter the now extinct "unaccountable mysteries."

He peered back into the interior of the hut. The light left no recess of his surroundings in shadow; it was extraordinary, that light. His assistants had already gone out to make their rounds along the line of construction. The hut itself was nearly empty, though it would not, he knew, remain so for very long. Soon others would join the solitary patient, one of the Negroes from Barbados, who lay altogether enfeebled, his respiration failing, having agonized with fever since the previous afternoon.

The hut, as you may already have surmised, served as infirmary for the entire construction gang working to bridge the Rio Abunã. Finnegan saw the Negro raise an arm briefly and went over to him. The fellow's eyes were wide open, but no trace of light was reflected there. Eventually he murmured something to which Finnegan nodded, as if he had comprehended the agony the man was experiencing. Poor moribund bastard with his coarse fingers clamped to the physician's sleeve; but Finnegan understood at once and leaned his head closer to the Negro's whispering. After all, what did it cost to listen to what this Barbadian needed to say. In any case, his delirium seemed to have subsided once the fever had ebbed at least momentarily during the night.

"Done frig myself royal dis time, dat so, doc?" the man asked.

Finnegan took hold of the fellow's wrist, mentally noting the fever's progress, although the gesture may have also connoted a degree of sympathy. He remained silent, in any case, and simply observed the Negro's struggle to reformulate his question.

5

"Must be I gone die now, right, doc?" he pleaded, only to conclude to himself, "goddom right," seeing that he would get no words out of the physician. "But you already fallin' down de same hole, doc," the dying man managed to mutter as he felt his whole body stabbing with chills. "You already fallen down de same Judas hole. . . ."

As if to the accompaniment of Beethoven's variations on "Ein Mädchen oder Weibchen," from Mozart's *The Magic Flute,* a rush of swirling waters swept over the bristling rocks atop the principal cataract of the Ribeirão Rapids. The sun was dazzlingly strong and millions of drops of vapor composed the iridescence of a delicate rainbow. A huge raft, secured by heavy ropes, was being towed patiently against the rapids as it rocked to the cacophonies of a raging current. Lashed to its timbers, a splendid black grand piano gleamed in the sunlight.

The men straining at the ropes, almost all of them Indians, steadfastly resisted the force of the rapids but with increasing desperation. For what did human strength avail compared to the vertiginous power of those waters? Yet Alonso Campero, the only white man among them, continued gesticulating and shouting, and even leaped onto some of the flatter rocks in a dangerous attempt to rally the others.

In a similarly agitated state, Alonso's wife Consuelo trailed after him alongshore, anxiously watching her husband scramble from one slab of rock to another. If she did not directly rail at the men, it was only because her mind was so intent upon its prayer—to all the saints imaginable, and with so many promises that, should the piano miraculously survive, she must surely spend the remainder of her days fulfilling her vows. In fact, the intensity of her fervor in entreating heaven was bested only by that passion with which she eyed the instrument in question.

The Indians were doing their utmost, but Consuelo saw all too clearly that much more was required: the violence of those waters surpassed the limits of any resistance and demanded absolute miracles to be conquered. So Consuelo Campero prayed unceasingly, stumbling about after her husband; her heart nearly breaking with each new complication; even an occasional blasphemy exploding from her lips, amid the more pious entreaties, whenever one of the men faltered and nearly lost everything.

That Alonso Campero was so clearly out of his element could only add to the burden of his present ordeal. Yet his principal anxiety did not stem from the fact of his having poured most of his savings into the purchase of the piano. After all, he still had his little shop in Sucre, where he sold band instruments, musical scores, and a monumental supply of trivial accessories geared to the countless variety of strummed instruments scattered throughout the city. No, if he was nervous it was because this was already the fourth grand piano that he had imported from Germany—to satisfy a dream of Consuelo's—and it must not be allowed to join the other three, somewhere at the bottom of one or another of the nineteen tributary rapids of the Rio Madeira.

His investment had been terribly steep, representing years of thriftful economizing. Yet it would have been far worse for him to have to witness ever again the morbid frustration of his lovely wife, her beauty despoiled by that streak of childishness that obsessively lacerated her spirit with its broken dreams. And as the only son of a Spanish family whose blood flowed back generations, he knew the price of failed expectation.

Alonso Campero was imposingly tall, as none but a Spaniard can be: the fine head of dark hair, the oval face of handsome proportions, the finely chiseled jaw and powerful lips to which a heavy mustache lent just the right touch of delicate sensuality. His robust physique—the broad chest, the powerful arms and legs—were moderated by his height, which only enhanced the note of sensuality, while his watery blue eyes seemed to guarantee him the perfect romantic demeanor that would ever absolve him in his dealings with the fairer sex in search of musical scores. In fact, no woman seemed able to resist a suggestion, however laconic, that sprang from his lips. He himself was quite proud of his abilities in this regard, though he was completely innocent of the powers of his virile magnetism, believing rather that his mastery of the sale of sheet music was due entirely to his knowledge of the subject.

Consuelo, on the other hand, understood only too well the captivating potency of her husband's congeniality. Had not she herself fallen victim to its sway? In the beginning, of course, she never even suspected what that merely amiable young man was fully capable of, any more than she was aware of how much more demonstrably seductive she grew with him each time she entered the shop to look for another piece of sheet music, the latest song in vogue, or an additional book of piano exercises.

Ever since his parents had passed away, Alonso had been running the shop by himself, and he seemed content with the simple tranquillity of his job, a specialization that curiously brought him into contact with two divergent worlds. For the cultured ladies and damsels of Sucre society, the Casa Santa Cecilia represented a very special affirmation of their own spiritual endowments, since there they could gather the printed music of Chopin, Mozart, and Beethoven. It was those and other masters who brought them particular pleasure on these rare evenings, otherwise generally so tedious, when a woman might finally manifest some talent other than simply culinary and thereby play a fleeting part in the cultural life of the city normally reserved to men. This, then, was the world Alonso showered with the romanticism of his demeanor, as each shapely client, subject to his gaze, would exit from the shop bearing armfuls of sheet music in exchange for equally endearing sums of money.

Yet there was another world to that same Sucre—of guitarists and mandolin players, of the musical bands from the interior, a more open-minded crowd of fun-loving, boisterous fellows who only came to the shop at the close of business hours. True, they purchased very little—scores for marches, strings for their instruments, reeds, turning forks—trifles which financially speaking seemed hardly worth the effort. Yet Alonso valued such sales for the link they provided him to that other demimonde: of bohemians, cabarets, bandstands, and bars. To such a world, however, Alonso certainly offered very little and prided himself rather on what he received: the opportunity to ask questions, a chance to satisfy his curiosity—the curiosity of a somewhat solitary lad who nevertheless harbored his own set of dreams, who fancied an occasional night on the town in the company of easy women.

There was no such ambience here, however, and Alonso Campero felt terribly uneasy: bellowing out his orders, spurring on his Indians, riveting his every nerve to the black grand piano.

* * *

8

Always, what came into his head was that sensation of feeling dislocated in time. It must have been like this, back somewhere in the Devonian period. Or, who could say, maybe the Cambrian . . . Collier felt locked away in the prehistory of the world.

The mist hung over everything. Nothing could be gauged with precision. Even the morning chill lost its edge in the seamless humidity. A vast, metallic, sweated hulk (its dark carapace camouflaged amid the greenish, vegetal surroundings) crept forward slowly, wheezing like some dinosaur. Stegosaurus? Brontosaurus? There were sudden splashes of chrome, as the mist spread forth in rhythmic intervals. The whole effect was like some monstrous, antediluvian exhalation puffing its breath into the frozen air, though in point of fact the heat was infernal. Insects hummed relentlessly and there was a grating sound, like metal against metal. The mist was scalding hot.

Collier heard that powerful wheeze, not unlike the aspirate hiss of a snake. He was not entirely comfortable with such mist, but the sudden ophidian sound seemed to reassure him. Still, mist and more mist pervaded everything, adding to and mingling with the steamed breath of the vast hulk slowly emerging, hardly moving at all, dragging along its monstrous weight with indolence and caution. Also concealed by the brume were the fevered commotions of the lesser forms of primordial life. Bloody animals, Collier thought to himself, always mucking about this time of morning, though you could never quite pinpoint where they were. Mist and steam, day after day, combined to transform the entire landscape into obsessive illustrations of the same prehistoric setting. So many vague shapes moving about among bizarrely cut leaves; and that one, too, *she* was there, in the mist, enveloped by it. Occasionally one of those shadowy figures would be startled by the points of yellow light that, like lazy fireflies, sifted aimlessly through the foliage.

The mist was heaviest nearer to the ground. The great, sweated hulk advanced laboriously, panting its vapors, squealing. This was somewhere along the Rio Abunã, on no particular morning, in the summer of 1911. In the Cambrian period it must have been so.

Stephan Collier, construction engineer, was about to face the worst moments of what technically would have appeared

9

to be a simple undertaking—were it not for thirty miles of marsh and swamps. Or the unthinkable working conditions his men were forced to endure. In fact, most of them would not survive, because the task was too difficult, because you could not make men adapt to so hostile a terrain. Collier would have liked to have been somewhere far, far away from it all, for he had no particular inclination to risk himself in this way. He knew he was not immune to every disease around, and whoever fell sick in the Abunã was a dead man. Working conditions were hardly the bloody forte of this insane project!

Collier could make out a gang of nine Barbadians carrying a rail through the swamp. The day was beginning to grow light. Soon the sun would burn its way across a cloudless sky.

The Barbadians had already begun to sweat heavily, their black muscles gleaming as they worked, wading through waters up to their knees. Collier had all together a hundred and fifty men there, under his direct orders. The job was to cut a railway through the marshy terrain of the Rio Abunã: seemingly not an impossible operation. After all, hadn't six Barbadians just lugged a rail over to where still others were hard at work opening trenches with picks and spades?

Our Collier was thirsty and his arms were lumped with swellings. Each time he would run his hand over his forearm, it felt as though he were touching the thick hide of a Saurian reptile. Actually, both arms had been savaged by mosquitoes, because Collier could not be bothered wearing a long-sleeved shirt. Unfortunately, work had taken him some twenty meters into virgin jungle, where he was soon set upon and sucked at by swarms of insects. His left elbow had quickly turned into a ripe cherry, while the right one looked more like a spongy, bloodied apple.

The heat by now was burning into the backs of the Barbadian workers, although they at least had the sense to protect themselves by dressing in buttoned-up shirts and long trousers. Still, it did seem an odd means of protection for laboring in such heat: it was already thirty-two degrees centigrade. The metallic luster of the tracks was nearly blinding in the sunlight.

Collier felt thirst and a stabbing pain in his skull. His great fear at the moment was of getting sick in the Abunã, though no one else there had any notion he might be afraid. No, Collier was too dry, too closemouthed a fellow, forever caustic in mood and manner. For one thing, he had to keep one hundred fifty furious workers in line—among them forty German trouble-makers, twenty Spanish cretins, another forty Barbadian idiots, thirty imbecilic Chinamen, not to mention the Portuguese, the Italians, and a number of other exotic numbskulls! Even a few Brazilians (one just as stupid as the next)! The most advanced professionally, though in the minority, were the handful of North Americans. The ones running the bloody show were certainly all North American, as was the project itself. Collier was the only Englishman, a rather old, rather obstinate Englishman. He was their construction engineer, but everyone working with him had come from the States, including the young physician, the locomotive man and his stoker, the mechanics, topographers, medics, and cooks. And Collier was responsible for them all—but only insofar as they were useful to the operation itself. Beyond that, it was up to every man to see to his own neck. Meanwhile, their construction engineer was thirsty and much afraid of getting sick, quite preoccupied with his own neck.

He watched as coolies cut and cleared a path in the forest, forging their way through the wall of jungle. Not far behind them were the Germans, digging up the larger tree trunks and leveling out the terrain. Gangs of Barbadians worked stolidly but meticulously at laying tracks along the newly graded embankment while groups of Spaniards—garnered from the repressive colonial system in Cuba—patrolled the camp as security guards, sometimes doubling as overseers. He watched them all, each man at his specific task, on work shifts of eleven hours per day with one break for lunch. And the image of every man was the same, regardless of his job or nationality. All of them were as ragged, exhausted, skeletal, and decrepit looking as any prisoners of a forced labor camp.

A Barbadian worker passed directly in front of Collier. He was a tall, lean fellow, staring up at the sky and wiping the sweat that literally bathed his black skin. The Barbadians were generally a healthy-looking lot, except for this one, who displayed a purulent mask for a face. Indeed, both his lips and part of one cheek were covered with a fungus that horribly maimed his features. Still, he gave a respectful nod to Collier. They had known one another a good many years, he and Collier. That Barbadian was a bloody good worker! And he har-

bored a deep respect—or who knows? a profoundly respectful
indifference—for everything around him, including for the
Englishman Collier. The suppurating mycosis grew more and
more inflamed as the heat intensified throughout the day, eventually provoking a truly maddening irritation. Which is why
the Barbadian was now scratching dementedly at his cheek.

It was not a pleasant sight to watch a man sweat and bleed
himself to death, scratching his face uncontrollably with the
blade of a knife or the thorn of a tree. But nothing made for
a pretty sight at that work camp, there on the banks of the Rio
Abunã—where Stephan Collier, construction engineer, had
somehow managed to plant himself.

The locomotive advanced slowly, spewing smoke. She was
a beautiful thing, like some fierce creature out of the Jurassic
period. And all around her on the edge of the jungle giant
Cretaceous trees, Silurian insects, Oligocene butterflies, and
Pliocene ants feverishly converged. Life teemed, promiscu-
ously so, while human beings went mad in that Cenozoic inferno.

Like the ants that marched back and forth along the leaves
and branches of the tree he had climbed, he was present but
he was also invisible. The *civilized* seemed totally unmindful
of his being there. He felt alone, confused, and wildly hungry.
The terrifying thing was the hunger: it clawed at him, ravenously. He had found little chance for sleep; yet he chose not
to leave the vicinity of the *civilized*. He was always there,
invisible. He could understand nothing of what it was they
were so desperate to accomplish. The fact was, no matter how
near he might be to them, there was no place for him to enter
their world. Yet, they could overrun the lands which—since
the time of the ancient customs, about which elders would
speak with such emotion—had forever belonged to his people.

Elders were all dead. Women had gone off to Santo Antônio,
where many also died; and those who survived now killed their
kurumi, as soon as they bore them into the world. What was
left of men among them, even the strongest, had likewise
fallen. So many had perished in the final confrontations with
the *civilized*—this, while he was still *kurumi*. Not that they
had in any way expected to halt the onslaught of the *civilized*.
No, they knew that the *civilized* were a fierce invader, worse

12

even than those Indians who, painted with fish ink, periodically ventured down the great river to attack, rob, and burn their villages.

Elders had once tried to speak with the *civilized*. They had gone up to them weaponless, with *kurumi* in their arms. But the *civilized* would not be spoken to, and they aimed their rifles. Not a single elder was spared; only *kurumi,* left crying there, who afterward ran to the villages and told of what had happened.

All of this had already taken place, long ago. Had he not eventually watched his own family die of the sorcery practiced by the *civilized*? Friends, brothers and sisters, mother, father, uncles and aunts: had they not agonized in fever while uncountable sores encrusted their bodies, oozing a foul stench?

Now he was alone. And there was no need to shun the vicinity of the *civilized*. He was invisible, like the ants.

The window of the confectioner's shop, with its opulent variety of sweets and candies, always seduced him. Day after day, whenever he came to Rio de Janeiro, before going up to his office he would quickly cross Avenida Central, proceed down Rua 7 de Setembro, hugging a briefcase filled with documents under his arm (for protection), then station himself for a few moments in front of the window at Colombo's Confectionery.

It was not the sweets that he relished particularly, but rather the *sensation* of coveting them, out of reach, beyond the glass of the display window. It was a habit of long standing which must have originated (or so he thought) in the poverty of his childhood, when the only sentiment permitted him was envy. A bit of a fatuous explanation, but one that he kept to himself like so many other intimate associations he had practiced not to reveal, the effect of which was to earn him his reputation for being a serious, objective man. Yet he put no stock in his own objectivity—he was too serious a man for that. He had learned that all objectivity was nothing more than God's way of manifesting Himself, through his particular mind, guiding his sentiments, his understanding, and directing his faculties to decide for the best. The fact of his continuing to placate a childhood habit—fixing his eyes greedily on that window of sweets—was most probably another of God's designs, but one

13

that he himself had not managed to entirely decipher, though it must have had its utility.

By that particular morning of 1911, captivated though he may have been with Colombo's Confectionery, Percival Farquhar was also one of the most powerful men in Brazil. His outward appearance could hardly be said to indicate his true importance. Indeed, there was little that was exceptional about him: short but stocky, straight chestnut hair, slightly bald, with a roundish face and dark eyes. The arm that determinedly guarded the folio of documents was moderately well developed, and its hairy forearm strained at the cuff of the white shirt he wore, cuff-linked by twin Peruvian gold coins. His clothes, generally well tailored, never exceeded the limits of good taste. His suits were dark. Our Percival was seldom seen out of his jacket or without one of his fine, silk ties.

So much for his appearance, however, because once he was heard to speak it was obvious his voice carried the unflinching self-assuredness of a scoundrel, the inexorability of the confidence man able to discourage any thought of retaliation in the minds of his interlocutors. Still, whenever he did gather his associates together, matters were generally conducted with the utmost discretion—hence his reputation as an "objective" man.

Beyond the circle of his increasingly influential organization, among ministers of state and politicians, he seemed to epitomize the energetic North American businessman. He seldom smiled, never promised anything, and rigorously discharged his contractual obligations. In this regard, he was equally hated and respected—something he understood perfectly well, appreciating as he did how in a country like Brazil (steeped in vice and not entirely democratic), objectivity, or what have you, was small virtue in the face of dissimulation. And the Brazilian variety of dissimulation seemed to have much in common with that infantile yearning, almost innocent voluptuousness, that he inevitably experienced when staring at the candies and comfits encased in their glass.

14

2

First there were shouts, then shots. Richard Finnegan left the dying man's side to go out and have a look, but not before completing his outfit by donning a most peculiar hat with a roundish brim to which was sewn a delicate netting that draped to his waist. The medics, two clumsy fellows recruited from the army following their discharge from active service, were just walking in.

"Another row?" the doctor tried to ask matter-of-factly yet was unable to mask his despondency.

"One hell of a fight between them Negroes and the Germans," the one volunteered as he helped the other to pull out several stretchers from the emergency locker. "Coming with us, Dr. Finnegan?"

"Any fatalities?"

"The usual."

They stepped out into the intolerable sunlight. The English engineer Collier, spattered with mud but striding along doggedly as usual, suddenly found himself confronted by the spectacle of the doctor and his aids. The engineer had yet to decide if he could actually stomach this Irish fool with his confounded ideas about playing doctor. There they were in their idiot hats, wrapped in mosquito netting, gloved and high-booted, Finnegan and his medics—looking like futuristic nuns. Collier smiled at the thought as he peered at the three of them.

The doctor returned the smile, running a quick clinical eye over the engineer's arms, noting the inflamed elbows. Those insect bites were already edematous and could become seriously infected without proper care, Finnegan surmised to himself but did not wish to draw attention to the fact.

"I see you're not wearing your protective clothing, Mr. Collier."

"Dr. Finnegan!" Collier's cry of greeting seemed almost sympathetic but the effect was quickly undermined by a sub-

15

sequent outburst of impatience. "Don't bother wasting your bedside manners on me...."

Collier never could decide whether to get into a fury or simply to resort to irony whenever he came across the doctor and his crew, dressed in those ridiculous trappings. Finnegan was just as perplexed on such occasions, for he still aspired to achieve a modicum of respect on the part of the engineer, at least for medically established rules of procedure.

"But Dr. Lovelace..." Finnegan began, by attempting to invoke a higher authority.

"You and your Lovelace can got to blazes," the engineer replied vituperatively. "Your Dr. Lovelace has managed to make my life positively hellish for the past ten years. At my heels every step of the way, he'd come a million miles if necessary, just for the pleasure of frying my balls. Even here, in the middle of the jungle, not a moment's peace from his pills or his swinish pronouncements!" Collier relented, however, seeing how disconcerted the doctor had become and, more importantly, not wanting to demoralize the medical staff in front of the work crew. "Sorry, Dr. Finnegan, but these filthy brawls among the men, the daily slaughter seems to be finally getting to me, I'm afraid. Every day it appears I have to break up another squabble which invariably ends in fatalities. It's not proper work for an engineer, I can tell you, it's work for a bloody idiot. These witless dunderheads kill each other over the most ridiculous trifles you could imagine." Then noticing that Finnegan was beginning to regain his composure, Collier added, "Besides which, your Lovelace hasn't got the faintest notion of what he's about..."

"I don't understand," said Finnegan, now doubly disconcerted.

"Never mind!" Collier realized that the medics were standing there, laden down with stretchers and with wire baskets full of dark, bulbous bottles that looked more like cases of beer than quinine pills.

"Mr. Collier, sir, I believe it's time to stop work and administer some of this quinine," the doctor ventured timidly.

"What? We've already lost too much time, not to mention the lives of five workers."

"Yes, I was told. I'll get the autopsies under way imme-

16

diately. I understand there are bullet wounds, that there is evidence of lesions...."

"I've had *enough* for one day, Dr. Finnegan. In any case, work is not to be interrupted. We have two hours to make up before the end of the day."

"But, sir, my orders are to dispense the quinine just before lunch. In fact, while I have you here, you should be taking your own as well; right, sir?"

"I'm not about to have another filthy pill, thank you. Makes me absolutely nauseous."

"Nauseous, you say?"

"You can stuff that clinical look of yours, doctor. And you had better not interrupt things before lunch with that rotten medicinal brew of yours. Instead, I'd try to come up with some antidote to this violence, if I were you...."

"The problem, sir," one of the medics interrupted, "is that somebody's going around stealing things, and the Germans suspect them Negroes."

"They're all alike, these Germans. Out of work and half-starved when the company found them. At Hamburg, the docks were crawling with them. The Barbadians are a different class. They know what they're about, at least when they're on the job. Professionals, that's what they are, and I know what I'm talking about. Worked with them in the canal zone, back in Panama."

"So Dr. Lovelace told me. You spent quite a bit of time working on the canal." Finnegan smiled. "He told me a lot about you and spoke very fondly of you. He said I'd be working with a very competent man."

"And a stubborn one, no doubt."

"Stubborn? I don't think that was exactly what he said," Finnegan replied, still smiling.

"Smile all you like, the point is I happen to be the engineer whose job it is to construct a railroad across thirty miles of the Abunã. Well, I better be bloody stubborn if I expect to do a competent job of it."

"I think it's taken a certain stubbornness and know-how to bring our civilization this far along," Finnegan attempted with rather questionable conviction.

"Our civilization, is it! I haven't heard that kind of drivel since ... our *civilization,* is it now? It would have to be some wet nurse of a doctor come down here to remind me of its existence. Here only a few weeks and already it's *civilization* we have to remember."

"They'll be blowing the lunch whistle in another couple of minutes, sir," Finnegan had the prudence to suggest, after consulting his watch to change the subject.

Collier pulled out his own watch and saw the doctor was right. "Damn! There goes another morning and we haven't laid a bloody millimeter," he concluded with irritation but allowed sheer exhaustion to outweigh his temper. "Well, give me your quinine pill but don't interrupt things now. Wait till the men quit for their lunch. Oh, and don't forget to have the guards on hand."

One of the medics shook a pill out of one of his bottles and placed it dutifully in Collier's hand. The other filled a tin cup with water and handed it to the engineer. He tossed the pill onto his tongue and swallowed it with a mouthful.

"These pills are enough to make a fellow queasy as a pregnant nun."

Finnegan snorted and walked off to find a bit of shelter under the shade of a tall palm. The medics trailed after him. They would wait there for lunch, when they could distribute the doses of quinine and see to the removal of the corpses. Meanwhile, Collier had turned his back on them and headed off in the direction of the site under excavation by the Germans. After only a few steps, however, feeling that familiar burning sensation at the back of his throat that signaled the onset of nausea, he suddenly whirled about in his tracks and shouted to the doctor:

"Take a look at me, lad! Do I have the face of an engineer? Is there anything left in me that even hints that I once might have been an engineer? Or that I was born and raised in London and am a subject of His Majesty King George V. Take a good look and *you tell me* if I have the least trace of civilization left in me after only one year in this filthy oven! I've become a sort of raving butcher, I've become an absolute heathen. . . . We'll all be barbarians sooner or later in this stinking hell, and I've had it up to *here* with Lovelace and his pills!"

A shrill whistle cut through his last words, making them inaudible. It was time to break for lunch. Finnegan picked up one of the wire baskets filled with quinine bottles and, ignoring

18

the engineer's outburst, walked over to where the workers were slowly gathering in line for their daily meal. He was hardly inclined to take Collier's outburst seriously and was even content to muster a plausible explanation for the annoyance he seemed to provoke in the old engineer. Yes, our Finnegan suspected that Mr. Collier, like most veterans in any profession, detested newcomers. Perhaps he was right. Perhaps Collier was annoyed by that apparent purity, fruit of the total ignorance of most novitiates.

Consuelo was a young woman possessed of a sweet disposition, but certainly not as infantile as her husband liked to imagine. What he was accustomed to regard as her childishness—and for Alonso, the term was not pejorative—had more to do with her innate capacity for perseverence, an intelligence that could cling to its dreams with such equanimity that there was no other choice but to help her to realize them. The case of the piano was exemplary. Consuelo's great dream had always been to possess in her own home a German grand piano—for her the most perfect of instruments in existence. Yet it was not something she dreamed of out of mere childishness. It was rather the effect of wanting to have the very best of something, which is no sin in this world. Although he could not possibly fathom the depth of his wife's desire, Alonso was nonetheless confident of its fundamental importance to her—possession of a fine grand piano—and since he cherished in his wife that very equanimity of her perseverance, and since it was her dream of owning a German piano that had caused them to meet in the first place, Alonso was determined to spare nothing to accomplish her desire. And Consuelo was grateful to her husband for such affection, for the determination he brought to bear upon this her highest aspiration.

She was extremely beautiful, even as a young girl, and now she had completely blossomed, blossomed in his very presence—he had watched her turn into a woman, and he felt proud now of having accompanied so intimately the day-to-day budding of her femininity with which she already seemed quite wholly imbued. Consuelo possessed the oval, slightly aquiline face of a true Spanish *dueña:* her eyes almondlike, and the curve of her brows following the same sinuous outlines so expressive of the urge for life and happiness that those eyes communicated. Her skin was not white, not milk white, but rather of a creamy texture, more congenial to the roundedness of her well-proportioned figure, with its long-legged suppleness crowned by the sudden waist that narrowed gracefully above the curve of her hips. Her mouth was almost scarlet, and her lips, not overly full, offered a tenderness whenever she spoke that never displayed gratuitous intensity. Consuelo was neither weak nor timid for the standards of decorum then operative in Sucre. Nor was she one of those modern, feminist inventions complete with masculinized habits, so common among the girls of richer families, who ran off to Europe and returned smoking cigarettes and mouthing crudities.

At the moment, however, Consuelo was deep in prayer as Alonso supervised the Indians, who were grappling with the ropes that stretched out to the raft while carefully avoiding any risk to themselves. Alonso had tried, in fact, to contract the very best among them, back in Santo Antônio; and he was spending a tidy sum of money with the promise of additional bonuses, depending upon the condition of the piano once it had made it through the rapids to the tiny settlement of Guajará-Mirim. Yet he had small confidence in any of those Indians; he found them all loutish in the extreme. They were strong enough, but they seemed to be summoning very little of that strength they clearly possessed in those arms now hard at the ropes. And he knew that if something should end up going awry, those savages would do little beyond what they were already required—simply tugging at some ropes.

The raft, at this point, was at the base of the most dangerous declivity of the rapids, tilting tremulously to the right as the waters buffeted it like some quixotic dike set in their path and throwing the men off balance as they expended the last of their strength to resist the watery assault. Noticing that one of the ropes was about to slip from the hands of several of the Indians, Alonso rushed to join them. Consuelo was not pleased to see Alonso go so far as to throw himself among Indians, but at such a moment, with the raft on the verge of being overswept by the waters, she stoically sanctioned her husband's resolve and redoubled her own vows: she would order mass to be celebrated every single Friday for the next year in the most beautiful church of the city, the Basílica Metropolitana.

* * *

20

The Germans had been digging a trench, their bodies sunk in water up to the waist. No one was saying a word and they appeared to be driven by a frenzy to finish the job as swiftly as humanly possible. A desperate zeal, Collier thought to himself. There were forty of them furiously demolishing a bank of yellow clay, widening the muddy channel along which clusters of diaphanous hyacinths hugged the ground in profusion. Collier observed the Germans as they strained impatiently at their task but he felt no sympathy for them. He knew that they composed potentially the most dangerous group, given the restiveness of so many months of unemployment prior to their arrival.

Collier felt moribund in the heat. The sweat had already soaked through his clothes in roundish stains under the armpits, at the small of his back, and between his legs. He watched as if from a stupor while a gang of Barbadians transported another rail to the vicinity of the Germans. The sweat was dripping from his neck, and his elbows were on fire with itching. He was wholly miserable in his wet clothes. From time to time he would tug at the seat of his pants like a child at his soiled diapers. And the thought came to him of what a shitting mess it was to have to stand there with wet pants and burning elbows. He swore at the sweat pouring steadily down one leg, trickling into his boot, and turning his sock into a hot, soggy waste. Still, he could not complain. He had better meals than the rest of them—he was one of the only men with a little color left in his cheeks—and, despite his age, he was probably one of the few chaps who could still boast of nocturnal ejaculations, because he had adamantly refused to eat any of the foods to which saltpeter was regularly added. At least he could cultivate a few sordid dreams, far away from that abominable work camp they were cooped up in.

The German workers had paused in their digging to look up at the Barbadians carrying the rail. The Germans had come to manifest a particularly hostile regard for these Negroes. Inexplicably, they had fixed all their fury upon the Barbadians, although they might just as easily have done it to the Chinese, the Spaniards, or any other nationality or race present on the line of construction. But for some reason they never paid the least attention to the Chinese or the Spaniards; or to anyone else for that matter, except the Barbadians, toward whom they evidenced an almost maniacal hatred. Perhaps the Germans had chosen this obsession as a kind of last resort with which to draw together the remnants of whatever might be left of an identity. Still, Collier saw no evil in such hatred. The Germans could do whatever the hell they bloody well pleased, so long as it did not interfere with the momentum of the construction.

From the Barbadians there came only a hostile indifference, as they clung to their own gregarious but private nature, defensively perhaps, alongside the impossibility of comprehending this hatred from the Germans. Yet, though they tried not to be drawn in by the insults and provocations, the Germans were crude and insistent, with comments that invariably dealt in abdominal indecencies.

One German worker, completely fouled with the mud into which he was mired to the waist, was boasting to his compatriots that as soon as he could return to the fatherland he would have a most lucrative enterprise to exploit. His nearest companion could not imagine anything other than a house of ill-repute filled with accommodating females. The idea of profit was extremely popular in the camp, much more than any dream of compassionate females since, after all, they thought, the one could always buy the other.

Collier was sick of sweating and had decided by now to have a break in the comparatively more amenable climate of his airless but shadowy tent. As a result, he missed the further remark by the befouled German to his compatriot, to the effect that, yes, he would open a bordello, but full of professional Negresses, the most practiced of which might be recruited from among the mothers of the Barbadians. Collier, in any case, would have had no idea what they were saying because it was all in German, and he himself spoke no German. Once he was out of earshot, however, the conversation switched to a broken English meant exclusively for the Barbadians. Yet the latter seemed not the least drawn in by the antagonism of the others, and matter-of-factly dropped the track in place. The rail landed with a metallic thud and the Barbadians sauntered off. A shorter German worker, his trousers in tatters, a rag tied around his throat to cover his burning shoulders, and his watery blue eyes filled with fury, continued in German:

"No one can tell me they are not the thieves...."

22

"Calm down, go back to work," a much older companion advised him.

"The dirty swines, I tell you it was one of those Barbadian bastards who sneaked into our sleeping area to rob me," the other repeated, clenching the handle of his pickax.

"You had better just do your work and forget about it."

"Forget about it? Do my work? Here I am with nothing but a lousy rag across my back because somebody made off with my shirt. It cost me a dollar and a half, that shirt, and now it's gone. I tell you it was the Negroes. It had to be them, I'm certain! And they stole my mirror from me, too!"

Cautiously, the Barbadians were trying to keep an eye on the Germans from the vantage point of just beyond where they had earlier deposited the rail. They discussed their apprehension quietly, so as not to be overheard.

"What you spose dis German arseness about?" one of them asked, incredulous at the intensity of hatred that seemed to radiate from the Germans.

"How you s'pose a mon can figure dat out, when dey talks English with such a occent. Is a real mystery, brother."

Meanwhile, the Germans had stopped work entirely. Now they amused themselves a bit by toying with the outrage of their fellow worker, while the Barbadians occasionally looked on with a seemingly indifferent curiosity.

"So the blacks have made off with your shirt, have they?"

"It happened last night, I'm pretty certain. This morning I discovered my bag had been opened and my belongings riffled."

"You must have been in a very deep sleep, Hans. I don't wonder the black, after helping himself to your shirt, helped himself to your behind."

"You can laugh all you like. Yesterday it was me, but tomorrow it might just turn out to be your shirt, you bastard, and your behind!"

"Calm yourself, Hans."

"When they hired me for this job, they didn't tell me there would be Negroes doing the same work."

"Eight *milreis* a day to put up with a horde of black thieves is asking *too much*."

"Look how they stare at us." One of them turned to face

23

the Barbadians and shouted, "What are you staring at, you black monkeys!"

"It's obvious that they are laughing at us, laughing at me. Some countries still exist where a Negro knows his proper place. I used to work in Africa, in Togo, on the cacao plantations. Back in Togo, a real worker could get out of poverty, a real worker could leave his country and go there to find his fortune, if he were shrewd about it. . . ."

"So how come you didn't become rich, Hans?"

"You must not have been very shrewd, Hans. That's probably why the blacks even managed to steal the shirt off your back."

The short German, barely able to keep the rag spread over his shoulders, suddenly climbed out of his hole and went up to the Barbadians, wielding his pickax like a weapon. That single morning without a shirt had already been enough to produce a severe sunburn. The skin of his shoulders felt as rare as roast beef and was still cooking.

"Hey, get back here! Have you gone crazy?" one of his companions yelled after him, already alert to the air of impending disaster.

Hans, however, refused to stop. He had decided. His back was blistering from the heat and he was thoroughly out of control. In a frenzy, he grabbed the first Barbadian he came across, shaking him by the front of his shirt collar. "I vant to know vhich von of you rob my shert," he asked in English, but so garbled that it was incomprehensible to his victim.

The Barbadian was astonished by the outright aggression. "In English, goddom it!" he answered in a humble but firm tone of voice. "Or I go have to finish dis discussion very uncomely."

"You better start opening your mouth, you shit," Hans continued, now totally in German. "Who broke into my suitcase? Which one of you stole my shirt!"

The Barbadian, understanding nothing, but a lot stronger and a lot taller than the German, breathed a sigh of impatience and disentangled himself from his aggressor with a few simple movements and a final shove. By now the guards had appeared with rifles aimed at the two groups of workers, fingers on the triggers. Hans, irritated but defeated, returned to his job in the ditch. Things began to settle down as the Germans got back

24

to their digging and the Barbadians went off to find another rail.

The young Hans, however, had not been appeased. His aching shoulders were a continual reminder that he had been robbed of the only shirt he possessed. Humiliated, he was a dangerous man. The guards had lowered their weapons, unaware that the young German's pride would bridge the gap from his fearful debasement to a vengeful retaliation.

No one saw exactly when he broke into his final run against the Barbadians, with both hands wielding the pickax high above his head. Yet, even with their backs turned, the Barbadians were instantly galvanized into awareness and instinctively readied themselves for some manner of response. It happened quickly and resulted, as always at this camp, in the very worst of consequences. One of the Barbadians nearest to the galloping German drew his machete from his belt and with a precisely timed movement swung the blade with all his strength, adroitly beheading his attacker.

A dry, guttural gasp escaped from every throat. The workers stood transfixed, in a sea of surprise that engulfed even the perpetrator of the sudden decapitation. The head of the youthful Hans—mouth open and eyes bulging—seemed to hang in space, spinning like a lopsided ball suspended by conflicting anarchical forces until it dropped. Meanwhile the body itself trembled, without releasing its pickax, then collapsed into the mud as jets of dark blood spurted from the rim of its neck. Yet the blade of the machete was spotlessly clean. It seemed impossible that it had just cut through an infinity of nerves, tendons, tissues, and bone to release a head from all its worldly possession. Indeed, the seconds it took the body to become one with the mud felt interminable. Yet already the water was tinged with blood. And perhaps it was the sun, gleaming off the edge of the machete blade, that had suffocated all movement—but only for an instant. . . . Once the youth's compatriots had recovered from their stupefaction and horror, they ran senselessly to the rescue, shouting imprecations and wholly possessed by something far more irrational than hopeless solidarity—something that bordered on the uncontrollable and the infamous in its bestial fury. Some of them frantically dragged the decapitated body out of the mud while still others groped in vain for the lost head. The rest took after the Barbadians,

25

tackling them headlong and reducing the camp to a murderous free-for-all.

Not far off, despite the noise of the locomotive, the stoker had picked up the sound of the tumult. He stopped shoveling coal into the firebox and signaled the engineer his intention to find out what was going on. It was a purely instinctual attitude since in all probability there was nothing unusual about this latest uproar, and he knew as much. Some misunderstanding, one worker trading punches with another, somebody killed, and there you are: that was that. . . . The locomotive engineer slowly brought the engine to a halt in a huge cloud of billowing vapor.

"God Almighty, if it's not another howling mess down by the trenches," the stoker muttered indifferently, though he was still curious to see what form it had actually taken.

"It must be them German fellers, havin' it out again with their Barbadian friends," the locomotive engineer surmised, punctuating his remark with a sharp spit of chewing tobacco over one shoulder.

He stepped down from the cab just as a reinforcement of ten more security guards trotted by, accompanied by the Englishman Collier. The locomotive man told his stoker to stick around and keep the boiler heated.

"The fellahs givin' ye a heard time, Collier?" he shouted, trying to catch up.

The construction engineer responded without slowing his pace there at the head of his men, all of whom were armed with Winchesters. "It's bloody hell, Thomas, as if we didn't have enough problems already with this infernal terrain. Everyone seems to have gone off his chump around here. The devil take it, it's worse than a war!"

The majority of the laborers had fled their tasks and prudently gathered at a certain distance from the conflict. The Negroes and the Germans, however, were still at each other's throats when Collier arrived with his contingent of security guards. The splashing of mud exuded a penetrating stench of swamp and stagnation. The engineer acted quickly to restore order.

"This is a place for work, not a boxing ring! Are you all demented? Break it up, that's an order! Have you lost your minds, you idiots!"

26

But the men would have none of it. They continued to fight, rolling in the mud, because by now the lust for blood was hammering in their veins and only the power of their own hatred would determine the outcome. No words, no orders could possibly register inside those fevered heads, which the caking mire had contorted into monstrous apparitions. Collier was no fool, and he realized that in a situation like this the muscularity of his build or the authority of his voice meant nothing more than the pointedness of his well-trimmed beard. He would have to resort to the only language they were capable of understanding if he wanted to put an end to this riot. He therefore took a Winchester from one of the guards and began firing it repeatedly into the air. Even this had little effect, however, as the men gave in to their madness.

"Act like dogs and I'll treat you like dogs!" the engineer decided savagely.

He directed the guards to spread out and cordon off the fighting from the rest of the workers. Once that was accomplished, their rifles at the ready, the men watched indifferently while awaiting further orders. Collier realized he must not lose control of the situation. The moment necessitated a drastic response or his authority would be completely undermined. This was conceivably our Collier's greatest virtue—to be able to anticipate whatever moment his power of command might possibly fall into question and to react ruthlessly, so that no one would be left with any doubts about his resolve. Almost casually, then, he lowered the Winchester, aiming it directly at the struggling rabble—specters of mud barely defined by their animal fury—and pulled the trigger. The rifle clicked emptily and the engineer threw it to the ground in disgust. He turned to his men.

"Open fire!"

The security guards, however, balked at the command. They did aim their rifles rather mechanically in the direction of their supposed targets, but they seemed to doubt that the Englishman really meant to order what would amount to a bloodbath. Collier swiftly walked up to the nearest one of them, shoving him aside and knocking off the fellow's straw hat in the process.

"I said open fire. . . . That's an order! Shoot the bloody bastards!"

The guards began to shoot randomly, almost without taking

27

aim, as if the target were the acrid swamp itself. The first to be wounded was a German, with a bullet grazing his head. Almost at the same instant, a Barbadian was struck at point-blank range with a bullet in the stomach, bringing him to his knees in a bloody mire. The deadly barrage quickly brought the men to their senses; they ceased fighting and stared back in terror at the guards.

"Stop, don't shoot us!" cried one of the Germans.

"Mercy!"

"Don't *shoot,* for the love of God. . . ."

Collier raised his hand to signal to the security guards that they should hold their fire. The men involved in the brawling were groveling on all fours, pleading for their lives. The engineer looked down at them without a trace of pity. The heat felt merciless and he took off his Terai hat to run a hand through his sopping hair. The survivors have began to stand up, cautiously, and back off timidly to their jobs. All of them were now grotesquely squalid, smeared with mud, and some were obviously bleeding from cuts and bullet wounds.

"Collect the bodies," Collier flatly instructed the guards.

The latter shouldered their rifles and began dragging out the corpses. There were five—two Barbadians and three Germans—so coated with mud that all of them seemed to bear the same racial characteristics: an earthen yellow the exact color of the thick mud on the banks of the Rio Abuná.

The idea of work seemed impossible now. Most of the men stood idly by, watching the procession of corpses with that irrepressible fascination the living nurtured toward the dead. A curious fascination that was apparently not to be sated by the glut of diurnal fatalities—as regular as lunch, or as the meager wage collected with each passing week in that simmering wallow.

The *civilized* were a difficult tribe to understand. From the top of a tall tree, invisible among the web of vines, he had seen everything and was frightened—not by the rifle shots but by the furious outbursts of hatred that the *whites* spewed forth echoing through the jungle. It also troubled him that, even though light of life seemed to be extinguished so often among the *civilized,* they possessed no ceremony with which to treat their dead. It was as if only the very act of bringing death to

hemselves constituted a ceremony, and this he found difficult
o accept. The *civilized* were powerful, nonetheless: they could
build great constructions and they always had food, though
hey did no planting or hunting. Yet every day he felt obliged
o withdraw in terror, because the intensity of hatred issuing
rom the *whites* was so painful to behold. He watched the
civilized who had wrestled in the mud now get up and walk
off in bitter silence. An older one of them, who was apparently
heir chief, came walking beneath him together with another,
as the two were lost in conversation. What they were saying
o each other was not difficult for him to understand; he had
already managed to learn to speak many of their words. This,
despite the fact that the *civilized* used a number of different
anguages; for he had observed that some among them did not
understand even the language of their chief.

"I wonder if we'll ever have a day without one of these
infernal quarrels?" the chief complained to the other.

"Yer Barbadians were likely at the bottom of it," said the
other *white*. It was he that could move the huge thing which
spouted smoke from one place to another.

"The Germans are just as bloody worthless."

"D'ye think there's ever any gettin' use' to all this misery?
Eight months here and, I'll tell ye, I've yet to larn to stomach
it."

"Come now, Thomas old boy, what gives you the idea anyone could ever stomach this place?"

"Whoever yer feller was invented the idea o' puttin a railroad
through here musta been daft."

"We're the ones who're bloody daft, for taking the job in
the first place."

"And pickin' the divil's own place to do it, what with thirty
miles o' nothin' but swamp ahead of us. And the workers up
to their ankles in that sickly yeller marsh, I never seen a water
so pukin' yeller. I tell ye, Collier, I ain't a man to complain
but walkin' in that stuff's sheer nauseatin'. The vomit o' very
nature—you work in it long enough and yer brain starts to
fog."

The chief among the *civilized*, as he nodded to the other,
walked over to where he had thrown the rifle on the ground.
It was a *Winchester*—a thing invented by the *whites* but that
his own people had learned to use as well. The *whites'* chief

29

finally picked up the weapon spattered with mud, with th
same yellowish clay that the other *white* had just referred t
as vomit. He could not understand the *white's* disgust for th
earth: mud was mud and he felt no repugnance for it, any mo
than for vomit, which was also a natural thing. The chief wa
wiping off the stock of the rifle, cracking off the mud that ha
already begun to crust upon it. The sun was fiercely hot b
now and the two *whites* were drenched in their own sweat
tormented by the clothing they wore that abraded their flesh

"You'd better get back to Mad Maria and move the dam
thing up a few more millimeters of track," the chief concluded

The other *white* smiled, but it was not purely a smile o
friendship. It expressed rather a kind of indifference, as h
pushed his engineer's cap back and began to walk over to tha
huge unknown thing that shrieked unbearably and spewed blac
smoke. On his way, the *white* ran into some others just arriving
A young *white*, almost his own age, and several companion
of more or less the same generation. These, however, were al
dressed in a very different manner with strange masks tha
descended over their shoulders but through which it was sti
possible to make out the faces.

His legs were growing numb from the uncomfortable po
sition he had had to take, high in the tree. He made his wa
cautiously down the trunk and fled into the jungle.

Percival Farquhar had to enter his own office by walkin
through the spacious, open quarters of his staff and their sec
retaries. The rooms occupied one floor of a small office build
ing on Avenida Central. Personally, he had no liking for thos
installations—the building was badly partitioned and overl
pretentious. The builder had obviously wanted to imitate th
French manner and then stinted on the proportions, as seeme
to be the case with all of Rio de Janeiro. After climbing th
slightly too narrow stairwell, he entered his offices, where th
air was suffused with the faint odor of perfume—but not fror
women. Every night, after office hours, a cleaning crew woul
arrive to sweep the floor and polish it with a sanitary solutio
he had ordered shipped here from the United States. To hir
the scent evoked a bit of some sense of order that was so sorel
lacking in his adopted land. Yet he did not complain, fo
Brazilian disorder was in certain respects providential to hi

purposes, the unsung patron of his entrepreneurial accomplishments.

The majority of his staff was North American but the secretaries were Brazilian girls, generally the daughters of well-to-do families, who had traveled abroad to learn other languages and other customs and had returned home with a desire to be modern and independent. Percival himself cared little for the modernity or the independence of these stylishly dressed ingenues, but they did represent to him the best available labor force in a land of rustic illiterates. He perhaps even liked his Brazilian office-girls and certainly paid them a salary well above that of the average for Brazil. Yet he refused to have such a secretary for himself. Privacy demanded otherwise.

Instead, he had called upon a North American lad who had arrived in Brazil as an employee of the U.S. embassy. Unfortunately, the fellow soon became embroiled in some sort of contretemps with the American military attaché and the ambassador had to let him go, but not before providing him with a letter of introduction to Farquhar, praising the lad's efficiency and suggesting he be hired into the firm. The boy wanted to stay here in Brazil, it seemed, because he was now married to a Brazilian, the daughter of a federal congressman from the state of Bahia. His name was Adams, one-hundred-percent American, and Percival had come to enjoy an enormous confidence in him.

As he entered his own office, Percival Farquhar immediately noticed the pile of brown manila envelopes on his desk: a sign that some American vessel was in the harbor with a shipment from the mother country. The manila envelopes were full of newspapers and other periodicals that were clearly out of date but useful nevertheless in supplementing his knowledge of what was happening back in the States, particularly during an election year.

In Brazil, the presidential election had already taken place the previous year. Marshal Hermes da Fonseca had come to power after a bitterly contested campaign with polemics from the newspapers, accusations of slander, countercharges, and threats of a coup d'etat. Farquhar's temperament kept him aloof from such polemics, but he was now preoccupied with the problem of this administration. His principal allies were members of the opposition. They had run on what they had dubbed

31

the "civil ticket," and had lost. He gave a tinker's damn about their "civil ticket" but would be sorely upset should the defeat of the opposition come to jeopardize his interests here in Brazil. His apprehension was not, as yet, a completely realized emotion but rather a state of alert that could immediately bring the necessary energies into play should that prove necessary. He had always counted upon the unpredictable character of Brazilians, and so he was not surprised suddenly to see in office a man who actually knew how to wield power. No, Farquhar was quite aware of the implications of having someone like Marshal da Fonseca as president of the Republic. The marshal had the power of the army behind him, the only truly organized force to reckon with in the whole country and one that functioned as a species of political club. Moreover, Marshal da Fonseca had already taken care, while minister of war under the preceding administration, to modernize the military forces. They were still insufficiently up-to-date for combat purposes, but adequate enough to sustain any man in power.

Among the stacks of large brown envelopes a small white one caught his attention. It was embossed in an elegantly modern typographical style but sealed, curiously enough, in the most traditional, even ancient of manners. There was no need for him to read the insignia in order to recognize the sender: unquestionably, one of his most intimate collaborators. Not an employee (the thought made him smile) but rather someone Farquhar had come to regard as a sort of private secretary of state. Certainly, Farquhar held him in high regard, estimating him to be one of the few Brazilians capable of combining a sensible modernity (witness the fashionable typography of the monogram) and a conservatism in the grand old manner (observe the red sealing wax into which the monogram had been pressed). Farquhar opened the envelope and removed its lengthy missive written in a delicate, nervous hand whose letters were nevertheless immaculately well-turned, as were the English phrases of which the message had been composed. Farquhar finished the note and sat down. As elaborate as it was, it said very little. A natural enough precaution on the part of his friend—not to put anything in a letter. Briefly stated, it amounted to an invitation for him to join the sender at the Hotel International—for a pleasant lunch, between old friends.

3

It was a large shelter constructed from wood. The two side
windows were screened in as well as glassed, and a door in
the back also had the protection of a screen. The screens, of
a fine mesh, were hopefully to prevent the entrance of mosquitoes. There was not much else in the way of comfort to this
infirmary beyond the four beds of a cotlike construction for
the patients, and bunks for the doctor and his medical staff.
The sickbeds had been laid out near the entrance to the infirmary, on either side of the door. At the other end, with the
bunks, a table, and a cabinet, was the doctor's corner. Dividing
the two sections, but isolated themselves by wooden screens,
were two slabs of rock which served as table for the autopsies.
There was no patient interned here at the moment. The single
Barbadian ravaged by malaria had died earlier that afternoon,
his mind still lucid, without having entered into a coma. Finnegan was finishing stitching up an incision in the shape of a
Y that began at the pubic bone of one of the German corpses,
continuing across the abdomen until it finally bifurcated where
the curves of the chest began. One of the medics was seated
at the table, compiling the report that the doctor dictated in a
droning voice. The rest of the staff were already asleep despite
the light of the hurricane lamp that hung from the ceiling
directly above the autopsy slabs. The other four cadavers,
having already been treated to their autopsies, were lying on
the floor naked and washed, cradled in tarpaulin. The one with
the decapitated head had been reassembled, with the head sewn
to the trunk in such a way that his shoulders were fixed in a
perpetual shrug, as if caught in some involuntary gesture of
disdain.

Finnegan exercised his trade with perfect clinical indifference. The heat had already given rise to that familiar process
of decomposition endemic to all corpses, and the smell was
hardly agreeable. Even so, the young medics managed to go
on sleeping while the doctor himself added the final touches

33

to his methodical labor, to all appearances without perceiving the penetrating stench of dead flesh. He was not terribly good at autopsies, however; he had not practiced a single one prior to his arrival in the jungle. In those early weeks, though, he would all too quickly perceive that performing autopsies in the jungle was to become as routine as delivering babies in a maternity ward. Death was the great diurnal harvester and seemed to look after its task with far more alacrity than that which they lavished upon the building of their railroad across the swampy morass of the Abunā.

Faced with his first corpse, Finnegan had actually felt somehow defiled. Not for any lay reason, mind you, such as disgust for a dead body or fear in the face of a defenseless human carcass. Not even from any vestige of human respect that might have arisen from his own Catholicism. No, as a matter of fact the feeling was due to an apparently misplaced sense of pride. For throughout his years of medical training, his teachers had made it only too clear how humiliating it would be to end up merely signing death certificates for a living, how menial the work of a coroner actually was: running about in subterranean corridors, cutting into corpses, writing up laborious reports in medical legalese. After all, was not the task of a real doctor to wrest the living out of danger? Was not his very notion of the medical profession encapsulated by a piece of sculpture that he had seen on the desk of the school's director while still in his first year? It was of a gentleman attired in an immaculately white dressing gown, a doctor who was trying to wrestle from the arms of Death, represented by a human skeleton, a young woman entirely nude and of such shapely curves that her Venus mound was positively thrust out from between her thighs like a soft geographical acclivity. The image had long engraved itself upon his mind, though not without a certain dose of irony, perhaps from the latent eroticism—or manifest one, he sometimes wondered—that the supposedly threatened but visibly healthy figure of the woman had allowed to surface. The director of the school had noted his interest in the sculpture and had suggested that he should acquire something similar for his consultation room when he graduated. It would lend an artistic touch to the decor and provide an excellent means to initiate conversation with some of his more timid patients— so the director had said. But now, after nearly thirty autopsies

34

and death certificates, the sensation of shame had begun to dissipate itself through sheer indifference—that same perfunctory indifference that they had so ridiculed in coroners.

Finnegan felt rather sleepy as he introduced the needle into the humid skin of the cadaver, rejoining the two borders of a deep incision that still oozed a bluish liquid—the last vestige of what had been blood in that body, yet had flowed all too quickly and throbbingly, propelled by its hatred. Finnegan yawned and tried to hurry his task. His eyes were already heavy, and he was quite aware that he would sleep like the dead the moment his head hit the pillow. Sleep had also been, initially, a motive of some preoccupation, as if all of Finnegan's sensitivity were dying within him. Not that he hadn't always slept well; he had. And rare was the nightmare or even the dream he could remember. Yet to sleep like a stone, that was something entirely new to him. At the hospital where he eventually completed his internship, he had worked every bit as hard as he did here, so it was hardly out of exhaustion. Perhaps it was the excessive heat, he didn't know. He would lie down around eleven at night and only wake up at five-thirty the next morning, when the locomotive whistle would signal to all the advent of another day's labor. And his sleepiness would already begin to manifest itself by around nine o'clock in the evening, when he would normally play a hand of bridge with the other lads if he had no one in sick bay to attend to. Richard Finnegan sensed that too many things had begun to change in his life.

The twelve Beethoven variations lay hidden under every leaf in the darkness of the night. The pervasive blackness densely populated with sounds muffled by humidity now cloaked Consuelo's sobs. Clutching a package to her breast, with unclad feet she fearlessly braved the perilous ground of the everglade, unable to glimpse where or upon what her footsteps fell. Everywhere about her the world was choked in the pitch darkness of a rain forest after nightfall. Consuelo wept inconsolably, her long fine silky hair disheveled and blighted by dead leaves and cracked mud. She could still feel the powerful arm restraining her by the waist, immobilizing her as she struggled helplessly, reducing her to total impotence as she looked on like a defeated bystander, forced to become party to a spectacle she had no desire to witness. It had all been so horrible. The submerged

35

rocks, the glaring sun mirrored by the top of the piano, the taut muscles of the Indians—the latter apparently brought to a standstill. The raft swaying, then Alonso grabbing the rope and coiling it about his body, the muscles and arteries of his neck tensing into a supreme effort. And then . . . but she couldn't believe it. Again she lost control and found release in a flood of other impulses . . . a cozy room, well-furnished, the fine chairs upholstered in damask with pile velvet trimming, her husband smoking a pipe, drifting off to sleep, a candelabra of six flickering candles bathing the room with a placid light, the onset of dusk much like any evening after work in the Casa Santa Cecilia, their living quarters at the back of the music shop with a separate entrance, the perfect abode for a young couple so much in love with music and with each other. Green silk curtains on the windows and walls carefully decorated with landscapes in gilded frames. A black piano, a tremendous piano and a young man in his striped suit smiling at her; a morning of practice at the university's concert hall; an empty auditorium, the chairs covered and the windows shut. A grand piano. Consuelo walks up to it, sits on the crimson velvet stool. Her fingers try out the ivory keys while the young man looks on, smiling, petting a fat cat mottled like a leopard . . . and the idea of something feline causes her to awaken slightly and notice the jungle cloaked in darkness and inundated with noise. But the raft was somehow grounded upon a huge rocky ledge, the water cascading over it like a breathtaking fountain. Until suddenly efforts stalled, the raft edged over and was torn off course, dragging down with it in its furious defeat a number of the Indians as it rushed toward the deadly gorge. A helpless handful of godforsaken savages with no time to disentangle themselves from the ropes. And Alonso! Consuelo swiftly turned her head only to glimpse her husband flailing at the rapids, carried helplessly along. She would have rushed to his aid, but a powerful arm now gripped her by the waist, dragging her helplessly back from him. She screamed and punched wildly but Alonso had already disappeared as the raft kept spinning, descending, accompanying the tempo of the onrushing waters while describing incredible swerves and graceful twirlings in and around the rocks. The piano, reflecting the glorious sunlight, proudly clung to the destiny of its conveyance. Consuelo was pounding her fists against the man who held her in his

36

rip, preventing her from hurling herself desperately below. He was a terrified Indian, who had clasped her by the waist more to shield himself than to keep her from her own folly. Just then the raft with its precious cargo slammed against a jutting boulder. At once the splinters went flying into the air; the grand piano shattered like a plaster toy and disappeared. All that remained were the sounds of the rapids, victorious now, for the Indians had fled—those who were still alive— frightened off by the death of Alonso Campero. They had seen him lose his balance and fall, the rope coiled about him, no help possible, and no way to unravel himself from the loops he had wound around and around his own waist. It had dragged him off, his body stretched out behind and his arms grasping for anything to hold on to, lacerated by the cragged surfaces of battering rocks. He was dead! Drowned! Not even a corpse would turn up anymore, because his body was probably roped somewhere to the bottom of the river, below the falls in those deep waters, full of trunks of fallen trees and the debris of other wreckage. Consuelo could walk no further, her legs felt torn to ribbons; a voice sighed, her own voice, amid the aleatory symphony of wilder sounds. The floor of the forest was wet and spongy, a thick carpet that seemed to undulate under her throbbing feet . . . the heavy curtains, green, and the windows of the conservatory, shut, now, for winter had arrived in full fury, salting the cobblestones and frosting the windows with ice. It was so cold now, but the young man's smile seemed to warm her. Consuelo sensed that he liked her, though they scarcely knew each other. But she was avid to learn what he was doing there at the conservatory, at such an hour: exactly the hour for her piano exercises. She had only made his acquaintance a short while ago and did not even know his name. He was the young clerk who had waited on her at the music shop where she had gone to purchase some sheet music. And it was to him that she had turned for information on the price of a German piano, of the very best quality—something she had always dreamed of owning. It would be expensive, the young man confided attentively as he made the complicated calculations there on the spot for her, quite good-humoredly, in fact, and even transmitting a special warmth that to her was a disturbing novelty. At home, the perturbation of that warmth troublingly persisted and Consuelo remained restive, walking

37

back and forth from the living room to her bedroom, feverishl
pacing, awakening the curiosity of her mother finally, a woma
normally quite indifferent to her only child and occupied mo
with her own world. Yet it was cold in the conservatory, an
so she warmed her fingers by rubbing her hands together eac
time she stopped fingering at the keys to bars of Chopin
Mozart, Offenbach. It was so cold! The cold crept through he
and for some reason choked a sob from her. The young man
however, still watched her, a blushing male with full lips draw
in a handsome smile. His look was thoroughly disarming
though Consuelo could not say why. She fell to her knees o
that spongy carpet of never dry leaves that covered the humi
floor of the jungle. She curled up against the trunk of a cashew
nut tree and slept without fear.

A crude structural framework, built of tree trunks, serve
as a place for workers to string up their hammocks. They sle
there, yes, but to characterize the place as a dormitory was t
euphemize rather cynically. The hammocks were lined up i
parallel rows with the "dormitory" itself divided into two wings
Security guards were posted every two meters or so. Eac
sleeper was protected by a length of mosquito netting whic
hung like a tent of gauzy spiderwebbing that completely en
cased its hammock. Yet the total effect was to offer seclusio
only from the mosquitoes. The rain was another matter, sinc
the "dormitory" was roofless. It was a sallow night of heavy
low-lying clouds which wholly effaced the customary expans
of pinholed starlight, where the Milky Way normally hovere
with a splayed solemnity. Exhausted men were snoring wit
intermittent groans in their sleep. Eventually there was a muf
fled commotion, carefully concealed from the Spanish senti
nels, issuing from somewhere within the Barbadian wing.
few shadows threaded their way among the hammocks in ab
solute silence. Now and then they stopped to communicate i
hushed tones, with barely a sound brushing from their lips
Then two of them, armed with machetes and treading on tiptoe
escaped into the darkness.
   The infirmary hut was faintly delineated by the surroundin
obscurity. It was the glow of illumination from twin side win
dows that had helped to pinpoint the bungalow. Suddenly, tw
figures loomed up in silhouette against the second window

38

while, inside, Finnegan continued his absorbed and somnolent revising of the copy of the postmortems. He was scrutinizing each page with excessive care out of a fear that his sleepy mind might well play tricks on him at such an hour. Our Finnegan loved perfection, you see, to such a degree that he was wont to check whatever had been written up by his medics and make still further annotations. In the meantime he had noticed an odd sound that seemed to come from somewhere outdoors yet had nothing to do with the din of insects. He became suddenly alert, for if he had digested one thing from this place, it was to be alert to the slightest abnormality. He looked up but saw nothing out of order in his infirmary: the dead persevered in their quiescent immotility; the medics were asleep. The air was leaden, as always occurs in the jungle shortly before a cloudburst.

Just outside, the two Barbadians continued to peer through the screened window. It was not their plan to smash it through; they only wished to estimate the situation inside and seemed to have found things more or less as expected. Presently one of them touched the other on the shoulder and made signs that they should proceed together to the door. The sound of footsteps on the bed of dry leaves surrounding the hut had by now fully ignited the doctor's nerves, as his eyes flashed vainly into every nook and cranny illuminated by the overhanging kerosene lantern. He felt the imminence of a catastrophe and was not to be disappointed, for almost at once the door to the infirmary gave way with a violent thud, and the doctor was stunned by the entrance of two Negroes in possession of a lethal-looking pair of machetes.

In the faces of these two intruders, Finnegan read something extremely profound, which he was nevertheless unable to fathom—something far more oblique than any sense of danger—a mysterious potentiality which barely disguised itself and so was doubly disturbing to him. The two Barbadians held their weapons so tightly in hand that their flesh seemed to have been drained of its circulation, to have turned nearly white in color, or rather a pale and frightening curdled brown. They breathed cautiously as they proceeded around the partitions and came upon the cadavers; whereupon that unfathomable potentiality in them seemed to intensify and Finnegan tried hard not to delineate the slightest gesture that might be mistaken for a

39

reaction. And so he looked on as inertly as possible, his ashen lips barely parted, a noise in his ear making an uncomfortable din as his heart beat so swiftly it seemed to be burrowing through his chest. Our doctor was, in fact, scared to death but he could not let it out; for if they should have any inkling that they actually had the upper hand, there would be no chance of his salvation. Second by second, Finnegan slowly watched the mysterious potentiality turn into evident rage—a familiar emotion, one that he could actually relate to, which allowed him finally to attempt to summon some courage.

"What is the meaning of this?" Finnegan protested in a firm and incisive tone, trying to imitate the manner of his superior, the Englishman Collier.

"Why you corry dem here?" one of the Barbadians arrogantly answered, pointing to the cadavers.

"What do you mean?" Finnegan responded disconcertedly, afraid they might have come there, for all he knew, to require him to bring the dead back to life.

"You ain't cut dose up, Doct' Finn'gan?" the Barbadian insisted flatly.

"It was only a matter of routine procedure. Nothing more could be done for them. Do you want to see the report?"

"Why you mess with de bodies dat way?" the other Negro asked him in a malevolently suspect tone, which only left the doctor more dumbfounded.

"I think you boys had better return to the dormitory and I will try to forget everything that has just occurred," the doctor mustered curtly, irritated because he was unable to fathom precisely what they were seeking and why, particularly, this preoccupation with the dead. "The remains will be sent tomorrow morning, as required, to the company cemetery, in Candelária. Now, if you have no further questions . . ."

One of the Barbadians violently flung aside the screens. Finnegan felt the Negro's rage intensifying as he himself watched the partitions tumble to the floor, awakening the medics with a start.

"No! You profanin' de corpses! Goddom white mon always haves to scromble up de dead!"

Finnegan was in the midst of recollecting, painfully, how expert these Barbadians could be with their weapons: they had wielded one of those machetes, with its cutting edge as sharp as a precision scalpel, on the neck of that unfortunate German. A single, perfect slice—worthy of a medieval executioner. The medics at the moment seemed to read the doctor's mind and sat motionless in their beds while their eyes danced from shining blade to shining blade.

"We already told de coptin no white man s'pose to hondle we brothers," the one Barbadian said menacingly, pushing Finnegan against the wall.

"Have you gone *crazy?*" the doctor groaned hoarsely.

The medics, still lethargic with sleep, stopped breathing suddenly as their strength began to drain down their legs into a puddle of feet as helpless as liquid lead. The other Negro, signaling with his machete, ordered them to line up next to the doctor against the same wall. Finnegan's mind had fired its last blank and his stomach had become so agitated as to give out its own form of long, guttural moan. The lamplight monstrously illuminated his surroundings while as if from a great distance footsteps now entered the infirmary.

"Well, Dick and Jonathan, I might have known," the engineer interrupted with a booming voice, breaking through the air of unbearable expectancy, and with that extinguishing almost entirely whatever mortal inclination the two Barbadians might have nourished toward the doctor and his staff.

The ex-aggressors wheeled about, almost stunned. Finnegan immediately relaxed and turned to his medics, now collapsed against the wall in a feeble effort to avert total loss of equilibrium. One of them went so far as to let out a long whistle; for the Barbadians were now incredibly docile.

"When they told me there was a row in progress over here, I said to myself, Scratch my butt if it doesn't turn out to be Dick and Jonathan up to their old tricks again."

"Nemmine, Copm Collier, we wasn't here to cause no trouble," one of the Barbadians replied.

"I know, Jonathan," the engineer answered him sarcastically. "And those machetes you've got there were just to prune the infirmary hedges, I suppose."

The security guards began to materialize in the fragmentary light that escaped from the doorway. They had accompanied Collier, of course, but had not immediately entered. The engineer preferred to impose his own authority single-handedly, leaving the guards to back him up only as a last resort.

41

"But dis Doct' Finn'gan, why he hads to be slicin' up de dead brothers dat fashion?" Jonathan stammered.

Only now could the doctor take the measure of his intruders, and what he saw was little more than two emaciated-looking men—the one called Jonathan was the taller of the two, his bony frame flecked with tufts of kinky dark hair—and both of them wretchedly underfed: pathetic creatures wholly preoccupied with primitive superstitions. Finnegan began to muse to himself what a truly ridiculous animal man, at times, turned out to be.

"Now, before we proceed any further, why don't you hand over those two little instruments," Collier suggested, and the two Barbadians surrendered their machetes without the slightest hesitation. "Your problem is simply a lack of sleep, lads. Guards! See these lads back to their hammocks."

The guards, however, were superfluous to the matter, inasmuch as the Barbadians headed back to the dormitory the moment they overheard the engineer's instructions.

"Pleasant dreams," Collier recommended in their wake.

"What do you mean, 'Pleasant dreams'?" Finnegan suddenly demanded, nauseated at the sheer arrogance of the engineer. "Don't you even plan to punish them!"

"Go keep an eye on them, and be quick about it," the engineer ordered the guards, paying no attention to Finnegan's demands. "We must clear out of the infirmary to give the young doctor here a little room to do some thinking."

The guards slouched off after the Barbadians while Collier continued to inspect the infirmary from where he stood. Finnegan for the first time felt a degree of genuine hostility toward the engineer, whereas until now he had been more the submissive boy busy compensating for Collier's continual belligerence with a shell of professional indifference.

"So, two men enter here, threaten me, almost kill me, and you have the gall, sir, to dismiss them as if nothing had happened," Finnegan protested now without bothering to mask his emotion.

"Are you hurt?" Collier asked. "Did they touch even one hair on your head?"

"I'm not injured, if that's what you mean. I'm quite fine, thank you. They did not go so far as to commit any wrongdoing, but they certainly didn't come here with good intentions."

"And by some chance is there anyone around here who *has* good intentions?" Collier's question came like a dry slap in the face of Finnegan's self-righteousness.

"It's not reasonable, sir," the doctor retreated into his professional demeanor to achieve validity through authority. "They invaded the infirmary. They left the dormitory without permission, and I can't say for sure, but God knows what they had in mind when they entered through that door. . . ."

"They were going to kill you," said Collier dryly.

Finnegan felt his irritation begin to ebb in the face of the engineer's objectivity. Collier knew his Barbadians and was totally aware of precisely what they were about. Finnegan, on the other hand, could only comprehend men through regulations, which in turn he viewed as a species of organic reductant of the work to be executed.

"The next time a Negro shows up dead, see that you arrange for an immediate burial," Collier stated bluntly. "I'll have no more of your delectable carving and trussing. You're running an infirmary, not a meat market."

"I have strict orders to perform autopsies on all fatalities. And the remains are to be buried in the company cemetery."

"Except for the Barbadians, Dr. Finnegan. You have my personal assurance in the case of any Negro fatality."

"I don't see a reason to treat a black corpse any different than a white one," the doctor countered in the same tone.

"I am apprised of your fine sentiments, doctor," the engineer replied, slipping into a rather Southern drawl for an Englishman in order to vent his irony; but he quickly resumed his tone of authoritarian aloofness that so nauseated Finnegan, to warn him: "From now on, any Negro we have the misfortune to lose, for one reason or another, is to be buried immediately by the edge of the railroad bed. And the internment is to be performed by the Negroes themselves. With no autopsy, is that clear? I am giving you an order!"

"Well, it's one I can't accept," said Finnegan impatiently, pacing back and forth in front of Collier. "What about the death certificate? And the coroner's report?"

"I wouldn't trouble myself, lad, if I were you. The dead are so explicit in this place that it's enough to have only a glimpse of a corpse to surmise the reasons for his undoing. Write whatever comes into your head, my boy—use your imagination. Nobody would ever give a thought to verifying the genuine *causa mortis* of every stinking wretch who's run afoul of this bloody inferno."

Collier promptly left, slamming the door of the infirmary and thereby echoing the harsh ring of his voice inside Finnegan's head. The medics, in the meantime, had finally relaxed a bit but chose to remain prudently silent. The doctor was still peering at the door that had been closed with such arbitrary violence, but after a few seconds he began to lift up the screens which the Barbadian had overturned. Rather spontaneously the medics mutually agreed with a mute nod to go back to bed, since the doctor in any case scarcely seemed aware of their presence at the moment, so busy was he gathering papers up from their disarray and rummaging through the material splayed across his desk. Presently, however, he became aware of their stares and, ignoring the state of shock still lingering in their expressionless faces, he quietly told them to wrap up the bodies of the Germans. His staff, in turn, received their orders with evident dismay, because they had been hoping for a bit of sleep to dissolve the tension in their neck and knees.

"Use the sheets they're lying on," the doctor instructed. "Then we'll bury the two Barbadians."

"Tonight?"

"Immediately!"

Close by the encampment of workers on the banks of the Rio Abunã, the locomotive engineer and his stoker were waiting for their soup to cook. Another pair of eyes was also mesmerized by the simmering broth as it foamed and bubbled in the iron pot suspended over the flames by an iron tripod. He was hidden in the jungle and he was ravenously hungry. Despite the fact that he had recently had some fruit to eat, he was still jealous of these other creatures; for the smell of soup was strong, indeed, though it would be difficult for him to have gained any share of that meal. He was not alone in that regard. The two *civilized* he was now observing enjoyed the privileged status of professionals in the company's eyes and, as a result, received among other benefits the waterproof tent behind them, which served as their own private lodgings for this sector of operations.

Thomas Gallagher, the elderly locomotive operator, was

44

bent over the improvised stove, stirring the broth with a large wooden spoon. The glare of the small bonfire was the only source of light in the vicinity and it scarcely illuminated the two men. The stoker Harold seemed to be lost in some intimate reflection. Still a young, muscular fellow with a squared-off face that seemed cut with hammer-and-chisel blows by a sculptor without talent. He was a stubby-looking youth, and his fiery auburn hair and freckled complexion showed him to be the son of immigrants, possibly Dutch, though there was no traceable descent to his name. He was simply Harold Appleton, born in New York City. Old Thomas was also deep in thought and so neither one of them noticed the shadowy figure that was moving stealthily through the undergrowth in the direction of the tent. Though human, the figure moved like a cat, stealing lithely along the ground and slipping silently into the tent. Harold the stoker slapped regularly at himself with the palm of his hand or swatted vaguely within the vicinity of his body, fending off the tiny nocturnal moths and other insects attracted by the fire.

"A good dose of gin laced with lemon juice would do very nicely right now, wouldn't you say," he asked just to break into the monotony of the night.

Gallagher answered provisionally with a noncommittal grunt, as he was busy ducking the mosquitoes that refused to be intimidated by the smoke from the cooking fire and insisted on sucking his blood.

"I can heardly remember the taste o' gin," he finally replied with an economy of words, more absorbed by the bitten tip of his finger, where a yellow blain had begun to appear.

"What kind of soup is that supposed to be?" Harold asked rather dubiously.

"Onion."

"Onion? That'll give us a hell of a halitosis."

Harold Appleton had never worked on a railway construction job before. Back in the States he had been a fireman on the regular railway lines and thus was only accustomed to proper timetables, fixed stations, and more-or-less tranquil rides through countrysides cultivated in summer and blanketed in winter. The truth is, he had not always been a fireman and had entered the profession only through the good graces of his friend Thomas. He was, in fact, unemployed (and dead drunk)

45

when they had met for the very first time, at a station some-where in New England. Harold was trying secretly to hitch a ride on a freight train, from out of the station yard, when he had slipped on the grease of a switching track and toppled directly in front of a waiting locomotive. Gallagher had dis-covered him there, lying across the track, when he went to give his engine her routine inspection before taking her out of the station. Harold was unconscious, more from alcohol than from the fall, although the gash above the eye had shed a considerable amount of blood. Old Thomas helped him up. It seemed the lad had no plans or destination other than never to return to New York, where he had been living by himself, was almost always drunk, and worked hefting furniture about for a moving and storage company. No, there was no going home again. Harold was already close to thirty with no wife or girl-friend. He was so timid, in fact, when it came to women that he would flee the very sight of them; yet the motive behind such behavior had continued to elude him. In any case, the women he came across hardly seemed attracted by his rough-hewn, squared-off jaw, let alone his always disheveled clothes stained with grease and smelling of bourbon. Still, two years later he was a changed man, healed by the energy and com-passion of Old Thomas, who treated him more like a son. Harold could never even think of leaving the old grump, not even when the latter, recently widowed, had decided to accept the invitation of a construction engineer named Stephan Collier to come down and work in this blasted hellhole.

"What was that ye were sayin'?" Gallagher asked, inter-rupting Harold's thoughts.

"Oh, nothing, only that onion soup you got there—we've been eating it for days on end."

"Well, what else have ye got in mind? The beans get here all mildewed and jarked meat is downright repellent to me nature. . . ."

"Hold on, Ol' Tom, I ain't complaining." Just then, Harold heard a noise coming out of the tent—field mice, he thought, or maybe a snake. "Onion soup ain't so bad," he added at the same time that he was trying to make out what the sound might actually be.

"Ye hear that?" Thomas said, turning to look at the tent.

46

"Probably just some damn animal again," Harold proposed in a casual way.

"As fer meself, o' carse, I'd take far better to a good meaty stew." Thomas had returned to the subject of food, reassured by the attitude of his companion.

"Well, we're not so bad off," Harold commented to humor him. "Onions, at least, have yet to be proven fatal ... even here." Still, he had a feeling something strange was occurring inside the tent. There was too much noise, and it was only because he reasoned so slowly that he had yet to feel more than simply intrigued. "What the hell was that?" he finally asked in alarm.

"What?"

"The noise inside the tent. Maybe it was my imagination."

"Yer not afraid, now, are ye?" Gallagher chided, but it was as if he were asking himself the question.

"Me, afraid? To be honest, Ol' Tom, I ain't never been not afraid."

"Well, what are ye afraid a, now?"

"Everything. You take that tent there, for instance."

The two of them now stood staring at the tent as if it held some terrible secret.

"I'm a fellow who lives by fear and fear alone, as if you didn't know," Harold continued.

"What are ye sayin', laddie? Gallagher's here, ain't he?"

"I guess, by God, I'll always be afraid, but right now I'm scared half to death just walking around this place. Day and night, it never lets up. At times I ask myself how the hell it can be worth risking your hide for seventy shillings a day."

"And who gave ye the right to be askin' yerself questions?" the old man challenged, trying to bury their fear in the charisma of his long experience, a tactic that generally hadn't failed him. "You listen to me, laddie. Ain't Gallagher's hair tarned white enough without lettin' more things quare up 'is head? But don't go troublin' yerself about it, laddie, bein' scared is natural enough. The Lard knows Gallagher's scared, I'll tell ye. Scared o' the heat that's enough te brial ye alive and scared o' the sickness anywhere ye step."

As he talked he began to take the pot from the fire. He carefully lowered it onto the crate, where Harold had set out dishes, mugs, and spoons.

"No, it's not that kind of fear," Harold confessed as the darkness began to take on an added density around the fire. "Agh, who knows? Maybe it is just the fear of coming down with some disease, of dying in such a place."

Old Thomas began to chortle to himself, which had more the look of a fit of coughing; and Harold stared up at him, trying to gauge his own sense of security.

"What's so damn funny?" Harold finally asked him.

"Oh, nothin', laddie, just somethin' out o' the past come back to pay a visit." Gallagher spilled some soup into each plate and then passed one to his companion. "Ye know when it was I felt most afraid in all me life? It was when I'd arranged meself a mistress fer the farst an' last time of all. A fine pace a stupidity, that was! At the time, though, it was piar suffacation. The problem had nothin' to do with the missus. She had no suspicions atall. She trusted me. We'd been married tree yars already with no kids. Suddenly me mother comes to spend a wake with us and I began to get a quare feelin' she knew I was up to no good with another woman. I could see it in her very eyes. At the time I was workin' in this office place and fairly wet behind the ears. Lard, your Gallagher was niver so scared in all 'is life, what with me mother mistrustin' me and me shar she was goin' te tarn me in to the missus any minute."

"You must have gone through hell, all right."

"Me mother was pretty sharp—" Suddenly Thomas stopped talking, for now he was certain that something or someone was in the tent. "Ye were right, Harold, it seems we got visiters."

Harold threw his plate of soup on the ground and watched the tent without drawing another breath. What if it was the Barbadians, armed with machetes, stealing from their belongings. He just didn't want his head lopped off.

"That's what I was afraid of."

"Quiet," Thomas warned him, reaching for his revolver and walking slowly toward the tent.

Something was moving about in there, something nimble as a cat, for no sooner had they begun to approach it than it vanished, dissolving into the pitch-black night. The two men cautiously entered the tent, lit a candle, and discovered that their bags had been broken into. All their belongings had been emptied onto the floor.

"They took a mirror from me," Harold remarked, sifting through his things.

"Me Swiss army knife went with it," Gallagher added.

They had nothing especially valuable that could interest a thief. Nothing that anyone could covet, let alone turn into a profit. The theft was wholly incomprehensible and, therefore, all the more frightening to them. It only augmented the climate of generalized mistrust that had now reached the point of impending explosion. And for Thomas Gallagher and his companion it was hardly the loss of penknife or mirror that filled them with foreboding. It was the fact that, from now on, they would have to disguise their suspicions whenever they looked at someone else, and that could be taken as a provocation.

The light was on in the bathroom and dimly illuminated the bedroom, which was otherwise sealed in darkness by a wall of window drapes. Percival Farquhar inhabited three adjoining apartments at the Hotel Avenida, which he had remade into drawing room, reception room, and bedroom. The three together, agreeably spacious and furnished discreetly with French effects in the Restauration style, were rented the year round in order to be kept at his disposal as a kind of center of operations. He felt, actually, a moderate affection for this hotel (always spotlessly clean) with its attentive waiters and efficient chambermaids; its great silent walls and dignified windows comfortably aloof from the incipient barrage of nightlife in downtown Rio de Janeiro. For it was always at the close of day that he entered those apartments—in order to resuscitate himself from that outer world of every day preoccupations, preferably by sinking back into a deep, cool, refreshing tub.

He was now stretched out upon his bed. It was eleven-thirty at night. The noises from out on the street had already begun to fade, but sleep would not finally descend upon him until well past the midnight hour. As he rarely accepted invitations to nocturnal gatherings (not a "night person") and held no particular fondness for the theater, let alone any other form of nighttime public diversion Rio might have to offer, this hideaway was generally his habit. Occasionally, however, Farquhar would indulge in a solitary walk, strolling along greedily and without any special thought in his head, merely savoring the richness of emotion such hours of sleeplessness afforded, because they were dead hours and, therefore, as delicious in their vacancy as an unexpected profit. And sometimes, as upon this occasion, such profit would assume a somewhat different contour—without, however, breaking the archetypal mold. Someone, in fact, was gliding about in the bathroom, whence there seemed to emanate a rather sylvan, though wholly civilized perfuming that lent mellifluous substance to the play of light and shadow. Percival had turned his head to observe the source of so delightful a chiaroscuro—moving about in the bathroom, turning on and off the faucets, tinkling tiny bottles together, drawing the curtains. Outside, the summer night was of a tawny vintage, the air refreshed by a sea breeze, and passersby shed too pale an echo to trouble the peace of his bed.

All of Farquhar's business machinations were moving ahead, although it was more a moment for waiting, a time of political change, of vagaries within the administration. Of course, the solidity of his undertakings was little disturbed by the cataclysms that shook the nation and caused its citizens to walk about with grave doubts stamped upon their visages. Lunch at the Hotel Avenida had been revealing in this regard and Farquhar had hardly touched his plate, asking questions, listening carefully, jotting down bits of information and drawing out all the material he could from his skinny little friend (so skinny, mind you, it was as if his scrawny body were a studied act of dissimulation meant to disguise his true stature). Farquhar's friend at his luncheon table had an oblong head in the shape of a balloon, a bushy mustachio, and a pair of lively but inscrutable eyes that seemed to dance beneath their yellow, bloodless lids. The head seemed that of a huge man's, misplaced upon the bony shoulders of a misshapen dwarf. He was an ugly man and had a sickly appearance, although he actually enjoyed excellent health and was known to be an energetic horseman. The name of this friend was Ruy Barbosa; he was a lawyer, full of vitality and perhaps the most famous public figure in all of Brazil. Curiously, his fame appeared to grow in direct proportion to the reduction of his political powers. Just the previous year he had run for the second time as a candidate for the presidency of Brazil, a position that he really did not seem to desire in any case. Farquhar had known this lawyer for three years now and had gradually reached the conclusion that the more Barbosa declined as a politician, the more quintessentially purified he became (by some species of moral compensation, perhaps?) as a jurist. He often behaved like a man of arrogant convictions and vainglorious demeanor. Brazilians (who always exaggerated regardless of their position) generally deemed him an infallible authority (when they liked him) or an imbecilic ass (when they didn't). To Farquhar's way of thinking he was neither. Percival Farquhar had become interested in Barbosa the day that his own affairs began to be drawn into the legal octopus of the country's juridical system, and Ruy's name was whispered to him as a species of legislative engineer capable of working his way through the hundreds of thousands of decrees, regulations, laws, amendments, and other federal, state, and municipal provisions — generally ignored by one administration after the other but always cited during the lengthy process of the negotiation of favors, when they would be employed as nudge or trap to garnish fat gratuities.

Farquhar had already heard much talk of Barbosa but refused to take the hoopla very seriously concerning that loquacious lawyer (anti-American in The Hague, pro-American in the Senate, and with no position at all in the final analysis). Besides which, hadn't this Barbosa character wasted a lot of precious time mooting questions of no import with respect to the proposed Brazilian Civil Code now being drawn up by Congress? Offering a grammatical critique rather than addressing its contents as behooves a proper jurist? And thereby damaging the pace of the entire project? Ruy Barbosa's philological incontinence was already folkloric in Brazil, and bordered on the ridiculous: the Civil Code was hardly a literary work, let alone a pretext for lengthy debates on the purity of the Portuguese language. Percival's estimation of Barbosa dropped even lower once he had ascertained the real motives behind this man's grammatical zeal. The little lawyer had hoped to be the editor of the Civil Code himself, and now he wished to humiliate the highly regarded jurist who stood in his place. That man was none other than Clovis Bevilacqua, with whom Farquhar was well acquainted as a serious, competent bureaucrat with no inclination—unlike the little gnome with the big head and sickly brown mustachio—to soft-shoe his way linguistically into the political limelight. Farquhar and Barbosa met for the first time in 1908, in a dingy room piled with books and papers on a floor of the Senate building. Barbosa spoke, buzzing like

51

a beetle, and like a beetle only revealed his innate capacities when he opened his wings and soared in and out of arguments as elegant as Tiffany glass. Little by little, Farquhar began to discover a man very useful to his own interests in Brazil, and beneath the artful facade of this wizened lawyer Farquhar slowly detected an ambition the size of which a born businessman like himself could only thank the Lord was wedded to the empty gestures and posturings of his playing at prominent personality. And so it was an alliance at first sight, although Percival Farquhar would never completely set aside a degree of circumspection, required whenever one deals with a man who refuses to measure the consequences of his own vanity. In the case of Ruy Barbosa, however, the valence of Brazilian dissimulation and vanity did seem to promise enormous profits where Farquhar's business dealings were concerned.

During lunch our Quaker entrepreneur had confessed his preoccupation with the direction things appeared to be taking in Brazil; he feared a possible military coup that would most likely sink the nation in those turbid waters of diktat and revolution so typical of most countries in the hemisphere, south of the Rio Grande. Political instability was venomously antithetical to his own interests, and Farquhar had eyed the turbulence that erupted in those first months of the new administration with growing apprehension. Barbosa was likewise discouraged and had already begun to play down his former Republican devotion. Farquhar happened to have been in the United States when two battleships from the Brazilian Navy were suddenly overrun by mutinous sailors threatening to shell the city of Rio de Janeiro. A state of siege had been declared and the revolt received a perhaps inappropriate response, since it was not really politically motivated—the seamen were simply demanding better treatment aboard ship and specifically the abolishment of the use of whips, which made their presence felt on Brazilian vessels as if it were still the eighteenth century. Although publicly amnestied, the sailors suffered terrible retribution at the hands of naval officials. The following May, hundreds of ex-mutineers were loaded into the pestilential hold of the ship *Satellite* and cargoed off to the Amazon jungle. Farquhar sensed that matters were hitting rock bottom in Rio de Janeiro and he knew that Ruy Barbosa had still not recovered from the upshot of Marshal da Fonseca's

itially conciliatory blandishments. Before he actually as-
umed the presidency, the old marshal (old as a sly fox because,
a point of fact, he was vigorously active for a middle-aged
man married to a sprightly lady of Cariocan society) had telephoned Barbosa and asked him to indicate possible candidates
or ministerial posts. Ruy's vanity had prevented him from
eading the invitation properly—no more than the formality
f a military man in need of legitimizing himself before politicians. So the lawyer suggested a number of possibilities,
with all the appearances of an intimate collaborator, but none
f his recommendations would pass muster behind the doors
f Catete Palace. Marshal da Fonseca filled his cabinet with
members of his own political coalition, completely ignoring
the lawyer's recommendations. During those following weeks
when the cabinet was to be announced and sworn in, Barbosa
turned into a most contumelious fellow, escaping to his sump-
tuous mansion, where he found solace in dictionaries, his principal source of diversion. Percival suspected that his friend's
fanatical worship of grammar was faintly onanistic and this
repelled him; although the marshal's manipulation of Barbosa
had been crudely managed, he had to admit. And to make
matters still worse, to the post of minister of public works and
transportation the president-elect had nominated one of Ruy's
bitterest enemies: J. J. Seabra, a stern politician from the
Northeast, who was quite capable of simply ignoring the lawyer's posturings and eclipsing him altogether with his own
electoral prestige.

Their luncheon had served as a predictably florid framework
or the exchange of favors and information. Farquhar had as-
essed the faces of the new administration as wayfarers amid
the political fog. Ruy wished to place at his disposal (in the
literal sense of the word, "to dispose of," and the farther away
the better!) the coquettish talents of one Luiza Rosalvo, a
frivolous, ill-tempered girl from Bahia who had been on intimate terms with Barbosa ("pampered like a favorite kitten")
and who now needed to be sent on her way before she should
become a dangerous nuisance. Luiza, it seems, had already
taken to asserting herself, and Ruy certainly could not have
such a girl invading his office, sitting on the edge of desks
with her ankles exposed while imperiously demanding favors.
Our Percival certainly saw no inconvenience to his request and

53

decided to send the petulant little flower packing to São Paul ("No farther, Percival? Well, no matter."), where she coul take a position in the more and more populous bureaucracy his electric company. He might have sent her, out of pu maliciousness, off to Belém, on the Amazon, where he ha controlling shares in the harbor, telephones, and tramways; even to Colombia, where he was moving ahead with negot ations to build several highways; or to Cuba, where he owne hotels, railroads, and countless warehouses. As a matter fact, even China was a possibility, for among the many holding of his sprawling empire was a lumber concession on the islan of Formosa.

In return for the favor, however, Ruy Barbosa could n manage to relieve his friend's anxieties. He was equally cog nizant of a difficult political situation and had just as man doubts regarding the wisdom of the marshal. Ruy believed th country to have veered off on an uncorrectable course an suspected that a republic directed in such a specious manner— shielded by a counterfeit federalism wherein the actual state served as little more than an elaborate nomenclature to hid powerful and corrupt local oligarchies—would inevitably be gin to crumble. Farquhar, therefore, should consider takin more decisive steps; he needed to penetrate the very machi nations of this new group of men who were firmly in powe and openly disposed to remain there for quite some time. Al most against his will, because to recognize as much was admit his own decline, Barbosa insisted that Hermes da For seca represented a very potent group indeed, ruthlessly dete mined to hold on to the reins of power; yet, this group c younger politicians, full of nascent intrigue, still wanted ver much to get to know Percival Farquhar, the Quaker magnate And if the situation was tense, it was all the more imperativ that Farquhar waste no time.

After several moments of pensive reflection, during whic he had occasionally raised a glass of champagne to his lips, only to moisten his thought, Ruy Barbosa finally made th following suggestion to his friend: that, to attract the favorabl attention of the present administration, why not make use o one of his more daring enterprises? Wasn't he building a rai road in the very heart of the Amazon jungle? Of course, Far quhar had any number of business dealings; some huge, other less so. The railroad was one of the latter; not being among the largest or the most important, it had slowly devolved to that lower order of preoccupations that hardly entered his head. And so at first he could barely understand why Ruy should propose, of all things, the railroad as a means to enter the confidence of the administration. Especially since the Madeira-Mamoré project—surrounded though it was by a somewhat purposeful wall of silence—had already provoked a number of attacks in the press, owing to, among other factors, the lack of competitive public bidding for such a lucrative federal contract. (A gross lapse on the part of his titular contractor the engineer Joaquim Catambry, a corrupt and highly authoritarian sort of fool without even the patience to disguise the sordid details of his methods of transaction.) That is, not until Barbosa explained that, knowing the marshal's fondness for feats of modern technology, it was quite possible that as president he would welcome an invitation to visit the site of construction, along the Rio Madeira. He must remember, Marshal Hermes da Fonseca greatly admired the Germans, was even something of a Germanophile, and strongly identified with the seeming Teutonic capacity to dominate the field of technological advances. Beyond the simple boyish admiration, however, there lurked the danger that the marshal's intimacy with the Germans might actually lead to the opening of the Brazilian markets to those capitalists of Berlin. Hadn't he been on a visit to Germany at the time of his election? Hadn't he been received by Kaiser Wilhelm himself? Wasn't he on intimate terms, as well, with men of such powerful Teutonic names as Krupp and Siemens? Even the Baron Rothschild was growing pensive over the possibility that the Germans could descend upon Brazil and begin to compete for the market. Barbosa himself had gotten wind of the fact that Rio Branco, the powerful Brazilian baron who was minister of foreign relations, had been receiving alarmed notes from his Rothschild friend, and yet Percival had the perfect trump card right within the boundaries of the nation itself—a *railroad,* the building of which was about to be completed, a feat that had defied a host of entrepreneurs as far back as the epoch of the monarchy. This railway was exactly the type of accomplishment that the marshal could not help but admire, and one that would finally gain Farquhar his access to the presidency.

Farquhar remained skeptical, though he did not completely disregard the suggestion. His lawyer friend, it turned out, was not only providing him with a possible mode of entry to the gates of Catete but also furnishing valuable information on the marshal's relations with the Germans. Farquhar had also surmised this connection and now felt himself cast in the anomalous role of patriot: defending the interests of North American capital investments, here in the tropics, against Teutonic intervention. When they parted company, in front of the hotel, he could see how relieved Ruy Barbosa was to be rid of Luiza Rosalvo, an emotion he seemed to wish to convey by scratching his mustachio and winking determinedly as if the light were irritating his eyes and the heat were making him suddenly itchy.

The silhouette in the bathroom switched off the light and came billowing into Percival's bedroom. She was quite naked, and her ample rump and roundish hips made him anticipate the taste of salt from her skin. He was positive she bore that voluptuous smile on her lips that could only be eclipsed by the dark, magnificent waves of her freshly washed, still damp hair. He could sense the eagerness of his own fingertips to probe the navel that marked the beginning of her downiness like the bud of a desert flower. Soon he would make his way through the dense foliage to the mound of flesh, softly undulating, that was her pubis. She was solidly fleshed, with a vibrantly delicious buttocks that tightened to his hands the instant he leafed the tip of his tongue gently between the petals of her vagina. She was a woman who could wield her pink passion in bed like a long-stemmed, gelatin rose. Percival Farquhar smiled at the thought as she slipped almost soundlessly into his bed. After all, here was a woman and then some; for with him was the most delectable mistress of Senator J. J. Seabra, implacable adversary to his own Ruy Barbosa.

4

The bodies of the two Germans were encased like a pair of stringbeans. An exhausted Richard Finnegan was seated at his desk, dozing on and off, practically falling from his chair sometimes and waking up alarmedly, while the medics were finishing up with the dead Barbadians to be buried presently by the edge of the tracks. The young lads worked taciturnly, ruminating their task as a bit of unmerited punishment, as if the doctor—after having found it impossible to stand up to the English engineer—were castigating them as a form of malicious compensation. And yet they sympathized with the doctor. After all, they were of more or less the same age and shared a similar faith in meticulousness. The effective knowledge and experience in medicine that Finnegan brought with him from one of the most respected schools of medicine in the United States, Johns Hopkins University, had considerably bolstered the confidence of employees in the health and sanitary services of the company. The reality was that before Dr. Lovelace had assumed the directorship of the division of medical services and begun to restore a little of its integrity by hiring youths like Richard Finnegan, to seek medical treatment at company facilities was regarded as an act of wilfully suicidal deliberation. In that earlier period, when the workers first began to arrive there, health services were represented by the presence of a half-dozen unsavory, unsuccessful, unscrupulous medics —for the most part old scoundrels who had lost their medical licenses for some breach of practice or other—"angel-makers" and quacks who had actually tried to run a monopoly on quinine pills, distributing them on the black market at two pennies per pill. And to complete matters, they would commit the worst sort of medical atrocities, such as administering violent laxatives or Epsom salts to patients suffering from diarrhea and thereby inducing fatal dehydration. One of these doctors was notorious for prescribing injections of potassium permanganate as an antidote against snakebite. None of his patients survived to attest to the effectiveness of the cure. With Lovelace, however, came young doctors like Richard Finnegan—altruistic, professional—who at least managed to slow the mortality rate among workers and could actually, from time to time, snatch a patient from the hands of death. One of the young lads working as a medic was particularly grateful to Dr. Finnegan, who had found him burning up with fever and sinking into deliriousness on the first day of his own arrival there as head physician. After examining the fellow he concluded he was really suffering from pneumonia, not malaria as the other physicians had diagnosed. Finnegan at once suspended the doses of quinine and concentrated instead upon the fever and the dark, infectious stain that like a cancer was blanketing his lung. The lad's recovery was considerably slowed by the unavailability of appropriate medication and proper diet, but in a few weeks' time he was out of danger and had begun to get his strength back. Eventually, he was able to assist once again in the infirmary, with that gratitude of those who have escaped certain death and have come to regard their physician with a devotion normally reserved for prophets or magicians. Thus, the irritation these lads felt at the moment was as nothing compared to the respect they accorded the doctor, even under such unpleasant circumstances. In any case, the incident would soon be forgotten, as would the very tensions and exhaustion of that particular night.

Awakening from his dozings, Finnegan gradually became aware of some vague shapes crawling along the ground. He concentrated his gaze and the shapes crystallized into three passing scorpions—one almost three inches long marched at the head of their parade. This largest of the creatures was charcoal gray in color, with a body that seemed constructed from plates of armor and with his pincers held high in order to camouflage his arms as if to look like antennae. Finnegan was ever observing scorpions. He knew their poison was enough to kill a man. Beyond that, he had not formed much of an impression. They were a brazen lot and exhibited a mysterious determination. They showed great strength, were devoid of emotion, and had invaded the infirmary in search of something that Finnegan was unable to ascertain. They were evidently headed in the direction of one of those wrapped corpses lying about, perhaps hoping to settle themselves among the folds of a sheet. Finnegan got up and with one leap smashed the leader and a smaller one who was following directly behind. The remaining one, instead of fleeing, stiffened its legs as if to gain added height in order to challenge the doctor, making frenzied semicircles around the boot that had proved fatal to his comrades. The physician, however, so hated that outrageous daring that he delivered a single blow with his heel, transforming what was scorpion into an amorphous paste. When Finnegan eventually raised his head from contemplating this accomplishment, a feeling of repugnance now invading his own body, he noticed that the medics had stopped working and were watching him. Clearly, there was no trace of annoyance on their faces. By smashing scorpions, it was as if Finnegan had somehow managed to renew his leadership among his subordinates and regenerate a sense of protectiveness and efficiency. Finnegan, disgusted, said nothing; he felt like what he would term a load of shit because to destroy three scorpions, a dozen scorpions, even a hundred scorpions signified nothing at all. It seemed little short of a confidence game to sustain his leadership through such fallacious behavior. Yet, the young medics appeared not to care in the least; they wanted to be grateful to the doctor regardless of the circumstances—as human creatures, all too fragile and in need of such lies.

As each day passed, Richard Finnegan grew more and more convinced that he also wanted to preserve his own admiration for Dr. Lovelace, the chief physician, by means of that very same fallacy. This recognition was at least a step in the right direction, though a painful one. Men lost their charm out here, and even one's idea of God ended up a bit tarnished in the midst of all this banal havoc. Finnegan was hardly a fervent Catholic. To some degree the simple contact with human cadavers dissected in anatomy classes coupled with his shock at the death of one of his sisters—precisely the sweetest and most devout of his sisters, he would have added—had distanced him from the Church; and if he remained a Catholic at all, it was more by virtue of a certain ethnic definition. Back in the States, all the Irish were presumed to be Catholic and alcoholics. Since our Finnegan did not drink, not even socially—he felt ghastly from it whenever he did—it was left to him to be Catholic. Still, he did believe in God; and the complexity of the human body—not the wrecked and frozen cadavers he would dissect in anatomy classes, but the incredible machine which showed up in textbooks, in colorful illustrations that seemed to palpitate with their various hues—somehow substantiated the presence of this apparently absent and arbitrary, sometimes benevolent but nearly always indifferent *Being*. And if Finnegan's faith was no longer what it used to be, it had merely been replaced by an admiration for men he considered in some way superior, wise: as Dr. Lovelace had appeared to be.

The previous year several professors of parasitology had managed to bring Lovelace to Johns Hopkins for a medical conference. It took place on one of those summer afternoons, when very few students were left on campus because of the vacation and only a handful of idlers with nowhere to go or no girl to go to bed with sat fanning themselves in the amphitheater of the medical school. Dr. Lovelace was an extremely refined-looking sort of gentleman with the air of an English lord about him as he discoursed with great humor, confidence, and joviality. The major part of his lecture was devoted to the diagnosis and preventative treatment of malaria and, in particular, to a detailed description of how he had personally developed a method for a prophylaxis en masse in a region where the disease had run epidemic: during the construction of the Panama Canal. This feat had brought him a certain renown and, at the time of his visit, Lovelace was considered to be one of the most important authorities in the field of tropical medicine. What Finnegan did not know was that the same Dr. Lovelace had been visiting all the medical schools around the country under the sponsorship of a firm called the Madeira-Mamoré Railway Company, with the unavowed purpose of attracting recently graduated medical doctors to work in South America, in one of the most inhospitable regions on earth. The company wanted young doctors because they were still relatively unspoiled, because they were still reasonably enthusiastic, and because they were cheaper and less demanding. Lovelace did not reap a good harvest at Johns Hopkins University that summer. Almost all the students there had already had their futures mapped out for them; they were the sons of millionaires who did not need to lift a finger to become established in their medical practices. Besides which, those who were on campus that summer with the exception of

Finnegan were students either just beginning their studies or, at best, a long way off from finishing them, students who had not gone home for the holidays precisely because they were trying to get as much coursework out of the way as possible through summer labs and seminars. Such interest normally declined only after the first two years or so, until, in the end, the students would become so saturated with their work that they would hardly be attending classes at all by the final semester. Finnegan would shortly graduate but had remained in Baltimore that summer: solitary, grieving, badly scarred by the untimely death of his sister Nancy. Nancy, married just a year before to a young lawyer, had died during childbirth at the end of last winter. It had come as a terrible blow to Finnegan because her death had been senseless, attributable only to the incompetence of their old family doctor who, almost totally deaf and with a pair of doltish hands, had refused to perform a cesarean in the fanatical belief that women ought to have their fair quota of suffering as mandated by the Scriptures. The cursed fundamentalism of that Protestant doctor had blinded him to the seriousness of the pains that his sister Nancy was experiencing: she had suffered insufficient dilation and a series of resulting complications that ended in death for her and the baby. Finnegan considered this a monstrous barbarity and was crushed by the fact of his not having been there himself. This, then, was the reason why Finnegan had not gone home that summer, preferring to walk the pacifyingly conservative streets of Baltimore, with its red brick houses in the Georgian style. He had also visited, without much conviction, the girl with whom he'd been regularly dating for the past two years—she, an English student—and attended occasional summer lectures, if only to reawaken the fonder memories of his freshman days. It may well have been his all-consuming sorrow that led him to fall into Lovelace's trap, given that he had never before demonstrated so adventurous a spirit, and was actually planning to dedicate himself to general practice back in his hometown of St. Louis.

After the lecture, Finnegan spoke briefly with Dr. Lovelace, who gave him his card with his home address, in case the young student should wish to enter into correspondence with the great doctor or, who knows, even work with him down in South America. The very same summer, before finishing his

61

studies and without advising his family of the fact, Finnegan
wrote to Lovelace, asking for employment. The address he
wrote to was Portland, Oregon, where the Madeira-Mamoré
Railway Company had a branch office. The reply came quickly
and he discovered that Lovelace was still in the United States
and only planned to proceed to South America at the beginning
of the following year. Lovelace suggested that they take advantage of the opportunity to travel at the same period, so that
together, they could get to know each other better and perhaps
avail themselves of opportunities for Finnegan to even gain
some valuable experience in the field of tropical medicine. The
trip was to be by sea and would take two months: up the
Amazon River, then the Rio Madeira, as far as the town of
Porto Velho. In December of 1910, now with a medical degree,
Finnegan found himself once again with Dr. Lovelace, this
time in Portland. They were to depart in several weeks' time
from New York harbor, on an ocean liner, a luxurious trans-
atlantic that would take them as far as Manaus. Lovelace was
extremely attentive to him throughout his stay in Portland and
instructed him in the principal ailments he would have to confront at the end of his journey. Yet the great doctor never lost
for a moment his keen wit and jovial demeanor, thus sugar
coating with a virtuoso irony the horrors that others from time
to time would whisper in Finnegan's ear, in the very direst
tones. The lively and sweetened *mots justes* that seemed to
positively flow from Lovelace's lips, however, easily eclipsed
the pessimists and Finnegan was now in this place, squashing
scorpions and performing autopsies, signing death certificates
and swallowing insults from an ill-disposed English engineer.
And Dr. Lovelace had lost his charm, just as God, his appeal
to the once unshakable faith of Richard Finnegan. He felt truly
like a load of shit as gradually he came to the realization of
the hole he had dug for himself, one with plenty of room for
other loads of shit who hoped to find solace in the false magic
posited by his presence there. Our Finnegan was tired and
wanted only to sleep. The young medics were smiling at him
as prudent in their behavior as the two smaller scorpions who
had paraded smartly behind their larger brother. Christ, it didn't
even occur to them how easily they could be squashed as well.
Lightning and thunder announced a storm.

* * *

The lightning flash followed by thunder awoke Consuelo, but she managed to open her eyes only with great difficulty. Her eyelids were heavy and drooped closed before she had the chance to adjust her vision and comprehend what that flash of light actually meant which cut across the membranes of her eyes and afterward exploded into a grave, rumbling sound. She felt the strong light penetrate her eyelids as she moaned to herself from the discomfort of her legs having fallen asleep, pricked by thousands of pins. There followed a series of lightnings that burst aglow one after another, remaining alight, illuminating the length of her body down to the tips of her toenails. Her toes, caressed by Alonso, his mustache brushing along the soles of her feet. Her feet were plump and delectable. How Alonso delighted in them. Alonso . . . Running his hand slowly over her leg, first one leg, then the other—never the two at once or with equal fervor . . . The stage of a small theater, the municipal theater of the city of Sucre, its auditorium filled with gaily dressed ladies as the carbide lamps slowly flashed on one by one. Consuelo walked onto the stage, though the curtains were still to be raised. She was nervous and the tight shoes pinched her feet, cutting the circulation off and releasing a thousand needle points into her tender flesh. Her clothes fit her tightly, too, and the heat had grown unbearable. The blood was rushing to her face, causing her to blush in fear and expectation. She clutched a sheaf of musical scores to her bosom. A fear both terrifying and voluptuous seemed to well up within her and was about to wrench out a cry when the curtain began lifting without a sound and she saw herself in the midst of a host of children dressed with fastidious care, who bowed in unison before the public that were already applauding, loudly clapping, like thunder. At the front of the stage stood three white upright pianos, like toys, with a backdrop of a starry, blue-skyed rotunda. Consuelo sat stiffly back in a velvet chair as three of the children walked over to the pianos, sat themselves down, lifted their little trained hands and played in unison: Chopin? She felt the water begin to drip from her face and thought it curious that the stage should be splashing everywhere as if it were drizzling, a fine drizzle, still not rain, indoors? A stage trick? Chopin? Alonso had begun to perspire, that was it, transmitting his own body heat to her body as well, the drops of sweat landing upon her shoulders, dripping down

63

her breasts, puddling across her abdomen and moistening her inner thighs while he rocked above her. But the streets, the troops scattering under fire from civilians? Her father telling her *It's the revolution! Bolivia never learns, so you must be careful and not to let your husband get mixed up in political intrigue.* Her father had had suspicions about Alonso, because he himself had no love for music. To be truthful, he had no love of anything—only Gongora and the history of Spanish grammar. Father? So gangly looking in his dark suit of cheap cloth, badly cut, slipping off his narrow shoulders, the sleeves too short to hide the plunge of the always threadbare cuffs of his shirt-sleeves. He disliked everything there was to like about Alonso, but still he presented no opposition to their plans to marry. Marry Alonso? So opposite from her father—an impetuous, wild, terribly handsome devil! And he sweated like a man but was not one to hurry pleasure. He liked to lie beside her in bed, stroking her body and uttering such loving intimacies they seemed like poems of love. Perhaps they were poems, those words he whispered to her? Or lyrical songs? Sucre had been declared the federal capital and the people were fighting to impose that right. A howitzer shell was lying on the street unexploded, like an aberrant egg. No one wanted to risk going near the missile until Alonso walked over, picked it up carefully, and tossed it into a sewer. It never did explode and lies there still. Someday, it may yet explode in the sewer. When? Alonso didn't know. What he knew best of all was music, scores, the chords of a guitar, tuning pegs, and compositions for the violincello. The *twelve variations:* a heavy, violent downpour broke upon Consuelo. She seemed to lose consciousness altogether or fall into a deep, empty sleep. Undisturbed by the water that was slowly drenching her helpless body. Gradually a house emerged, and she was seated on the piano bench drinking a chilled glass of something so refreshing as she listened to the lesson which a dark-complected little girl, her hair in braids, was attempting to execute with a flurry of supplicating glances directed toward the teacher beside her. But Consuelo was distractedly caressing the piano, a lovely grand piano imported from Germany. The little girl showed no talent, only bad coordination. Consuelo finally interrupted to demonstrate how her pupil ought to perform her lesson. Consuelo played crisply, fingering rapidly across the immaculate keyboard which filled her with exhilaration. Until the keys began to crumble and sink into the maelstrom of water, when she opened her eyes and felt dizzy, and at the same time was aware from the smell of ether that she had to be in some hospital. What had happened? Alonso was staring at her disconsolately. She was pregnant, four months into her term, but now she felt a cold ache ebbing and flowing there below, and an emptiness. The baby? Lost? The shock of realization compounding the intuition of loss. She could do nothing to save the toy, hurled into the abyss of furious waters. The room, empty now. It was raining outside. Alonso was the strange man in the mustache who leaned over to hug her and caress her hair. She felt herself responding to his touch, but noticed that he was hiding something in the other hand kept behind him. And she grew ever more curious, as always. How she loved to read other people's letters, intimate diaries and confessions, to learn the secrets of another being. Consuelo kept asking what he was hiding behind his back but Alonso preferred to prolong her suspense. Until she could stand it no more and he brought out a lovely brochure: a catalogue of German pianos. He might have been asking for her hand in marriage with that catalogue. She wished to marry him and she wanted the piano. Her kiss of gratitude was accepted passionately and the rain poured down with terrible flashes of lightning. Yet all was so comforting.

The lightning illuminated the crumpled ace of hearts that Harold Appleton had just discarded onto the top of the crate. Gallagher gave no particular response in the expression of his face. The game hardly interested him; it passed the time or was supposed to. Old Thomas Gallagher disliked the thought of problems. It could have irritated him that he had been robbed, but he had long ago learned to resign himself. Wanting nothing in the way of complication in his life, he preferred to know his place and empty his head. He had been striving these seventy years now to score a perfect zero in the great summation of the things of this world. He was an efficient and solitary self-cancellation, with no undue ambition or depression. What more could one ask for than to be able to run a machine that always followed the same path bound by the protection of its tracks and the security of its signals. Each

65

station along the way was another mark of his own reassuring insignificance. Already by adolescence he had lost all trace of whimsy. He was poor, had always been poor, had fought to manage every forkful of food that entered his mouth, and every bite of food was a victory commemorated in total apathy. His only point of pride was in the absence of dreams: he had no wish to climb nor to conquer in life. Nor did he know rightly what it was precisely "to conquer in life." He could only surmise that to do so was to have plenty of boxes of Havana cigars, plenty of money in his pockets, and *colleens* by the score—"much disposed te farnicatin'." It would all be very complicated for him, especially the *colleens*. He mistrusted women and preferred to possess just one of them, at home, *farnicatable* when he wanted her, though low on the enthusiasm. The rest of them were far too dangerous, lining up like tramps for a tryst with the rich; and whoever was after that, any woman who would submit herself to such queuing up for a wealthier poke, was capable of anything at all, of sheer madness. And Old Thomas had no stomach for madness, which is why he had actually come to the rescue—like the good missionary to conformity he was—of the young Harold Appleton, when one day the lad stumbled crazy drunk and fell in front of Gallagher's locomotive. And now Harold was becoming more and more like him—at least he hoped so—so as not to get into complications either. For our Harold also nurtured a mistrust of women. The lightning flashes and thunder surely portended one of those early morning heavy rains.

Stephan Collier came ambling over among the flashes and darkness to sit down and watch them play cards. The game hardly seemed governed by any rules and Collier found it difficult to follow; but, who knows, perhaps it was just a matter of being bloody fed up.

"Don't you chaps ever think of turning in?" Collier asked.

"With this storm coming up?" Harold responded.

"Think we'll actually have some rain?" Collier insisted.

Thomas could see the engineer wanted to do some talking. He knew the signs because they had worked together a fair number of years already, starting way back in Panama.

"Ye can be sure of it," Gallagher affirmed smilingly. "Me rheumatism ain't in the habit o' lyin' to yers truly."

"Rheumatism, is it? I should recommend you for a chair in

he meteorological branch of the company," Collier chided, trying to shrug off his irritation.

"Care te join us fer a hand," Gallagher ventured, trying to help in some way. It was always thus between them.

"No thanks, I've no bloody patience for games."

"Problems, is it?" Thomas insisted, trying to make Collier open up. "It couldn't be that fine bucko of an Irish doctor gettin' on yer nerves now, could it?"

"He's a decent enough chap," Collier granted. "It's not entirely his fault."

"Almost met his Maker wi' them Barbadian fellers," Thomas offered, hoping to goad his friend into a bit of conversation, thinking it might do him some good.

"He did look a bit peaked, I'll warrant you," said the engineer smiling, a touch of perversity in his voice. "Thought he was about to wet his pants."

"Heard-workin' feller, though, ain't he."

"No compunction about committing a few idiocies every now and then."

"Ye haven't much sympathy for the lad, have ye, Callier? Yer no mystery to me."

"Rather too diligent for my taste. Nothing personal, of course."

Thomas gathered more or less what the engineer meant by his remark. The doctor was close to making a horse's ass of himself by refusing to recognize the mess he'd landed in.

"He'll be larnin' quick enough this ain't exactly the place far bein' diligent," Thomas agreed. Yet he had no complaints about the lad, who appeared to be a decent sort of worker, and he hated to see him make a horse's ass of himself.

"If it does rain, we'll be having quite a mess on our hands." The change of subject seemed to indicate that Collier also hated to see the young doctor make a horse's ass of himself but he wasn't one to admit the fact to anyone.

"Would ye believe it's already stearted?" Gallagher replied, feeling the drops of rain on his shoulders.

But the engineer, at least momentarily, forgot about the rain because a strange procession had begun to emerge out of the night. It was the medics carrying two cadavers wrapped in sheets. Collier stood up, set his fists against his waist, and, dumbfounded, observed the ataxic caravan. He hadn't expected

67

this, the little sod of a pious physician had passed the limit Collier had the distinct impression that Finnegan was delib erately provoking trouble.

"Hey, you blithering idiots!" Collier howled. "What the blazes are you up to? Where are you going with those corpses?"

"Following orders, sir," one of the medics replied sheep ishly, much as a raw recruit would reply to a general when caught practicing some sort of minor but degrading asininity.

"We're about to bury them, sir," said the other, also wholly intimidated.

"Don't tell me you have the Barbadians there," Collier asked and his voice slit them open like a razor.

"Yes, sir," one of them whispered hoarsely.

Collier turned to Thomas. "It's not possible!" Then he faced the medics once more, trying to keep a calm voice: "Take them back to the infirmary at once, and don't leave your quarters till the sun is up."

"Yes, sir. But, sir . . ."

"Get *going!*" he howled, making it clear there was no al ternative.

Thomas had begun to laugh out loud, unable to control himself now that the situation had evidently turned comic, as the medics about-faced and lolloped off as fast as they could under the circumstances. Collier caught a whiff of the loco motive operator's laughter and nearly gave vent to the impulse himself. It seemed a whorishly comical situation, all right, that this bloody Irish fool of a physician had finally concocted for himself. On the point of fucking himself royally and still acting like the clown.

"Gallagher, you old fox, I'll tell you one thing: if we do get rain tonight with you and your rheumatism, I'm going to send you out to inspect a couple of square miles of Caripuna Indian country," Collier concluded, walking off to his tent, which was pitched in the vicinity.

In a moment, Thomas had turned to Harold and they were staring at each other in astonishment because a peal of laughter had just ripped through the night from somewhere off in that general direction.

When the rain should fall he would have to find protection. And it certainly was going to rain hard this time. Yet he had

68

no *maloca,* had no home: no father or mother, no sisters or brothers, no relatives of any kind. Everything about him amounted to hunger, terrible hunger. Occasionally he would manage to steal some food from the *civilized,* then devour it without even noticing its taste. At other times he would contrive to catch a fish, then fry it on a campfire and bolt it down, always forgetting about the taste, because he was feeding himself to stay alive and to staunch the hunger that gnawed obsessively in his stomach like a half-dead rodent. He was gaunt now in stature, his skin flaccid and clayish, having lost the dark vigor of his race. He seemed shorter, as each day he regressed further into a state in which his senses mattered very little; he was becoming decrepit. The act of stealing from the *civilized* had no real connotation of robbery in his mind. He was taking from the *civilized* whatever fascinated him and he presumed that the *civilized,* possessing so much, would have no objection. He was dressed in a pair of foul, stinking shorts and had not worn anything else for over a year, taking them off only when he would decide to have a bath in the river and therefore undress himself to go into the water. He did not understand yet that shorts—this pair a gift from one of the *civilized* traveling in the company of the benefactor Rondon— could also be washed clean. These shorts were hardly to be called cloth anymore, so encrusted were they with dirt, earth, urine, and excrement. He reeked but did not perceive his own stench, for he had lost all capacity to sense himself. Entirely cut off from the world around him, he had gravitated around the *civilized,* contenting himself with their leavings. He had no illusions, no dreams or hopes of one day becoming at least friends with the *civilized.* Brothers of his had tried and had died of it . . . or ended up working savagely hard in Santo Antônio, always drinking, without their women. The fact that the *civilized* lived without women made him absolutely certain there was no possibility for acceptance among them. If only women were living there with them, if only the *civilized* would marry normally, he might still contemplate at least finding such a woman for himself and becoming one of the *civilized.* Without the bridge of a woman, there could be no illusion left to nourish. His own wife had been a Tacuatepe maiden with a very good name in the hierarchy. He also had hierarchy because from quite a young age he had acted as initiator of ceremonies,

69

and he knew all the music and rituals for each occasion. She
had been a very spirited little maiden with white teeth; dark
brilliant eyes; and pointed, little brown breasts. She had yet
to formally take leave of her childhood and had undergone the
rites of initiation only a short time before coming to live with
him. She worked very hard, preparing the meals correctly,
going to the hammock with him every night he wished, and
never wandered after young boys to make mischief in the forest.
They lived in a *maloca* along the Upper Mutum-Paraná, not
far from the uplands of the Pacaá-Novo, together with a group
of some twenty families, all with lots of boys and girls, to
whom smiling elders would tell amazing stories toward the
end of each evening. Contact with the *civilized* was minimal;
occasionally they ran into them along the river and would barter
fruit, skins, fish, and meat for bits of cloth, for knives and
mirrors. Men appreciated the knives; he had always wanted
such a knife and now he possessed three good ones. Women
preferred the clothes and mirrors; he could remember how they
laughed into the mirrors, making faces and sticking out their
lips. How comical when his wife would sit down near the
campfire at night, before going to the hammock, and make
faces that filled her with contentment! The *civilized* seldom
came to *malocas,* and whenever they did so they would not
sleep there. They refused even food or drink. His people were
quite peaceful and prided themselves in being more cultured
and more complexly organized than the *civilized*. If one of the
civilized suddenly appeared at their *maloca,* they would naturally all come out to receive him and show friendship, to
pacify the *white*. It was what elders had always said: of all the
tribes the *civilized* were surely the most fearless and the most
dangerous, because they would kill with no reason—neither
for making war nor for performing any ritual among themselves. They killed simply to kill, hitting with their rifles even
those who had come to the bank of the river to make signs of
a joyful welcome. The *whites* of the *civilized* and even those
of darker skin seemed more fierce than even the Shavante and
the Bororo, more fierce than the Paressi. His people were not
thus. The *civilized* had named his people Caripuna and had
invented the legend of Caripuna ferocity because the men wore
two macaw feathers, yellow ones, stuck through the nose. It
was a lie, of course. Such feathers were only worn for specific

ceremonies to recall how they had once upon a time made war—this, such a long time ago that no elders among them could claim to have participated in such battles. All men of his people had repudiated war, long ago. Yet the *civilized* preferred the lie and began to kill people from his *maloca*, or to entice youths to run off to promises that were never kept. Elders grew preoccupied but, no longer listened to, chose to lie down in their hammocks and say farewell, preparing to cross the land of the living to the other side. Preparing to die, say the *civilized*. It was even preferable that they were no longer there when the *civilized* who called themselves *seringueiros* turned to making war one early morning; and thus they arrived shouting and firing their rifles into the *maloca*, causing all to flee into the forest. They had come to steal women, and he suddenly realized that probably because the *civilized* did not have sufficient women among them they needed maidens to marry them. Clearly his people could have reached an understanding with the *civilized;* had they not done so before, when the Paressi had needed women and they had come to an understanding concerning marriage? The *civilized*, though, rejected understanding and preferred stealing women and shooting men. On one occasion they had even tried to steal his young Tacuatepe, but she had refused to go and had struggled and screamed with such fury that a *civilized* opened her up with a blow that began at her chest bone and finished between her legs. He found her dead inside an earthenware vessel for making tapioca, floating in the already darkened blood and her legs wide open where flies were circling and landing. At that time, their *maloca* had had hardly any families left; most of them had fled to beyond the mountain range of the Pacaá-Novo, or were already dead, or living among the *civilized*, working as *seringueiros* and getting drunk on *cachaça* in Santo Antônio. He had buried his young Tacuatepe girl and then resolved to live closer to the *civilized*, imagining that he could thus find some manner of better comprehending them and perhaps pacifying them a little. But the *civilized* were strange in all respects, and he was becoming weaker, and slowly dying of his hunger.

Farquhar reached out to the side and discovered that the woman was no longer with him. He opened his eyes; it was still dark. The open window had allowed a cold and uncom-

71

fortable wind to chill the bedroom. He got up, dazed with sleepiness, and closed the window, then tried to sleep some more. His bed was naturally in some disarray, but still it hardly seemed plausible that just a little while ago an incredible woman had been there. Only on his side of the mattress were the sheet crumpled and twisted. It was a huge bed, all right, but still— to have the sheet drawn tightly over, on the side where a delicious cunt ought to have been lying? She was an intelligent whore, that one, thought Farquhar—didn't let herself be carried away by the sentimental bullshit of most Brazilians. Percival had assumed that she would want to stay the whole night and had not bothered to even check if that were actually so. In truth, he did not appreciate it when these women wanted to stay with him until morning because, generally, he found Brazilian women to be just too damn sentimental, mistaking a good night's lay for a firm commitment. This whore, on the contrary, had placed that fuck in the proper perspective—a strictly professional transaction. Percival Farquhar felt a bit envious of J. J. Seabra. Certainly the bastard had no inkling of the vein of rich ore to be mined in that woman. He would be willing to bet on how Seabra went about treating such a mistress: as if she were just like any other young succulent nugget fucking him for his money and worthy of no more consideration than that given to the ordinary French strumpet. For Brazilians, he had long ago surmised, the height of sexual refinement was to be found in the mercenary appetites of the European streetwalker, generally of Polish extraction, who tried to be taken for French in order to command a better price on the market. Rio de Janeiro was swarming with these ambitious tarts who made of their physical exploits a species of commodity for the veneration of French culture. He personally couldn't give a cow's shit about French culture and detested anything that had to do with France. The French reminded him of nothing so much as of a thoroughly ruined man, or of all the formerly rich, or even of that cheap variety of pretentious swindler who tries to hide everything behind his fancy words and a good education. The whole mania for the French—a bit too effeminate to his way of thinking—might well prove eventually to be the undoing of the Brazilians. First of all, because the Brazilians themselves had never been rich and hardly ever bothered to hide the fact they were poor. And second of all

72

as con artists they barely passed the level of the crude, neophyte pickpocket trying to work the White House in hopes of palming the wallet of the president of the United States! The simple fact of the whore's having been so objective and unfettered by all that Gallic bullshit was already reason enough for her to enter into his good graces, and should she continue to do things right she would certainly earn more than his trust. For the moment, however, he was treating each wet lay as an investment; and he expected to soak up quite a profit. Farquhar, in fact, had the greatest veneration for the principle of profit. Indeed, he had come to believe that profit was perhaps God's finest creation. In nature, was not everything a source of profit? Our Farquhar was convinced that a shrewd God would never have acted thus for nothing. Hence, the lay, realized with such expertise, her perfumed body steeped in its ritual of flawless toiletries, was as promissory as a bank note deposited for a fixed term and compounded daily.

Farquhar realized that he was not about to sleep more; it was always thus with him: awakening, he found it constitutionally impossible to doze off again. He smiled at the notion of how dirty the language of his thoughts tended to be. They sounded in his head almost constantly, these words he would never permit his lips to utter. For when he spoke, he never had recourse to gross expression, preferring to ply his interlocutors with persuasive arguments and a vocabulary so chaste, who could possibly not believe him immediately? But in his thoughts, however, he was still that uncouth lad from York, Pennsylvania, who would lace each sentence with half a dozen swearwords, although he had never in his life uttered a single blasphemy or any imprecation involving what was Sacred. His parents had refrained from reprimanding him for mouthing obscenities because they believed it was all a matter of age and would happen, in any case, according to the dictates of the Lord God Almighty. And they were right; with the passage of time their son Percival had learned that he must moderate his language and temper his impulses if he wished to make any headway in life. To be sure, he had quickly made up his mind not to be a "manure hick," living off crumbs and attending church on Sunday with a pudgy wife who fucked seldom and suckled frequently. Precisely what had happened to his father, who never could restrain himself and even as an old man continued to bellow out the crudest vulgarities over nothing at all or at the worst possible moments, when the bank would deny him a loan, for example, or the harvest was a disaster. Impropriety of language was linked to poverty, in his own mind, as inextricably as French culture was tied to his notion of a confidence game. And our Percival surely took pride in embodying the best characteristics of American society: he was a man of action who knew how to make a buck, knew how to get the best deal, and knew how to cheat in such a manner that the victims would nearly always end up thankful for the fact and sometimes insist on even becoming his friend. Privately, he considered himself the greatest highbinder of his time, and the word to him was an intimate crown of laurels. Because the real value of each and every son of a bitch in this world like himself lay in the rest of the world's tacit agreement that he was only a son of a bitch for the well-being of mankind and the health of the economy. All highbinders should, in fact, be considered benefactors of the human race. (This, too, was the will of God.)

The light of day had arrived, slowly entering through the closed slats of the blinds from the frosted glass of the windowpanes. With the light had come the heat, but a good heat, for the room was never particularly stuffy at this time of year. It was only in January and February that Rio began to feel like a hot loaf of bread, but he would always manage to be somewhere else during that time. Still, Rio de Janeiro had become for all practical purposes his permanent residence. Long before 1902, when he first initiated business dealings in Brazil, he had already singled it out as a country ripe for *his* expansion, but within five short years his expectations were to be eclipsed by the reality of his successes. It had all come to pass, however, in 1902, during a reception at the Brazilian Embassy in Washington, D.C., where he ran into the then current minister of industry, transportation, and public works, a fellow named Müller. Farquhar had attended the reception in the company of several friends who already held large interests in Brazil and talked of nothing but the vast possibilities of that gigantic country off in South America. Farquhar himself had just become rich, through a takeover of the May, Jekyll & Randolph Railway, owned by "King" John, now his employee. It had only been a relative victory because "King" John was already

74

tired and had proved himself to be an easy mark. Perhaps he had trusted too much in Farquhar simply from a yearning to play that classic role of victim who remains peculiarly attached to the swindler who has duped him. Lauro Müller was a corpulent sort of fellow, with pale milky skin and cheeks spattered with a variety of freckles. He would hardly have looked South American at all, were it not for his rotten teeth. Quite by chance he had settled himself on the same settee where Farquhar happened to be sitting, sipping a glass of champagne. They began to talk and Müller presently blurted out that he was growing quite fond of Farquhar, whom he considered to be a lunatic, for Brazil needed lunatics of his stripe since only such lunatics were capable of investing confidently in the future of such a country, without the prospect of an immediate return. The comment left Farquhar curiously intrigued, because it seemed to smack of an invitation and because he enjoyed the notion of being viewed as a lunatic for no apparent reason. Perhaps his interlocutor was actually aware of the source of his fortune; there was no lack of individuals disposed to point out how he had managed to amass—in less than three years, and starting literally from scratch—the sum of five million dollars. Although the novelty of being judged a lunatic finally struck him as rather unctuous, he did decide to look into Brazil. Besides, the novelty of the rest of South America had more or less faded with a succession of lucrative investments, especially the enterprise in Colombia that in three years had returned more than four times the capital invested—an enterprise, by the way, that he had managed to have almost totally financed by the Colombian government. So in mid-September of that same year he finally disembarked in Rio de Janeiro, where he was welcomed by Lauro Müller. At a party given in his honor he would quickly get to know a certain J. J. Seabra, at that time the minister of justice and domestic trade, whom he immediately assessed as one of the most cultivated highbinders he had ever had the good or ill fortune to encounter. Next to Seabra, the likes of Lauro Müller couldn't pass for better than a well-educated pup, capable of doing tricks for the price of a bone. Also at the party was the president, Rodrigues Alves himself, who confided that he believed one hundred percent in foreign capital since, after all, wasn't everything that existed of the best in this country a product of foreign labor and capital? Farquhar found it difficult not to grow fond of the president of Brazil, and through him began to cherish the country itself. Under the tutelage of Rodrigues Alves, Rio de Janeiro would finally turn into a genuine city: the tortuous colonial alleyways would be demolished; tenements and the grotesquely wretched *favelas* would be banned from the downtown area; and even yellow fever would be combated with a certain diligence, though this also engendered a rather unexpected outbreak of popular resistance when the poor and ignorant spontaneously ignited in mistrust of the obligatory vaccine. Farquhar got excited enough to enter the hotel business, expanding things little by little into other sectors. He adored Brazil, because it afforded him such tremendous profits and because its people, the Brazilians, behaved in such delightfully arbitrary fashion—much as an audacious playwright might attempt to turn his dramatic flop into a hit farce.

This very morning Percival Farquhar would begin to move his pieces into position for his game of rapprochement with the new government. J. J. Seabra was to be checkmated precisely where he least expected it, and the attack itself would come from within his most impregnable fortress: the bedroom of his own mistress. Percival was more than confident of the outcome. The whore to whom he had entrusted the major thrust of his procedural machinations clearly possessed, in addition to a crackerjack cunt, the finest brain in the whole country. And he had promised to make her rich and happy for the rest of her life. (A highly rhetorical pledge but one that, given the circumstances of its utterance, he could honestly confess to having meant to keep, at least in part.) As for what had to be mounted in public, for that he would turn to Alexander Mackenzie, his authorized representative in Brazil. They were to meet later that morning at the office to discuss just how Mackenzie was to pull the strings, affording Farquhar the unmistakable pleasure of watching puppets dance.

On the following day, the principal newspapers in Rio de Janeiro carried a telegraphic dispatch from New York City, signed by a journalist of impeccable repute, declaring that the Madeira-Mamoré railroad was one of those feats that would forever mark the history of the continent. The dispatch went on to make a number of additional claims for the project, all boastfully to the taste of Brazilian readers, and then added a

North American statistical touch to reassure one and all that what they were reading was the unabashed truth. An undertaking in which 12,000 hammerstrokes were sounded to the mile; in which, to cover that mile, 400 pieces of track had to be laid. With 366 kilometers of track needed to produce the construction of the railroad, the Amazonian forest would thus have to ring with the symphonic reverberations of some twenty-seven *million* clangs as a veritable orchestra of sledgehammers rose and fell upon each and every spike, before the job could be completed! J. J. Seabra was rather astounded to hear from his mistress, that same morning, that she harbored such a passion for railroads, never having set foot on a train in her life. Women were such a goddamn mystery! And seemingly in honor of this feature they promptly enjoyed one of the most remarkable copulations in the history of their affair.

5

The rain that fell behaved more like a solid that had suddenly atomized into a thick gas from which there was no adequate means of protection. The engineer Stephan Collier was crouching inside his tent feeling wholly fed up. Here would be another day lost. Theoretically, this was not yet the rainy season, but the tropics were beastly tricky and the rains would suddenly arrive with a sluttish violence, engulfing with a ravenous liquescence whatever section of rail might be then under construction. At first Collier used to panic at the mere sight of ashen clouds encroaching upon the sky. Now he simply chafed because the whole world about him was about to dissolve, literally, and nothing provided even the illusion of substance, let alone certainty. Everything grew damp and pulpy, with a pungent smell of aqueous clay exuding vestiges of life and death. This unmistakable odor would soon penetrate everything and produce in any man a brand of immobility, of glum passivity, as the wetness gradually pervaded his body like a disquietingly sticky, cold sweat. Only the most determined workers now passed by the front of Collier's tent, carrying out some minor chore. Occasionally some splashes roweled by the wind would invade the tent itself and oblige Collier to squint up his face to shield his eyes. Light was still dim and precarious, as if the darkness of night had given way not to daylight but to an ashen and opaque obscurity. Through the opening in the form of an inverted V that provided a doorway to his tent, Collier could glimpse the railway bed that ripped a hole through the jungle where it lost itself in a shroud of rain. Mad Maria was trundling in reverse, shooting thick eddies of steam into the air. Activity among the workers had virtually ceased. Collier felt horribly useless, while all the problems gathered futilely in his mind. Even taking into consideration the natural difficulties of the terrain, construction had fallen far behind schedule. Yet in the midst of the driving downpour, the engineer would have liked to have simply assumed a stoical attitude,

78

out it was something he had never managed to learn. Even as a child he had lived on the offensive; he was a fearless organizer, implacable as granite. Perhaps for this very reason he was always at odds with the scum of the earth; his life had always been this restless encounter with the challenges imposed by the dregs of mankind. Not that he considered himself in any way superior. Or if he did, it was only to the extent that he permitted himself to be led by them, because life was bloody short and, to die, all you needed was to take a quick slide in the wrong direction. Men were living in a time when the pitch of voracity rivaled even the intensity of those violent tropical rains.

Richard Finnegan had his umbrella up and stood spectating as two Barbadians dug the graves to bury their twin compatriots butchered in the previous day's fighting. The umbrella was nothing more than a useless convention in that downpour, and the doctor was wet and shivering with the cold. Collier seemed to be following the flashes of curiosity and misgiving telegraphed by the physician's shifting facial expressions. An ingenuous sprout if there ever was one, Collier calculated instinctively, and to think he could be a thousand miles away from here if he weren't such a sugar-coated fool. In fact, the flimsy idealism of the fellow was causing Stephan Collier far more irritation than the pluvial destruction of his supposed timetable. It may have been a sign that our engineer had not been entirely corrupted by all about him and still took some interest in his fellow man. He was yet, in his way, an idealist and this self-revelation was at the bitter heart of his irritation. He would have preferred to wield a more impersonal nature of the sort which makes of professional efficiency a weapon against all manner of disturbance. His anxiety, which he kept secret closeted in his tent, seemed to torment him precisely because it was still human, when what he should have been is a good hornswoggling son of a bitch. The thought reminded him of Mr. Farquhar, and the recollection bore the odor of a swampy irascibility. Mr. Farquhar was the only scoundrel he knew who could fashion from all the horrors of the world a collection of grandiose accomplishments because they made him profits. He and the young physician did not fall into the same species of animal as a man like Mr. Farquhar. Collier would have liked to belong to that family of beings who had never allowed the world to torment them since the world itself was wholly in their service. Bit by bit his perspicacity would reveal itself in these subtle self-questionings, and he had come to regard his Mr. Farquhar as an invisible infection which the eyes of the world regarded as nothing more serious than a benign little scar.

Despite the implacable cascade of rain, the Barbadians had managed to complete their digging and now were grappling with the two wooden boxes, lowering them into the graves. Finnegan was mussitating a Catholic prayer of some sort, the only visible sign of religious service. The physician always had a prayer in his mental back pocket for those of his patients who finally proved impermeable to his ministrations. As the Barbadians commenced to shovel the mud back into the holes, Collier left his tent and set out in the rain. Within the first five steps he was soaked through but remained undaunted. Finnegan noticed the engineer approaching and stared blankly, doubts fulminating in some long-lost part of his head. He viewed all this effort as rather meaningless and futile.

"If we'd buried them yesterday..." he recalled pointedly to the engineer.

"That simply wasn't possible."

"But why not, I don't understand?"

"Perhaps you were hoping to provoke a rebellion among the Barbadians?"

"But, Mr. Collier..."

"That's what I said: a *full-scale* rebellion."

"But, sir, how in God's name can a simple burial inspire a revolt among the Negroes?"

Collier stared into the eyes of the doctor, and Finnegan took it as a flat insult—exactly as Collier had meant him to do. This witless ass of a doctor had better start to fathom that no man was exactly the equivalent of an illustration in his anatomy book. Not all the world was Catholic and stupid.

"The Negroes, my dear boy, have little respect for anyone while he's *alive*. But once a man dies, the body becomes sacred."

"You don't mean to tell me you take such superstitions seriously," Finnegan challenged with a strong impulse to give the engineer a swift kick in the balls, because he detested that "dear boy" tone of voice.

80

"Right, doctor. You go ahead. The next Negro to die here is all yours. Mind you, these fellows are marvelous creatures and the finest workers of the lot. The only ones who really know what they're about. They never cause me trouble but they do cling together. And I pity the first man who dares to lay a hand on one of their corpses."

The doctor adjusted the shoulder of his shirt, which seemed to be distending from the weight of the rain. Collier kept staring him in the face.

"All this is quite absurd," Finnegan insisted.

Collier took pleasure in the uncertainty of the doctor's voice and he allowed a pause for the wave of nervousness to wholly inundate the lad. Finnegan responded with a nervous twitch and eyes deepening to an uncontrollable fullness quite appropriate to his youth and inexperience.

"I know it's absurd. But what do you know that isn't absurd, my dear boy?"

Finnegan was a hairbreath from succumbing to the urge to lift his knee with a lightning reflex, right up between Collier's legs.

"Fuck you," he grunted instead.

"Excellent," Collier replied, "you're finally learning."

"Fuck all this absurdity."

"I couldn't agree with you more," he said, nearly adding a final "dear boy" that might have proved his undoing. "The fact of the matter is they don't allow us to touch their dead, and there's nothing we can do about it. Fortunately, the company's only concern for a man is when he's alive; after he's dead, he's bloody well funked it in any case and certainly of no further interest to us."

Finnegan responded with a lengthy silence while the Barbadians, indifferent to their conversation, continued to tamp the mud on the graves.

"Have you ever heard people talk about zombies?" Collier finally asked him.

"Zombies?" the doctor echoed, bewildered. "You're not going to tell me you believe in that crap!"

"No, I don't believe in that *crap,* as you call it. To me it's just like Catholicism and the rest—they're all varieties of feces."

Finnegan hardly felt the brunt of the insult because he had

81

long ago worn out his religion like a spare part that still lacked its replacement.

"They simply believe the dead can return to life and the body become a slave to whoever can possess it," the engineer concluded.

"Mr. Collier, this is getting downright whimsical."

"You'll find it dangerous, doctor, not comical."

"A dead body cannot come back to life. It's a fact."

"It's rather what you think."

"It's superstitious to imagine anything else. Primitive irrationality."

"It's your lookout, doctor, but I advise you to keep your distance from any dead Barbadians if you want to continue to be able to wear a tie."

"Zombies," the doctor muttered under his breath as Collier walked away. He stared at the graves with the only certainty he could muster now: these two would never be troubled by anyone again. And if ever they did have to leave their graves, it wouldn't be until the Day of Judgment.

Two simple crosses made of wood indicated the site, but the sea of mud made it nearly impossible to distinguish their respective graves. No one else remained; the Barbadian diggers had fled for cover and Finnegan was now completely alone. The graves sank to the periphery of his vision as he stared up in awe at the wall of jungle. The dignity of the trees washed by the rain suggested a momentary solace from himself. Then a few objects strewn upon the muddy earth drew his attention, and he walked over to have a look at what they were. To examine them more carefully he actually knelt upon the graves. What he found there were necklaces hung with medals, with lead bullets, and several teeth. He picked one of them up with his free hand, still holding his umbrella with the other, and held that position while examining the strange piece of handicraft. What he discovered somewhere between shame and fear was that these teeth were *human*. Dr. Finnegan would have preferred scorpions.

Consuelo Campero had no inkling of where she was but felt she had somehow contrived miraculously to escape the forest and the rain. She was in point of fact lying in a soft bed, covered by clean sheets, and this was no delirium. Yet she found herself impossibly fatigued, wanting only to sleep, to rest, and perhaps never wake up or see the world again. Little by little she lost all sense of irritation from the light beating down upon her closed eyelids, as the red intensity faded into paler and paler shades of pink, until disappearing into an ashen silence of blissful unconsciousness. The unbearable crashing of rain and thunder was over. The storm had seemed bent upon tearing up every last tree in the jungle and sending it hurling into hallucinated flight. The crashing of thunder had at a certain point startled Consuelo out of her lethargy and caused her to leap to her feet in the blinding darkness. The din of the down-pour bored into her head like the echo of a driverless horse and wagon juddering madly down a cobblestone street. The trees trembled in the wind with animal whistles while each leaf strained unimaginably before it was torn from its branch and sent spinning through space. She began running with no sense of direction, hugging the sheaf of musical scores to her breast as she moaned in desperation. Her wail was similar to that of the leaves, only less phantomlike, closer to that of a frightened woman reduced to the behavior of a child quavering in an empty house with no light. Consuelo ran because she could not believe how nature could encompass such violence or that eventually—when the downpour should cease, when the trees should stop their danse macabre—the jungle would return to its former state of lush tranquillity. The extremity of nature was like a lie, finally exposed, and she preferred not to open herself to so potent a revelation. The wind and the rain pum-meled her body and she was assaulted by the smells of the jungle: the odor of wet earth, the sickly perfume of macerated leaves, the fetid redolence of mashed fruit. Each mephitis was an alarming reminder of the furor of the storm—or so she imagined and was thus goaded farther and farther into flight. She ran without regard for the thorns or spikes of leaves and grass that lacerated her flesh and tore her dress to undulating shreds. Her wet skin was wholly insensitive to pain and the cold rain commingled with her blood. By then the darkness seemed welcome because with no visible destination she was not obliged to choose any particular path but could follow her inclination and go on blindly running, stumbling, flailing, crashing against the parting branches and twisting free of the clumps of roots that tangled about her feet. Now she almost savored the running, her breasts bouncing and the rainwater flowing down her neck, eddying between her cleavage, flooding her navel, and rushing between her thighs. Consuelo was moist to the core and had never known such wetness in her life. Not even after having just made love with her husband Alonso she lay soaking in her bath, her body soaped and her hand slaked between her thighs with the easy lethargy of sated lust. In the tub the water offered none of the violence of such a rainfall; it was more an enticingly vulnerable pool, a corner of repose. Yet, no matter how hard she ran she could not outpace the image of Alonso, whose face materialized forever in the darkness. It bobbed wet and disembodied, only to be swallowed in the whirlpool of the rapids with a splash that froze like a necklace of incandescent pearls. And she noticed with a fright how his hair had lost its dark sheen, which so thrilled her, to the furious cascade. And remembered the times when she would get out of the tub, still wet, and Alonso would rush in to throw himself at her knees, to embrace her thighs, to plant a kiss on her moistened curls. She would laugh and protest gleefully; it was part of the same amorous impulse that made her grip his hair and feign resistance. But he had vanished in the rushing torrent and she was fleeing in the midst of the scouring tempest.

Consuelo had no recollection now of how much time she had spent in the storm; she felt comforted by the white sheets. She must have run incredibly far for her legs to be so numb and swollen. The bottom of her feet ached and her long toes burned painfully; there was something of the soft sponginess of the drowned about her flesh. A memory as impersonal as an anonymous dawn brought to mind the instant she had finally fallen, no longer able to summon strength to get up and run any farther. Her hands could not get a grip upon the foamy leaves. She saw a light approaching and heard indistinguishable voices amid the thundering of the rain. Suddenly a face was observing her. Just before she fainted she caught a glimpse of human feet and imagined she must have fallen into the hands of savages. Consuelo had no way of knowing that the face had belonged to a Chinaman, who was heading a search party there on the muddy slope of the mountain. A routine job after such a storm, because it was common for the workers to seek temporary shelter somewhere in the forest and then end up losing

84

their way when they attempted to return to camp. With the Chinaman were six others, coolies as well, who in the midst of the maelstrom might easily be mistaken for a pack of wild Indians.

The rain ended shortly before midday and a merciless sun began to bake the mud. Collier stood before a team of workers who were busy clearing away the effects of the deluge and the resulting erosion. The engineer was trying to assess the damage, already certain it was no bloody joke. Several giant trees had fallen at the edge of the clearing, though the wall of jungle hardly seemed diminished. With trunks of over four meters in diameter, not to mention the accompanying branches, they would require hours of work to be removed. And in such a slough, whose waters seemed to rage up out of the ground itself, the mud accumulations were acutely dangerous and could swallow up a man should he grow careless on the job. Feverishly, Collier's laborers attempted to disentangle what was left of the equipment, most of which had been reduced to twisted wreckage. The large timbers, planking and railroad ties that had been used to construct a makeshift bridge, across which the railway line might provisionally pass, were now a tangle of debris and branches intertwined by the fury of the floodwaters. Tracks had been partially torn awry and lay dazzlingly contorted in the sunlight. As Finnegan walked up to the engineer he could sense Collier's despondency.

"The rain must have washed out about thirty meters of track," said Collier flatly.

"Sir, I suppose you've heard that four men have disappeared?" the doctor reported somberly.

"The force of the water was enough to slue these tracks like boiled macaroni."

Finnegan caught the bitter irony of the words of the engineer and attributed the taut severity of its tone to the fact that Collier's work zone had been transformed by a single thunderstorm into something resembling a sunken branch of hell, as if nature herself were impelled by satanical forces. Several workers were struggling to retrieve a corpse from the ubiquitous mud. The body blended into its sepulture of twisted boughs, while the effort to extract it produced tremulous undulations of the mire.

And those pulsations of mud caused a queer palpitation deep inside the engineer, who could no longer hide his dejection.

"Four more deaths!" Collier wailed.

No one could offer any words of consolation to the engineer, so complete was his discouragement. The doctor felt too intimidated because he had himself witnessed the filling up of the trenches dug by the workers and the ensuing rush of furious waters against the foundation works, eroding everything in its path. The maelstrom had been unequivocal, annulling all solidity, and Finnegan could easily estimate how much the damage would cost the engineer. Collier may have been an implacable fellow, but under the present circumstances he was thoroughly defenseless. Nature had wrought a species of unpremeditated havoc and her fury had swiftly resulted in wholesale calamity. The doctor observed that all of the engineer's self-assurance had been crushed; Collier was completely self-absorbed, with no hint of braggadocio, stifled now by his own impotence.

Old Thomas, the locomotive operator, came over to his friend and put a hand on his shouder.

"I never in me life saw anythin' like it," he commiserated.

Collier said nothing, and his silence was as moving a confession of defeat as any he could muster. He was no longer the obdurate engineer; he was a man so entirely defeated that, for the first time, even Finnegan could glimpse how old he really was.

The locomotive operator began to cough embarrassedly as he tightened the fingers of his hand on the shoulder of the engineer. Collier simply shook his head. Whenever a storm of that magnitude was unleashed by nature, its waters were vicious enough to slash like razors, so incapacitating his men that they could barely comprehend an order, let alone carry it out. The corpse had already been disentangled from the branches and mud, and the workers were now dragging it over to a dryer bed of clay. The unfortunate creature had been torn apart and his legs were missing. Finnegan drew nearer the corpse, which seemed more like a lump of humid, grimy dough into which a pair of clean, human eyes had been inserted. The doctor could still glean from those misty eyes the final agony of the man, the look of a gullible pawn who had found his moment of truth in the very instant he was being rent apart as a human being. Finnegan surmised the man had probably not died from the loss of his limbs but rather from suffocating in the mud. As a physician he could only speculate whether, before death, the deceased had been aware of his own legs being wrenched off his trunk like useless branches. One of the workers had just fished out of the mud what appeared to be a large dead frog and tossed it onto the harder ground beside the corpse. It was the hand of a man, limp and putrid.

"It's the divil's own donnybrook," Thomas admitted with disgust.

"Reminds me of the Civil War, Thomas: no bloody weapons to fight with."

"Right ye are," Thomas sighed in compliance, "ye die o' the heat, ye drown in the muck, and if by some marvel ye manage to get around all o' that, it's diarrhea and malaria alinin' up te kick ye in yer arse."

"That's not the only violence," Finnegan interjected, wrapping the severed hand in a piece of cloth.

"One month's work wrecked in a couple of hours. Makes me spew to think of it," Collier said coldly.

Finnegan suddenly realized that it was not the loss of life that had so dispirited this Englishman, but the damage to his almighty timetable. The discovery of this fact nevertheless produced no negative reaction in the doctor, who contented himself by squeezing the enfolded member between his hands as if the human creature it represented were the most distant thing from his mind. Twisted tracks were far more explicit than a corpse without legs.

Just then a gang of coolies walked out of the forest, carrying a stretcher. The engineer looked up and caught sight of the mud-caked body.

"Well, gentlemen, here comes another corpse," he said resignedly.

"Mista Corrier, Mista Corrier! Rook what we find," shouted one of the Chinamen, "a rady!"

The engineer's face broke into a smile, because somehow this discovery was exactly what was wanting—a woman found in the middle of this rotten jungle, with Farquhar's stinking railway halfway down the drain, brought as much relief as a crude expletive in an aristocratic drawing room.

"Where did you find her?"

"She raying ona glound, Mista Corrier," answered th
Chinaman, still excited. "Over ona mountain, about free ki
rometer dissy way," he pointed back into the jungle.

Finnegan signaled the men to set the stretcher on the groun
and proceeded to examine the woman.

"Any indication of where she came from?" Collier contin
ued. One look at her had been enough to tell him she was n
ordinary woman, not one of those occasional down-and-ou
prostitutes who sometimes drifted into Santo Antônio.

"She no speaky, Mista Corrier," the Chinaman replied. "Sh
just ry rike dat since we put her ona stletcha."

"She's obviously in a state of shock," Finnegan commented
"I think she'll be all right, though. Take her to the infirmary.

The Chinaman handed a wet and crumpled package to th
engineer. "She cally dis, Mista Corrier."

Collier opened the package and examined its contents, an
what he saw was no less surprising than that fainted woma
lying there on the stretcher.

"No identification?" Collier asked, quite aware that every
body was waiting to learn the precise reason for that look o
surprise that had already vanished from his countenance.

"No, Mista Corrier, onry have a package," the coolie con
firmed, with the same look of curiosity as the rest of thos
around him.

"Music," Collier said abruptly, leafing carefully through th
soaked sheets of paper with an effort not to tear them. "Blood
musical scores: Chopin, Liszt, Beethoven, more Chopin..."

The coolies solicitously lifted the stretcher from the groun
and trotted off after the physician in the direction of the infir
mary. Collier closed the booklets full of music and threw ther
worthlessly to the ground. At the same moment some shoutin
came from somewhere in the vicinity of the workers' dormi
tories. Another beastly row, the engineer sighed to himself an
unconsciously reached for his holster to make sure he ha
brought his revolver along. His fingers basked in the still-coo
touch of metal as he hurried over to see what was happening
He came up behind some Barbadians who were casually ob
serving the general pandemonium.

As soon as the rain began to fall, he had looked for shelte
in the hollow of a giant root. Hunched over, with his fac

88

resting on his crouched knees, he hugged his ankles while the darkness dissolved everything into a single void and the only sounds were the rain and the thunder. They danced a mayhem portending the powers of all that was beyond him. Yet he did not feel afraid; he was so accustomed to the extremities of nature he could not begrudge her the right to revolt since, in any case, she had the omnipotence to do so. To him each tree, each gust of wind, each drop of rain represented a particular variety of intelligent spirit that wished, for good or ill, to enter into contact. He was the one who lacked all strength and had lost the paternity of his people. He stank of urine. He wanted to rest and let the tempest unfold around him. His back, however, had begun to ache: a twinge that ran down his shoulder blades and sorely affected his breathing. He tried, therefore, to anticipate the moment when his back should be relieved, since he was cognizant that the pain would pass if only he could stand up once more on his feet and stretch himself a bit. As it was, though he found himself in an awkward position there in the hollow of the root, there was still the odor of earth and rotted wood, a good and friendly smell. And when the rain should finally end, he would get up and stretch and try to steal a bit of food from the *civilized*. The rain, however, grew heavier and his hollow, located on a sunken stretch of terrain, began to fill with water. To him his hollow had transformed itself into a voracious mouth soon likely to swallow so much water; the only thing left was to escape and seek some other shelter. He struck out into the rain, still reverent before the lightning flashes that streaked across the sky high above the copse of giant trees. Reverence was essential inasmuch as life could be devoured quite innocently by the storm. How perfectly lucid of the cosmos to unleash its violence which, once unleashed in the form of rain upon the forest, would wet the earth in a thoroughly wise and benign sort of way.

How different from long ago when his ancestors had lived in a world that never rained because water was guarded in a nutshell hidden away in the sky.

Whenever ancestors had wanted to have a drink of water, or take a bath, or wash off newly born *kurumi*, they had to ask the jabiru storks to please bring water in their long beaks. Jabiru storks were, however, a perverse lot who liked to be angry all the time. Occasionally they refused to bring water to the Caripuna, so that many ancestors had died of thirst or become so filthy that they finally ceased to be human beings.

It was then that the three sons of the great chief, or *tuxaua*, Unámarai fell prisoner to a giant jaguar who happened to slaver all the time. This huge jaguar did not think of eating the three sons of *tuxaua* Unámarai, for he needed them to catch his slaver because he was forever dribbling all over the place and each time that a drop of his saliva fell upon the earth it turned into a centipede or some other such stinging creature. The three boys came to spend their days catching the jaguar's slaver in giant gourds and then spilling it down a deep, deep hole. The same three brothers would then take turns during the night so the other two could sleep, but they soon got tired of all this effort until the youngest one of them dreamed that if they could only give a great deal of water to the jaguar he would stop all his dribbling and they would all three sons of *tuxaua* Unámarai be free once again. The oldest youth liked the idea of his younger brother and knew that the dream had been inspired by their father Unámarai, also a great shaman. So the eldest brother ordered the youngest one to go look for a jabiru stork and ask it for water to give to the jaguar to drink. But he warned his little brother to be very careful because jabirus could be quite dangerous and, in any case, if irritated might refuse him any water. The youngest brother told the eldest not to worry, that he had thought of a way to please a jabiru. And off he went. He walked and walked through the jungle until he came upon an old jabiru meditating at the edge of a river, waiting for some fish to appear for him to spear with his beak and eat. Then the youth, the youngest son of the chief, changed himself into a lungfish and began to swim back and forth in front of the jabiru, splashing about to give the stork a laugh and waiting for the right instant to turn back into being a person. But the jabiru, seeing a lungfish happily splashing about, quickly skewered him and thus swallowed the boy. Meanwhile, the eldest brother had had a feeling that something might go wrong with his youngest brother's plan and went after him. He found the jabiru, looking all too satisfied and walking contentedly along the river bank, so immediately he knew what had happened. To save his brother, he swiftly changed into a motuca fly and landed on the beak of the jabiru stork, giving him a sting and sucking a drop of blood out from his brother. The

90

motuca that was the eldest son of Unámarai flew far away and became a person again, vomiting the drop of blood and blowing on it until his brother came back to life. The youngest brother then leaped up smiling and playing but the eldest one only scowled and told him to be quiet. You were careless, the eldest scolded him, and you let the jabiru eat you. The little brother looked at the ground and listened, but without the smile on his face. You hardly seem to be the son of our father, the eldest insisted. And the youngest brother became even sadder, since it was obvious that his brother meant that his mother had perhaps been sleeping with the wild creatures at the time he was conceived.

Then the two remembered the middle brother, who was alone catching the slaver of the jaguar.

They knew that they had better work quickly to find a solution because the middle brother might soon grow tired and fall asleep, letting some saliva from the jaguar fall to earth, creating more and more dangerous creatures. Let's sleep once more, said the eldest brother. Who knows, perhaps we may dream another solution to our problems? And they slept. On the following morning, when they awoke, the eldest brother had dreamt nothing. But the youngest felt contented because, in his sleep, he had found an answer. And he said to the eldest brother, All the water that exists in this world is kept in a huge calabash gourd hung by liana vines somewhere up in the sky. The jabiru flies there to take all the water he wants. We must climb to the sky and punch a hole in the great calabash with our clubs. But we will have to be very careful because the calabash is also filled with man-eating piranhas. So they performed cigar ceremonies, blowing out the smoke, and along the ladder of smoke they climbed into the sky. There they saw the immense calabash hanging down, suspended from two well-twisted liana vines. The eldest brother climbed right onto the calabash, while the youngest held his club high and gave a hard whack to the outside of the gourd. He had managed in so doing to make a small crack and the water began to pour out, forming rivers and all else that exists of pond, lake, marsh, and cataract on earth. Watching the water flow from the calabash, the youngest brother became distracted and a fish stuck his head out and devoured him. The eldest brother, who was hanging from above, saw his brother be eaten. He held on to the liana, trying to figure out which of the fish had eaten his little brother and, in doing so, caused the calabash to swing back and forth. With each arc of the calabash more water spilled out and made another storm on earth. Until today he remains there, trying to catch sight of the fish that devoured his little brother. The calabash swings from one side to the other and more and more water surges out through the crack, rushing forcefully to escape and thereby creating the hard rains, the tempests, and floods.

This, then, was a day when the eldest son of *tuxaua* Uná-marai must have swung the calabash very hard, trying to find his brother. And he himself was trying as hard to find a suitable place of shelter from a terrible storm. It rained heavily and he ran to where the *civilized* had their *malocas*. He hid himself under a tarpaulin and liked it there because it was warm and water could not get through to wet his skin further. It was there that he would remain until the rain should have passed, happy, half-asleep, drowsing, when he was suddenly awakened by a group of the *civilized*. He attempted to flee but one of the *civilized* grabbed him, and then another. From his pockets fell mirrors, combs, pens, pencil stubs, a penknife, and other trinkets that he had taken from the *civilized*. All that he possessed was quickly stripped from him, including the pair of filthy shorts that had been the gift from the men who were traveling with the benefactor Rondon. The *civilized* seemed angry and struck him over and over, flailing him and making him cry out with pain. Then he vomited blood, his lips were split, and his eyes so puffed he could barely see. That was when the worst finally happened. The *civilized* held him securely on the ground and stretched his two arms across a railroad tie. One of the *civilized* then took out his machete and struck off his hands at the level of the forearms. He swiftly lost consciousness in the midst of the thought that he was about to take the journey to the other side and must prepare to meet his ancestors. The stumps of his arms were the only part of his body still to quiver, like the beheaded necks of chickens, spouting thin gushes of blood. He did not see the chief of the *whites* hurrying toward the *civilized* who had done this to him, along with other armed men. He saw nothing at all. He was too preoccupied with holding on to the fact that he would shortly see his ancestors

92

and must find some explanation as to why he was arriving from the other side without any hands.

The brilliant green eyes of Alexander Mackenzie would have sat beautifully in the head of a young and sensual woman, but they were sorely troubling on that severe, delicate, almost lipless countenance with its wrinkled eyelids crumpled like parchment. Farquhar, however, entirely appreciated the extent to which such a face imposed respect and almost always settled matters far beyond any arguing. His representative in Brazil, Mackenzie was the kind of man who imposed respect, of the incontestable sort that exuded power by its easy airs of naked familiarity with money. At times Mackenzie could be truly terrifying, and, were it not that this was Brazil, his truculent methods could, to Percival's mind, be qualified as damned imprudent. Mackenzie was a refined thug, without subtlety of any kind, capable of sacrificing his own mother if the transgression could bring him power. That was the difference between them. Mackenzie wanted naked power, he liked power, while Percival preferred to accumulate wealth instead, a much greater form of power and never so perilously explicit. Still, he could deal with Mackenzie quite objectively and involved him only in the insipid world of the delegation of powers that were ever a manifestation of his will. He could even allow Mackenzie to carry out orders as if they were a product of Mackenzie's own personal power—an icy fellow, that Mackenzie, cunning and yet rather frank about it.

Alexander Mackenzie had lived in Brazil for the past twenty years and spoke perfect Portuguese. Rarely would he visit the United States anymore; behind his flinty exterior he felt a real love of Brazil, especially for Rio de Janeiro. He had an exquisite mansion in the posh Cosme Velho district, surrounded by tall palm trees and flamboyant tropical flowers. He was unmarried; perhaps it was his very coldness that kept him aloof from the opposite sex. It was also more than likely that he preferred solitude to the mere idea of partitioning power with another human being. He was going on fifty-five now and he looked his age. The sedentary life of Rio, the occasional dabbling in his garden behind the mansion followed by long siestas after ample lunches, had softened his university football player's build into a protuberant belly that his finely tailored suits barely managed to conceal.

Percival Farquhar was well aware of the fact that his representative was no hermit, being of course privy to the intimate details of the lives of his employees; but he did not interfere, judiciously informing himself only to avoid unnecessary surprises. He would almost never visit him at his mansion because he felt profoundly ill at ease in those luxuriant gardens where Negro adolescents in a state of semi-undress strolled about pruning plants or watering flower beds. Mackenzie kept some ten such employees in his service—all in the flower of their manhood—whom he regularly contracted from the various coffee plantations in the interior. This was Mackenzie's "secret," a secret that was nonetheless rather celebrated among the Carioca cognoscenti. Among Rio high society he was nicknamed "Mrs. Daddy," and Farquhar had found out through the mistress of J. J. Seabra that her impetuous minister could only refer to Mackenzie as "that nauseating Yankee fairy." Percival therefore needed to isolate his representative from the prerequisite public maneuvers involved in approaching the new administration. In Brazil, as in many countries, virility was less important than money, but in the present instance it was probably better not to let the former dubiously taint the latter. Mackenzie was still an extremely powerful force to reckon with, even independent of his connection with Farquhar. He could work in the wings, smoothing things over with a timely bribe or two to mollify the hardest edges. As director of Brazilian Light & Power, he had enormous experience in this particular level of "management." In 1907, in what Farquhar still regarded as a blatant imprudence, Mackenzie had actually bought out the mayor of Rio, a Mr. Passos, for two hundred thousand *cruzeiros,* thus achieving a monopoly on electrical energy in the federal capital. The concession generated a scandal, with the newspapers attacking it by suggesting that though Mr. Mackenzie was undoubtedly a productive and enterprising gentleman in many respects, for which he had undoubtedly earned himself a reputation, must he be "allowed to transact thus illicitly" in the affairs of the capital of Brazil? Even Ruy Barbosa showed his indignation, in a heated article for *Imprensa,* where he disclosed that Mayor Passos had actually

94

boasted at a party that he knew he was committing an illegal act and felt confident he could ride out the storm.

"I've been told they surmise that we financed the opposition," Percival was explaining to Mackenzie. "Is that actually what they think?"

"On the contrary, they know that we didn't," Mackenzie insisted. "I followed to the letter the instructions you mailed me, and I would hardly have been inclined in any case to lend assistance to the opposition. You know I can't stand Ruy Barbosa."

"But now the government's playing deaf and dumb," Farquhar concluded smiling.

"Why the smile?"

"I was just remembering what Ruy Barbosa had to say on your behalf. The little weasel loves nothing better than a bit of healthy, dirty double-dealing. Don't you think so?"

"He's a fool."

"Not quite, he knows how to land on his feet."

"Which means nothing. He may land on his feet but he's full of hot air. If somebody dared him he'd knowingly walk on coals. Then he'll finally go up in a puff of smoke or burst wide open."

"But our problem isn't Ruy Barbosa, it's the government. They're suspicious of us, Mac. My request for concessions in Paraná has been shelved indefinitely, and on the flimsiest of pretexts: they say there are Indians down there who need to be protected."

Mackenzie did not stir in his easy chair but stared imperviously at his employer. Finally, he shrugged his shoulders. "I know; Indians. Some excuse."

Farquhar pressed the palms of his hands together above his desk. "They want to squeeze us like grapefruit; they know we produce *rich* juices."

"That Paraná business may take a little time," Mackenzie continued, "but it's ours, I can tell you. No one is going to take that plum from us."

"Still I'd like to see the matter settled once and for all, but it's not our only problem. Last week several inspectors from the Ministry of Health paid a visit to each of my hotels, here in Rio. They refused to accept the usual payoff; they weren't even the same inspectors. It worried me."

95

Now it was Mackenzie's turn to smile and he repeated Farquhar's gesture, squeezing his hands, but rather obscenely.

"If anyone's to squeeze juice around here, you can be sure it's us. We're the only ones who can tell a good piece of fruit."

You're a son of a bitch, all right, Percival mused to himself then added aloud:

"Nonetheless, I have ascertained from very reliable sources that our position vis-à-vis the government is not very salutory at the moment. This is a fact, Mac. I don't know who might have spread this story of our financing the campaign for the opposition. It could have been the English consortium, or even that French group that's never forgiven us for winning the concession to build the Madeira-Mamoré. For the moment, the source of it all is quite immaterial—we can deal with that later. Right now, what we need to do is improve the climate of our relations with the present administration. I have tried to get to see the president personally, but they keep putting me off by saying his calendar is absolutely booked for the rest of the month. That's a bad sign. It never required an appointment to see the president before. I could walk into Catete Palace whenever I wanted."

"But now the president is in tight with the German consortium."

"It's not the Germans—they're not even interested in the same sector of the economy. They've consistently shied away from any investment of capital in the public sector."

Suddenly Farquhar began to laugh at himself.

"What's the joke?" Mackenzie asked, a bit irritated.

"The Germans are menacing Rothschild's goose with the golden eggs. Old Paranhos—you know, *Baron* de Rio Branco, the *minister* of foreign relations. Well, it seems he's had his wings clipped. They tell me this Marshal da Fonseca is a rather obstinate fellow, quite his own man. They say he doesn't defer to anyone, now that he's president."

Mackenzie's expression was quite relaxed and complacent again. His green eyes were watching with laughter like two drops of creme de menthe diluted with ice.

Farquhar then mustered the most casual voice he could: "I want you to give me a hand with something. I want you to draw their fire while I launch a little surprise attack. I mean to walk into Catete by the front door again. And I've come up

96

with a plan, a good one, where you'll play the principal part, Mac...."

"I'm listening," said Mackenzie, feeling the delicious heat of battle already throbbing in his temples.

So Percival began to spell out his plan. He liked his plan, and it pleased him that it had been born of a suggestion from Ruy Barbosa, a casual idea espoused at a luncheon for the exchange of favors. The little gnome had marvelous antennae and Percival Farquhar couldn't get over his capacity for political hanky-panky.

BOOK II

Arbeit Macht Frei

6

Jonathan and his compatriots knew very well why they must preserve the integrity of the dead. What they failed to perceive was why they should profess a faith so entirely at odds with other religious practices on Barbados. They had no idea that, as newer Barbadians, they had different roots than the majority of Negroes who had long ago joined the Anglican church or else converted to any one of a number of Protestant sects as was normal for Barbados, a British possession in the Antilles. There had been a great deal of persecution on account of that difference, with the Colonial authorities prohibiting the religious ceremonies attendant to his faith while tolerating a diversity of other cults of African origin. This anomaly arose in part because the Negro population of Barbados was made up of slaves garnered from a multiplicity of African tribes but predominantly Congo, Aradas, and Nago. A great number of such slaves were originally Moslems but over the generations had lost all ties to their faith and adopted in their stead the religious practices of their masters. The ancestors of Jonathan and his compatriots, however, had not belonged to any of those tribes or even been brought directly to Barbados to work on the sugar and tobacco plantations. They had actually been captured in Dahomey and transported to a canebrake in Haiti, bought there by a French planter. They were of the Fon tribe— not Moslem—and remained faithful to their tribal cults. They worshiped the serpent Dā, eternal mother, and the spirit Legba, origin of all fertility. With the passage of time elements of their original beliefs were conjoined with the compassionate Catholicism of their French owners. Many supernatural entities, the Fon spirits, or *loa,* gained the names of Catholic saints and Fon prayers assimilated French Creole vocabulary. The serpent Dā was the vitreous eternity of Dâgbé, the All Powerful, to whom the Fon offered blind adoration while his divine potency would spew forth like creamy dust in a creative surge, between good and evil, to sweeten or embitter human existence in this

act of consummation ministered by priest or shaman mixin
potions and bleakly fasting amid the parched, chestnut-brow
savannahs of Dahomey. The serpent kept watch over planta
tions of peanut, millet, and sorghum; illuminated the dawn
with scintillating green; was manifest in the transport of giraffe
as they knelt to eat the tender leaves from budding orang
trees. Thus, Dâgbé glided sovereign as an untiring lover wh
goes from one pallet to another, satiating his women thoug
never purging himself of his own enthusiasm. Out of the va
black profundities he was conjured and beseeched on beha
of man's necessities, and come he would to bewitch the stil
closed eyelids of naked virgins in the opaque misty hours befor
dawn. The Fon would offer their prayers to the sandy earth c
Samorné, its pebbles carpeted with greenish moss, and to th
forests draped with lianas like canopies of leafy brocade; c
the nearby repellent Allada, with its herds of wild pig; and i
Whidah, with its brambles bristling like the hair of old hag:
Dā-vodu shimmered in the rippling waters, the parched desert
the humid slopes, the trails from village to village with the
huts of mud and somnolence. The Fon women, whose cor
cinnity of flesh was heightened by their taut dark skin anointe
with animal fat and fragrant with the odor of burnt chips c
cow dung, would beseech Legba. They represented all th
colors of the rainbow and had incorporated in the luster of the
eyes the beauty of Ayida-Hwedo, mother of blossoming. Legb
would arrive with the fleetness of the gazelle and the virilit
of the lion. For he was the great Papa Vodu whose untirin
penis fecundated with spurts of semen milky as the dew upo
the verdant pistil of the grasslands. Legba drank cow's bloo
mixed with curdled milk; he slung himself between women'
thighs, kissing with his organ brimming with enchanted bloo
the moist entrance of Ayida-Hwedo that every woman pos
sessed for the pleasure and joy of man.

Then one day, in the early eighteenth century, a Fon villag
was attacked by Nago warriors and many of its men and wome
were taken prisoner. The Nago traded their prisoners with a
Arab merchant for millet, metal utensils, and hashish. Th
Arab merchant, in turn, sold the Fon to a French slave shi
for a handsome profit. The ship cast anchor outside of Por
au-Prince and auctioned its cargo in the marketplace. Like othe
Fon slaves before them, also brought there by slavers, thes

102

were quickly scattered over a variety of cane plantations. Their tribe represented only a minority of the living property of Haiti, but voodoo was already sovereign. In the hot Haitian night its discordant rhythms would cut through the bitterness to liberate the good and evil *loa* with endless invocations to *"Damballa, langbesi ouida."* All along the impenetrable mountain trails crisscrossing the border of Haiti and Santo Domingo it was the witch doctor who ruled, together with the *caco* guerrillas of Christophe and Dessalines, the chimerical *bocors,* and the fat Grande Mamaloi as supreme *mambo.* Their faces were tattooed with the sign of the phallus, the circle of the vagina, the heart of Ezili, as well as three stripes and three disks to remind their initiates of the triple path and the triple circle embodying the mysteries of voodoo.

The great slave rebellion began in 1793, with what was actually a profane celebration of the *bombeche,* or carnival week, to the hallucinated outbursts of a young virgin who had leapt before the multitude and, shaking her breasts like two puddings, incited the men to change themselves into black scorpions or rainbow serpents. The reign of Toussaint L'Ouverture was about to be born with all the fragility of a glass toy and yet become one of the great mysteries of the Antilles.

Fearing pillage and murder, the French cane planter who had purchased his Fon slaves at auction abandoned his estates and moved with his slaves to Barbados, where he married an English wench, a prostitute to be exact, and became rich a second time by planting tobacco. The English, however, were not so complacent about the practice of voodoo and the Fon slaves little by little forgot their Creole, adopted the English language, let their syncretic Catholicism lapse and celebrated their voodoo rituals in secrecy. Jonathan and his compatriots were the descendants of those ill-fated slaves from Dahomey.

Jonathan himself had grown up in a poor household where the family worshiped in the living room, the doors bolted and the curtains drawn, offering furtive homage to the Fon deities; where they acted out the complex alchemy of cures and magical potions; and where above all they ministered to their dead. For the dead, they believed, could sometimes be reanimated—not revived exactly, merely reanimated, like a puppet, and thus enslaved and obliged to commit murder or perform forced labor. Jonathan had never seen one of these poor creatures

which his grandmother had called *zombies*—the living dead—
but during construction of the railway along the Panama Cana
he had heard a terrifying story. An old Nago had told him o
how an avaricious agent for manual laborers, himself a black
as well, had shown up at the start of the digging with a line
of some ten or so silent creatures. They were dressed in ragge
clothes clotted with earth and they walked as if they had ye
to awaken from the most profound sleep. The overseer aske
who these men were, but the agent dismissed the question
calling them nothing more than a gang of half-savages wh
still spoke their African dialects and understood nothing of th
languages of the whites. Since the agent was asking for onl
half of what was normally paid the other men, the oversee
took them on and sent them to work a distant area whe
excavation and leveling of the terrain was barely under way
The silent toilers worked from sun to sun without a singl
pause to rest, to slake their thirst, or fill their stomachs. The
seemed impervious to hunger and proved to be the toughes
workers the whites had ever seen. So it was natural that i
time they had achieved a certain reputation. One day a tear
of engineers came by to get a closer look at these laborers wh
never spoke, never caused trouble, and performed their almos
inhuman exertions with not a sign of protestation. When th
observers arrived, the chief engineer asked the agent to lin
the men up for inspection. The agent grew fearfully agitate
and offered all kinds of excuses until he realized there was n
way around it but to lead his men over to the whites. H
bellowed out his orders and soon they had gathered, India
file, eyes without expression. To the whites they seemed rathe
sickly looking, despite their capacity to behave with reasonabl
vigor. They looked bloodless and their Negroid complexio
was surprisingly drab and pale. The chief engineer was munch
ing on some peanuts and offered them each a handful. The
accepted humbly but began to chew them whole, without re
moving the shells. The Negro who had hired them out seeme
to fall into a helpless panic, actually began to cry, pleading fo
forgiveness, though the whites could not imagine what ha
come over him. But hardly had the men begun to swallow th
salted nuts when they commenced to let out terrifying shriek
and flee. The Nago explained to Jonathan that the living dea
must be fed only a light soup and no salt since when zombie

took salt the spell was broken and they had to search frantically for a place to rest. And thus it was that these men had acted: they began to run and shriek until they finally reached the cemetery of the construction company, where those who perished while at work on the canal were customarily buried. Each one of the ten rushed to a different tomb and began to dig frenziedly, but their first contact with the earth produced a stench of rotten flesh—their own!—and they crumbled into lifelessness. The whites subsequently verified that they were, in fact, the workers who had already died but been dug up from their graves by the unscrupulous agent apparently familiar with the powers and incantations of voodoo. Two days later he himself was found stone dead, with no apparent signs of violence other than the wide-open eyes still glowing beyond the tomb as if they had glimpsed the abominable in the final seconds of life.

With an ancestral dread Joñathan and his compatriots were fearful that they, too, might be exploited after death since the whites seemed to have little scruples about profiting from the rapaciousness of some evil *hungan*. And so they had made a pact not to permit any fellow Barbadian to be taken advantage of by the whites and to see that, once dead, each of them would be shielded by voodoo so that all could eventually rest in peace, free from servitude, forever after. Thus, when one of their number should die, he was to be interred by the others and to have his grave discreetly looked after for the following three days until his corpse should begin to decompose. The witch doctors, after all, only had the power to reanimate those cadavers yet to have rotted to pieces; once they had entered into a state of decomposition, irretrievably returning to dust, they could no longer serve as zombies.

On certain nights particularly illuminated by the moon, such as this one was, the Barbadians would gather in some secluded spot, light a bonfire, and chant before their *loa*-deities, intoning a language that for them had lost all meaning:

Yi…yi…yi…yi!
Yi…yi…yi…yi!
Yi…yi…yaa!
Yi…yi…yaa!
Garder en bas gaillard;

Ou oue iune bout de couteau;
Ou oue iune tete poisson;
Ou oue iune bom borri;
Prends, yo—porter—
Bai moins.

No one dared to go and watch them because they seemed to sing and dance an obscure appetite for survival from the inferno in which they found themselves. Indeed, with each movement they appeared to awaken some memory of their forefathers: the fluidity of the leopard that quiescently prepares to spring; the tenuously prolonged grace of the flight of a falcon. And in the odorous sweat of their own bodies they found solace against the lost scents of women (discreetly lowering their heads wrapped in flamboyant *coussabes,* while disrobing to welcome their men ardently between their legs). Only Collier the engineer had been invited, once, to attend one of these ceremonies, as a gesture of friendship and confidence. Collier understood only too well that this rite danced in parabolic rhythms was both a camouflage and a rapture of the will to live, an exalted mode of sensuality that carried these simple people through all their historical adversity and humiliation. And since the engineer was rather accustomed to feeling displaced in time, he saw in his Barbadians who had worked for him for so many years the deprivation of mankind at the duplicitous hand of fate.

On this night, the engineer had hardly finished his dinner and turned to scrutinizing in the light of his tent the building plans etched on rice paper, when the Barbadian Jonathan appeared. He had not come merely to seek authorization to hold rituals once more around a bonfire. No, he looked nervous and preoccupied.

"What's your problem, Jonathan?" Collier asked, still shuffling with his roll of plans on the table.

Jonathan had squatted on the earthen floor with all the hollowness of a tormented man. "Copm Collier, I come bout my brothers."

"What's bothering your brothers?"

"Dey gettin' all riled up 'bout de money, Copm Collier."

"You chaps must be making near double what they gave you up in Panama!"

106

"It weren't only us, coptin. De men is sick of riskin' derselves. Dey been tricked an' dey knows it. Dey want out, copm, while dey still got dere hides."

"And you, Jonathan, are you also sick of it?"

Collier's question was completely beside the point and he knew it. Jonathan shuddered imperceptibly from the effort to separate Collier from the company. He knew the company was rotten but he struggled against applying the same judgment to this engineer with whom he had so many days and nights in common.

"I got no one leff on dis earth, Copm Collier."

"Don't you have family in Kingston?"

"Dass de way de world go, Copm Collier."

"What do you mean? Are they dead?"

"All dead, from d'earthquakes dat hit Kingston. 'Cept my brother dat were in Cuba at de time, working on a Sponnish sugar plontation. We hod two houses bock dere in Kingston, but de quake come and dey crumple like paper."

"Sorry, Jonathan, I had no idea. When did it happen?"

"Dat were in nineteen seven, almost five year. I were still up dere in Panama, busy workin' on dat canal. I take de first boat home but dere was nothin' leff, nobody."

"Nineteen seven, that's the same year I left."

"By dat time you were already leff Panama, coptin."

"Well, it's a damn shame, Jonathan. I wish I'd known..."

"Instead de houses and all so forth I finds myself in de rubble. Never even could find de bodies. Earth just swolla everythin', I s'pose. Dey aint' but me leff."

"What made you come to work here?"

"What else were I s'posed to do, coptin. Got nobody."

Collier paused, then added: "You didn't answer my question, Jonathan."

"If I be domn sick of all dis? Well, I tell you one thing, Copm Collier, if I be fairly sick of all dis business, it were more for de men dan for dis old bones."

"For all those scum?"

"You gots to realize, Copm Collier, I just goin' through de motions, nemmine to get all riled up for what dey payin' me down here. Only reason be to stick my neck out is for dem others."

"Have you lost your senses, man? Either you stick your

107

neck out or you don't, but it had better be for yourself and no one else while you're about it!"

"Maybe dat how de motter stand for you, Copm Collier. Maybe you still got a inside to get all riled up over, but dis old—"

"Enough of this drivel!"

Just then some harrowing, guttural cries splayed open the night like a burst of glass over dying embers. Collier swept the plans off the table and concentrated all his attention on the ghastly howls issuing from somewhere over in the vicinity of the dormitory.

"What in blazes?"

"Dat have to be dem German son of a bitches," Jonathan muttered, the words bubbling through his saliva.

"What the hell are they howling about now?"

"Dey howling bout nothin', Copm Collier, they just d'lirious, dass all."

"Delirious?"

Jonathan was minutely calculating the reactions of the engineer as he continued to explain: "'Bout ten of dem sick since yesterday. Dey figure to hide de fact long as nobody spill de beans to Doct' Finn'gan."

"Sick?" Collier was about to explode. "But it isn't possible, man! Not with all those mucking medications down their swinish throats!"

"Dey stop takin' dem pills."

"What! You mean they've been off medication?"

"Dass right, coptin, dey hidin deres so's dey can sell it to de ones afraid of gettin' sick down here. Dey pockets two *milreis* a pill."

"Trafficking in their own death, my God," Collier groaned to himself, too stunned now to explode.

"Twenty-four *milreis* come de end of de week."

"Witless porkers, nothing on their minds but bloody profit!"

"But y'see, coptin, come de end de month, dem fellas got dereself a awful tidy sum."

Collier felt an irresistible urge to bash Jonathan in the cheek in reply to the seeming obscenity of the remark. The howling was so wretched, however, it momentarily stifled the impulse.

"You're not up to something similar, are you, Jonathan?" the engineer eventually queried his companion, half wishing the answer to be yes, so that he could spring like an animal upon the Barbadian and pound him to a bloody pulp.

"Now, what you take me for, Copm Collier?"

Impotent in the face of his unvented fury, the engineer stalked out of the tent and vanished into the darkness. Upon reaching the wing of the dormitory occupied by the Germans, Collier discovered the physician pacing back and forth and looking as astonished as a newly violated virgin. The medics were obviously jittery: the kerosene lamps shook in their hands, exacerbating the danse macabre of the flames that starkly illuminated the tangle of fetid hammocks—each twisted by its occupant's palpitant delirium. The afflicted clasped to their bosoms the tattered clothes that served for blankets as their bodies contracted into such bizarre positions that they gave the impression of being jolted by electricity. Their disordered movements would suddenly coalesce in demented expressions, the result of instantaneous nightmares which, with piercing cries, would gradually subside in a wash of momentary oblivion. The physician seemed lost at sea amid the waves of contorted hammocks, impotent before it all and sweating profusely. The shock had gradually emptied his face of all expression the way the sun might melt a snowman. At the sight of the engineer, Dr. Finnegan hastened to where he stood as if to ask to be pardoned for what was somehow happening. But old Collier himself was thrown off balance as well by the unexpected turn of events—to such a degree that he could take no pleasure in the apparent defeat of this Irish flea of a doctor.

"Sir, I simply cannot understand!" Finnegan pleaded, as if bracing himself for a recrimination.

Collier quickly lowered his eyes but almost regretted the fact when he beheld one of the stricken slavering and groaning with disturbing authenticity.

"They're running absurdly high fevers," Finnegan complained with the bitterness of someone caught completely unawares. "There is no way for this to have happened!"

"They were looking for trouble," Collier snarled, still staring at the body convulsed with pain, "and by God they've found it!"

"But with the doses of quinine they were taking this is simply impossible; it cannot be happening."

"They weren't taking the quinine. . . ."

Finnegan heard what the engineer had said and yet the words seemed nebulous and faint. The physician could not comprehend that men would deliberately expose themselves—actually permit the vector to deposit, by means of its salivary glands, millions of parasites which had already begun in their asexual cycle to infest the tissues and bloodstream. This was logic beached on the shores of the absurd, and Finnegan, feeling catastrophically ineffective, gave vent to his own frustration.

"It's not possible!" the physician in him insisted.

The engineer acquitted himself of the doctor's exclamation: "They were selling the damned pills."

"How did you find out? It's the only way to explain this epidemic."

"Never you mind how I found out—what matters is they're going to *die!*" Collier was vehement with a desire to see them dead as an example. "Of that you can be certain!"

"They won't die if taken immediately to the hospital in Candelária," Finnegan—once more the competent physician—replied curtly.

The howls of pain grew hoarse and lush with desperation. The victims alternately throbbed with delirium or were convulsed with cold as they succumbed to the effects of the fever. Collier ran a hand through his hair with an air of determination.

"If you haven't got the means to solve this thing here and now, then it will have to wait until morning."

It would be an exhausting night for the physician. He would trace the delirium of those miserable laborers who had bartered their own health like a cheap rag. The initial consternation had already worn off his brow. Despite the writhing limbs and pop-eyed stares of his patients, the hoarse and broken German phrases flung out like garbled comminations of the unconscious, Finnegan had already settled down for the long siege ahead. Only he and the medics stood among the stricken—aside from the engineer, waiting for his response.

"I can do nothing," Finnegan confessed. "It happens to be an attack of malaria falciparum and its parasites have entered the brain. It might have been the intestines, in which case: diarrhea. With the brain the result is delirium. The prophylaxis for this form of malaria is not difficult but I have not the proper medical resources at my disposal, as you are well aware. Here, my treatment can only be preventative."

110

"You mean to tell me that they have to go on howling like this?"

"Until they fall into a coma. It's horrid, I know, but there's nothing I can do to help them."

"But they could keep that up all night long, isn't that true?"

"It's difficult to estimate how long they might sustain the delirium. They all present signs of acute cachexia."

"Then we'll have to consider our own sanity and that of the men. No one can get any sleep during these bouts of delirium. And the men need their sleep, by God. . . ."

"Everybody needs to sleep, but I have nothing with which to sedate these men."

"I realize that, Dr. Finnegan. So I'm afraid we'll have to settle for an improvised solution."

"Improvised?" Finnegan pricked up his ears, for he had sensed an ominous lassitude behind the engineer's choice of words.

"Oh, we've already tested it several times." Collier signaled the security guards that had been prudently posted between the scantlings marking the corners of the dormitory. The guards, their weapons down but still within reach, recoiled instinctively, intuiting what the Englishman was about to exact of them. "You there . . . and you!" Collier shouted. "We'll tie them to their hammocks."

To the physician's ears Collier's orders were like slaps of embarrassment and humiliation. Having proven his own medical futility, he had opened the floodgates of the English engineer's repressed penchant for violence.

"This is outrageous," Finnegan managed finally, as if the protest had merely eroded from the banks of his gaping mouth.

"Don't interfere," barked the engineer.

Methodically each patient—with his gaunt mask of desperation and eyes burning like incandescent vials—was held in place by two Spanish guards while an additional number worked perfunctorily to bale him into the sweat- and urine-soaked folds of a fetid hammock by harnessing the spastic, anemic, and fever-ridden torso in progressive spirals of coiled rope. The nervous reactions of these doomed Germans would seem to have petrified into a series of apocalyptic sculptures crafted by the genie of the grotesque, sovereign in the Abuná, were it not for the shrieks that horrifically mimed a last vestige

111

of the human. The physician, meanwhile, was mainly concerned with removing his medics, in order not to be considered party to such a brutally depraved therapeutic. The medics were still clinging to their kerosene lamps like the last turbid bulwarks of their disenchanted illuminations. They gathered around the doctor who now hesitated to abandon his patients from a suddenly unraveled thread of shame. Collier, however, seemed to be positively swimming in activity, spitting out orders upon the receding wake of the physician's incompetence.

"Tie them good and tight. We don't want anybody breaking loose in the night."

A final guard helped Collier stuff each yowling mouth with rags, then complete the gagging with some strips of cloth tied from between the jaws around the back of the neck like a barbaric bridle. The cries grew muffled to brumous sighs of desperation.

"Careful not to cut off the poor bastard's breathing," the engineer recommended. "We don't want anyone dying of asphyxiation."

Soon they were all tied securely into their hammocks. And yet they strained to break free in a fulmination of muscular contortions accentuated by the moonlight, the fever, and the silence. Only their panting—like maddened horses on the brink of death after a suicidal gallop in the desert—still occupied that silence. Indeed, strung into their hammocks, they rather resembled the larvae of a monstrous insect; pupae, ready to break out and liberate the imago of some nightmare; chrysalides, projecting their winged deliriums through the ebb and flow of a muddy void.

"You will have to pardon me for saying so, sir, but this is one of the most repugnant spectacles I've ever been a witness to in my life."

Finnegan spoke with the bloodless bravado of the helpless, while Collier's rejoinder reflected mere fatigue.

"Repugnant or not it's the only way to shut them up. Otherwise we sit up all night while they howl like a pack of wolves. And for what?"

"By tomorrow they'll be dead," the physician retorted flatly.

"We all have to die sometime, with or without a gag."

"This is plain murder."

"Quite possibly!" The engineer eyed him sternly, then added: "Why don't you enter it in your report . . . ?"

"You, Mr. Collier, sir, have shed all decency. You've gone to rot as a human being; I hope you know that."

"Do your sniveling elsewhere, doctor. I'm in no mood to be edified."

"I never imagined a civilized man could stoop so low."

"Bravo, my boy! It almost gives me pleasure to hear that, as it may be the only sign that I can still survive this inferno. If I were you, my little lad, I'd dispense with a bit of that rancid decency and start tiptoeing through the sewer you seem to have fallen into. And another thing: don't clothe yourself in civilization; it's rather hot for that sort of thing down here."

Finnegan's shoulders sank in discouragement. The engineer was certainly on firmer ground than he, with all his tender anxieties over seeking out the good in a place where there was clearly nothing but turmoil and exploitation.

"Go back to the infirmary and try to get some sleep," Collier advised him. "By the look of you, *Dr.* Finnegan, you've had better days yourself."

The emphasis on the title of doctor irritated young Finnegan even more than Collier's calling him "my boy" or "little lad." Yet he felt too disadvantaged by the sheer power of the engineer's modus vivendi to counter with reasonable or effective argument.

"If they're still alive tomorrow," Collier added, sparging the flow of thoughts the physician struggled to cup in his mind, "we can arrange for their removal to the hospital at Candelária."

"I can hardly go off to the infirmary," Finnegan answered. "I belong here, where I can keep an eye on the situation."

"As you like." Collier shrugged and went off.

The medics were impatient, seeing that they might also forfeit the privilege of sleep that night, despite all the effort to silence the cries of the stricken. Finnegan noticed the general restlessness of the lads and signaled them to withdraw. Let them go back to the infirmary and have their rest, he thought, if that's what they want. The other workers climbed back into their hammocks and fell asleep almost at once. The physician continued to wander about the dormitory, checking his patients, such as they were, and when he looked up for a moment he found that only the guards still remained standing. All the rest

113

were sleeping and the dormitory echoed only the relaxed symphony of human sleep in which fear had been vanquished by
fatigue and where the only discordant note—like an anach-
ronous cadenza—was in the perseverance of the doctor. Some
hours later, as he seemed to hear strange noises emanating
from somewhere in the surrounding jungle—was it singing of
sorts?—Finnegan succumbed to sleep, vanquished at last by
his exhausting watch at the foot of a mast from which bifurcated
a sea of hammocks in all directions.

An instant after he fell asleep Nancy came over to play
beside him, which did not surprise him. Richard Finnegan had
four sisters: two older ones, Flora and Cynthia; and two younger
than he, Nancy and Katherine. He loved them all, but especially
Nancy. Born when he was not much more than a year old,
Nancy Finnegan had grown into a sweet and lovable little girl
with flowing hair and longish legs. She maintained a preference
for baggy, comfortable clothes and always talked as if she had
divined his every thought. It was almost two years now since
she had died in childbirth. Oh, Nancy was dead all right; yet
there was nothing strange in the fact of her coming to play
nearby him. Indeed, nothing could seem strange to him now
that the logic of the nightmare had been transferred to daily
life in this inferno. Why shouldn't the banalities of ordinary
existence come to animate the images of sleep?

It was the death of this sister, in any case, that had more
or less led to his present state of disintegration in this insane
locale. On the heels of her pointless martyrdom, the insensate
brutality that surrounded her passing, Finnegan could only
despair of his vague projects for the future. So it was to this
state of mind that Dr. Lovelace's overtures of challenge and
excitement presented themselves. And what could now com-
pare to those possibilities of adventure which a smiling Lovelace articulated with such energy and good humor. Yet in the
final analysis, had not his actions resembled those of a sulking
schoolboy who preferred running away from home to reality?
And what had he left behind, besides the death of a sister?

Nothing!—not even the impatience of his sweetheart with
her slender volumes of verse tucked under her arm and her silly
dresses always crumpled from her habit of sitting on the campus
green to savor Blake in her spare moments, nor her blushing
look whenever he touched her arm or brushed his lips against

her perfumed hair. Finnegan still recalled the lustrous sheen of her blond tresses spread over the rug where they lay together on the floor of his fraternity room, with the noise of the carousing in the main hall downstairs filtering benevolently up into their own intimacy. She had scarlet lips, rather delicate, like arched filigrees through which her voice whispered upon her breath while he undressed her unhurriedly because there was no need to hurry. How often had he mined the geography of her body: the multiplicity of curves that unveiled themselves as the dress was lifted up over her head without the need for her to get up from where she lay; the tumescence of her breasts which he could not stop touching even after he had sheathed himself to the hilt in her foamy passage; her pleading fingers that seemed to beg him to penetrate her even further, to dig deeper, to mine her furiously.

Finnegan had been rich enough not to fear for the future; he could have relaxed into the tepid facility of preestablished lives just as easily as he succumbed to the sadness that inevitably overtook him once he had overflowed into the fruity interior of his now forgotten mistress. Perhaps the simple fact of his having been a child without disadvantages—always money in his pocket, able to study at the finest schools, outfitted in the best of clothes (incidentally frustrating the negligent air he always hoped to effect)—had somehow paved the tortuous way that would lead him into the trap. In any case it was to be the death of Nancy that would serve as final pretext. All the shielding that money could buy had not been sufficient. Very much to the contrary, it had amplified his frailty in the face of all seductions. He knew as much himself. Indeed, to him his sweetheart was hardly so different from the others—those compliant nurses from the hospital where he had worked for a time. They were all the same, weren't they? And now even Nancy was playing just as Dr. Lovelace had played, with him, in Portland—merely a bit surprised at his sudden disposition to accept a position in the Madeira-Mamoré Railway Company—like a fisherman who had thrown out his lines to hook a catfish and then reeled in a salmon! After signing the contract there in the drugstore where they were sipping piping cups of hot chocolate, he sat back to Lovelace's discourse on tropical disease:

"I bet you haven't heard the naughty tale of the Countess

of Chinchón? Of course you haven't. You see, before our even
knowing the cause of malaria, its effective treatment had already been applied with astonishing effect." Lovelace spoke
with the cloying impertinence of a true flimflammer, but Finnegan only caught wind of exotic spells that seemed to emanate
from the soaring blue smoke of the great doctor's pipe. "Ah
yes, Countess of Chinchón, a remarkable woman! Spanish
nobility, I think. So beautiful that even legend has refused to
describe her, leaving it to us to imagine freely her physical
charms. Myself, I prefer to think of her as rather youthful—
nearing thirty, let us say—with pale, porcelain shoulders that
had never known the sun despite her living in the tropics.
Always secluded in the shadows of baroque alcoves, lavishly
ensconced in great beds with mattresses of goose down and
sheets of white satin, or reflected in the salons of marble colonnades and gilded ionic capitals. They say that she lived in
Peru, 1630s or thereabouts, years of gallantry amid an already
well established system of colonization. The silver of the Andes
crammed the holds of ships and the treasuries of kings, financing all sorts of extravagances: divinely aromatic spices,
exotic perfumes and textiles brought from the remote quadrants
of Asia on camelback. You can't imagine . . ."

Yet poor Richard Finnegan imagined things only too well
in certain spheres and this was evidently one of them.

"No matter when the countess's lovers arrived they would
find her shamelessly eager, moistened by a cold sweat—and
this above all when their rendezvous took place in the hours
just prior to dawn. The body of this impenitent wench would
tremble so—would perspire as if lasciviousness ruled her every
fiber, as if each centimeter of flesh were consumed by a fire
that left her insatiably frozen while fueling the passion of her
every lover. She burned, yet the cold she felt resisted and her
passion was never consumed. Exhausted at the end of an evening, with no one left at her side in bed, the profligate countess
would suddenly grow terror-stricken as her head began to ache—
to throb unbearably with shooting pains of blood! Yet it wasn't
remorse that made her head pump so; she was ill and didn't
know it. The fevered sensation that she felt in the wee hours
of night was a symptom of malarial fever characteristic of the
most intense moments of its infection. The probationary cold
that suffused her body in nowise represented the vespers of

116

er communion, the anticipation of a lover's touch—it was *malaria*. The sweat that bathed her skin was not the juice of lovemaking realized with ardor—it was *malaria*. Eventually, she was obliged to withdraw from Lima for a week, to a place where there were no lovers to account for those early-morning ecstasies, and still the attacks occurred and the countess knew now for certain that she was possessed of something beyond the sin of luxury. An Indian sorcerer was called in and he fed her a brew concocted from the bark of a certain tree. The countess miraculously recovered. Gone for good were those odd, albeit voluptuous symptoms of profligate, predawn fever. Her lovers—when she finally returned to Lima—found a less wanton but more robust mistress. And in homage to her cure the tree from whose bark the medicine man had brewed his liquid extract was immediately baptized the Chinchón. The most active chemical ingredient to be found in the tree would eventually turn out to be the basis for all therapeutics in the treatment of malaria: quinine."

Finnegan had hung on his every word at the time, but later on he would see the worth of such eloquence. Sheer rhetoric! Because Lovelace was almost Latin in his manipulation of words for their own sake. Forget the ardors of a Spanish countess in the arms of her paramours. Malaria was both horrendous and insidious. It crept over one like the consummate cat burglar, reduced men to yellowed tatters as its parasites secreted their pigmentation into the cells of its host while coursing through the bloodstream. In the masks of its victims, the fable of the countess drew an atrocious blank. No cheap thrill here, you old scoundrel, only the foul routine of mortality.

And the young woman? Nancy? No, the one who had been brought in unconscious. She was already recuperating. Finnegan had had her placed in bed, had arranged some screens around her to protect her privacy, had removed her torn garments and washed with a disinfectant her lacerated body, bruised and scratched by the leaves and thorns of the jungle. She was beautiful to look at. Perhaps the long absence of a woman had finally begun to reflect itself in the urgency of his ministrations. Her body was lovely lying there asleep, not unconscious, merely asleep. In a state of shock, perhaps, but sleeping nonetheless, with her breasts rising and falling to the rhythm of her breathing. Her eyelids half-open at best in the periodic, partial glimpse

117

of an exhausted female who had literally torn her way throug the forested night and now lay helpless in a nebulous state o sleep. Who was she, this woman? He did not know. She hadn' even a name. Countess of Chinchón? Why not? Were not he incoherent mutterings in Spanish and did they not include however inarticulately, a Spanish masculine name? Her las lover, perhaps. Or, who knows, the famous sorcerer-savior At least she was clean now, relieved of her tattered garment and dressed decently enough in a change of masculine clothes Shirt and pants, both his own. They were the blue-stripe pajamas that he had brought down here in his luggage but neve taken out because as the physician he had come to sleep half dressed for any contingency. Sometimes the young girl woul open her eyes, dark eyes that opened fleetingly with a burs of anxiety which thoroughly disconcerted the doctor. Inert an vulnerable where she lay, the girl breathed to the rhythm o her sleep and even took her food without visibly awakening Nearly a week had passed since her arrival. Did she attrac him? Yes, though he would not own up to the fact. Eventuall the state of shock she was in would loosen its hold and sh would begin to emerge from the cold limbo of unconsciousness He felt certain that she had experienced some trauma, some thing awesome enough to have driven her from the livin though not yet to the dead. What had she been doing in th forest? Beyond that incredibly feminine body there before him he could discover nothing: all was an amorphous mass in locked memory, a nameless totality muted and mutilated b her past. She opened her mouth only to be fed, her dry throa swallowing with difficulty, her chafed lips caressed haltingl by a swollen tongue. The secrets she bore fascinated him Excited him? Aroused his curiosity, he told himself. For hour he would stare at her, confounded; but her secrets resisted hi scrutiny, hiding themselves and enslaving him, dominating hi will. Her arrival was like a thunderbolt from the unexpected as his first conversations with Dr. Lovelace had been roman ticized flashes of lightning. Yet she was palpably there; sh existed; he could feel her as he examined her, as he sponge off her forehead or with his stethoscope now and then listene for any sign of internal malignancy in the breath that emerge from those curves aflame with sultry perspiration.

Then there was the second patient—equally unexpecte

118

he Indian with the amputated hands. The men had avenged
hemselves by imposing a brutal, Islamic sentence. The thief
f tiny, almost trivial objects—pencil stubs, pens, mirrors,
eckerchiefs, penknifes—his sentence carried out, wept con-
tantly now with a poignant passivity. He had innocently pro-
oked his own tragedy by robbing inconsequential objects of
alue only to men so wretched that a stub of pencil was like
sliver of gold. That the Indian had been saved at all was a
mall miracle. The thirst for vengeance on the part of the men
vas obviously not limited to cutting off his hands; they had
learly intended more. The had wanted to kill him, or at least
o transform his whole body into slices of meat with a rain of
·lows from the machete. The amputation was but a prelude
hat had been thwarted by the arrival of the engineer Collier
vith his Cuban security contingent. Even so, Dr. Finnegan did
ot hope to save him. The wounds had spewed a great deal of
·lood—the Indian appeared to be a grotesque fountain cha-
·tically dissipating itself when finally brought into the infir-
nary livid and debilitated. And the doctor had none of the
mergency equipment to perform the needed surgery. Still, he
vas obliged, almost out of inertia, to work on those sectioned
xtremities, fighting to staunch the hemorrhaging and to close
he vessels hanging open like miniature mouths which instead
·f screaming were vomiting blood.

It took Finnegan nearly three hours to sew up in a rudi-
nentary fashion the tissue which had already begun to recede
round the exposed bone. Yet the Indian held on to his life
nd it looked as if he might survive. It was ghastly, to be sure,
vith no transfusion—nothing!—but a force of a different na-
ure seemed to sustain him and draw from some unknown
rovenance the needed replacement of blood. Yes, he would
urvive if the wounds did not turn gangrenous. It was not a
retty sight: the forearms ceased at midlength, culminating in
alls of reddish, swollen flesh.

The curious thing was how neither patient would speak;
iey moaned, even wept, but uttered not a syllable. When the
ndian ventured to open his eyes, he observed the doctor from
state of terror, wholly ignorant of the physician's purpose or
ntentions whenever the latter was obliged to approach him in
rder to administer medication or check his condition. The
ndian's fear was discomforting but understandable. The girl's

119

indifference and her abandonment wounded Finnegan mor deeply, disconcerting him completely. As each humid nigh unfolded, the doctor would minister to his patients until fatigu overtook him. Then Nancy would come to play beside him by his bed, and time finally usurped the logic of things.

Finnegan proposed to send the two patients off to the hos pital in Candelária the moment the opportunity should aris There they would receive proper treatment and the Indian coul undergo additional corrective surgery and perhaps receive pair of protheses as well as an indemnification from the con pany. He was aware of similar situations that had arisen in th Abunã even before his arrival: Indians who had suffered am putations for one reason or another, legs lost to gangren stumps outfitted with prosthetic latex limbs shipped in fro the United States. Until the opportunity presented itself to ge them out of the Abunã, Dr. Finnegan would work to spar their lives, above all the Indian who had suffered such a unspeakably violent physical trauma. The girl was already o of danger; the superficial abrasions were healing nicely am she was probably more in need of attention than of medicatio

Nancy, who was dead, would return to play close by hi bed and he did not wish to break the spell. There was no silenc in the Abunã, and such dreams reached out of the memory lik latent caresses. On that night Nancy drew near and bent ove his chest; her loose-fitting clothes seemed to want to fall fro her nubile figure like a superfluous integument. Our Finnega suddenly opened his eyes in the nether light of early mornin he had felt a chilled breath close to his face and he turned ove frightened. Then voices came to him whispering a distant cor versation and the breathing turned out to be nothing more tha the matinal breeze. The Barbadian Negroes were already sittin up in their hammocks. The other workers slept on because th sun had barely begun to announce the new day with a viole tinge to the clouds.

Finally, Dr. Finnegan got to his feet. His limbs were numbe and ached accordingly. It had been an absurdity to spend th night sitting there among the hammocks. He had hardly man aged to sleep really. He stretched his body and worked t animate the circulation by shaking his arms and legs. He no ticed when Jonathan vaulted out of his hammock and watche him approach.

120

"Doct' Finn'gan, look like you done slept right dere de whole night."

"I did."

"How dey be doin'?"

"I don't know, I still have to examine them all. But if even one of them managed to survive it's a miracle."

"Gen'ly dey is dead in de mornin'."

"You mean you've already seen this sort of thing, Jonathan?"

"Dat right, Doct' Finn'gan, if a sick mon get de deliriums, de coptin tie him up and gag de mon so de rest of us get some sleep."

"It's barbaric!" Finnegan muttered, more for his own benefit than that of the Barbadian beside him.

"I wants to put a certain motter to you."

There was no aggressivity in Jonathan's tone of voice, any more than there had been intimations of solidarity with respect to the doctor's espousal of repugnance. The Barbadian seemed not to attribute the slightest importance to the brutalization of the physician's patients. Finnegan let the numbness of his limbs dissipate itself through the vent of growing indifference that seemed to well up now within him. He remained silent.

"I go tell you why we ain't s'pose to let de dead be touch," Jonathan said without irony, though the situation itself did not cease to be encumbered by the grotesque. "It were Copm Collier dat—"

"So, it was Collier who made you come to me."

"De coptin don't made me, de coptin ask me."

"I'm still half-asleep, Jonathan," Finnegan said to put him off.

"Sorry, Doct' Finn'gan, but I haves to be workin' fore long."

"The day's already breaking," Finnegan replied, breathing in the cool, misty morning air.

"Dey ain't no doct's like you believe in voodoo?"

"Voodoo? Is that some kind of religion?" Finnegan asked, deciding to be diplomatic.

"Is our religion," Jonathan declared, unperturbed.

"I thought you were all Protestants—Anglicans or something."

"S'pose I tell you we really be Cath'lic? Den what you say?"

"Catholic?"

121

"Is not too common, I tell you dat, Doct' Finn'gan, but den I figure de history bout Barbados not too familiar to you mostwise anyway."

"I guess you're right about that."

"But you pro'bly knows dat most all dem islands dere is inhob'tid by de Africans. When de African slave come to de islands he find de Indians already long dead, decimated by de white mon."

"Yes, I have some vague idea of all that."

"Well, de Africans dey also hod dere tribes de way de Indians hod deres. And dere ways and religions, too. And we is de d'scendants of one dem tribes: de Fon tribe."

"How is it you know all these things, Jonathan?"

"I is *hungan*," Jonathan explained.

"You're *what?*"

"I a priest of de voodoo. I haves to know all t'ings dat dere is leff to us, even dough we already loss much of de ways of Africa."

Shrieks of delirium, slave ships, countesses, black angels in the form of serpents—Jonathan related thus the history of his people. The living dead, more free in their prison beyond life than the lives now shackled with *Plasmodium falciparum*—there was nothing left in the world to confound the young physician and he thought of himself now as freed from further surprises forever and always. Meanwhile, Jonathan's story, like some whispered commotion, silhouetted memories of prismatic yesterdays and resuscitated legends, parables, and animal sacrifice with tinctured words that slackened with exhaustion into feebly rancorous anecdote. Finnegan knew, of course, that the stricken patients were surely dead after their comatose state, when nightmares were finally pacified on the edge of nullification, with cardiac paralysis asphyxiating the brain. They would be no more than stippled corpses stiffly laced into their hammocks in stately rigor mortis. Still, Jonathan abandoned himself totally to the rapture of his tradition, where the dead could return to life when animated by greed, while the chary logic of the physician dismissed it all as nothing more than primitive fantasy. Indeed, he almost shouted back at Jonathan that the worst thing of all is to be exploited while still alive

122

because, after death, when life has already irrevocably departed, the body is not even the specter of what we once were. Dear God, thought Finnegan with an additional dose of expletives, the worst disease of all has to be the idiocy of man!

7

Minister Seabra, or J.J. as he was affectionately called by his partisans, was a very special breed of politician. He had not come up from the bottom—slowly widening the circle of his prestige with successfully petty forays in the manner of those who escape the dregs and manage to pinnacle themselves through sheer ambition. No, J.J. was a man who had always been great—of a strong and fearless temperament, wealthy and powerful, frank and authoritarian—because he was a landowner with his roots firmly planted in the soil, although he had joined the generation of city dwellers, gentlemen farmers, seigneurs from the sugar mills who would more readily recognize the bouquet of a wine than the sweetish odor of molasses boiling in the great cauldrons. His most obvious connection to the heroic days of the "big houses" and the vast cane plantations lay in his virile carriage: head always erect with unfeigned arrogance and bushy black brows tufting the forehead as if to protect the eyes from the remorseless sun of the backlands—chestnut-brown eyes watered with intricate Ibero-African genetic permutations, not to mention a great-great-great-grandmother whom an itinerant French portrait painter back in the eighteenth century had depicted in colorful Portuguese costume, like some peasant from Estremadura, but with her ears cut and stretched to hold ornamental spools and the dark skin of her face wrinkled like parchment and as ritually scarred as any pure-blooded Indian's. The painting, framed in gold, nearly opaque with the dust of years in the backlands, hung in the study at his mansion, up in the Santa Tereza district, where J. J. Seabra now resided.

J.J. was at the moment seated in his study, whose windows opened onto the hilly slopes of the neighborhood covered with greenery and threaded with steep roads along which elderly Europeans, mainly English and German, were treating their pedigrees to early morning strolls. Seabra was actually one of the few Brazilians to live in Santa Tereza, which also served

124

s the location for a sanatorium for tuberculosis, not to mention
 haven for a number of old-world retired pensioners who were
till tempted to try this final amalgam of the heat of the tropics
vith the temperate serenity of the springs which recalled their
native lands. Santa Tereza was indeed a refuge and Seabra
iked that. Along with its solitude it offered the pleasant sen-
ation of being able to loaf about high above the city of Rio
le Janeiro, where life had already fallen victim to the mod-
rnization begun by Prefect Passos, with its clouds of dust and
plaster rising from countless demolitions, high up into the ever-
plue sky, and its widened avenues elbowing their way through
he clutter of scaffolding that still framed the new construction.
n that stately three-story dwelling, set on a hillside of gray
ock mottled with whitish stone bubbles, he lived with his
vife, with a small staff of household servants, and with the
omfort that he had at least for a time escaped the administrative
ustle and bustle of Catete Palace. Here the silence was broken
only by the insects and the birds, or by gusts of wind rising
up from the sea and rattling the window sashes.

Seabra's wife was born and raised in Salvador, Bahia; white,
vith blond hair that recalled the Dutch invasion, she possessed
a scrupulously Calvinistic shrewdness that he could ill account
or given that she had been raised with nuns in the habitual
Catholic boarding school. Yet she had been ardorous, almost
predacious for his company, and soon became the mainstay for
all his most daring political undertakings. With the onset of
middle age, however, she had suffered a decline: relegating
herself to housedresses and—since he had agreed for a second
ime to serve as a cabinet minister—refusing to accompany
him on public business. Seabra still felt the same strong at-
raction to her, her short stature disguised by a slender figure
and the straight blond hair that rendered her even more willowy
and enticing. And he continued to worship in her the old
shrewdness that infallibly produced instantaneous judgments
of people—a thing of which he himself was generally incapable, even after weeks with a person—and which had served
him incalculably in the advancement of his political career.
But now she would only vanish into her alcove and therein
distract herself by reading French romances and furtively light-
ng up Virginia-brand American cigarettes, which gave off a
tepid, sweetish-smelling cloud of smoke that hung suspended

125

beneath the ceiling of her closeted boudoir. Whenever he entered those chambers to sleep, or to attempt to convince her to come along with him to some festivity, J.J's nostrils would be stung by the acrid smoke that had almost become one with the smell of her flesh by now. Indeed, what was his wife but a wisp of smoke? In fact, what was the whole house but a tenuous wisp that had somehow managed to drift high above the anterooms of Catete with its tallowy politicians and its perfumed generals girdled in threadbare frogs and verdigris copper buttons.

Our minister was attempting to make some headway through a voluminous legal brief while searching for an important political dispatch which must be delivered that very afternoon into the hands of the president. The documents related to a rather hazy contract with dubious entrepreneurs for the construction of a series of public schools in three northeastern states. To further that very procedure, on the previous day, a number of congressmen and senators from the political caucuses of each of those states had paid him a somewhat untimely visit in his chambers. The building of schools in this particular case had little to do with improving the nation's system of education. The politicos who had paid him call in their wrinkled suits, passing their hats from one hand to the other, pragmatically equated each proposed edifice to a determined number of votes. It was electoral mathematics which had actually motivated them, obliging them even to descend upon his study like that, perorating vulgar hypocrisies that he forced himself to endure—between the emotional bearhugs of their arrival and the jovial handshakes of their departure—with the skeptical certainty that he had also indulged in such behavior himself, numerous times in the past.

Yet it was not the problem of the building of schools, nor the pending legal action involved (favorable, obviously), that troubled him. He had already decided to concede what these northeastern bosses were after: to open to public bidding the referred to public-works projects—thereby delighting some half a dozen greasy regional bosses who would wangle the necessary votes for the administration in the next election by brandishing revolvers, not primers. And Seabra himself, who was preparing to run for governor of Bahia, would thus have prepared solid terrain by gathering the faithful for the moment

126

n which he would have to confront the force of circumstances
n the electoral state. No, what troubled him was the insistence
of his mistress, whom until then he had regarded as little more
than a frivolous child with milky white limbs and blushing
cheeks—-the daughter of Portuguese immigrants, whom he had
lifted out of the gutter from the Mata Cavalos slums where she
was living with her parents at the back of a fetid grocery store—
but whose temperament was now suddenly altered by new
exigencies that she was beginning to proffer with the same
cast-iron Calvinistic spirit as that of his legitimate wife!

There on the table at which he sat perusing the document
in front of him, though unable to focus his concentration, was
the clipping from the papers that she had given him the previous
night and which now thoroughly distracted him. It was a news
item datelined New York which spoke of the Madeira-Mamoré
railway, a project currently under construction in a remote
sector of the Amazon rain forest.

Customarily, J.J. visited his mistress once his office hours
at the ministry were over, around six o'clock in the evening,
before proceeding to his refuge and his wife back up in Santa
Tereza. He had lodged this lovely young creature in a small,
discreet cottage over in the São Cristóvão neighborhood, to
which the coachman could drive his victoria with its two horses
at a comfortable twenty-minute trot. The house in itself was
modest, set back and protected behind a narrow front yard
filled with fruit trees, whose bounty was avidly coveted by the
passing street waifs. The stratagems of these urchins when
tempted by the fruit thoroughly amused his mistress, diverting
her from her daytime solitude when the only other compan-
ionship was provided by the maid.

Seabra's mistress was nineteen but had begun to think like
a mature woman—something J.J. showed no liking for in the
least. When he had questioned her as to why she had cut out
the item concerning the railroad—never having suspected her
even of reading a newspaper, not to mention concerning herself
with such a matter as this—she limited herself to indulging
him with a smile of snowy white teeth, not uttering a word
but simply reclining against her pillow and stretching her cres-
cent, rosy thighs half-open, in a gesture that accentuated the
gentle bulge of her sloping cleft lushly garlanded with curly
blond tuft. He had not insisted, but noted nevertheless when

127

the clipping was deftly placed in the pocket of his jacket hung
on a chair near the bed—a gesture for which she had little
need to shift her position since she could simply stretch out
her arm enough to deposit the folded paper as she sometimes
had done to remove his money. After their lovemaking he
observed in the expression on his mistress's face, as she pretended to sleep, a cold tenacity quite at odds with the engaging
passivity of their first times together.

As for the text of the clipping, he had read it already a
hundred times; it was both insipid and disturbing and he could
merely suspect at this point what its true significance might
be. The railroad under construction was a project tied to the
interests of the North American capitalists, forces which had
openly helped to finance the opposition in the last election.
This was the hand of Mackenzie with his young, black-boy
pets. From the portrait on the wall J.J.'s great-great-great Indian
grandmother gazed down upon him with the sadly apathetic
commiseration of those who may no longer counsel.

How to discover where the trap lay? Was it, in fact, a trap?
He dismissed the question. Our J. J. Seabra was no fool: years
of political juggling in public life had whetted his instincts to
such a degree that infallibly he picked up the scent. But to
pick up a scent was not necessarily to track down the game,
find the contours of the trap, or manipulate it to his own
advantage. Then again, he could hardly run to his wife and
show her the crumpled piece of paper. Women had a sixth
sense and his wife might conceivably detect the odor of her
rival while going straight to the heart of what for him seemed
nothing more than empty propaganda. Propaganda? Hardly!
No one heard anything about that railroad anymore. The newspapers had been silenced by hefty bribes just as the contract
itself, he knew, to undertake the project in the first place had
been secured through payoffs and swindles. And now suddenly
here was the railroad, enigmatically resurfacing after three
years of purposeful silence: hailed as an extraordinary undertaking, a technological feat!

Where did his mistress fit into all this? Almost no one was
aware that he even had a mistress in São Cristóvão: he had
never appeared with her in public; he avoided confiding the
fact to any friends, even of the most intimate sort; besides
which, President Hermes da Fonseca was a man of rigid moral

128

standards and simply would not tolerate such moral transgressions. The marshal habitually extolled J.J.'s fidelity to his wife, harshly reproaching with the same breath those senators and congressmen—his supporters, yes, but who let themselves be seduced by power and unctuously parade about town accompanied by scatterbrained *cocottes* and tawny-skinned *morenas*. Da Fonseca was implacable, to be sure, with respect to certain strains of moral misconduct among his close aids and had recently cast off even his old comrade in arms, the jovial Major Quitanilha, for having abandoned his wife to go and cohabitate with a certain German girl from Espírito Santo. Not even the arguments on behalf of racial purity— the major in question was married to a woman of evident African descent—had moved the adamant marshal. Only the youngest of his supporters—and among these only bachelors, those with *discretion*—were permitted to visit the house of Tina Tatti, or the notorious Eudoxia, without calling down upon themselves the inevitable wrath of the first executive of the nation. For this reason, and out of the naturally sedentary inclination of the provincial who still abhors the customs of a federal capital, Seabra sought to conceal his conjugal escapades. Certainly the wench from the house in São Cristóvão had not been the first; nor would she be the last!

Likewise, Minister Seabra intuitively shunned the fashionable places of the moment and was almost never to be seen at the Politicians Club, on the Praça Tiradentes, or at the wrestling clubs scattered about the Avenida Central. Neither was he inclined to gambling in or lingering about those literary salons which he found to be altogether too tedious and affected for his ancestral, backlander's verve. A few times, it was true, he had attended with his wife—once it had been founded, in the same neighborhood of Santa Tereza where they themselves resided—the famous salon of Dona Laurinda Santos Lovo. There, a select crowd gathered every evening for vapid conversation and piano recitals, reading sonnets and sipping Tokay. Through that orientally baroque salon passed the likes of the Baron Homem de Melo and the Counselor Ataulfo de Paiva along with international celebrities such as the ballerina Isadora Duncan and the poet Paul Adam. J.J.'s wife was similarly disinclined to indulge in the fawning conventions of those swankily attired pretenders and sat aloof in her chair, silent and withdrawn, contemplating the golden silks from China, the carpets from Persia, the bronzes and jades representing figures from out of the Confucian pantheon, and later listening without much interest to some poet or other with flowing locks and a feminine pallor recite his most recent *oeuvre*.

J. J. Seabra, with his own nose for things, associated such an atmosphere with the sweetish smell of vanilla and gradually limited his visits, then finally eliminated them altogether. His name was never to be cited again by gossip columnists, except should they raise their sights a bit to comment upon some political matter. No, he preferred to keep his distance from such *blasés;* indeed, from all the snobbish rubbish and foppish refinements of the *jeunesse dorée*. Most of them had no real wealth in any case and barely managed to sustain the facade: dying of hunger but lavishing themselves with garish jewels, mother-of-pearl, platinum, and lapis lazuli; then dusting off the dubious results with a dose of ochre and face powder. Seabra kept aloof from it all—a professional politician who had twice assumed the duties of a minister of state; an immensely wealthy man, but one whose fortune was solidly rooted in the abundant riches that generations of Seabras had managed to extract from the rustic backlands of Pernambuco. Indeed, hadn't his forefathers faced ferocious Indians, rebellious Negroes, wild outlaws, Dutch interlopers, and pirates of every nationality in order that one day a young J.J. might study law in the capital of Recife and there become a professor with advanced republican ideas, exalting in the American Revolution and despising the reactionary oligarchs who still refused to surrender the reins of power though they were choking on their very putrefaction and nepotism while staunchly resisting the ascent of new ideas? From Recife he would eventually make his way to the federal capital in Rio de Janeiro, where he adamantly refused to surrender to the languid gestures of the more cosmopolitan *carioca*—he was a politician, not a *raffiné!* He did not, of course, wear shabby clothes but merely continued to dress as he had always done in Recife: soberly, in white cotton suits, with no hint of affectation.

In the light of all this, it was impossible to figure out how they had discovered his mistress or what they actually planned to do with her now in order to extort from Seabra something he could barely guess at. And this was no mere contrivance

130

of old Mackenzie's; the tactics were of a Machiavellian subtlety that the American did not possess. Mr. Mackenzie, J.J. knew for certain, was too direct a person for all this: a man without subterfuge. If he wanted something, he didn't beat around any bush; he walked into your office and after two or three cordial words came directly to the point, made his offer; you accepted or refused. Yet the clipping did indicate that Mackenzie had at least some hand in the matter, and Seabra knew he had better look to things, cautiously, without diverging from his routine, since he knew that in the face of any danger there is always the possibility that the one who is menaced can turn that very threat to his own advantage.

On this same morning, immediately upon arriving at the ministry, J. J. Seabra sent a messenger over to the office of Alexander Mackenzie, summoning the American to an unscheduled meeting of the so-called Public Utilities Commission. It was to be held in the conference room at the ministry. He should be there without fail that same morning at eleven o'clock, promptly.

The Public Utilities Commission for all intents and purposes existed only on paper and was rarely convened. The few times that its members had actually held a meeting they had generally dealt with some plea for concessions in a new factory or a rescheduling of payments on loans to the economic cartels therein represented. J.J.'s intention was to approach Mackenzie after the meeting and force everything out into the open. He would invite the American into his chambers and then take the clipping from his pocket and place it on the desk. If Mackenzie were involved in the matter he would react to the ploy immediately and give himself away. The messenger, however, returned with the news that unfortunately Mr. Mackenzie was not to be found in Rio at the moment; he had left for São Paulo three days before and no one could say precisely when he would return. And to complicate matters, there would be coming in the American's place still another *gringo*, a certain Adams Mackenwieks. J.J. immediately recognized him as an ex-employee of the American embassy who currently worked as general manager of Mackenzie's business conglomerate. Since the Americans were quite aware of the relative unimportance of such gatherings, the fact of their sending over a representative signaled that there really was something in the

131

air. As far as J.J. was concerned, however, he was going to await the return of Mackenzie himself because he had little confidence in this Adams fellow, married to a Brazilian and frequently seen attending the worldlier salons held at the mansion of Sampaio Araújo, on the Rua Voluntários da Pátria. Nevertheless, when the meeting was finally adjourned—after twenty minutes of jawing over a new hydroelectric system to generate power—Adams Mackenwieks remained in his seat while the others filed out. Seabra signaled him to follow him to his private chambers.

"Some difficulties in São Paulo?" he plied Adams casually.

"No, no problems. Mr. Mackenzie is simply there on a routine visit, nothing more."

"When will he be back in Rio?"

"Quite possibly by the end of next week."

That was too long; Seabra could not allow himself to risk so much time. The scandalmongers would place everything in jeopardy by then because, in Rio de Janeiro, scandals had the habit of spreading like epidemics. He eyed Adams but espied no crack in the ease of his demeanor; the American had long been trained never to let others know what was on his mind. He also had the habit of pretending not to have understood whenever it came to someone else's expectations—above all, someone in government. The minister impulsively drew the newspaper clipping out of his pocket and placed it on the desk. He did so against his will, cognizant of the risk he was running. No reaction could be traced in the American's expression, not so much as the blink of an eye. After a few seconds of complete silence, Adams finally addressed him:

"Minister, I can't tell you how sorry I am that Mr. Mackenzie happens not to be in Rio at this moment."

J.J. shrugged his shoulders and began to fold up the clipping once more to return it to his pocket.

"Certainly," Adams cloyingly persisted, ". . . certainly Mr. Mackenzie would have been pleased with the chance to speak to you like this. I am merely his subordinate, without direct authority to make policy decisions. Yet I am also sensitive to issues, and can claim even a certain intimacy with Brazil. The minister must be acquainted with the fact that I am married to a Brazilian."

"Yes, I am," Seabra replied coldly.

"Well then, may I suggest that such intimacy and real empathy leads me to surmise that at this juncture that the minister could possibly have need of our services—that is, of something that Mr. Mackenzie may be able to provide. My own humble position should perhaps exclude me from pleading Your Excellency's confidence; yet it would be a pity not to be of assistance only to discover too late that the matter was actually within the reach of my managerial powers."

"I would like urgently then to speak to your Mackenzie," the minister responded stiffly, like a man about to surrender.

Adams smiled his commiseratively humble smile.

"It happens that there *is* someone here in the capital whom, were you to speak to him, you would find quite as knowledgeable as Mr. Mackenzie himself, perhaps even more so. He could easily speak with Your Excellency should the minister deign to receive him. He just might be able to find a way of helping matters, and as discreetly as Mr. Mackenzie himself."

Seabra had been mulling his alternatives with which to surprise and crush this Adams fellow. He could not bear to have this miserable subordinate dare walk into his office like this and make veiled threats to him.

"Mr. . . . ?"

"Adams Mackenwieks, sir."

"Mr. Adams Mackenwieks, I don't believe your intimacy with Brazilians has done you much good."

"I don't follow you, sir."

"What makes you think I might need the assistance of your Mr. Mackenzie?"

The American's face reddened and his jaw fell to suck in his breath.

"I was merely suggesting; a supposition, Your Excellency."

"No one here is in need of any help, *Senhor* Adams, least of all from your Mr. Mackenzie. And should I ever run into difficulties, it would hardly be him or, for that matter, any other American from whom I should require—let alone request assistance."

"Pardon me, minister. I had no intention of seeming impertinent: far be it from me to contemplate such temerity. Yet the minister seemed to be suggesting this whole time that he might well wish something from us, that is, from Mr. Mac-

133

kenzie. And since I was sent here today as his legal representative, I thought it best that I at least inquire."

"I can appreciate your interest. I really do, however, need to speak urgently with Mr. Mackenzie. But with him only . . ."

"Could not the minister speak with Mr. Farquhar?"

"Farquhar?"

"Yes, Percival Farquhar, director and president of our company. He's here in Rio."

"I believe we already know each other."

"Well, there you are. He's just as understanding as Mr. Mackenzie but with considerably more power at his disposal. Mr. Farquhar heads the entire firm; he's the owner, as Your Excellency himself is no doubt aware."

"Yes, I'm familiar with Mr. Farquhar. I think he might do perfectly well in place of Mackenzie." J.J. stared into space for a few seconds and then suddenly broke into a smile: "Yes, perhaps he's exactly the person who ought to hear what I have to say."

"It would be a pleasure for me to communicate this to Mr. Farquhar and arrange for an appointment."

"Let me first take a look at my calendar."

"Of course, Your Excellency."

The minister opened a magnificent appointment book bound in pyrographically tooled leather, then paged through it slowly, moving his index finger carefully down each row of annotations penned in a small, meticulous hand. He raised his head the moment his finger encountered a blank hour.

"All right, inform Mr. Farquhar he may have his audience tomorrow at five o'clock," he concluded to the American, then took his finger off the datebook and brought his hand down forcefully, as if to slap his desk, banging vehemently instead on a bell.

Immediately, a subordinate entered and drew himself to attention before the minister, mutely awaiting his instructions.

"See the gentleman out."

Adams got up from his chair thoroughly disgruntled, unable even to have ended that frustrating interview with a suitably spirited repartee. The subordinate preceded the American to the door, where he opened one of the French partitions and stepped aside to let him pass. As Adams was about to cross the threshold, he heard the minister call after him.

"Senhor Adams! You can tell your boss he's just lost all his concessions in the state of Paraná."

Adams Mackenwieks stopped in his tracks as if struck by lightning. He clasped his hands together and bowed slightly in a quick gesture of leave-taking, though without turning to reveal his livid countenance as he swiftly escaped from the office; nearly running for his life, it seemed to Seabra. His subordinate now stepped out and closed the door behind him, leaving J.J. alone to savor his apparent victory with a smile. So it had all come down to the sordid maneuverings of the Americans! He would show them who was in need of help. The poor *gringos* seemed to think they had discovered a breach in his administration—in his character, to be precise. Well, he certainly didn't consider *himself* a vulnerable man, because no female was ever going to cross him with any childish caprices. He could see the Americans were trying to find some way to penetrate the new administration. The election of Marshal da Fonseca had lost them the emoluments of office. Indeed, rumors were afoot that they had actually financed the unsuccessful "Civil Campaign" of old Ruy Barbosa. For a moment he reflected upon Ruy Barbosa, once a powerful enemy but now at seventy little more than an antiquated oddball living off past glories, off a pride that sometimes bordered on insanity. Still, Barbosa might also be behind it all; he was someone who would take great pleasure in seeing J.J. take a tumble, get tossed out of government, wind up with his entire career ruined by unseemly scandal. And Ruy himself would be the first to drag J.J.'s name through the mud in one of his tedious newspaper columns, where he could resort to his usual pedantically anachronistic parlance; no doubt to exclaim that Mr. J. J. Seabra "ought to be running a lupanar instead of a branch of government," because Ruy was the type who enjoyed dusting off a dead word the size of *lupanar*. Hadn't he already done so once or twice when writing about J.J.'s participation in the elections in Salvador for municipal superintendent and city council? Seabra had backed Júlio Brandão, a young politician who would certainly back him in his own future bid for governor of the state of Bahia. Barbosa, on the other hand, had backed the incumbent, João Santos, with an almost visceral adherence that shed significant light on the extent of the dissolution of his former prestige.

135

After lunch Seabra went to Catete Palace where, between two and three o'clock, he had his daily meeting with the president. The marshal was more and more confused each day by the nation's political turmoil, seemingly engendered by the maneuverings of the state oligarchies. That very afternoon he had received alarming news from São Paulo—a state which had refused to support his candidacy—making it clear that there was a conspiracy afoot within the upper echelons of the "Public Force," a powerful military police organization that virtually controlled the state, with a firepower the equal of or superior to the federal troops assigned to that sector of the nation. Rumors were flying! And they pointed to a combination of economic interests who were supplying money to the seditious. In particular, the name of Rodolfo Miranda—nothing but a front for the shadowy participation of the powerful Pinheiro Machado—appeared with disturbing frequency in these reports.

The marshal was a man of robust constitution, his pale skin thoroughly leathered by the sun, from continual exercise in the open air, and his every gesture of a dignity that made a lasting impression. Seabra considered him a sort of Prussian officer surreptitiously thrust to the head of state by a masterful stroke of blind fate. Well, at the moment the Prussian spirit of Hermes da Fonseca was beset with attacks from all sides. Yet he proved incapable of losing his composure—no matter that his peculiar temerity might just as easily lead him blandly straight in to hell, given his ever-courteous bullheadedness!

Seabra presented him with the legislation involving public school construction in the northeastern states, with a favorable opinion and a memorandum detailing the corresponding decrees it would require. Da Fonseca opened the portfolio and commenced to examine it carefully, raising questions as to the number of children who might benefit, whether the minister of education was prepared to increase the number of teachers assigned to those states, and a number of other matters related to the proposed legislation. Seabra, by now accustomed to this sort of detailed scrutinizing by the president, offered the kind of answers that the idealistic ears of Hermes da Fonseca preferred to hear. Thus, instead of saying to the president that the schools were only going to benefit some local politicians—thereby winning them over to the administration—he answered

136

that nearly three hundred children would receive an elementary education from those very schools and that the problem of staffing them was a state matter, not a federal one, and therefore the minister of education needn't trouble his head. He failed to mention, however, that the additional teaching positions were simply manna for the local politicians who could fill them with ward bosses and other supporters of a character who certainly would not be permitted near children of school age, were this a country that actually troubled itself about its future. But this was, after all, Brazil. And it would be not only difficult and dangerous, but also highly unprofitable, to try to change any of it. In any case, the president appeared to be satisfied with his explanations, as well as his budgetary estimates, and promised to expedite the legislation that very afternoon, since it necessitated only executive approval and was not subject to congressional jurisdiction.

At the close of their meeting, just as Seabra was about to leave, the president informed him that he had good news. J.J. came back to his seat and stared at Hermes as the latter rummaged through another portfolio on his desk.

"J.J., you remember that invitation to participate in some shindig to honor the founding of the Association for Commerce in Salvador?"

"Of course, marshal. I was the one who handed it to you."

"It's to be in August, correct?"

"Exactly, the first week in August."

"Well, J.J., I have decided to accept the invitation. It will be a pleasure to visit the state and lend support to the merchant classes."

"Our own friends there will certainly be euphoric over this, I can assure you."

"I imagine so. . . . I have already asked the minister of the navy to arrange transportation for the presidential party, and I want you to accompany me."

J. J. Seabra felt both pleased and comforted. He had delivered the invitation three weeks ago but had not expected the president to accept. Not from a lack of interest, mind you, but rather because the problems with São Paulo were so on the mind of the marshal that Seabra had assumed that they would keep Hermes there in the capital for the time being. Now the president was once again demonstrating his courage and his bullheadedness; and by accepting that invitation he was—under the pretext of attending a useful solemn brouhaha—attacking on two fronts. By going off to the Northeast, he would prove to his enemies in São Paulo that his administration did not really regard the threats from their quarter as any danger to the status quo. By visiting the state of Bahia, he would be lending key support to Seabra as his candidate for governor, in opposition to the dominant oligarchical powers. No other news could have pleased J.J. more at that moment than this confirmation of his prestige in the presidential camp. He took his leave from the executive chambers with the radiant expression of an inveterate gambler who, hopelessly in arrears, suddenly breaks the bank at Monte Carlo.

In this high state of gratified spirits, Seabra walked briskly through the halls of Catete Palace imagining the disgruntlement of his Bahian adversaries and in the process nearly forgetting that now he had much more cunning and possibly dangerous enemies right there in the federal capital. As a result he also did not notice when a smiling Colonel Agostinho, the new aide-de-camp replacing the unfortunate Major Quitanilha in the military office of the president, approached and took him by the arm.

"Well, minister, you seem quite happy today."

J.J. grudgingly allowed himself to return to reality: "Afternoon, colonel."

Colonel Agostinho possessed an altogether special charm, that of cold efficiency won by long years of study at the Academy of Saint Cyr, in France.

"Might you spare a few moments, minister, for a quick conversation in my office?" the colonel asked.

Seabra was in such a good frame of mind that he decided to accept the colonel's invitation, although he felt more inclined to make off directly for São Cristóvão. "Why not, colonel. It would be a great pleasure to have a chat."

The two of them headed down the stairwell side by side to the ground floor of the building, while the colonel indulged in apologies for the momentary state of his office.

"I still haven't had the time to even begin to straighten things out down there. The offer of the post was totally unexpected. I was still in Paraná when the president called me.

We're good friends, you know. I served with the marshal in the ministry of war. An extraordinary man, don't you think?"

"Yes, he is an extraordinary man," Seabra said dryly as something began to pulse at the back of his mind, throwing him into alert.

When they reached the door to the office in question, the colonel stepped aside to make way for Seabra. The minister entered a small, stuffy room, nearly a cubicle, crammed with stacks of papers that obviously had little to do with the Military Advisory Council. It was rather as if all the branches of Catete had agreed to consign their dead archives to this oversized cabinet.

"Major Quitanilha was most generous," the colonel observed with sarcasm. "He apparently allowed all sorts of things to gather down here. And you can see how little space there is to begin with."

Seabra watched the colonel settle himself into a chair behind the diminutive desk and then found himself a seat in a rather ungainly armchair. He waited silently for the colonel to broach whatever matter it was that wanted discussion.

"I don't intend to waste your precious time, Minister Seabra." The colonel exuded too much confidence, as if he possessed some secret weapon hidden away somewhere in that overstuffed crypt. "The president by now has certainly communicated to you his plan to travel to the Northeast, to take part in some cockamamy affair or other. He came to this decision early this morning and immediately informed me of his intentions. Personally, I don't like the idea of this trip at all. I consider it a danger for the marshal to be away from Rio at such a moment, when São Paulo presents every sign of impending rebellion. Since the invitation originated with you, Minister Seabra, I felt I should like to hear your opinion before I express my own to the president."

J.J. was staring attentively at the colonel, searching for any clue that might indicate the true motives behind this conversation. It was already obvious to his alerted senses that, however sincere the colonel's apparent preoccupation, it was only a pretext to couch more fundamental concerns.

"For my part, Colonel Agostinho," he finally replied, "I believe the president knows quite well what he's doing. Traveling to Bahia shows any troublemakers in São Paulo that this administration is strong enough not to be intimidated by threat of that sort. And at the same time the trip will reinforce hi prestige in the Northeast."

"You are not, I take it, unaware of the situation at th moment in São Paulo?"

"On the contrary, colonel, I'm quite familiar with what' going on there—and in Bahia."

"Excuse me for being so frank, minister, but what seem quite clear is that it is *you* who will benefit politically by th marshal's trip to Bahia. You stand to gain more than the *federa government* by this visit!"

"I am going to forget what you have just said, colonel though I confess not to have the slightest notion of what yo had in mind by saying it. I am a minister in the service of th government who also happens to enjoy the utmost confidenc of the president. I am likewise a candidate for governor o Bahia. My possible victory would only constitute a furthe victory for Marshal da Fonseca. I see no contradiction betwee state and federal politics."

"A thousand apologies, Minister Seabra. I seem to hav expressed myself rather clumsily."

"No, colonel, you've expressed yourself quite clearly as matter of fact," Seabra commented, getting up to leave.

"Minister, are you familiar with what happened to Majo Quitanilha?"

"Afternoon, Colonel Agostinho."

Seabra was headed for the door, but the colonel still con tinued, only louder:

"Poor Quitanilha," he chortled with obvious relish, "he' been transferred to Fort Príncipe da Beira, out in the sticks o Matto Grosso. They say the mosquitoes there are the size o elephants!"

"The giant mosquitoes of Fort Príncipe have nothing o certain insects right here in the capital," J.J. retorted wit visible irritation.

"Oh, *Seabra!* Is it true that the Southern Brazil Lumber an Colonization Company's concessions have been canceled i Paraná?"

The minister solidified in his tracks, as if he were haulin a huge cart that had suddenly mired in the slough. "How di you happen to learn about that?"

140

The colonel smiled, shrugging his shoulders. "You know how news gets around, minister."

So, the pressure had already risen to the Palace itself; Seabra, in an instant, realized he had better act swiftly if he wished to survive. Without wasting so much as another word on the confident colonel, whose stare grew more and more impertinent, J.J. scoffed and turned his back upon him, then headed out to his victoria stationed in front of the Palace. He ordered his coachman to proceed as quickly as possible out to São Cristóvão. His blood was boiling over now, as he felt once again the hunted backlander whose self-respect has been impugned and therefore clamors for exemplary satisfaction.

Matters were becoming perfectly clear: the entire plot was unfolding before him as the victoria rocked over cobblestone streets. Major Quitanilha had been the first target of their conspiracy, and they had bagged him quite innocently. Perhaps the Americans had hired that beautiful little *fräulein* in the first place, just to manage her cheap seduction of the major and estrange him from his conjugal duties. In place of Quitanilha there was now this Colonel Agostinho, an ambitious rascal—aspiring to the rank of a general—who was fresh up from Paraná, where he had no doubt been wholly seduced by the Americans. With the colonel, the Americans were practically on the president's doorstep: everyone knew the marshal placed absolute trust in that nonetheless fatuous military fellow with his skinny waxed mustache, his gold-rimmed pince-nez, and his superficially polished demeanor, if only because he was thoroughly acquainted with all the most advanced techniques and secrets of modern military life. In fact, the colonel knew more than the majority of Brazilian generals put together about how an efficient and professional army ought to be run. Indeed, he had proved to be the marshal's right-hand man during the reform of the armed forces, when da Fonseca had served as minister of war under the previous administration. It was none other than the colonel himself who had nearly single-handedly conceived of, organized, and then carried out the famous military maneuvers of 1908, right there in Rio de Janeiro—the first ever by Brazilian troops and the occasion of an unprecedented outpouring of surprise and admiration by the public at large. As a result of this alone, he had won the undying confidence of the marshal and the invidious hatred of a fair number of generals who felt themselves looked down upon by their own hierarchical inferior.

Well, his connection to the marshal was a fact of life: the colonel enjoyed the intimacy of the presidential hearth and his opinions seemed to be valued on the level of absolute truths. It was also a fact that he could reduce J. J. Seabra to ashes. And there he sat, that petulant man in his dusty office full of old stacks of paper, already scouting for the American interests. He was Mackenzie's man, all right, and by his proximity to the president he was worth more than all the other ministers put together if he knew how to manage things. And J.J. was convinced that the colonel was not a man to commit any rudimentary follies.

Although night was falling, an oppressive heat had begun to drench Seabra's body in sweat, and his soaking clothes chilled him from the effect of the humid breeze provoked by the vehicle's motion. He undid the knot in his tie and began to unbutton his shirt, relieving his neck from the snugness of the collar. He was beginning to experience the relief he sought and so did not go so far as to remove his jacket, which had already become wrinkled from the crouched position he had assumed, as if he were hiding, in the corner of the upholstered seat of his victoria. On the Rua de São Cristóvão where his mistress lived, there were no public streetlamps and the lane was already immersed in that quiet darkness of the onset of night, when the only sounds to be heard are of silver and china, for this was, after all, the dinner hour. Yet if the darkness was so prevalent, it was also because the majority of families in that neighborhood lighted one room at a time—economizing on gas, since there was still no electricity there—and at nightfall it was usually the dining rooms or kitchens, toward the back, which received the first light.

The victoria pulled up before the house and the tired horses breathed heavily, nodding their heads in relief. Seabra leaped down from his carriage and swiftly made his way through the narrow front yard with its fruit trees and then bounded up the steps. The front door was ajar and the house dark. He called to his mistress while fumbling for a candlestick. No one answered and he grew uneasy. She almost never left the house, much less at that hour when he was accustomed to call on her. Finally, he found a candelabrum on the sideboard and struck

142

match to light the wicks. The room suddenly materialized nd looked to be perfectly in order, clean, peaceful, and un-isturbed. He picked up the candelabrum and set out for the ther rooms, calling her continually, with no response. She as nowhere about, she had gone out, and that was not like er. It was a small house and his search was quickly ended; e was now in the alcove, seated on the edge of the bed, andelabrum set upon the floor and throwing shadows up in very direction. He noticed that her wardrobe was ajar, got up nd flung the doors all the way open—he was stupefied! in-redulous! his mistress's clothes were no longer even there! None of her silk dresses! None of her sheer camisoles! None f her boots of English leather, her purses, her fans, nothing! he had vanished: without warning and without explana-ion. . . .

He sat once more on the edge of the bed and discovered to is relief that he was neither sad nor really surprised, that he as actually quite serene and that his faculties were operating vith appreciable clarity. He had no desire to fathom his mis-ress's behavior; he simply wished for her to disappear truly nto thin air and never more show any sign of her existence in his life. Deep down, even though the smell of her presence n that bed still awakened in him the old appetite, he somehow njoyed the fact that she had eluded him. After meditating for while, he realized that the room was swelteringly hot; with he windows closed there was barely a whiff of fresh, breath-ble air. And then he noticed that someone was crying: a carcely perceptible sound, but without a doubt a woman's obbing.

He took up the candelabrum once more and headed for the ack of the house, into the kitchen, where he first suspected he crying to be. But there was no one in there; only the cold vood stove and the pots and pans hanging from their hooks n the wall. Yet the sobbing existed and now it seemed to be coming from just outside; from the small terrace where their clothes were washed, and then dried in the sun, among a tangle f clotheslines. Near the stone tank, seated on a box, protected by the darkness that reluctantly gave way to the light of the candelabrum, Seabra finally discovered his mistress's maid, quietly sobbing the soft sighs of one who had been crying for ours.

143

"What happened?" he demanded to know.

The woman could not respond and he took her by the arm lifting her gently. She was trembling; she was also an ex-slave and the crying now metamorphosed into a pale convulsion of fear.

"What happened?" he insisted.

Her countenance still reflected that abrasive look of fear although the threat had already dissipated sufficiently to enable the old woman to summon renewed strength, though not enough to allow her to speak. Seabra supported her while he led her into the kitchen. He forced her to drink a glass of water and stood by waiting. Little by little she regained her breath like someone nearly drowned who had been saved at the last possible second.

"Oh, sah, dey come and took Missy away!"

"What do you mean, *they?* Who took her?"

"I doan know, sah."

"Tell me how it happened!"

"They done knock on dat door and I goes to answer. They be two men: one short-like and the other, he very big. They say to me they come here 'on your master's behalf', they very words, sah, I swears to God. So I invite them both in to sit down and I goes in to call my Missy. She was sat right here in the kitchen, but she say something wrong about all that and scold me for lettin' the gentlemen in. But I told her it was already too late, they be sitting in the livin' room, and Missy she decides to go in and talk to them. Then I doan rightly know what happen next. I jus' standing here in dis kitchen and I hear de missis scream. My lord, I ran in to help, but the gentlemen, they tells me I better stay put if I doan wants no harm to come to my missis. Well, sah, then dey goes off with the poor child, Lord forgive me!"

"And what time was this?"

"They comes round in de afternoon, sah. I swear 'twasn' but four o'clock."

"And had you ever seen these men before?"

"No, sah, never! Nobody evah been here before. Only Missy's mama every now and den. Once a month for de money."

Seabra made an effort to calm the old woman; he then instructed her to continue looking after things there at the house and await the return of his mistress. Everything would be taken care of and nothing terrible was going to happen. He asked that she not open the door to anyone nor go out into the neighborhood where she might be tempted to gossip. The old woman promised to obey with the sincerity of an ex-slave burdened by the guilt of what may have happened to her mistress.

Seabra himself was seemingly calm. Whoever did not know him might have suspected that he was resigned—and been wrong: the demeanor of calm was, in fact, a measure of the rage which now gripped him. Someone would pay dearly for such audacity! After locking all the windows and doors of the house, he climbed back into his victoria and ordered his coachman to continue on to Santa Tereza.

He arrived at home earlier than was his custom, still perplexed and with a deplorable look in his eyes. His wife was relaxing in the living room, reading something. She saw immediately that her husband was unnerved; it had been a long time since she had seen him in such a state—as far back as when he had not yet ceased to be either young or impetuous. In a way she was pleased to discover him thus: the desperation she could read in her husband's eyes rekindled her memories of the good times when they were both young and impassioned, when they confronted the vicissitudes of life as one. Seabra scarcely acknowledged his wife and proceeded directly up to his room. She closed the book she was reading and immediately followed him up the stairs. She wore an opaque salmon *robe de chambre* that hid the contours of her body in its opulent folds of Chinese silk. In his room, she found him already changing his clothes. She felt it better not to question him while he was still undressing, and she turned to the matter of finding him a clean change of pajamas, which she took out of a drawer and placed on the bed. Her husband, now naked, sat down on the edge of the bed, beside the pajamas laid out upon the quilt like a ghost that had taken substance within the corporeal dimensions of the white fabric. She quietly sat beside him and, in a characteristic gesture, caressed his hair; he failed to respond, which indicated the degree of difficulty he was in—a sign that she could intervene.

"Don't you want to tell me?" she asked in her timid voice.

Her husband began to speak, with his head still lowered, almost hidden in his hands. She gazed indulgently at his gray hair and powerful neck. He was telling her everything: his

145

apprehensions, his suspicions, his mistress in São Cristóvão, her disappearance at the hands of intruders. She might easily have been disgusted by the revelation of a mistress, but as his wife she felt too much the mistress of their entire conjugal universe to take the matter as anything more than an unfortunate but unavoidable accident. She had long ago entrenched herself in the cynicism of middle age and was prepared to accept, albeit remorsefully, even betrayal by her husband. Still, the pain of it was tempered, to a degree, by his willingness to confide everything to her—a fact from which she slowly drew her comfort. The important thing, now, was that her husband— and therefore herself, and more emphatically their world— was under attack. There was an imminent menace hovering over their life, hers and that of her husband. They must be powerful forces to be threatening Minister J. J. Seabra: a pow- erhouse of the Republic, her husband, her conquerer! And given the measure of this menace, she had no doubt as to what should be her husband's recourse.

"How could I ever not be behind you, Zé. You must give these scoundrels a lesson they'll long remember, to keep them in their place."

Seabra raised his head and looked at his wife.

"You mustn't go on like this, Zé," she said proudly. "Strike back! And show no mercy!"

Two hours later there was a knock on the door of the house of Adams Mackenwieks, who went unconcernedly to answer. He was still awake because his eldest son was running a mild fever and had yet to fall asleep. His wife had already retired, to try to sleep a little, and failed to hear when her husband went down to find out who could be knocking at this hour of the night. When the American opened the door, he was seized and dragged out into the night. The street was wholly deserted and someone very powerful held him by the throat and across the mouth, nearly choking him. Then suddenly the world itself seemed to collapse upon him—crushing his stomach, his chest—as punch after punch laced with blows from a rubber billy rained down upon him. The attack did not last more than a few minutes, but Adams had lost all notion of time. When he had passed out completely, without having had managed to utter a cry, the men dumped him back inside the house and slammed the door closed. Adams's wife was awakened by its

146

violent thud and got out of bed, half-asleep, calling for her husband. The pale light which was always left on in the vestibule at night illuminated Adams's body, stretched out in a pool of blood. She screamed and froze where she stood, watching her husband's hands clench slowly into fists, then open like flowers.

8

If somebody was searching for sanity, thought Finnegan, this was certainly the last place on earth he should come to. In the course of the past week the volatile irrationalism of malaria had begun to strike down its victims indiscriminately.

The ten Germans who had inaugurated this series of fatalities had been found quite dead, of course, on the following morning. Ten macabre sacks of bones still encased in yellowed, emaciated, icy parchment were unraveled from the fetid hammocks like crystalized sweets prepared for a madman. Next, it was the turn of one of the young medics from the infirmary, immediately followed by four Chinamen and one of the Cubans from the security guard—all of them out of their minds with deliriousness and uncontrollable shuddering, gagged and roped in identical fashion until they lapsed into a coma, then death. Dr. Finnegan no longer attempted to arrest the onslaught of fatalities: they did not, after all, fit into the moral space he had allotted himself in which to lead his own life, and each fatality struck him, therefore, as another premeditated insult against his person. Even one medic, his closest assistant, who knew all of the dangers explicit in his behavior—even this medic had preferred to risk his life for the sake of a few coins, an option Richard Finnegan regarded as too patently absurd to be actually taken into consideration. True, money had never meant very much to Finnegan—he had always had it—and he refused thus to believe that for a handful of the same somebody might be capable of trifling with existence!

Yet miraculously the Indian with his truncated limbs and the young girl found in the jungle, exceptions to the rule that seemed to govern all else, were now recovering and thereby provided at least a symbolic reminder that his function here as a physician was to save lives, not sign death certificates. The girl actually helped a bit with the work of the infirmary. Although she clung tenaciously to her privacy and was always somber and morose, she did occupy herself without anyone's

148

asking with small duties: sweeping the floor, tidying up, even administering medications whenever the doctor solicited her assistance. The Indian, however, was as yet unable to walk about, his recuperation slowed by the incredible severity of his condition; besides which, the doctor had noted the edemas on his feet, the result of parasites that had dug their way into the calloused hide of his soles. Even with the natives, these parasites burrowed through the flesh to pocket their eggs, provoking papules, pruritus, and severe inflammation. Dr. Finnegan had already treated similar cases among the railway workers. The treatment of the Indian's case was harrowing by comparison, but he had managed in the end to eliminate the parasitosis. The girl, whom the doctor had already discovered was named Consuelo, took to caring for the native, learning the necessary prophylaxes for both his arms and his feet, so that the poor savage had already developed a certain dependence upon her. At these times, if Finnegan insisted, she would allow the doctor the exchange of a few pleasantries. He had not regained sufficient courage to ask her once more what had befallen her in the jungle, since on the previous occasion he had tried, she had regressed to such a degree that he had feared her very life must be in peril. But what he did know was sufficient: her name, Consuelo; and that she was a beautiful girl, appealing; Bolivian; and a widow.

Both Consuelo and the Indian were awaiting an opportunity to be taken downriver by the first available transport to the town of Porto Velho. The Indian would be sent to the hospital in Candelária, where he could fully recuperate, and Consuelo could likewise find accommodation there until the company reached a decision as to what to do with her—unless in the meantime she demonstrated more signs of her own inclination which she might present personally to the administration. Finnegan, who at first had been irritated by the absence of any conveyance, now nourished the unconscious desire that at least her trip not occur so soon. In some manner that woman who refused to smile—always very quiet, speaking only when essential, always grave and sad—somehow replenished him, providing sustenance in the midst of so much insanity. Almost as if to strengthen his desire, Consuelo apparently showed no impatience to be gone. Of course, neither did she exhibit any wish to remain; it was as if she had lost the capacity to aspire

149

to anything. But poor Finnegan had already grown accustomed to her, to the zeal with which she would sweep the floor, to the affection which involuntarily flowed from her whenever she cared for the savage. She was such an awesomely beautiful woman that she caused our Richard to forget all his woes. Outside, the world could be damned!

Yet outside, the world simply went on. Wagons passed loaded up with railroad ties, cut from eucalyptus, imported from Formosa. Atop a diminishing pile of sleepers some workers looked on as Arkansas mules hauled off their wagons in the direction of a flooded terrain. Off to the other side, a host of Germans and Barbadians were laboring to unclog a canal, filled with water, which extended in its breadth of approximately a meter to the perpendicular ledge that formed one bank of the Abunã riverbed. All along the length of the canal there was feverish activity, with men at work in rolled-up pants absurdly attempting to preserve their rags from the mold and ruination of the mud.

While some of the workers were struggling to deepen the canal, to shore up sufficient furrow in order to reroute the flow from the river's torrent, others went about emptying the wagons of railroad ties. The general effort proceeded in silence, but Richard Finnegan could see the exhaustion in each of the men out there, and smell the indifference that momentarily fostered cooperation among Germans and Barbadians.

Up in the cab of Mad Maria, Old Thomas Gallagher was also watching attentively as he slowed his locomotive to a stop. The Englishman Collier, up there beside him, did not bother to wait for the driving wheels to screech to a halt but swung out to the stirrup of the coal tender and leaped off onto the wet and slippery ground; sliding but quickly regaining his balance, he headed off in the direction of the wagons. He knew well enough why each wooden tie had had to travel over half the Earth to reach the Abunã, and to prove it to himself he picked up a piece of older cross-tie, cut from pine, and squeezed it with both hands, mashing it into splinters. Eucalyptus was now being shipped from Formosa because it had proven resistant to the myriad variety of termites in the Amazon. Sometimes the English engineer would shiver at the notion that such termites could very well gnaw through his bones, were they given the opportunity. He dismissed the thought by turning to

150

the Barbadians, just beyond him, who were packing the quag with multiple layers of tree branches gathered from the rain forest. It was to be the new roadbed along which the railway would run: a more solid terrain and immune to flooding. The compacting involved protracted labor: the Barbadians took from ten to twelve hours just to advance two meters, because the bedding of earth and branches needed to be at least ten centimeters thick. Since they had been at it for over a week now, they had produced a length of compacted strip that looked to Collier like a flat, gray, woven mat rolled out upon the yellow loam of the swamp.

Onto this packed surface a few meters of track had already been set down perpendicularly upon the parallel series of Formosa sleepers like jaws of teeth that had yet to be braced. The tracks laid most recently were now being braced onto the ties. Collier carefully inspected their progress and was satisfied: once again, his Barbadians confirmed their deep knowledge of the art of constructing a railroad. The engineer headed back for the locomotive and shouted:

"Thomas! Bring her up!"

The locomotive engineer signaled back to Collier with a three-ring sign, that affable American symbol for good humored confidence—in this case, in the newest five meters of track. Collier began motioning with his arm for the vast hulk of locomotive to crawl toward him, while Old Thomas set Mad Maria to work: a blast of steam from her iron petticoats, a metallic pant, and the wheels commenced to skid and screech against the track. Mad Maria began to roll slowly off the solid ground of tested tracks and onto the new rails nestled in their bed of matted branches. The Englishman nervously anticipated the mastodonic progress of cowcatcher, driving wheels and trailing truck over the newly compacted sector. Gallagher handled her gingerly, easing her on to the new section, while behind him his stoker agitatedly followed the operation with palpable vigilance. Finally, Mad Maria ground to a halt at the end of her five meters, where the tracks had yet to be braced onto the sleepers. Stationary, she still billowed giant puffs of steam. Collier scudded along the ground, slightly hunched over, examining the resistant strength of the underpinning. He covered the length of the locomotive, at times walking backward; the work seemed to hold and he signaled Thomas to back off. Mad Maria began to belch with steam and roll off in reverse. Collier stood mesmerized on the bed of the tracks, momentarily seduced by the hypnotic, incremental effect of any locomotive's rhythmical monotony.

When the clouds of steam had dissipated from his mind and his surroundings, the Englishman discovered that the Barbadians—with a dedication seldom envinced in this vegetal cauldron they called the Abuña—had also paused from working and were observing the testing of their labors with rapt attention. The results seemed to have brought a faint air of contentment to the expression on their faces, a flash of professional pride that already appeared to be dissipating at a velocity equal to that of the departing locomotive. Yet the Englishman sensed it and was gratified: a germ of compensation that ought to have been cultivated immediately for its fleeting potential. The locomotive, however, had already reached the older terra firma and the Barbadians had turned back to their tasks. Collier's minuscule victory likewise evaporated as he was once again confronted with the dour prospect of crossing those floodplains stretching out before him. The landfill would have to surmount some fifty meters of supine bog, of which at this point no more than twenty meters had been adequately compacted, upon which barely five stinking meters of track had been laid!

By nightfall, Dr. Finnegan found himself struggling to deal with another three cases of malaria falciparum. A German and two Chinese had been brought shrieking to the infirmary. The doctor, already familiar with the treatment they would receive should they continue to howl that way, had decided to prescribe strong sedatives, even though such a treatment would only hasten their demise. Still, it was by Finnegan's standards a much more humane solution than the gags and ropes of the English engineer. At the moment, Finnegan was seated pensively at his desk, occasionally looking up to see Consuelo carefully ministering to his patients. He had taken up his writing pad and begun reviewing his notes. Consuelo moved quietly about the infirmary: an enigma whose very strangeness was heightened by her borrowed masculine garb. She was wearing the physician's clothes and Finnegan could almost feel himself inside them, close to her body—a not disagreeable sensation

152

hat he savored little by little, as a thirsty man might sip his last drops of water. The sick were settled in their cots, and Consuelo, assisted by the medics, moved from one bed to another vigilantly mindful of any change in their condition despite the obvious fact that in a matter of hours they would be dead in any case.

On Consuelo's bed lay a copy of a North American magazine which she perused for its illustrations, since her command of English was barely rudimentary. From the start, communication had posed a problem which Finnegan had eventually resolved by a species of code language he himself had half invented, half improvised from his lessons in high school and through phrases he had coined from a small Spanish-English dictionary. Consuelo, however, could not be counted as wholly ignorant of the English language. She had also had her classes at secondary school and could even boast certain advantages over her physician: counting to ten, for example, or distinguishing the days of the week—subjects which eluded him in Spanish. Yet the patois of empathy over language drew them together and they grew to understand each other in a provisionally satisfactory way.

The doctor had ceased to be able to concentrate and began to leaf rather aimlessly through his notebook, skipping entire pages, overcome by the enormous lassitude of an exercise in futility. The pad was filled with notations—a detailed account of the kind of treatment the English engineer had dealt out to his critical patients—but the physician knew his reports would never be given any serious attention by the company's administration, that he was only pretending to himself if he thought that his notes might serve to denounce the arbitrary cruelty of a man empowered, after all, by the company. The logic of management would hold that Collier was merely safeguarding the advancement of the project; what more could one ask? It was hardly a crime to send a few doomed patients to their rest in order to assure the vast majority of workers a sufficient amount of sleep. Indeed, the health of each remaining worker was of paramount importance, since only a well-rested worker could be expected to produce adequately on the following morning. The doctor shook his head and peered into space: it had struck him suddenly that all his principles were crumbling before his very eyes and he, too, had become an accomplice.

153

The physician fascinated by the wonders of science had alread
ceased to exist in him, for he was redundant—no, worthless!—
because he was nothing more than his predecessors: the oblig
atory but nominal "company physician." Everything and every
one could proceed without him, even to the grave!

He got up from his desk and went over to the bed of th
nearest patient, where he stopped, put his arms behind him
and observed the helpless mortal sliding imperceptibly yet inev
itably toward death like water vanishing into the bottom of
funnel. Turning abruptly from his patient he noticed somethin
on the plaque over on the wall which posted the infirmar
regulations. He moved closer to see what it was and to hi
own surprise—at the sound of a resounding slap—discovere
he had hit the plaque with the palm of his hand as if to smit
his own directives. The medics stopped what they were doing
and turned to regard him; even the girl took a mild interest i
so unsuitable a gesture on the part of what she supposed to b
a personality like Finnegan's. He himself was unaware of thei
attention, with all his concentration fixed on the palm of hi
own hand; then he walked over to his desk where he opene
a drawer with the other hand and took out a magnifying glass
With this instrument of enlargement he returned to scrutinizing
the identical piece of anatomy. The others hung back with a
air of suspicion normally reserved for the potentially insane
Enlarged by the magnifying glass, the palm of the physician':
hand was discovered to contain the unsightly remains of
smashed insect. So it isn't only the friendly scorpions who
enter here with impunity, the physician thought to himself
even the mortal enemy infiltrates here; and he cursed aloud:

"Fucking anopheles! How the hell did you get in here"
Nothing around here seems to do any good: not the screens
not even the damned mosquito netting! If these little blood
suckers really put their mind to it, none of us would survive."

Harold Appleton and Old Thomas gave scant attention to
the menace of the anopheles; they had other problems, at the
moment, involving an entirely different species: Mad Maria
by name, broken down since late afternoon with troubling
symptoms in her boiler. The two of them had set three kerosene
lamps down inside the cab and were busy working on her, with
a variety of parts already spread out upon the ironclad floor.

154

Thomas Gallagher was a fanatical mechanic and for the moment had disappeared almost entirely into the mouth of the boiler. Although the boiler had been cooled down with water, the metal was still lukewarm inside there and the temperature high enough to be uncomfortable for any man, even an Irishman! Old Thomas was fairly sweated up by now, scrutinizing short lengths of iron pipe, eyeing joints, screwing and tapping whatnots.

"Nothin' atall!" he grumbled from inside the boiler. "Then if it tarns out to be some sort o' congestion in one o' her main pipes, ye've got nothin' to replace it with!"

"Ain't I always been telling you we need a couple of spare parts around here, just to have on hand," Appleton whined back. "But the management of this unholy alliance turns a deaf ear: *economize,* that's all they come up with—economize!"

Curious about the prognosis for Mad Maria, Collier had walked up just in time to query, "What's going on here? Economize what?"

"Everything," Harold replied, washing his hands of the whole matter already, just in case they failed to get her running again. "The company never sends us nothing we ask for."

"Jesus God A'mighty, will ye take a look at this!" said Gallagher, climbing out of the boiler.

Just inside a part, some sort of insect had managed to install a makeshift mud construction which must have hardened from the heat. Thomas picked up a screwdriver and began to chip out the obstruction, the substance of which had taken on the consistency of bedrock.

"How in tarnation did the little bugger get in there in the first place?" Harold wondered incredulously.

"It had to have been on a day when we left her idle," Collier surmised amusedly. "One fried insect less to contend with, despite the redoubtable fortification."

"Wha'? 'Twill warm ye in there, all right. With the hate bakin' the mud and sealin' yer escapement valve here 'tis amazin' the little feller didn't blow us sky high," Gallagher concluded. "O' course 'tisn't as if there's a part to replace it. But don't fret yersel', Collier, there's no law agin' me cleanin' this one."

"And you say you've ordered parts from the company?"

155

"I can't tell you how many times, Mr. Collier. They jus'
never pay attention."

"Yer administration reminds me o' the story o' that Irishma
who gev up ateing altogether. T'ought he could save mone
that way and buy the fabric he gev his wife to make himsel'
bigger clothes."

"I know, I know," Collier interrupted, "and he wound up
earning a pair of wooden pajamas for himself."

"The only one stingier than the administration is Ol' Tom
himself," Harold chided.

"Is that so? Well, what are you saving your money for?"
Collier asked, turning to Gallagher.

Gallagher kept chipping away at the obstruction in the par
with jabs of the screwdriver, but chuckled in response to the
Englishman's question, thereby ignoring the stoker's remark.

"Amn't I savin' it for me ol' age?"

Collier smiled. "Yes, but just when do you plan to star
your old age?"

"I'm damn near seventy, sonny. It must be about time."

Appleton, the stoker, had begun to feel slighted by these
two accomplices in old age and hastened to break in: "And
what about me? What am I supposed to do with the money
I'm putting away around here?" He asked with an anguished
sincerity, having little to share with two old men. "I can tel
you nothing occurs to me in this part of the world, but if
ever get out of here alive I'll probably think of something."

"I think I may return to England. Buy a house in Londo
or somewhere nearby and grow definitively old like a suc
cessful English mountebank."

"Me curse on the cold there, I'm no longer fet for the
dampness. It'ud play the divil with me rheumatism."

"You've become a regular tropical orchid, Gallagher," the
Englishman chaffed.

"Have I now?" Gallagher puzzled the Englishman's clas
sification with a certain skepticism. "D'ye know what I'm goin
to do with all me money? I'm goin' to kape it to buy a mau
soleum fer mesel'. A rale monument, to be set in the cemetery
of me old village. Built outa merble, with an epitaph an' all
HARE LIES A TOMFOOL SON O' DAMNATION WHO LARNED TOC
LATE HOW THE WORLD AIN'T NOTHIN' BUT A BOOBY TRAP!"

156

"Aw, you're always complaining," Appleton protested, "even in the grave."

"I find that very touching," Collier interjected. "Personally, however, I plan to drink my money. What I miss around here is a good splash of gin, or better yet a couple of ounces of bourbon. But this place has all the earmarks of a nuns' boarding school crossed with a forced labor camp."

"Speaking of women, don't you miss them as well?" Appleton's question was as much a personal one to himself, since he hardly knew what he thought about them either, though he did seem to miss them.

"A good, stiff drink comes first," Collier replied unhesitatingly. "Women leave you with a far more serious hangover."

"Wha', colleens! Troth, I've even forgotten what they are," Gallagher exclaimed.

"The worst of it is I'm no seventy-year-old," Appleton confessed self-consciously.

Collier gave him a paternal smile. "Women, drinks, and for Old Thomas here a mausoleum. We seem to be dreaming, gentlemen. Well, it's our only prerogative in this bloody hole."

Gallagher had almost completed the work of clearing out the obstruction. Nocturnal moths circled the kerosene lamps in their suicidal instinct. Collier fell silent thinking about how much dreams seemed to fill the lives of everyone caught in a situation like this. The chaste dreamers of the Madeira-Mamoré .. the scum of the earth that star-gazed while they masturbated—all of them the subjects of Mad Maria, queen of the iron road . . . the lady general with metal thighs and steamy breath . . , In the darkness of the night, blacker than the metal from which she was fashioned, the Englishman imagined her, infusing her with a life of her own.

They had named her Mad Maria; the men had baptized her thus. For Collier, there was something contradictory in the choice of the name. It was hardly a suitable appellation for an iron horse. In the Latin tongues which were spoken in South America, *locomotiva* is, of course, the feminine gender, which might have explained the effort to identify that efficient powerhouse with a female. Yet, it happened to have been men whose native tongue was the English language who finally dubbed her Mad Maria, and in English the word is neuter: "locomotive." At first, Collier was convinced that this circum-

157

stance could be explained by the habit of North Americans t
christen calamities such as hurricanes and tornadoes with fem
inine sobriquets. Yet the locomotive had proved over and ove
that it was no calamity. On the contrary, for a madwoman
Maria carried out her duties quite rationally. And though
woman, she was gallantly resisting where many strong, har
men had already been humbled. In a real sense that locomotiv
governed everyone with her caprice and indifference. She wa
like a queen bee in a hive of corrupt and routed worker bees
And she was ever-present, imperturbable, day after day starin
down at her workers from behind all her nuts and bolts, lickin
the tracks with her iron teeth.

It was she, Mad Maria, the Iron Queen, the unattainabl
woman, who even drank for Collier—not bourbon, but oil—
and made love to his men in her bed of mud. Of course, n
one else thought such things; none of the men lying out in the
hammocks, back in the dormitory, guarded by sentinels, ha
ever given a second thought to her presence; only the enginee
Collier. Only he knew how deluded his men were as they se
about laying a carpet for her to tread upon. A battalion o
vagabonds secured at a fixed price but imagining themselve
in the skin of a Sir Walter Raleigh, spreading their own cape
upon the mud so that she might cross unsullied in her metalli
boots. Only pirates and ruffians the likes of a Walter Raleigh
however, would be predisposed to such a gesture; just as onl
such a rabble of starveling wretches, gathered from the fou
corners of the globe, could be capable of thus squandering the
lives simply to unroll a metal carpet so that Mad Maria migh
finally pass.

There she stood, as if sleeping, while Thomas Gallaghe
the dedicated gynecologist, busily penetrated her womb. A
times, Collier wondered to himself if such a queen might ac
tually be loved by her subjects. No, he concluded, it wa
unlikely because the queen bee was not, properly speaking
loved by her worker bees. And she must probably have realize
by now that her indifference was reciprocated completely. N
hatred and no love; merely that indifference with which he
ragged subjects laid—each day, another section—her roya
carpet. Seen from a distance, such a mode of behavior migh
have even been taken for romantic.

* * *

On the following day Mad Maria majestically spouted clouds of vapor as her sighs of screeching metal filled the air. All round her, the earth crawled with the enterprise of her workers. A great stretch of tracks had already been put at her disposal, fixed into the coarse matting of compacted earth and tree branches. These rails, which stood out brilliantly in the midst of the sallow terrain, were like twin vigorous strokes of tarnished ink left by tandem brushes. Off to the side, the Germans had begun another day's work on the drainage of the canal, a stroke of yellow water gleaming in the sun. The railway pressed victoriously across the swamp, eventually succumbing to the abrupt hiatus of a sheer drop formed by the gorge of the Rio Abunã. The river was not terribly wide—no more than twenty meters from bank to bank—a distance to be spanned by an iron bridge, the basic contours of which were already in evidence. A great many men, the majority of those employed along this entire sector, were wholly given over to the task of its construction. The sun, as always at this hour, was fiercely intense and the men were dolorously performing their tasks in water up to their waists. A whistle suddenly shattered the crystalline miasma.

The workers stopped whatever they were doing, simply dropping their tools in place, and proceeded to climb the steep slope of the riverbank. Slowly, they formed ranks, row upon row, like soldiers of a failed army preparing to surrender. Stephan Collier appeared, accompanied by his armed men; and with him, the doctor and his crew of medics. It was the engineer, however, who began to administer the quinine. One of his security guards was toting the bottles and Collier personally placed a pill into each man's mouth. Another guard then handed the man a tin cup filled with water. Collier watched with his pistol drawn, attentive to the modulation of the fellow's Adam's apple to make certain the tablet was actually swallowed. Only then did he move on to the next man. Dr. Finnegan and his assistants, dressed in their protective garb, hardly passed for more than the comic spectators of what was nevertheless an eminently medical transaction. It was for this reason that the physician in question was impatient, irritated, and humiliated. Besides which, the operation—conducted as such—proved time-consuming and laborious for everyone involved, what with the scalding sun up above and an atmosphere of ill-feeling

159

and mistrust all around. When the last man had finally swa
lowed the emblematic host of that bizarre eucharist invente
by the English engineer, the empty bottles were handed to th
doctor, who passed them on to his nearest assistant.

"Excuse me, sir," said Finnegan, lifting back the nettin
covering his face as he went up to the engineer, "I must te
you I find this entire ritual unnecessary."

"Don't tell me the doctor's pride is hurt?"

"It has nothing to do with pride or anything of the sort.
am merely pointing out that your behavior around here seem
to offer lamentable examples of an arbitrary willfulness."

"Willfulness!" Collier looked at the doctor without emotior
He was beginning to tire of this physician. "Look here, m
lad, I'll have no more of your saintly drivel."

"I'm afraid you will," Finnegan retorted.

"Very well, doctor, what would be your suggestion to avoi
this clandestine trafficking in quinine?"

Richard Finnegan had no answer. Indeed, he had never give
thought to a solution.

"Or do you actually believe that these vagabonds will b
moved to behave by a bloody sermon or two?" the enginee
continued.

"It's their own health that's at stake," Finnegan pleaded, a
if irritated with himself.

"*Health* you say," Collier snarled. "To blazes with you an
your fatuous health! What concerns me is the efficiency of m
labor force. I will not tolerate the disturbance of men rack_
with fever or maddened with delirium."

"Your attitude is insane!" The words escaped from Finne
gan's lips before he could censure them.

"Perfectly correct, doctor, what we have here is akin t
bedlam, for which there is no other way to act than I do—c
do you see otherwise?"

"It's you, Mr. Collier, who have turned everything here int
a madhouse."

The Englishman looked genuinely surprised at the doctor'
misreckoning of their situation. Richard Finnegan was provin
to be more ingenuous than even Collier had allowed, and fc
the first time the engineer—against his own will—began t
feel a degree of compassion for the physician. "Me?! Am I
by any chance, the author of this absurd project?"

160

Finnegan shook his head, less from a conviction that he himself was misguided than from a sense of there being no point in carrying on the conversation. Despite his acquiescence, Collier became insistent.

"Was it I who invented the idea of this confounded railroad that is meant to lead a train from no place to nowhere, out here in the middle of the jungle? Come now, my lad, the most I can be accused of is playing idiot—perhaps one of the worst cases, but, still, a simple idiot, like everyone else."

The physician, however, wanted to have done with this disputation: "You have no business interfering in matters of health."

The ensuing burst of laughter from the engineer bitterly wounded the young physician, and Collier tried to make amends for his poor behavior:

"You needn't worry, Dr. Finnegan, I'm not about to go around handing out prescriptions or taking anybody's pulse. If I force this rabble to swallow pills with the barrel of a Winchester to the ribs, it's no reflection on my part of any preoccupation with their health. I'd like nothing better than to watch this pack of scum breathe their last—but only after I've made my use of them. And another thing: if one of these chaps so much as hesitates to swallow, he'll find a hole in himself big enough to toss a whole bottle of pills."

"I'm beginning to understand," Finnegan almost whispered. "At heart you're really a rather decent human being."

"If there happens to be a category," Collier professed disdainfully, "that invariably makes me puke, it's that of a 'decent human being.' It's a category I wouldn't try out on me again— do I make myself clear, Dr. Finnegan?—unless you're looking for a good bash in the teeth."

That same afternoon Thomas Gallagher checked into the infirmary with a burned arm. It was not very serious: the result of an accident with the pressure valve, which had spewed a few drops of steam onto his arm. Finnegan treated the injury, a sprinkling of reddish blisters down the forearm, with perfunctory silence, and the old Irishman felt compelled to draw the doctor out with a bit of conversation.

"A difficult feller, that Collier, ain't he?" Gallagher began.

The doctor regarded him questionably.

161

"Sorry, doc, I can see y'ud prefer me to drop the subject."

"You needn't worry." Finnegan smiled. "Collier's not such a bad guy, just a bit on the edgy side."

"Ye really feel that way, laddie?"

"Of course I do, Thomas. The problem is *he* can't stand *my* guts."

"Blarney! Ye've simply got to ge' used to his eccentricities."

"It's quite a life we lead here, isn't it?"

"Y'are still a young fella, amn't I right?"

"More or less, Thomas."

"Well, be the holy, why'd y'ever choose a place like this to come to?"

"For the same reasons you did, I imagine. I'm no different than anybody else."

But Gallagher refused to believe him and overcame his own reluctance to pry into the boy's private life to suggest, "At yer age a fella still has his prospects ahead of 'im, nearly any o' them better than to kape rottin' away down here in the jungle."

"This doesn't strike me as the worst of possibilities. I simply accepted the invitation of Dr. Lovelace. I think you know him, don't you?"

"Like the back o' me fingers. Met him in Panama..."

"Well then, you know what an extraordinary man he is, a thorough professional and highly regarded back in the United States. I attended one of his lectures on tropical pathology. I was impressed by the splendid work he had carried out in Panama. He convinced me that I should come work here; I'd always had an interest in parasitology."

"Parasites 'ud be the one thing ye wouldn't run shart of, down here," Gallagher surmised, and the two of them laughed a bit longer than was necessary.

"You have to realize, Thomas, my life had been laid out for me. As soon as I'd received my degree I was to have taken up offices—totally equipped, mind you—in the most expensive, ideal location in my hometown."

"Where were ye barn, doc?"

"Saint Louis, Missouri."

"A fine part o' the world."

"You know it, Thomas?"

"Visited the place, quite a long time ago."

162

"This business of having one's life all mapped out started to get to me: it was like being sentenced without parole."

"We all feel that way when we're younger, laddie."

"Anyway, I accepted Dr. Lovelace's invitation without much hesitation. It had come along at just the right moment."

"The right moment, ye say. Ye want to hare what I think o' that idea?"

"Why not, Thomas? It's no longer very important in any case."

"Ye can't change things, that's the truth," Gallagher proclaimed, secure in his conformity, "but I do believe ye took a tumble into Lovelace's trap; that I do, doc, 'cause in this land o' damnation there's certainly no possibility o' doing anything."

"I don't agree, Thomas, but it's difficult to explain exactly what I hope to accomplish from all this. If you were Collier, I suppose you'd get a good laugh out of what I'm about to say."

"I see nothin' to laugh at, me lad."

"Thanks, Thomas."

"Fer what? What ails ye?"

"Well, what I was about to say is that out here in the jungle we're waging a kind of struggle. It's a war of civilization, moving forward, vanquishing barbarism. In any kind of war, generally, terrible things will happen. Yet man always manages to make the best of it. Perhaps in the future, a number of medical discoveries will very likely be computed into our sacrifices here."

"D'ye truly believe that, doc?"

"Let me try to be more specific. In this region there exist a great many little-known diseases. The medical profession is ill-prepared to deal with them, and if man really hopes to conquer this jungle, we first have to find out how to eliminate such diseases."

"Ye mane to convince me that progress depends upon me crawlin' on me belly through the likes o' this slime?"

"It's the white man's burden."

"That's what yer Lovelace fella likes to say."

"Yes, it's one of his expressions. He has the idea that civilization can only progress through adversity."

"But what's the need fer this infernal stretch o' the globe?"

163

"Thomas, this part of the globe isn't so infernal as you think."

"No? Then tell me, what's the good of it? Any gol' here? Any rebber?"

"Of course there's rubber. Who knows? Maybe gold as well. That's exactly the point! Underneath this seemingly invincible jungle could lie incalculable hidden treasures. The rain forest itself is a treasure. Who can say whether we won't have to make our presence really felt here some day. For that we would first have to know how to deal with various diseases, how to dominate nature here."

Finnegan grew animated the more he talked, about things which for Gallagher held no special significance.

"Troth now I never in me life gev much t'ought t'all that."

"That's understandable enough."

"Well, laddie, I'm already an ould waster mesel' but with the high-mindedness o' young fellas like yersel' we're bound to win out over all this in the end."

"It's not so much a matter of high ideals. It's just confidence in what we've set out to accomplish here. Which is the reason why I deplore Collier's attitude toward things. He acts like he's already been beaten; he's lost the wider perspective and concerns himself only with what's immediately at hand."

"Still, he's got to ge' his railway built."

"I know, but the railroad represents much more."

"Wha' but Collier's a professional."

"No one's denying that."

Old Thomas remained pensive for a minute, as if he were calling to mind the many episodes he and the Englishman had lived through together in places like this. "Collier, Collier," he finally sighed, that look of complicity which excluded the physician stamped on his face once again. "I suppose he really has gone a bit sour this past yare. He's rached the point where the wrong step an' he'll sink like a drownded rat—ye know what I'm sayin', doc? But he's a character all right. Did ye know he was an artillery captain in the Confed'rate army?"

The doctor looked confounded. The more he heard the less he could fathom such a man who seemed to him to have always been in the vicinity of some railroad or other under construction.

"They gev him two medals for bravery afore the war ended,"

the old man continued, screwing up his eyes. "After that he went back to England and got himself a degree fer engineerin'. Those days ye'd think twice afore ye'd own up to havin' a diploma. On the iron trail they measured the size of a fella by how many pints o' porter he could spill down his gullet. And, by God, Collier knew how to wet his whistle! Then next thing ye knew he was lavin' fer India or fer Panama, or off te Wyomin' throwin' up a bridge fer the Union Pacific. Be the holy, if they ever take to fillin' public squares with statues to railway engineers, they'd build ten o' him just fer what he done in the United States."

"The English immigrant who built America!" the doctor said facetiously.

"Pautratism? No, he never gave up his English citizenship. Always claimed to be livin' in America just like it were India or anywhere else. When he was taken prisoner at the end o' the war be the Union Army, they t'ought he was a spy fer Queen Victoria. He narely went to the scaffold. Now he has a good laugh over it whenever he sits down and thinks back to them times. He's..." Gallagher suddenly had a pained expression.

"Something wrong?" Finnegan inquired.

"Me arm," he said patiently.

"That'll be all right soon, the burns were only superficial."

"Ye'd think I'd be accustomed to them be now. Me whole life's been one steam burn after another."

"I had pegged Collier for one of those Englishmen born and raised in India," Finnegan confessed.

"At bottom he's never been anything else, a veritable sahib of the British raj."

"A what?"

The days passed: dolorous and less than revealing for a young man as deeply troubled as Richard Finnegan. Work on the bridge was practically completed by the end of that week. It was a simple truss bridge with a short arc of iron chords and tie braces held together by bolts and clinches that the workers were still fastening into place. The roadbed itself was supported by iron girders floored with wooden ties. The compacting of earth and branches had proceeded as far as to the edge of the bridge, but tracks had yet to be laid that far. The Germans were busy with work on the bridge. The Barbadians continued setting track in place, advancing the path of Mad Maria toward the crossing of the Abunã.

Pacing back and forth along the trajectory of the railroad bed, the English engineer supervised the meticulous labors of his Barbadian crew, verifying the quality and precision of their efforts. He was completely absorbed by—and seemingly contented with—the progress of construction. The deaths from malaria had been halted finally, and within the last few days, there had been signs of heightened productivity. Thumbs in his belt, Collier surveyed the forward march of the tracks. He was surprised consequently when his Germans, as if responding to an internal order, dropped their tools and began to gather together on the bridge. For some moments this coalescing group seemed not so much to move as to absorb other Germans who had been at work in the more distant vicinities from the bridge and now were adding to their number. And though they did not advance or utter any threats, they certainly were exhibiting a mounting hostility. Collier surmised their intentions and turned to face them; with a glance over his shoulder he reassured himself that the Barbadians were still at work and would play no part in what was about to unfold. Since the bridge had yet to be completely floored, the Germans were in no position to retreat and could only come forward in the direction where Collier stood waiting. Behind them lay an empty space some four meters across and ten meters straight down into the abyss of the Abunã.

Collier waited. He felt calm as he observed his Germans. It was not quite the same attention he gave to the details of construction—there was a touch of hatred in his eyes. He had his revolver in his belt and kept a hand ready, wiping it on his thigh.

"What's going on here, gentlemen?" Collier shouted to them.

The Germans kept silent.

"There's still two hours left on this shift," Collier insisted, his nervousness putting an edge to the threat in his voice.

One German worker broke ranks. "Ve are not going to keep vorking sis vay."

Collier recognized the fellow: a lad of little more than twenty, rather strong physically, although the demands of such labors

166

had already reduced his physical stamina as well as his capacity for such impertinence.

"I suggest you get back to work jolly sharp and drop this idiocy."

Collier's tone was ugly and disdainful; yet the Germans were not impressed. The lad advanced further in the direction of the engineer. Collier's eyes darted about in search of a security guard. It was always the same, he thought to himself disgustedly, whenever you needed them they were nowhere about.

"Ve have thum sings to settle vith sa company first," the lad challenged bitterly. "Sen ve go back to vork."

"The company has nothing to say to derelicts," the engineer crowed, "not while there's work to be done on that bridge."

"Se bridge can go to hell!"

"Just what are you after? You and your friends want to lose your jobs? I've a bloody mind to ship you back to the shithole we dug you out of back on the Rhine. . . ."

"Sat's fine vith us!"

"You chaps had better give some thought to what the company is capable of doing with you."

"Sa company better sink vat a mess of sings ve can make right here!"

"And you better bloody—" but Collier paused and then adopted a more conciliatory tone. "Look, the best thing for you chaps is to pick up your tools and get back to work on that bridge over there. Then maybe I'll forget about all this."

But just then another worker, also in rags but skinnier, with his eyes seemingly popping from their sockets, came up behind his companion who had been facing Collier alone until now.

"It is not possible, Mr. Collier," he said pleadingly, "not possible for us to work this way with the paltry crumbs you give us."

The first lad was now emboldened by his pathetic companion. "Sis work is not fit for dogs," he argued. "Ve must have better conditions. You make us vork elefen hours a day and for a zalary zat not even a ragpicker vould accept. You're killing us here."

The engineer was losing his patience. Work was already at a standstill because of the unintentional adherence of the Barbadians who had now put their tools aside and turned to observe the impasse.

"Of all the damned cheek," the engineer retorted. "I'm not to blame if you've been played the fool. You should have thought of all this when the company agents showed you your contracts. This is hardly the place to discuss it."

"Any place is sa right place too demand vat is just. Any time is sa right time to give up sis insanity and stop behaving like fools!"

"No one gets cured of being a fool," the engineer said furiously.

At that, the lad lost his head and made for Collier but his companions managed to drag him back. Collier had drawn his revolver.

"Then this is the only argument you chaps will understand," he said, now waving it at them defiantly.

The Germans retreated, frightened now. The weapon in Collier's hand seemed to have an identity of its own—sovereign, to be sure—that threatened not only the protestors but the engineer as well. He looked at the revolver and repented of having drawn it in the first place, let alone waving it in the air and threatening the workers. It was the worst possible choice, he knew, and he tried to minimize the damage.

"All right, men," he concluded, replacing the revolver in his holster, "back to work. Nobody has time to be discussing salaries at the moment, least of all me. Besides, I haven't the authority. Let's all get back to work. There'll be plenty of time tomorrow when you have the day off. That's right, tomorrow's Sunday, a day of rest. Take advantage of it to do some reflecting on the foolishness we were about to get into. Everybody back to work! I can assure you it's better than a ridiculously inconsequential strike. . . ."

Finally, the security guards began to appear. The engineer was still haranguing the stragglers back to their tasks. Meanwhile, as if sniffing out a possible tragedy, the physician and his medics had arrived on the scene. The guards were already forming a line of defense between the engineer and the bridge, preventing any last-minute change of intention on the part of the Germans.

"Everything is all right," Collier soothed them. "Lower your weapons; we've all settled down, haven't we, men?" And he nodded to them, smiling.

The guards obeyed, lowering their guns, but were left standing without knowing what to do next. The Germans looked to one another silently and began to pick up their tools. The Barbadians were already back at their tasks. What little excitement was left in the air soon died, as several of the Germans began to slam additional planking into place toward the far end of the bridge. Things returned to normal and Collier appeared to have made his point in the skirmish.

"Well, that put paid to that," the engineer confided to a bewhiskered Spaniard who seemed to be in charge of the guards. "But don't take your eyes off those fellows. Tonight I want a double guard posted by the German wing of the dormitory. I won't have one of these louts appointing himself chief troublemaker while I'm trying to get some sleep."

"Si, señor, I will double de guard," the whiskery one replied.

"These Germans have turned out to be quite a scurrilous lot," the engineer sighed.

In the meantime, the doctor, followed by his medics, had approached the circle of guards surrounding the engineer, and Finnegan himself elbowed his way through to face the engineer.

"You continue to defend your sleep quite admirably," said the physician, smirking ironically. "Congratulations on the good work."

"What did you say?" Collier asked, turning to him.

"I said you've done an admirable job. A real accomplishment, worthy of the great sahib."

Collier's fist landed squarely in the doctor's face. Finnegan never even saw it coming. It flattened his nose and landed him on the ground. A thread of blood was already seeping into his mouth, still gaping in astonishment.

9

Adams Mackenwieks, hospitalized with fractures of the ribs, arms, and left clavicle, was already written off as far as Percival Farquhar was concerned. How could someone allow himself to be surprised like that? Mackenwieks had demonstrated himself to be shockingly injudicious; obviously he had been unable to recognize the complexity of the game afoot and, consequently, had failed to safeguard himself from such unforeseen possibilities. Farquhar, having decided to challenge a man like Minister J. J. Seabra, had been conscious from the very beginning of the inherent dangers in such a plan. He had thoroughly studied the agglomeration of facts surrounding the career of this northeastern politician and therefore appreciated to what extent Seabra was capable of an explosive style: he could arrange an assault, even a murder, with the same benevolent air with which he attended baptisms and confirmations to widen his constituency.

On the afternoon Farquhar had decided to set his plan in motion, Colonel Agostinho had telephoned his office. The news was not terribly serious. Seabra had just been with the president but, for some reason, had not communicated to him his plans for canceling the Southern Brazil Lumber & Colonization Company's concessions. Was he worried? Was he having second thoughts, or did he disdain his opponents entirely? Whatever the case, it had been a good moment to begin. Now, however, Farquhar felt irritated with the results: nothing was turning out as he had planned. Mackenwieks, laid up in the hospital, had struck out completely. Seabra's mistress, contrary to his expectations, had refused to collaborate—she wasn't the selfish little slut he had imagined; that is, not quite. They had been obliged to take her by force—to actually kidnap her! Something in that woman kept her from betraying her lover; as if she had a hunch the better business deal would prove to be Seabra! The little strumpet was being kept under guard, hidden in the staterooom of a freighter anchored off the Quay

170

haroux. The ship flew a Panamanian flag and was transporting quipment for one of Farquhar's own enterprises. They would ever think to find her there—even if the minister ordered his oons to comb the entire city, they would never imagine to ok there. Yet all these precautions were, in practical terms, failure if the lousy cunt should persist in her refusal!

The worst of it was that this was not our Percival's style. razil was still too rowdy a country for someone like Mr. arquhar and his sophisticated brand of shenanigans. By opting r violence, he had to admit he was entering a terrain where J. Seabra had the upper hand. The minister had risen through ure violence; he was hardly the sort of scoundrel that civili- ation demanded; he still believed in the older, more drastic ethods. Farquhar was conscious of the need to be aware of ch tendencies and ready to manipulate them to his own ad- antage. What he struggled to achieve in such a country as is was the right chemistry between his inspired shenanigans nd the no less inspired violence of Brazil herself. Especially ow that the country was changing, the political turbulence gnaled rather the end of a whole epoch, which Brazilians felt onfident was already behind them with the proclamation of e Republic. By adapting his own peculiar mountebankery to e Brazilian style, Percival hoped to create the precise method quired by this period of transition through which the nation as about to pass. Unfortunately, this also turned everything to an adventure, which bothered Percival. He did not like to ave adventures; no authentic scoundrel ever does. To be a coundrel, for Farquhar, was the kind of science in which each iven was computed, every move established, no surprise en- iled. Percival Farquhar knew that profit could not be sepa- ted from this scientific spirit that underpinned his own ulduggery. And there was no other way for him to justify e turbulent spirit of most Brazilians, if not because of the xcessive dose of adventurism that seemed to characterize nearly verything that happened in Brazil.

Yet beyond adventure, which still betokened something holesome to the rigorous patterns of Percival's thinking, there as a less palpable problem about Brazil. Yes, Brazilians were dventurers, but in addition they cultivated something far more currilous than mere adventurism: the Brazilians prized accom- odation! Percival Farquhar detested that tepid and decadent

171

spirit of accommodation. He considered accommodation to be incompatible with any form of modern civilization. The modern world—in order to construct and produce wealth—must avoid accommodation. The ruptures were essential to progress and certainly nothing should be allowed to stagnate in mid stream when either shore held out the possibility of earning. In his bids at mountebankery, there had never been any room spared for accommodation. The internal logic of his highbinding was as rigid as that of a game of chess: chance and the imponderable were relegated to the lowest order of probability. In the highest form of con-artistry—free from any physical violence—there was surely no margin for tricks or reversals. Sheer mountebankery was so highly respected precisely because it resulted from something more akin to divine interpolation. But rarely was someone in Brazil imbued with pure mountebankery; for the violence was so antithetical to the almost mystic sophistication of the truly great bamboozlers.

The day proceeded slowly. Farquhar was sweating it through. He had been awakened early in order to visit Adams Mackenwieks at the hospital. The young Brazilian woman married to Mackenwieks received him with her head bowed and an air of total incomprehension. The violence, she could understand; what remained a mystery to her was why it should have been enacted upon her husband.

While Farquhar was still in the hospital, the police arrived. They were there to begin their investigation. Mackenwieks's wife had actually called the police before informing anyone in the office! Another unpardonable error on the part of Adams, not to have instructed his own wife never to confide in anyone outside of the office—above all, the police! The officers were two dusky mulattoes with oily hair and seedy suits. One of them had a gold crown, without any luster, amid his upper front teeth. Neither of the officers smiled, however. They had a mammalian melancholy, something animalized that Percival was fond of detecting in the hybrid manifestations of Brazilian miscegenation. One of the policemen was seated next to Mackenwieks's wife, questioning her rather diffidently.

"You are the wife?" he asked.

"I am, yes," the woman answered, her eyes still puffy from a night of crying.

"Was it you who called the police, senhora?"

"Yes, I did!"

"Could you explain once more what happened, senhora?"

"Again? I've already told the police, I don't know how many times!"

"I'm sorry, senhora, but I'm afraid you'll have to. You see, we're from Special Detectives. We've had orders from above to take over the case."

Farquhar suddenly pricked his ears. "Officer, could you be a bit more specific about those orders from above?"

The officer turned to him.

"In what sense, senhor . . . ?" he offered tentatively, waiting for Farquhar to identify himself.

"Farquhar—Percival Farquhar."

The policeman stood up at once and extended his hand.

"A pleasure, Senhor Farquhar. I'm Inspector Eustáquio Guedes," he said amicably squeezing Farquhar's hand and then presenting him with his card.

"I presume, then, you're in charge of this investigation," Farquhar finally commented after examining the calling card, where he read that the officer had a law degree and a diploma in criminal investigation from Scotland Yard's police academy, in London.

The idea of this softspoken Negro's having sat in an English academy was altogether amusing to our Percival, but he avoided the impulse to smile. For a split second he watched an ironic expression on the face of a certain Stephan Collier, construction engineer, appear and then vanish in the sunlight dazzling the window of the hospital room. The inspector was still addressing him.

"You can appreciate, senhor, a man was brutally assaulted. We are as yet unaware of the motives for such an attack. It was not the case of a holdup. And the victim is a foreigner who enjoys the highest esteem in Carioca society. Nothing has happened quite like this in some time. The authorities are extremely troubled. It may have been intended as some sort of provocation."

"I see," said Farquhar curtly.

The wife of Adams Mackenwieks was still quite shaken. She had not slept at all since the incident had occurred.

"You'll excuse me, senhor." The inspector bowed to Far-

173

quhar and sat down next to her. "I must continue with the investigation."

Farquhar acquiesced with a nod and returned to the bed where Adams lay asleep under the effects of heavy sedation. Still, Percival kept one ear open to the conversation between the officer and the lady.

"He was unconscious. Not a sound out of him. I thought he was dead!" The wife began to weep. "It was savage. I simply cannot imagine why they did this to my husband. He has no enemies. He's a good man!"

"You mean there's no one you suspect, senhora?"

"No, no one."

"You noticed nothing out of the ordinary about your husband that night?"

"Nothing. We were worrying over our eldest son. The boy had a fever—a chest cold, you understand, and he kept refusing to eat or to sleep. My husband is very affectionate with our children, and he was with my son when they knocked at the door."

"It was your husband who answered the door?"

"Yes, he went himself. We weren't expecting any visitors but I don't think he would have been suspicious of anything. He didn't even call me. He had already sent me to bed, to rest a bit. We generally go to bed early."

"And why, when the police arrived, did someone inform them that Senhor Mackenwieks had tripped on the steps?"

The wife winced and Farquhar, staring out the window at the activity on the street below, quickened his attention.

"They said that?" she asked incredulously.

"That's what was said. It's in the police report."

"That's not possible," she ventured hesitantly.

"Who actually summoned the police?"

"I did, naturally. I sent a servant boy running off to the precinct. Then I gathered my wits and telephoned the embassy. The police were taking so long to arrive."

"When the police did arrive, senhora, were there already other people who had come to the house?"

"Why, yes. Two employees who had driven by car from the embassy, and a colleague of my husband's, from his office."

"Was it you who spoke with the police?"

"No, inspector, I was too distraught. Friends lifted my hus-

174

band onto the couch in the living room, checking to see if he was still ... One of them decided to summon a doctor. I was led to my room and given a sedative. Still, I didn't manage to sleep ... such a horrible night!" She began to sob.

"Senhora, I'm sorry," the inspector said gently, "but I have every reason to believe that someone has tried to hide from the authorities the facts that have led to your husband's tragedy."

For a few seconds, Mackenwieks's wife stared at the inspector in disbelief, then looked to Percival Farquhar for some kind of explanation. Slowly, she was growing to suspect that there was something sinister behind the injury to her husband. Something she had yet to fathom. Something terrible and mysterious that only Mr. Farquhar himself could have the means of knowing. He came up to her and placed his hand on her shoulder. She was still crying.

"Do you really think it necessary to go on with these questions, Inspector Guedes?" Farquhar inquired politely but with the clear implication that he might do better to desist.

"I'm afraid it's my job, Senhor Farquhar."

"Yes, but she's obviously very shaken by this whole incident. And I doubt that what she has to say will be of much use to you. You know how emotional it must be for her."

The inspector reluctantly rose from his chair, closed the notebook in which he had been making his notations and stood tapping the cover with his pencil. "Perhaps you are right."

"Could you spare a minute of your time, inspector?" Farquhar motioned him aside.

"However much you require, Senhor Farquhar."

Percival led the inspector out into the corridor and closed the door of the room behind him. The other police officer, not knowing what to do, had stayed, leaning against the wall and watching the woman shake with sobs.

Farquhar got directly to the point: "You still haven't told me who sent you over here...."

The police inspector, however, was suddenly offended.

"Senhor Farquhar, a man was assaulted. It's the province of my division to investigate the case and bring those responsible to justice."

"I doubt that's going to happen, inspector."

"I'll not allow you to talk that way, Senhor Farquhar."

"Listen here, Inspector Guedes, perhaps you really are well-intentioned officer who wishes to behave professional But this case is no ordinary case. This assault was no ordina assault. There are a number of disturbing implications lying the back of this incident. You seem like a reasonable man me, inspector, and an intelligent fellow. I wouldn't like to s you embarrassed by all this."

By the look on the inspector's face, Percival realized th the man was simply a professional, innocent of the who intrigue. He was there with the best of intentions, propelle by nothing more than professional zeal. It was unforgivable Farquhar's eyes. A man like that could make things uncor fortable for Percival Farquhar, without ever realizing the fac Nothing more problematical than an incorruptible pup in tl woods!

"Listen carefully to what I am going to tell you," Farquh began in a soft, persuasive tone. "This man was not assaulte Do you understand? He has suffered no offense. He simp tripped and fell on the stairs. It was only an accident."

The police officer listened with an air of patent disbelie The thing was familiar enough to him. He had even had son similar experiences in the past: it was another case of priva scandal—very common to the upper crust of Carioca societ in which police action would only become a hindrance, e larging the furor. The gradual change of expression on tl inspector's face was not lost upon Percival Farquhar, who car little what the officer was actually imagining provided he d not begin to get in the way.

"Very well, Senhor Percival," said the inspector, donni his Panama hat, "I will convey your declaration to my sup riors."

He opened the door again to Mackenwieks's room and si naled the other officer to join him. The two then retired silence. Inside the room, the wife was still crying. Perciv was not entirely relieved—his plan seemed about to erupt in a crisis and he did not take a shine to the feeling of panic th seemed about to embrace him. The wife looked up at hir straining to have a precise picture of this ominous man throu the tears that were clouding her bloodshot eyes.

"What's going on, Mr. Farquhar? Why have they done th to my husband!"

176

"It was an accident, don't be worried." It was Percival's attempt to assuage this woman, and he chose an intonation of voice that would not externalize the panic actually threatening to overwhelm him. "Your husband will soon get well. He suffered no serious injury, thank heavens. He'll soon be home. And I'm going to see to it personally that he has a proper convalescence—a vacation, that's what you both need, a nice long vacation. A trip somewhere, how's that? The company will pay for everything. It's my pleasure."

Farquhar had no confidence in that woman: she was weak and dependent. For that matter, he had no further confidence in Adams either. Adams Mackenwieks had shown himself to be an easy mark. Who was there to rely on? This violent type of game was (positively!) a far cry from the style of Percival Farquhar.

That same afternoon, as he looked over some waybills in his office, Farquhar had a visitor: a polished gentleman who introduced himself as a functionary from the Ministry of Justice. The visit provoked no particular anxiety on the part of Percival Farquhar, and this would prove to be the first time he had erred in his assessment of the nature of things. (It would leave him rather rankled.) The gentleman was brief: he had come to ask Mr. Farquhar to accompany him to the Ministry of Justice, *immediately;* he was to have an urgent interview with the minister himself. Now the minister of justice happened to be a certain Rivadávia Correa, whom Farquhar did not know personally at all. What he did know was that the minister was an extremely exacting jurist, an astute politician, and a man of few friendships—all of which was disturbing. In the various turbulent cases that had come before him in the initial months of the da Fonseca administration, Rivadávia Correa had proven himself a hardliner. He had only promulgated much against his will the amnesty decree, voted by Congress, for the navy mutineers, and then had fully supported every conceivable instance of arbitrary punishment that was to befall them once they had returned to their ranks. A man of even fewer words than friends, the minister was notorious for the curtness with which he treated absolutely everybody, even the most powerful representatives of the state oligarchies. The people characterized him as a rancorous bigot who liked to foment persecutions. Nevertheless, Farquhar was not impressed by the invitation, though he willingly acceded to it and even accepted the ride in the functionary's automobile, driven by a rather contemptuous-looking chauffeur.

Once in the ministry, after waiting for more than a half hour (a slight air of humiliation drifting across his brow as he watched the time pass), Percival Farquhar was summoned into the cabinet office and met by the glacial stare that issued from the pallid visage of Minister Correa. He was an imposing man, fully charged with the power that his post conferred upon him, but in an unnatural way, almost ostentatiously, with a kind of presumption that stretched his power far beyond the limits of ministerial function. After pointing to a chair, he observed Farquhar for a moment, as if both to intimidate him and to appraise his secret thoughts. Percival, however, was not a man to be intimidated, much less to be mined for his thoughts.

"Senhor Farquhar, you did not tell the truth this morning to Inspector Guedes," the minister began, his voice grave and flinty but to no effect. "What were you trying to cover up?" he added, as if aware of the fact.

Percival's response was no more than a thin smile of superiority; he felt himself quite untouchable. It was that heightened and very gratifying sensation of sitting beyond the reach of stupid men who only played at power.

"You may be getting yourself into rather deep waters, Senhor Farquhar. A man in your organization was barbarously assaulted and you persist in claiming it was nothing more than an accident."

"He slipped on the stairs," Farquhar replied cynically.

Little by little, the minister's pallor was displaced by a flush of ferocity.

"You, sir, are a liar!"

It was something Farquhar had not expected and it extinguished his smile.

"That's a grave accusation, Your Excellency."

"Far graver is your attempt to hide the facts from the authorities!"

"I am not hiding facts, sir."

The minister touched a bell and waited without taking his watery eyes from Farquhar, the flush of fury turning now into triumph. The door to the office opened and five policemen entered with two manacled prisoners. Both prisoners were in

178

a terrible state, their faces horribly disfigured and their clothes in rags. One of them, the shorter of the two, had his upper lip split open. Farquhar understood immediately and tried to appear coldly indifferent, like an experienced gambler who has just been dealt the worst cards in the deck.

"These men, Senhor Farquhar, apparently helped Senhor Mackenwieks to fall down those stairs. What have you to say now?"

"I don't know these men. Are they Brazilians?"

"They are Brazilians. They work on the docks. They were discovered carousing over in the Mangue district, spending a great deal of money and indulging in a free-for-all. They were detained by the police because they were suspected of being thieves. After some interrogation . . . they *suggested* that the money had been paid by . . . *you*, senhor. . . ."

"I deny any such accusation!" Farquhar snarled belligerently.

"Don't interrupt me, Senhor Farquhar; you'll wait till I'm finished!" Rivadávia Correa shouted even louder, indignant at such presumption.

Farquhar felt his strength beginning to forsake him.

"You, senhor, ordered these men to assault your own employee, though I cannot imagine the reasons why."

"This is a ridiculous farce," said Farquhar resignedly.

"Very well, you insist upon denying these charges." He gave a sign and the police officers dragged the men out of the office. "You seem to underestimate us, Senhor Farquhar. We are not afraid of economic power. We have information that the group which you represent aims to create problems for this administration. We know, for instance, that you helped to finance the opposition in the last elections. Now your friends intend to undermine the president."

"This is not true at all."

"What is true is that you can be expelled from this country and have your holdings expropriated, Senhor Farquhar. You depend upon federal concessions, upon federal money, and upon the good will of the federal government. You should have remembered that, Senhor Farquhar."

"If the intention, Your Excellency, is to frighten me, then this farce has been a waste of time."

"Then, to you this is just a farce?"

"It is, and you know it as well as I do."

The minister fixed his eyes on Farquhar's with that same jellied quizzicality. A few seconds passed this way and the cabinet office took on the smell, to Farquhar's senses, of must and old papers. The drapes of creamy velvet were as still as an oil portrait.

"I have a mind, Senhor Percival Farquhar, to expel you from my country."

The man was deadly serious, Farquhar knew—he meant every word. Rivadávia had obviously been taken in by Seabra and was acting, in his fashion, motivated by the solidarity among ministers. The conversation moved icily to its conclusion.

"I intend to consult the president in this matter. Consider yourself faced with such a possibility, Senhor Farquhar. Good day!"

As soon as he reached his office, Percival Farquhar telephoned Catete Palace, only to discover that Colonel Agostinho had been sent off to Niterói. Farquhar had never felt so humiliated, but he still had J. J. Seabra's mistress in his power. He told himself he must not be impulsive now, even though at that moment he would have liked to take that obstinate whore and make her vomit her brains out. Instead, he sat himself comfortably in his chair and attempted to put his plans back together. Perhaps he had gone too far in an undertaking that bore little resemblance to his own peculiar style. He finally decided that the most prudent thing to do was to get in contact as swiftly as possible with his confidant, Ruy Barbosa. The old lawyer would know how to analyze—with his cold impartiality—all the facets of these new complications and come up with a proper diagnosis of the future. The afternoon was still stiflingly hot and Farquhar hardly noticed the passing hours. Suddenly the telephone rang, and when he picked it up, it was J. J. Seabra.

"Listen here, you son of a bitch. I can kick you out of the country with one good boot in the ass!"

"And I can put an end to all your political ambitions, Minister Seabra." Farquhar's voice was filled with sarcasm. He despised conversations on the phone. "But let's get together and talk things over like civilized people."

180

"First hand over the girl your thugs have kidnapped from that house in São Cristóvão!"

"First things first! Let's talk things over. I think neither one of us has much to gain with all that's going on."

Seabra suddenly slammed down the receiver. Farquhar was not surprised. And he knew that shortly he would be face to face with this same minister for a definitive play of trumps. Percival Farquhar still nourished hopes of becoming great friends with J. J. Seabra—a paradoxical hope, perhaps, but Percival Farquhar felt rather at home with the likes of that.

10

Consuelo Campero became irritated on Sundays: a sign that she was beginning to possess the will to live again. Her irritation was not manifested in an obvious way. Richard Finnegan perceived it as a kind of halfhearted thing one early morning—in her manner of walking. She would take a few long steps from place to place, putting all the weight of her body on each leg. It was hardly her usual manner—silent and fluid as a perfumed breath (at least to Finnegan's imagination, which found in her something of a refuge). Consuelo seemed to be filling, without knowing it (or, who knows? perhaps she even suspected as much, but she was so quiet and discreet), the empty space in Dr. Finnegan left by all the privations he had thus far undergone. True, she simply loitered about the infirmary, still alienated from the rumblings of the world about her, but she was like a locked door through which the young physician might escape if only he had the courage to open her. The real company for Consuelo was the Indian with the amputated hands. The doctor had baptized him Joe—Joe Caripuna—and the Indian took a liking to the name. He had proved to be reasonably intelligent and, what is more, gifted with an exceptional memory. He was already speaking English better than Consuelo, and he delighted in talking to the doctor, asking questions about the world of the civilized and everything else that came to mind. During their conversations, Consuelo would remain surprisingly mute, but her eyes were attentive and emboldened the doctor. Meanwhile, she would spend her days beside Joe: helping him about, changing his bandages, hastening from one end to the other of the infirmary to carry out orders while still attending to the pleas of the Caripuna. In the last few days, Dr. Finnegan had managed to surprise a smile on her lips while the Indian was addressing her—with some ridiculously funny comment, no doubt: the fruit of his ignorance of civilized customs.

Consuelo fought instinctively to shun the oppressive invitation to desperation which haunted her life. Her struggle surfaced with a growing frequency and now demanded satisfaction. She was, after all, still a young woman, and her youth throbbed like an exposed nerve. Her hands were always moist and she never stood still; a vigor flowed through every muscle of her body and a smell like damp clothes exuded from her dark tresses. She felt as if something had come undone, inside of her, but as if it had at the same time liberated a force that was previously unknown to her. This notion pleased her, for some reason, and provided a consolation. For she had lost everything, or so she imagined, and had become a woman set loose upon life. In anguish, Consuelo saw herself as an old sponge desperate to absorb the last remnant of liquid in a desert. At the same time, everything affected her unexpectedly, sometimes importunately. Her body even rebelled against the sentiments that were attempting to take refuge in her mind while rending her heart. She had already begun to permit herself to weigh what might be her actions on the following day; she no longer clung to the present moment as if it were her exclusive existence. As a result, she had turned irritable on Sundays in the same way that she had come to dream calmly during her nights. The Indian was improving in proportion to the extent that she forced her own depressions to retreat into the farther recesses of her mind. She was fond of this Indian, with a sort of pity that she hoped she herself might arouse in others—the Indian had no hands; she had also suffered an amputation, though invisibly. Her husband was dead—a thought which now only provoked a shiver of consternation. She had yet to resign herself to this unmanageable fact; at times she had an enormous hungering for the presence of her husband—for his flesh—and she would succumb to weeping at the impossibility of it all. She wept because her desire had remained a prisoner of the past, although she had no fear of satisfying such desire with another flesh, another presence. She suspected that she was becoming cynical, which sometimes left her curiously proud rather than fearful. I am a woman, she would think at such moments, I am a stroke of destiny, despite my will. The thought did not free her but was sufficient to lift her apathy from her. Some nights (now that her nightmares had dissipated), she escaped even dreams; her sleep was a white void. There were only certain mild sensations: an orchestra of violins and pianos, happy conversations, and her body wrapped in the arms that she knew to be his—Alonso's!—and how they danced, how his hands, the heat of his soft palm resting upon her shoulder blade, how they spun across the floor, moving imperceptibly without anything separating her body from his, her hips swaying, massaging his penis—oh, it was too much to bear!—and the soft brush of his breath upon her neck . . . oh, not to awaken from what finally had become a dream! She imagined she must probably even mutter things occasionally in such a state of lucubration, representing the rebellion of her young flesh. She suspected what she must be capable of saying and, after waking, would become afraid of perceiving any sign of complicity in the eyes of the young physician. A strange man, still young himself, but as slippery to grasp as soap.

To a certain degree, Consuelo Campero had come to detest the doctor. He had seen her nude—not exactly naked because she had been wrapped in unconsciousness while he had undressed her, but nude as a sigh, as a breath, as a secret revealed by force. And the physician appeared to be omnipresent: he had been at her side when first she opened her eyes and her whirling thoughts were urging her to abandon this life. Then at whatever hour of the night she awakened, there was the young Dr. Finnegan, solicitous as ever, offering her still another glass of water, which she would drink down in almost a single gulp because her thirst was truly insatiable. His omnipresence was adroitly managed; it both supported and comforted her in a fashion she could hardly explain: a mellifluous tenderness? a sweet dedication? a furtive masculinity insinuating itself through the solicitousness he continually bestowed upon her? She felt the man in him—he was a man, with that masculine ampleness she had already experienced in her Alonso—and here the rebellion of her own flesh also revealed itself.

Whenever Richard Finnegan was absent from the infirmary, and this would occur practically throughout the entire day, she would amuse herself with the Indian. Joe Caripuna had incredible aptitudes and asked the most unlikely questions. He even confessed to her that for a long time he had suspected that the civilized (as he called them all) did not have women. He could not conceive of their actually marrying and having children. Such confessions were endearing; and here Consuelo

184

ould break into a smile—still remote, but a smile nonetheless. The Indian likewise enjoyed being playful and hardly lamented the fact of no longer having hands; it was as if they had never existed and consequently should scarcely be missed. In a certain sense this was, practically speaking, the truth: Joe had extraordinary ability with his feet, for picking up tiny things from the floor, for taking up magazines and paging through them, for moving each toe separately as one might move the fingers on one's hands. One day, for Consuelo's amusement, he carried off a small miracle: he picked up a box of matches, opened it, took out a match stick and struck it, causing it to light! Then, to top it off, he brought the match stick up to his face and extinguished the flame with an amused breath of air. Consuelo liked Joe Caripuna; he did not drown himself in woeful effusions—he had courage, or some such thing. And whatever it was, it thrust her forward and obliged her to reconsider life. Thus, the two of them helped each other without either asking anything of the other; they survived by sustaining each other, in a symbiosis of sorrows that melded their struggle to recover each of their destinies that had gone awry.

The prodigies of the Indian did not go unnoticed by the physician—they were, first of all, amusing. The Indian likewise revealed a strength, a very special energy which wholly escaped the young doctor and which raised that creature without hands above them all. It was not passiveness, nor resignation in the face of tragedy; the Indian was possessed of an emotional aplomb that left the doctor astonished. He had managed, through the vitality within him, to provide a fresh stimulus to Consuelo that was already affecting her. When compared to that of the Indian, ordinary tragedies were quickly reduced to their proper proportions: they were no longer even tragedies but rather an emptying, a deflation of the sacred. Indeed, that Indian had something sacred about him—smallish gods who completed his absent hands. It was all strange, comforting, but inexplicable. Richard Finnegan realized that pity did not apply to the Indian; perhaps this was the very thing which most perturbed our physician: a tenderness which emanated from Joe like a hallowed breath. The Indian was a complete entity, not exactly an entity, more a personality whose hands had become suddenly invisible and for this very reason more present than ever. I am incomplete and I have hands, thought Richard Finnegan, and

185

I do not deserve the compassion that I feel for myself. Some times I'd like to explode at this Indian, to vent a hatred of h ingenuity, but it's simply impossible. This Caripuna frighter me, because by fulfilling himself thus in his incapacity, h annuls my self-commiseration. Yes, my self-pity is ridiculou before him. I have my hands ... I have my people ... I hav yet to truly suffer. Son of a bitch! Here I am, a Catholic suffering by proxy! Poor Finnegan was actually a man of gen uine good will; but for that very reason he was wrecking him self—or so he judged. The only recourse that had been availabl to him was to become a conniver; yet the Indian had manage to confront the world through the more dangerous door courage. What Finnegan now hoped for was to somehow mer sharing in the work of the Indian's frailties, in the same wa that Consuelo Campero had gained access by permitting tha the savage rent in her life should begin its cicatrization.

It was Sunday and Consuelo was irked. She had no ide why she must remain a prisoner on Sundays. Outside there, large number of armed men were still congregated to stan guard over the dormitory. They had actually spent the entir night like that. Consuelo was unaware of the essential ritua that was played out on Sundays: a collective bathing of th workers. This bath had been invented by Dr. Lovelace as pa of the program of hygiene and preventative care. In fact, how ever, what Consuelo was forbidden to behold amounted to fairly depressing scene that would probably have shocked he sensibilities and not her morals. Around ten o'clock each Sun day morning, the workers would gather, naked, in a line tha terminated before a wagon. All laborers were obliged to tak one weekly bath; only the sick were excused from this gro tesque pageant. The wagon served as a dais where the me would mount—four and five at a time—and admit to th forceful spray of triple hoses manned by security guards. Th ambience was that of horseplay, but a horseplay incapable ameliorating the embarrassment of many of the participant particularly the elderly. The men, while up on the wagon, wer required to rub cumbersome soap bars over their bodies an thereby remove the cumulative filth of seven days' labor. Som of the antics were aggressive—shoving a companion acros the slippery floor of the cart or banging one another on th head with the soap—and provoked smiles appropriate to

186

oungster's boarding school. The timid were, as always, the
est targets and generally had to endure being hoisted on the
houlders of their rougher fellows, in triumph, only to be dumped
nto the platform, defenseless and alarmed, sliding about help-
ssly under the powerful jets of water purposefully directed
their most susceptible extremities.

Each worker, already undressed, awaited his turn holding
e week's soiled clothes under his arm. Before climbing up
brave the water jets he would dutifully drop these personal
gs into a huge wicker basket stationed there for that purpose.
he old clothes would eventually be incinerated. Once any
orker had decided he was finished with his douche, after
mbing down, he received a bundle of new, clean clothes that
immediately used to cover his still soaking body. Only
otwear was not changed, and the worker often took another
oment to get into his shoes or boots, tossed in the vicinity
the cart and invariably in deplorable condition. Obviously,
e professional class of worker did not participate in such
gradation, for they had access to a group of five private
owers installed just behind the agglomeration of their tents.
rofessionals had the privilege of bathing every day, should
e desire overtake them. . . .

Consuelo Campero, already irritated by this confinement to
e infirmary, felt even more alone once the Indian was per-
itted outside to take in the sun. Thus he became part of that
lective audience of guards and technicians sitting in camp
airs, observing the bathing, and sometimes even participating
the horseplay.

As always, Collier presided—especially on this Sunday of
eated tensions which did not appear to cool down under the
olutionary showers. Gallagher, his eyes half-shut in the glare
the sun, was conscious of the tense expectancy emanating
om the engineer.

"There ye are now, Collier, they're as calm as pups."

"I don't know, Thomas, they don't forget so easily," Collier
plied.

At the moment it was a group of Germans who were soaping
their bodies under the jetting spouts of water.

"They never showed up for their palaver?" the locomotive
an inquired.

"Not a peep. I was in my tent the whole morning, waiting."

187

A young German began to scrub himself with ashame[d] arrogance.

"If we didn't force them to take baths, they'd rot to death[,]" Collier remarked, watching the lad.

Gallagher, however, could not take his mind off the rebe[l]lious strike of the previous day. "I t'ought we had it there f[or] a minute, yesterday."

Collier turned to him with a look of commiseration. "I[t] true, I nearly lost my head drawing my revolver like that. [A]s soon as I'd done it I regretted the whole thing."

"They weren't exactly organized, were they?" the Irishma[n] reflected.

"That's what I'd suddenly realized. They must have simp[ly] decided on the spot—there was clearly no premeditation."

They watched the young German get down from the wago[n.] He refused the set of clean clothes held out to him by one [of] the guards. Instead, he walked over to the basket where he ha[d] deposited his rags and rummaged through the filth until [he] found a still-usable outfit. Thus, he covered his nakedness.

"Will you look at that miserable bastard," Collier grunte[d,] "not even the dignity to take a clean change of clothes. [He] prefers those filthy rags."

"A new set o' clean rags 'ud cost the fella five *libras*. Th[at] 'ud be twenty *libras* fer one month. That's quite a jingle."

"Good God, Thomas, don't start in on me with your Iris[h] mathematics! I'd pay a *hundred libras* if it meant I could chang[e] my clothes just twice a day in this infernal heat. . . ."

Gallagher remained silent. He knew full well that the E[n]glish engineer, who earned a salary fifty times greater than th[at] of any other worker, could hardly grasp the meaning of th[e] gesture of revolt on the part of the youthful German. To Collie[r] the results of such wretchedness were merely repellent.

After lunch, Collier and Gallagher dragged their canva[s] chairs over to the huge patch of shade where Joe Caripuna wa[s] already asleep in his hammock. Three tremendous-looking ing[á] trees spread their shadowy circle of branches that the sun faile[d] to penetrate. There they could sit placidly together. The e[n]gineer, using a sheet of heavy paper, fanned away the hea[t.] Gallagher had stretched out, dozing off almost as soon as h[is] bottom hit the chair. A few cooks and their kitchen help we[re] clearing the lunch tables, collecting dirty plates and dismantlin[g]

188

the makeshift awning that had been set up for the handful of professionals. The glare from the sun beyond the trees considerably accentuated the shadows on the ground, and the sprinkling of men still walking about seemed to be making the effort out of pure daring. A few squalid dogs were snarling over the remains of the repast, and the relentless heat produced to the eye an oven of tremulant forest beneath the mutilating but perfectly transparent curtain of humidity, now evaporating. Bit by bit Stephan Collier also succumbed to the heat, and the hand with which he had been fanning himself finally loosed the cardboard sheet, which finally flopped from the chair to the ground. Our engineer was at last subdued by an overpowering sleep that not even the swelter seemed to affect. Yet peace had little chance in a place like the Abunã, and pathetic scenes such as a sleeping Collier were fleeting at best. Eventually, security guards appeared—uneasy, staring at each other, surrounding the engineer, uncertain as to whether they should awaken him. But Collier, always a light sleeper and accustomed to the necessity of a ready response to anything, awakened suddenly, rubbing his eyes and staring questioningly up at the guards. The one in charge, with the imposing whiskers, finally stepped forward:

"Señor, the Germans have fled. . . ."

"Fled? It's not possible!" Of all things, Collier had not expected this. He refused to believe it. "No one runs away from here!"

"They ran off, señor. We don't know where they went but they're no longer anywhere in the camp."

"They must be around, they've got to be somewhere! Keep looking. . . ."

"I tell you, señor, they've vanished."

The engineer stood up, visibly constrained.

"They can't be very far, they know nothing about these parts. They haven't the faintest notion of how to travel in the jungle."

The beleaguered *jefe* of the guards wiped his mustache, then his forehead. "They have taken the doctor with them, señor."

"Finnegan! Gone off with that rabble? I can't believe that he's taken it into his head to defend the downtrodden!"

"I do not think so, señor. He was taken by force. The Bolivian girl as well. We naturally checked the infirmary; it has been plundered totally. By the look of it there must have been a terrible struggle. Everything has been overturned."

"And the medics?"

"Dead."

The engineer scratched his chin. It was turning out to be quite a Sunday.

"Dead, you say . . . All of them?"

"The bodies are still there in the infirmary."

"What could they possibly want with Finnegan and the girl?"

"I have no idea, señor."

"God be with that girl. . . ."

The Spaniard nodded his head.

"Let's have another look at the infirmary," Collier said finally.

The Caripuna began to babble something and Collier turned to him briefly. "Don't be worried, we'll straighten this mess out."

But the engineer was hardly sure of that. The Germans were bloody well disposed to anything and might easily slaughter the doctor and the Bolivian. He looked at the Caripuna and surmised that once again the Indian had escaped certain death. If he had been in the infirmary, by God, they would certainly have murdered him! Those Germans still bore a furious grudge against him. Collier kicked Thomas Gallagher awake and told him to stay with the Indian. Then he stalked off with the security guards.

The interior of the infirmary seemed to have been hit by a cyclone. Furniture, papers, everything was scattered over the room. Hanging from a crossbeam in the ceiling were the two medics, necks broken and expressions of indescribable suffering etched into their faces. Just below each body, the accumulation of feces released when the sphincter muscles had relaxed in the final seconds. The medicine locker had been broken into and looted of practically everything, including toxic substances and poisons that had been kept in a special compartment. The Barbadian Jonathan was sitting on the overturned locker.

"Okay, Jonathan, what happened?"

"Nothin', Copm Collier."

"Nothing? Come on, Jonathan, I know you well enough, what happened?"

190

"It were all dem Germans...."

"I know that much already."

"Doct' Finn'gan were still alive."

"And Consuelo?"

"It look so...."

"How do you know?"

"I sees de whole thing, coptin. The Germans, dey tie dem up and corry dem off with dem."

"What else?"

"I were right here in dis infirmary when de whole thing unravel, mon," Jonathan slowly confessed, raising his head little by little from the furtive posture he had assumed from the beginning. "I tellin' you, I come here with de Germans."

"You?"

"I knowed since last night dey goin' run off today, right after lunch. Dey also thief de storehouse. They go here to thief some medicine. Only thing dey wants was dat quinine, but Doct' Finn'gan say no way. Dat put dem furious and dey decides to corry off de doctor and de lady. Dey think Finn'gan and de lady make two good hostages, case de comp'ny tries and do somethin'."

Stephan Collier stood there listening, nauseated by Jonathan's confession.

"I very glad to go with dem Germans," the Barbadian continued. "I were de one to saddle and load de mules. Just so long's dey take me. But dey dump me on my black arse. Dey says dey won't have no niggers with dere likes. Dey leff me here, Copm Collier, dey frig me good. I ain't take it here no more, coptin. They could had put me up dere on a rope with dem other boys, dey could had hung dis old bones with de rest of dem and I b'lieve I be a hoppier mon by dis hour."

"You're a damn fool, Jonathan. If you wanted to leave, you didn't have to do it this way."

"That does beat me, mon. How'm I s'pose to knows what way when you see de sort of place it comin' now. You 'member any door goin' take me out of dis hellhole, coptin? Each day passes is a real mystery to me. I finish with dis arseness! What dis comp'ny payin' ain't worth dry spit! The onliest thing dem Germans ask for is a little less hard farin's, and you go grobbin' you gun!"

Collier flushed and turned his head away slightly.

"If de coptin go scromblin' for guns, what dem others goin' do? I say, Jonathan, you might's well put in with dem Germans. I go have to 'scape with dem or I go be dead dead."

"Well, you're finished now, Jonathan. You have no idea of the mess you've fallen into."

"Nobody ain't have to tell me, Copm Collier. I ain't have any luck for long time, coptin, maybe since I was born."

It was almost four o'clock in the afternoon; it would soon be getting dark. The night would prevent any effective pursuit; the patrols would risk an ambush. The apathy of the engineer was like the last distant flickers of a thunderstorm out on the horizon. His sigh filled the air with an impalpable vapor of anxiety and defeat. He nodded to the guards and motioned them to take the Barbadian away.

"All work here in the Abunã is suspended indefinitely! Tomorrow we pack up and head back to Porto Velho." All the presumption had been drained from the engineer's voice and he was now, as ever, an old man displaced in time. "Just when we were managing to overcome all the bloody delays..."

A tiny fraction of this timeless inferno had been breached, it was true, but the inferno itself stood indestructible. Out of place in time, none of the men on the Abunã could imagine that Collier's eyes were moist with tears.

BOOK III

Someday We'll Probably Laugh at All This

It was close to eleven o'clock at night when a small vessel pulled alongside the Panamanian freighter that had been anchored for the past two weeks at Quay Pharoux. The small vessel belonged to the Brazilian customs fleet in Rio de Janeiro and carried twenty armed men on board. Hardly had it pulled up to the enormous iron hull of the cargo ship when a man shouted through a megaphone that the ship's ladder should be lowered and that it was a matter of a routine inspection. On the rail of the afterdeck appeared the figures of the sleepy-eyed captain and some sailors. All very surprised, they obeyed the order nevertheless without resisting. The ladder was lowered and the officials boarded ship, the silence of the harbor night broken by their footfalls on the wooden rungs. When they finally reached the bridge, the same man who had given orders on the megaphone presented himself to the captain and informed him of their purpose there. The captain nodded his head in assent and the man ordered his subordinates to go over the ship with a fine-tooth comb. The operation, however, lasted less than half an hour and the small craft immediately put off for shore again, carrying a woman on board.

Once the craft had docked, the woman was placed in a victoria that trotted off into the night. The woman looked to be rather dazed, hugging her valise of clothes, seated between two gentlemen. The victoria juddered through the deserted streets in the direction of the São Cristóvão district. To the extent that the carriage approached its destination the woman began to present signs of growing uneasiness, but neither of her attendants uttered a word to her. The horses trotted on, the coach rocked, and the woman was jostled against one man and the other, though she made every effort to avoid this.

Locked behind a sternly dismayed expression, J. J. Seabra's happiness struggled to be released. How could he have suspected that his powerful enemies would act with such inexpertise, piling up error after error, leaving such clear tracks that one would almost think they were on purpose. He could not give vent to his happiness, however, because though he would soon have his mistress back, she must still be dealt an exemplary punishment. The fidelity she had mustered at the last moment in no way compensated for the fact of her having consorted with his enemies behind his back. She had let herself be seduced, thinking she might exercise some power over him— she was a shrewd woman, but not sufficiently shrewd to alter one iota of his existence. The incident had been instructive and now Seabra was about to administer the necessary corrective.

No, she was not the first mistress and she would not be the last. J.J. still loved his wife, it was true, but the relationship that remained between them was rather sad and lacking in fantasies. The years of marriage had elapsed in direct proportion to the lack of savor that had matured to tedium. His spouse, with her very practical approach to life, had methodically reduced their encounters to merely epidermal contacts which for him were hopelessly insufficient. J.J. also knew that many of his friends' wives, imprisoned by their marriages, had acquired lovers. His wife, never. She was too proud a woman, and, in the logic of her thinking, to seek out another male was akin to begging for some lowly succor; and help was something she would never seek from anyone because she thought of herself as above anyone there was to ask. And so his wife was slowly growing old, withering into a pinched cruelty that left Seabra both fascinated and reassured. Yes, the women that he had— his mistresses—were only women. And the one who was soon to be in his presence was nothing more.

Seabra began to remember how he had met her. It had been the beginning of the year, when he was visiting the site of some drainage projects in the Mata Cavalos district. He had noticed a young woman passing by, almost a little girl, with chestnut flowing hair and white skin that was burning in the morning sun with a temperature he admired in women. J.J. imagined how rapidly her heart must be beating under the heat of that sun, and he was seized with a desire to feel her pulse, to put his ear to her breast and indulge himself in that wondrous pit-a-pat that was a heart beating out its spasmodic, vital rhythm. The girl was walking, almost skipping along with a package under her arm. She entered a filthy-looking cheap saloon and he finally decided to do the same—with his entire entourage, for a tonic water. The saloon was too beggarly to have any; its regular customers were contented enough with cheap brandy and hard rum, the only beverages available. The atmosphere was repellent: a perennially filthy wooden counter was all, with no place for a customer to sit down. Well, it was hardly an appropriate setting in which to waste one's time savoring something, in any case. The girl was no longer there when he entered with his retinue. There was only the Portuguese immigrant, flustered and flying about because he saw his establishment suddenly being visited by clean, respectable gentlemen—a far cry from the habitual roustabouts and manual laborers who sipped their alcohol in the smoky shadows of the night. Seabra wasted no time and demanded an immediate investigation with respect to the girl. He had soon learned everything there was to know about her. It would not be difficult to arrange a meeting.

Their first rendezvous together had taken place that very same week. Her parents gave little importance to the whereabouts of their daughter; they were too wretched to realize that she was already growing up and beginning to feel the world descending upon her—a life without prospect—like the mountain of garbage in the inner courtyard of the tenement where she lived. Seabra simply called for her one morning and they took a ride through Boa Vista Park. She was obviously delighted to be sitting there in his victoria, yet from the beginning had also exhibited a captivating reserve—she was in no way silly for her age—regardless of her worn and baggy dress which had obviously belonged to someone much older, probably her mother. When he finally touched her, trying to listen to her heart, he could feel how she was trembling. Suddenly the inert warmth of her had taken on a different quality and he knew there would be no problem: she was his.

The house at São Cristóvão had belonged to a crony of his, from Pernambuco—a sickly fellow whose move to Rio dated back to Imperial days. Their first weeks together there were of such luminescence, as they passionately discovered each other, that her life took on a refulgent complexity which she had never suspected even to exist: expensive dresses, strange menus, baroque jewels, and reclusion in a cloud of perfume that positively transformed her until she metamorphosed into a woman who moaned aloud while her lover took his pleasure.

197

At the same time, she became a female who looked for new justifications. She acquired a higher level of ambition. She was being corrupted, and in the process she began to confuse acceptance with virtue. It was at this juncture that there appeared the emissaries of the American with the black hair and the caresses moistened with saliva whose whispered promises, like skylights, opened thrilling new perspectives. With her seclusion now broken by the intrusion of the American, she not only had everything she could want but had excitement as well: she was even carrying on a private life of her own; she was no longer exclusively her powerful lover's property. She felt no guilt—she adored the mystery of it all, and within the perfumed cloud of the world she inhabited she felt highly flattered. Until fear intervened and she stumbled: the American wanted to play for higher stakes with her but she was ill-prepared to go as far as that sinister Quaker had in mind. She thought of escaping, of running alway, but the cloud suddenly thickened, darkly this time, and she became the prisoner of her own nightmare. In the cabin where she was kept prisoner after rejecting the offers of the American, she was truly terrified and wished she could throw her impudence into the sea—drown her former rebellion!—but no, now she had lost all pride and was nothing more than a frightened woman. No one would forgive her! The victoria rolled to a halt in front of the house in São Cristóvão. A light burned in the living room. She walked mechanically up the steps, one hand primping her hair. Inside, her lover had heard the carriage pull up and the horses pawing the pavement. Seated in the living room in a comfortable chair, Seabra waited.

His mistress entered, displaying a hauteur she did not possess—a false confidence she hoped to pass off as an implicit sign of suffering. Such armoring disintegrated completely once she felt the glacial stare of J. J. Seabra. She threw herself upon her lover who had risen to meet her and was instantly repelled by a violent hand that hurled her against the door. She remained cringing against the wall in shock, staring at her lover, praying that the tears would somehow flow from her eyes. She believed that men respected feminine tears, but the tears would not come—she was alone and could not cry.

J.J. leaped at her and delivered a heavy slap. She spun about at the dry noise of its impact but did not fall.

198

"You whoring bitch!" Seabra growled.

When he attempted to repeat the dose, she instinctively dodged the blow, though she remained where she stood. Seabra's hand cut through the air in futility, and his mistress felt the smell of hatred emanating from his frustration.

"It wasn't my fault," she moaned in a weak voice.

"I don't want to hear anything from you . . . shut up!" he hissed at her.

"But I must talk with you," she ventured, with the excitement rising in her voice as she gathered her courage, though she had not the least idea of its source, "you need to hear me out."

"You're all alike," he muttered in disgust, for he saw how quickly she had shed her fear and that was too much to bear. There he was, brimming with hatred and this, this woman was ballooning with courage right before his eyes!

"I didn't betray you! It could have been worse. . . ."

She was right, of course. It had been a semi-betrayal, and the truth of it had somehow softened his rage, though not entirely. His mistress stood there, staring at him, and there was something disdainful now in her demeanor. Seabra was at a crossroads.

"I'm tired," she said finally, untensing her body and tentatively relaxing.

"How many times did the two of you meet?"

"I had nothing to do with him," she said feebly.

"How many times!"

She shivered and felt her face burn: she was blushingly ashamed.

"Only twice," she begged sadly.

"You filthy whore . . ."

"It was nothing."

"You rotten tart . . ." There was stubborn hatred mounting in his voice.

"He never even told me what he actually wanted. . . ."

"I have a mind to tan the hide off you."

"He forced me!"

"Because you allowed him to."

She lowered her head but the tears refused to come. Seabra's feeling of humiliation cried out for vengeance and he wanted to smash that proud face. He went to work on her. Something made his mistress slow to react, as if she strangely did not want to escape from the violence that was raining down upon her. His heavy man's hand rose and fell, methodically whacking her face. There was a certain lassitude on his part as well: a meticulous doling out of punishment, like the blows of a patient sculptor carefully disfiguring a piece of his work. Her countenance swelled: her lips were split, the eyes were virtually sealed behind the twin puffs of swollen eyelids, and the cheeks of her face seemed to want to leap off and stick to his hand. But she did not cry; she stood unyieldingly—a few times her knees buckled under the blows, but she refused to collapse. J.J. was exhausted. His hand also burned and was swelling. His mistress's face had become a red and violet debacle.

That night our Seabra enjoyed the sleep of the just. At his side there snored a dull and subservient wife. The world seemed back on its proper axis and happiness about to resurface once again, wiping the slate of life clean of all marks of its former severity. The only thing J.J. might have done better to remember was how easy it all had been, but he hardly wished to dwell on the subject. After all, now that he had his mistress back in hand, who could threaten him?

Percival Farquhar had left the Ministry of Justice in a state of shock. Rivadávia Correa was bent on demonstrating his power and his threats had to be taken seriously. Then when Seabra had called to harangue and insult him, Percival began to feel a bit more secure. Yet he urgently needed to change techniques; he positively did not take to violence. Farquhar had already been apprised that it was not politic to attempt violence with the dominant class—in Brazil, the powerful had long been accustomed to staying on top through violent application, so they knew precisely how to react. After J. J. Seabra had slammed down the telephone, Percival sought to redirect his thoughts. In a certain sense he was alone: his closest collaborators had prudently withdrawn to a safe distance at his own express orders. They must not be implicated if matters ran amuck. Farquhar was like that: preferring to assume open responsibility for the actions and consequences of all he conceived. It was one of the ways he had earned the admiration of those with whom he habitually surrounded himself. His lofty highbinding required absolute fealty, which only he himself could provide. His thoughts were difficult to organize at such a time; the recent violence had partially obstructed the fluidity of his reasoning powers. For no other reason—he urgently needed to transform the very rules of the game!—Percival Farquhar went out to find his friend, the lawyer Ruy Barbosa.

Wholly aloof from contemporary events, Barbosa was nevertheless hardly surprised by what he told him. Farquhar hid nothing of the essentials from his adviser, as together they sifted out details. The lawyer grew positively enthusiastic, although initially he had been irritated at the audacity of his enemy Seabra. To recognize that Seabra had shown perspicacity and wisdom was a rueful pill for the old advocate to swallow. Yet his own intelligence, long attuned to discerning improbable points of connection or contradictory juxtapositions, happily outpaced his petty hatreds and personal prejudices. This was precisely what Percival admired most in Ruy, especially when the cynicism of the lawyer's conclusions would emerge dressed in such exemplary, rhetorical pomp.

Barbosa was in his malicious glory, his recent ostracism had turned out to be agreeable to his nature, sugarcoating his otherwise poisonous sophistry. After their painstaking examination of the configuration of recent events, Ruy ordered tea to be served while he still ruminated on what he had just heard.

"And his mistress?" he finally asked with a grin of satisfaction that caused his mustache to dance, "how was she?"

Farquhar, who had been waiting expectantly, answered with a dry disappointment: "Very likable."

"Very?"

"Very. An extraordinary woman."

"He likes attractive women; it's part of his vanity."

"She would make any man vain."

"I can believe it. A pity how Seabra can confuse things."

"Confuse things? What?"

"Everything. He thinks that by frequenting beautiful women he can cultivate his own vanity. That's rather asinine, don't you think?"

It was not a subject to interest Farquhar and he shrugged his shoulders. The lawyer comprehended the indifference of his friend and became serious now, holding his cup of tea by the handle with two arched, slender fingers that like a pair of white snails slowly raised the beverage to his lips.

"But do you understand my position, Ruy?" Percival remonstrated, dashing the cup back into the saucer because the tea had gotten cold. "Seabra is no laughing matter. He sent his toughs over to beat the daylights out of poor Adams and then managed to convince the minister of justice, that Rivadávia fellow, that I was the one who ordered them to do it!"

"I wouldn't pay much attention to Rivadávia Correa—in the first place, he's a total idiot."

"Yes, but a powerful idiot who can give me quite a headache if he puts his mind to it."

"And your Adams Mackenwieks? How is he faring?"

"He'll be okay, the blockhead. Just a little battered up, that's all."

"I take it you don't like him anymore."

"You might say I've lost confidence in him. He was too easy a target, which showed how careless he had gotten."

"Oh, he's a decent fellow and he'll learn."

But Percival had the impression of having acted too impulsively in front of Ruy Barbosa and the sensation was a bitter one for his own sense of pride.

"In any case," Barbosa asked, deftly changing the subject, "have you decided on your next move?"

"Not exactly, but I intend to avoid any further violence."

"Quite correct of you, Percy."

"The problem is that as long as Seabra's mistress is still in my hands anything can happen."

"Who was it suggested kidnapping the girl in the first place?"

"Well, originally I was the one who got in contact with her—very intimate contact, if you get my gist."

The lawyer could not help but smile at the thought of Seabra's mistress spreading her legs to Farquhar without the minister's having a clue.

"She was clearly a woman and then some," Farquhar continued. "In our last encounter she seemed to have agreed to urge Seabra to approach us. I told her that I intended to take the minister and his retinue to Porto Velho, for a visit to the railway under construction there. It promised to be quite a trip, of course, and I think she began dreaming of higher stakes, suddenly imagining herself strolling arm in arm with her precious J.J., inspecting the construction site. After all, she had thrown in with me for the pure adventure of it; she never asked for money."

"Of course, her J.J. is already rich."

"Yes, he's rich; I know. But money doesn't seem to concern her. She'd come to me because she thought it would give her pleasure. But when I sent for her to leave Seabra, she refused. Colonel Agostinho went out and found some men, and they brought her away by force."

"Were they the colonel's own men?"

"Two ex-soldiers. He gave them orders to bring her to me one way or another. They dragged her out of the house and brought her to a warehouse of mine on the Rua da Alfândega. It was a surprise to me, I must say. I managed to relocate the girl on one of my ships anchored in the harbor with a load of equipment still on board. She's still there. She refused to col- laborate. She won't even eat her meals."

"What fidelity."

Barbosa had said it the way one might say, "What a com- edy."

"Seabra must have lost his head when he discovered the woman was no longer in the house," Farquhar continued dispir- itedly. "The same night he ordered the assault on Adams. Colonel Agostinho swore to me they were Seabra's men."

"I didn't realize that Colonel Agostinho had so little liking for Seabra," Barbosa confessed, delighted at the discovery.

"He detests the man and for rather stupid reasons: he claims that his promotion has never come through because of a con- spiracy of some kind in which the minister has played a prin- cipal part."

"Fascinating. What a pity the colonel is such an ass. I got to know him personally while I was in Europe. He was serving as military attaché to some Brazilian embassy. He's rather affected, I would say even repellent. Full of pretentions! It seems that he went to officers-training school in France and fancies himself the supreme authority on military matters here in Brazil. Nothing more than a bungling fool, of course, though certainly the type whom another bungler—someone like da Fonseca, for instance—would inevitably turn to.

"It's true, the marshal seems to be crazy about him; the colonel's on intimate terms with old da Fonseca."

"When you told me that you were going to place Colonel

Agostinho in charge of the affair, I remained silent, but you must have imagined I did not entirely approve of the idea. Are you quite sure that he's a man to be trusted?"

"He's helped us enormously and now he's going to help us even more."

"I don't know how much help he is, engendering Boeotian situations with Seabra."

"He's just a bit impetuous, that's all."

"That might be, but he ruined a perfectly good plan. We might have obtained a judgment against Seabra. The parents of the girl should certainly have been convinced to take him to court, whereupon their daughter could testify how he had seduced and degraded her. A scandal would ensue; the minister, ruined. But his mistress can no longer serve any such purpose."

"She's nothing but a hindrance now. Even more so were she to be found on a vessel chartered by one of my companies."

The lawyer suddenly looked up at Farquhar, then continued to stare at his Quaker friend.

"But she *should* be found by Seabra, and on that very ship," Barbosa announced triumphantly. "We must give him all the evidence against you."

"What are you getting at?" Percival asked in perplexity.

The lawyer became vexed. "I don't choose my words idly, Percy. What I meant to say was what you understood me to say. Nothing less, nothing more."

"That's like feeding myself to the dogs! Seabra would have me right where he wants me and he could play with me like a toy."

"Seabra's games are far smaller than yours, Percy."

"So much the worse, you're asking me to descend to his level, Ruy."

"Quite the contrary . . ."

"I'm not sure I follow what you're getting at. . . ."

Ruy Barbosa looked at him with a smile, but Farquhar hardly troubled himself now about appearing rather pathetic before this diminutive man who resembled more a talking worm.

"Look, Percy, from what I can understand you wish to have done with all the violence—isn't that right?"

"Exactly, I don't like it. It doesn't agree with me."

"I couldn't concur with you more, but unhappily for us it

204

is still the method of the mediocre minds who continue to govern us."

"But I'm hardly ready to give up."

"You needn't, you're going to win, although Seabra doesn't know it."

Percival Farquhar leaned forward on the edge of his chair, eyeballing Barbosa as if he intended nothing less than to pluck each word from those pursed lips at the moment of their ripest articulation.

"He must find an easy trail that leads him straight to the girl," Barbosa explained. "Easy, but not obvious. Seabra is stupid, all right, but sometimes his country-bumpkinly intuitions serve him well. His thugs will pick up the girl and he will have every possible proof of the fact that it really was you who perpetrated the sequestration of his mistress in order to pressure him. He'll hardly be able to contain himself, from sheer vanity. He'll imagine himself to be quite the minister— attracting such powerful interests as yours—and he'll try to blackmail you. You will allow him to threaten you, of course, even to take your money. You will buy him while he imagines himself to be extorting from you. By the time he discovers the truth, Percy, he will have so compromised himself that there'll be no turning back for J. J. Seabra."

Percival Farquhar was once again fascinated by his dwarfish advocate, whose plan would run as smoothly as a pocket watch. His only question was whether Seabra, a wealthy man, would let himself be bought so easily. It hardly occurred to Percival Farquhar that he himself was one of the richest men in the world and that, in comparison to his own wealth, Seabra's was little more than that of a man modestly well off. Most modestly, indeed.

12

Under different circumstances he would have vomited. The odor of rancid fat penetrated his nostrils, clawing its way to his insides and leaving a bitter taste in the back of his gullet. The position in which he found himself was also beginning to play havoc with his circulation: his limbs were starting to grow heavy and tingle; he no longer had feeling in his toes beyond the disagreeable cold that had enveloped and sensitized his toenails. Richard Finnegan was a prisoner of the renegade Germans and felt himself hanging on the edge of obliteration, rocking from one side to the other inside one of two hogsheads strapped in tandem across the back of a mule, tied up, with no possibility of escape. The ropes bound his hands to his legs, obliging him to remain seated in a single position. On the other side of the same mule, in another hogshead emptied of its lard, the Bolivian girl was being transported in more-or-less identical fashion. Finnegan strained to listen for some sign that might indicate Consuelo's condition; he could not call out because they had also gagged him. There had been moans in the first few minutes—she had struggled more than he—but by now all was sinisterly calm, and the mule padded his way through the rain forest with none of the initial alarm at so strange and rebellious a charge.

The horde of desperate men who were cleaving their way through the perilously swampy forest of the Abunã had as their leader a short, stocky youth with wild dark hair. His name was Günter, but everyone knew him as the Moor. He had no vocation for leadership but circumstances had propelled him to the forefront of his companions. He was alert but fairly perplexed at the moment, although he did not feel afraid. In truth, he was incapable of being afraid. At twenty-five, he felt already old and without hope. Nevertheless, he was among them all the one who was the most obsessed with the idea of escape, and this had turned him into a leader.

The Moor had been born in Hamburg, virtually on the docks,

where he grew up to become a stevedore. His mother was a streetwalker who flitted from one cabaret to another, climbing into bed each night with any man who would pay her a trifle and returning home every morning at dawn drunken and crumpled up like an old sack. As far back as he could remember she had always worked as a harbor slut, a skinny whore with her sagging, shriveled breasts forever peeking out of the filthy clothes she would wear around the house. House? A rubbish-filled cubicle on the outskirts of the port of Hamburg. She had not been born in Hamburg, but where she had come from or how she had become a prostitute he had no idea. Even her age was a mystery because she had always seemed so old to him in the light of day, then so young when night fell and she would emerge painted and smiling. For all he knew she was still making the rounds of the cabarets in the city, hanging on the necks of sailors, fornicating with drifters from the far-flung continents of the globe. She used to boast that at least her cunt was international, and her laughter had filled him with repugnance. He had never known his father and suspected that neither did she have the least idea of who had sired him with a hurried bolt of sperm in some chance encounter. Günter more or less suspected that the stories she told him regarding his father were no more than the mindless fantasies of a broken-down whore. They always began with a Turkish officer—an admiral or a general, the rank did not matter so long as it was sufficiently high—and were related with tenderness or rancor depending upon the state of her spirits at the time. This man without a face—with only his sperm—had made wonderful promises to her; they were passionately in love, but then one day he had disappeared. He was never seen again. She grew desperate. He had left her pregnant and she began to lose customers. She had never actually worked in a house of prostitution—she detested the idea as a form of imprisonment—preferring the risky, less lucrative whoring on the streets; picking up clients in the doorways of dance halls and cabarets, leading them into dark alleyways or vacant lots. When her pregnancy finally prevented her from going out at all, she took refuge in the charity ward of a hospital and there he was born. Günter was raised in the cubicles and bedrooms of his mother's profession, sullen and aloof, his mother as his only companion, until at the age of fifteen he found himself in serious trouble, implicated in the delivery of a shipment of opium. Günter was sent to a reformatory, where he suffered a year and a half of violent discipline. Finally, he had managed to escape and, since the institutional authorities only concerned themselves with those unfortunate enough to remain in their care, Günter was never given a second thought, returning to the docks of Hamburg, though not in his mother's care. From time to time he ran across her, on some street or other, where she would shed a few tears and avoid the subject of his moving back in with her. But Günter already understood that he must live by his own wits—the fact of that woman's having given birth to him was incidental, as fortuitous as her having picked up a Turkish officer rather than anyone else in the first place.

Now he wondered if this desire he felt to flee from the Abunã—potent as the desire that had led him to escape from the reformatory, and later from other varieties of prisons—was not a legacy of the abhorrence his mother had always felt for the cloistered tenor of all bordellos. On the Abunã, the ambience of the bordello was perceptible: they were clearly no better than prostitutes, with the added aggravation of never fucking, only abusing their strength in exchange for paltry sums of money. Still, Günter was not a man in revolt; he had no clear perspective on life and no intentions. The only thing he had on his mind was escaping, freeing himself of the prostitution of the Abunã, eluding the snares of the company, never again picking up a sledgehammer to pound a spike through a sleeper on a railway that defied comprehension. Günter had never been able to puzzle out anything remotely resembling a scheme in life, because the future had always been a closed door to him—more and more closed, less and less accessible.

The wave of unemployment that swept through the port of Hamburg, in 1909, had filled the streets. Strikes were barbarously suppressed by police; numbers were killed when soldiers opened fire on the crowds. Hundreds of honest workers began to commit petty thefts like picking pockets, spurred on in their wretchedness by hunger and desperation. In that same year a group of North Americans visited the harbor and its vicinity, inviting laborers to come work in America. Multitudes had already gone to America and amassed oceans of money. America mesmerized one and all, and soon the contractors had signed up four hundred men ready to embark. Among those four

ndred misguided dreamers was Günter, the Moor, who
arded the fragile-looking freighter that proved to rock on
en the calmest of seas and seemed ready to split in half
henever the waters got choppy. Yet America was more than
e continent and it seemed that none of the men—at the
oment of signing their contracts—had bothered to inquire as
where, exactly, in America they were going to work. Not
ving been asked, the North Americans had said nothing.
nce again, destiny was making a fool out of Günter. It was
t New York they were heading for as, fifteen days later, they
ossed the equator and the ocean phosphoresced to a different
imate. Twenty days later, they dropped anchor in the harbor
Belém, in Brazil, and the majority of men realized they had
en double-crossed. This was no America of their dreams:
is was an inferno! Twenty men tried to jump ship but were
prehended before they reached shore. They suffered the cruel-
t retributions: imprisoned in the scalding hold, with no food,
ith no air to breathe. They were even rumored to have been
rtured (Günter could not swear to it; no one could) but what
as certain was that eighteen had died and were buried in
elém. The German consul came aboard but did not speak
rectly with any of his countrymen; he limited himself to an
amination of the employment contracts presented to him by
e North American agents. As documents, they were in order,
d the consul was never seen again. Even the most rebellious
til then now began to submit; and Günter waited, without
riosity, to see how Porto Velho—the ultimate destination—
ight turn out to be. Those still left with a capacity for hopes
d dreams now fixed them on the same place. Günter remained
oof—trusting in no one, he had no use for the others on
ard.

Yet here he was, cutting through the jungle, leading this
nd of raggle-taggle refugees scraped up from the port of
amburg. He knew all those anxious faces and comprehended
e aspirations of each one of them. Their destiny lay in his
nds like a cruel irony, but he hardly gave a damn for the
ct—he only wanted to escape. And now even flight was
oving impossible: the jungle grew dense; lianas embroidered
to the trees proved tough as iron and impervious to machetes;
xuriant clusters of flowers fell from the crown of towering
lm trees, insulting with such staggering beauty the anguished

209

path of the fugitives. The striated wall of green vegetati[on]
wrested their strength from them, and the darkness grew wi[th]
the intensity of their exhaustion. The jungle offered no excu[se]
for life; it was simply another prison. The miasmic humidi[ty]
split the rotted trunks and the sounds of a teeming vegetal li[fe]
ruptured by fugitive footfalls added a dying echo to the alrea[dy]
futile effort to hack a path through the dense, millenial bed [of]
rotted, damp humus. Günter and his companions neverthele[ss]
persevered, with varying success, sloshing through the gre[en]
waste, with a spontaneous, often illogical decisiveness bo[r]-
dering on a madness that only their thirst for liberation cou[ld]
have allowed and increasingly confounded by the chilled r[e]-
verberations of the night that was rapidly closing in upon the[m]
with a lugubrious resonance. Palm trees and lianas; chestnu[t,]
rubber, mahogany, and hibiscus; bushes, giant ferns, and cree[p]-
ers leaped up in sudden flashes from mercurial drops of de[w.]
Günter refused to look to either side because the whole disord[er]
of the forest brought to mind his own confusion. Like himse[lf,]
the jungle seemed not to have any purpose; and through h[is]
soul ran the most contradictory reflections. Only the darkne[ss]
itself reigned over the path they were cutting, and the featur[es]
of each man faded into the shadows like washed-out silhouett[es]
in perpetual motion. Their watery eyes burned as—Indian file—
they advanced along the rough-hewn trail they were scarri[ng]
through the jungle. A single file of men and mules padde[d]
tentatively into the night.

They had managed to steal off with eight beasts of burde[n]
loaded with provisions stowed away in wooden hogshead[s.]
The hogsheads had served as storage containers for grease a[nd]
lard, which made for an intolerable odor, an abominable sten[ch]
that now seemed to these runaways to epitomize the very sti[r]
of the company itself and of all the work on the Abunã.

At the head of the line trudged the team of men charg[ed]
with opening up a trail. Several of these men had alrea[dy]
performed this service for the company and now furiously s[et]
the pace, but the jungle did not permit itself to be penetrat[ed]
so easily. The whole forest resisted, interposing florid and la[cy]
obstacles amazingly impervious to the blows of axes and m[a]-
chetes or yielding only to the additional darkness all aroun[d.]
To counter this lack of light and hopefully continue their fligh[t]
throughout the night, a few of the men began to light kerose[ne]

210

amps, but the resulting illumination proved insufficient—a pale glimmer that scarcely encompassed a ridiculously small circle about each one of the lantern bearers. Meanwhile, the men's restlessness, added to the severity of the trek, had begun to affect the beasts of burden. The mules now followed nervously—their instinct ferreting out the danger—and they complicated the progress of the march by vacillating, by digging their hooves in until a whiplash once again drove them reluctantly forward. The crude trail was actually more like a species of tunnel through which they blindly burrowed their way. A maddening silence guided each one of them, but the silence did not meliorate the anxiety to forge ahead, to wield the ax feverishly against interlocking branches, to tear away lengths of liana vines by hand. Like a herd of cattle, the fugitives tore through the treacherous vegetal symmetry which centuries of violent humidity had multiplied by species almost to the infinite.

Günter followed, a little behind, leading one of the mules by the bridle. He kept an eye as best he could on the frantic efforts of his companions to cleave a trail through the frozen verdure of the rain forest darkened by nightfall. Clouds of insects, meanwhile, flowed over the exposed skin of the Moor. The mules occasionally stumbled and upon their backs the hordes of insects also fell like a rain of grain. The trek had become a maddening trial and error of advances and stalemates, which only compounded the agony of the two prisoners. For Consuelo Campero and Richard Finnegan were being jolted about inside their hogsheads like sides of beef, sliding about in the fetid grease that coated the interiors and transformed twin prisons into dank, penumbral caverns. Consuelo's arms were already manifesting signs of the onslaught of insects and she wanted to die. She had lost weight and the repugnance that she felt for her clothes, thoroughly soiled with lard, gripped her throat like a burning phlegm. Her hands were swollen and purple; they seemed like two bulbous frogs. And from her bruised mouth came indistinct moanings, as a painful indolence seared her brain and scoured her temples. On the other side of the same beast, Richard could not take his mind off her. The mule was stumbling along a few meters more, a few meters more, but had suddenly stopped short in bewilderment; the muscles of its back flickered with nervous shivers, because

211

insects were biting through its hide and sucking its blood. Each shiver produced a jerk of the hogsheads, and Finnegan slid forward, banging his head against the staves, or lurched backward, whacking his spine. The insects were also mired in the grease, where they struggled until they expired, while the captive physician asked himself in desperation where such madness was to take them. The sensation of being irremediably screwed was uppermost in his mind, and his thinking veered toward the maudlin and pathetic. Dr. Finnegan, however, finally began to detest even the pathetic, and in the solitude of his hogshead—rolling and tossing from side to side—he came to abominate his sterile ambition. Perhaps if he had known how to protect Consuelo a little better, she would not now be there beside him, feeding the demented fancies of a gang of desperadoes. Consuelo herself had faced them with courageous defiance; she had struggled, screamed, bitten, while he stood passively observing. Indeed, she had defended his locker of medicines with more alacrity than he had. He was a weakling all right. The snares had long ago been imbedded in his every act. Perfectly defined, he was no more than an imbecile—the imbecile doctor!

Since childhood, that perfect imbecility had lurked within him. Richard Finnegan had grown up totally suffocated by women, surrounded by little girls and housemaids who worshiped him because he was the only male in the house besides his father. Wasn't his favorite prank to hide himself for hours at a time while his sisters and their girlfriends would hunt for him through the house, shouting his name, pleading with him even to let them tag along to his hiding place, in order to sit silently together and experience all sorts of naughty sensations of the flesh? He liked to do that, especially with Nancy, while the others would become excited in turn with what Nancy had to tell them, though their desires were never realized. And wasn't he, in a certain sense, hiding now, although the hiding place made no sense because Nancy could hardly come here to call him; like Consuelo, she was also imprisoned, but forever, in an inaccessible hideaway. His arms and legs—from the immobility imposed by the ropes that bound him—tingled and ached. His tongue was dry and swollen; his teeth hammered; and the pressure of the gag on the corners of his mouth seemed to tighten more and more. But how was Consuelo?

as she still alive? And if the Germans should decide to take
eir pleasure? They were capable of committing any infamy!
nnegan grew more and more afraid of the possibility—what
e positively could not endure was the thought of her being
olated in his presence, and his dread of this was greater even
an his fear of dying.

Günter felt his legs begin to drag with the heaviness of lead.
is strength was giving way to sheer exhaustion. He had lost
l sense of time, and it seemed to him that they had already
en walking for days on end. In reality, however, they had
rely put four hours of flight behind them. The men at the
ad of the line were also showing signs of depletion; there
as an exasperating sluggishness to the manner in which they
ere now hacking out the trail. The successive halts appeared
 grow longer and the progress of their march, shorter and
orter. The mule that Günter led by the bridle was panting as
 possessed, his quivering nostrils contracting and dilating
neath the wan light of a lantern. No one said a word, panting
 well, struggling to move on, to remain on their feet, to
ercome the lassitude that had finally infected even the most
perhuman efforts. The Moor, just like his companions, in
e few hours they had spent in the jungle, appeared to be
rribly marked up. Indeed all their clothes were in tatters and
ost of their bodies exposed. Arms and legs festered with
oody scratches and other inglorious signs of their maddened
ght. Yet worst of all was the exhaustion, stronger and stronger;
d the attempts to overcome it more and more feeble. A new
lt finally awakened Günter from his stupor: two men had
llapsed up ahead, and the others were milling around in torpid
tonishment. Günter dropped the bridle he was holding and
mbered over to the spot. Yes, two men had fallen, overcome
 exhaustion, while the others had finally allowed themselves
 be dominated by inertia, staring at their unconscious com-
nions with somnolent indifference.

"What's going on?" asked a panting Günter, in German.

"We're too tired," sighed an old man with a long beard.

Gunter bent over the prostrate figures to verify whether or
t they were, in fact, still alive. They were: they were sleeping
ke stones. They probably hadn't even fainted but just gone
 sleep, overworked to prostration, nothing more than that.

"They're sleeping," Günter announced to the others.

213

All around there had already gathered a circle of abject silhouettes, avid to follow the example of the two inert figures on the ground.

"We cannot endure any more of this," croaked the bearded old man. "We'll all fall apart."

"Why don't we stop here for a while?" someone suggested.

Günter noticed the hands of one of the men who were stretched out on the ground: raw flesh...

"The hell of it is we are still very near the railroad camp."

"After all we have walked?" asked the bearded old man.

"It's just that we have lost all notion of time," Günter answered despondently. "Actually we have hardly covered more than four kilometers."

The crushing fatigue appeared to be drawing the fugitives back to reality. Their flight had begun to seem an absurdity — even Günter no longer felt sure of what he was doing but refused to vacillate in front of his companions.

"Do you think we're doing the right thing?" speculated the bearded old man.

"We're getting away, aren't we?"

The Moor had responded without much conviction and the old man began to look really frightened. The others were grumbling doubtfully among themselves.

"I suppose we might as well stop here," Günter concluded. "They won't be hunting for us during the night. We can get an early start in the morning."

But Günter's words had convinced no one. The fugitives were gathering around their sleeping companions and the mutterings grew louder.

"Don't let go of the pack animals over there!" Günter shouted. "All the food we have is inside those barrels. If those mules run off we'll really be finished."

The prostrate figure lying closest to Günter's feet now opened his eyes. The poor fellow panicked at the sight of the crowd gathered around him and tried to rise, but his strength failed him and he lay still.

"He's awake," the old-timer remarked. "I figured he was done for."

"I told you already, Gustav," the Moor hissed back at the old man, "they were only asleep."

214

"I'm all right," said the man, opening his eyes again and recognizing his companions.

A burly lad, more or less the same age as Günter, stepped forward and knelt down beside his waking companion. "Feeling better, old fellow?"

"Tomorrow I'll be back in shape," the man assured him.

The lad was of more or less the same stature as the Moor, but for the blond hair flowing back over his shoulders and the tattoo in the form of an anchor on his chest. The lad looked up at Günter.

"He'll be fine by tomorrow."

Günter nodded and stood up. "Let the other one sleep. I think we'll all feel better if we sleep a little."

The lad got up at the same time as the Moor, following him with his stare. "There's only one other thing..."

Günter stopped.

"... that's for the Moor to explain how we are going to get out of this place."

"I don't think I heard you properly," Günter replied ominously.

"You heard right, Moor. I'm asking how you expect us to get out of here."

"By not losing our heads, that's how. Everything is working out so far."

"You call this working out?"

"What did you expect? Don't be a fool, boy. You ought to have realized that this wouldn't be any picnic—this is a savage land!"

"Exactly, Moor, which is why we have no idea how things will turn out."

The lad was clearly speaking for everyone, and Günter, knowing it, felt incensed. He had no wish to be their leader; for his part, he would have preferred to flee alone, without the responsibility of enduring the cowardice of others.

"Well, what's the matter with you, boy? Are you shitting in your pants with fear? Why didn't you stay behind with the English engineer, licking his boots!"

The lad lunged off to regain his composure, eyeing the Moor with rage over his shoulder. He would have liked nothing better than to explode but he was still hoping that Günter really did have a solution.

215

The Moor perceived the lad's dependence upon him—the same as that of the great majority of his fellow fugitives, all of them handing over leadership to him *spinelessly*—and the reflection filled him with repugnance.

"I ought to have known I was dealing with a gang of weaklings," Günter said, scowling at them all. "You ought to be wearing skirts, the lot of you!"

"Listen here, Günter," the bearded old man interjected, "we just want to discuss the thing, to hear how you actually plan to carry out our escape. We only want you to be reasonable with us. . . ."

"I'm not about to be fucking reasonable with any of you! I didn't invite anybody to go running off with me, did I?"

"You told us that you had a plan for escaping," the old man continued serenely. "We were all equally humiliated by what happened on Saturday afternoon—that filthy engineer with his revolver, the only kind of additional pay we would ever see from that company. He left us with nothing, and you had a plan of escape."

"*My* plan, foor me *alone*, Gustav!"

"I know—I think we all understand that. But where one can flee, so can a hundred."

"But a hundred men with courage, not a hundred little whining bastards!"

"You needn't be so aggravated with us."

"But why didn't any of you open your mouths while we were still back in the camp? Before running off like this! Why were all of you silent? Like cows ruminating in the fields at everything I said!"

"We couldn't very well discuss things then; we were being watched. Or have you forgotten how they doubled the guard?"

"Well, now it's too late for questions or comments—there's no time for anything but getting out of here."

The sullen lad walked up to the Moor again. "I'm getting fed up with your yapping, Moor. I'm already up to here with your arrogance," he said swinging a hand, "and so is everyone. You know what I think? You're not about to take us anywhere! You don't really have any plan of escape. The only thing you knew was how to run away from the camp. And you only got that far because the nigger decided to throw in with us. It was

216

his idea to steal the pack animals! You never even would have thought of *that!*"

Gunter stared at the lad with a mixture of defiance and stupefaction.

"You want to know the truth?" the lad asked, turning to the others. "He hasn't got a plan and we're going nowhere."

"It's true," Gustav added fearfully, "we could be walking in circles."

"Our friend the Moor, here," the lad remarked sarcastically, "did not even remember to bring along a compass."

The men were beginning to grumble that they knew nothing of the terrain, that they didn't have a chance, that what they were attempting was completely insane.

"Why don't you save your breath, the lot of you?" Günter scowled. "We still have a lot of ground to cover before reaching the Rio Madeira."

"And just how do we get to the Rio Madeira!" one of them fumed in desperation.

Günter sensed a genuine fear taking hold of them all.

"By continuing north," he said, softening his contempt. "I know that some of you are frightened. I am also afraid, but such fear has nothing in common with behaving like a coward. We're not cowards! We simply couldn't stand it anymore, under those conditions. Meantime, our contracts with the company won't be concluded for another three months. And by then we'd all be dead—if we didn't decide to escape! We'll hit the Rio Madeira, all right, and we'll take it down to Manaus. That is the plan!"

Old Gustav eyed Günter nervously.

"Let's be reasonable, Günter," he finally ventured. "I also agreed to run off. So did we all; no one was forced to go. But perhaps we were all a bit too hotheaded. And maybe now is the time to reconsider things more carefully."

"You think that we should give up? Go back?"

"It's no longer possible to go back to the camp; they would treat us like chattel."

"Then what is there to discuss?"

"How are we supposed to make our way down the Rio Madeira? Swimming? Do you have any idea of the distance we will have to cover to reach Manaus?"

"It's a great distance, obviously, but not impossible."

217

Yet the Moor was already starting to doubt himself whether it was really possible to survive such a trip. Just four kilometers of jungle had already provoked an attitude of surrender among his companions. The months of grueling labor, poor diet, and sheer exhaustion had broken something in them all. They were burned out and they were men on the brink of disaster.

"You still did not answer my question," the old man challenged Günter.

But the Moor simply dropped to the ground, stretched his legs and stared silently at his companions. Soon everybody else had followed his example.

"The only thing to do now is sleep," he concluded.

"How are we supposed to feel like sleeping, Moor, if we still have no idea what we're supposed to do when we get up tomorrow?" It was the same burly blond, although the others were obviously of the same opinion.

"The plan has not been altered in any way. We simply take the barrels and turn them into floats for a raft, once we reach the river."

All were listening to the Moor in silence, waiting for someone else to say something.

"I think it's insane," old Gustav finally remarked. "We could never reach Manaus by simply floating down the Rio Madeira."

"And what do you suggest, old man?"

"We have two prisoners with us, Günter. One of them rather high up on the company payroll. Who knows? Perhaps we could strike a bargain for his safe return."

"Wonderful idea, Gustav. We all know how fond the engineer is of the doctor. I can just imagine what his answer will be—a bullet up the ass!"

"I do not believe he would be so ready to sacrifice the doctor."

"They would sacrifice their own mother," the lad sneered, agreeing this time with Günter.

"Then there's no escape," the old man retorted.

"I know what it is you're after, Gustav," said Günter threateningly. "You want us to go back to the camp—our tails between our legs—whimpering for forgiveness, isn't that it? Go up to the engineer and tell him we've been a couple of bad boys but we've all learned our lesson. Isn't that about the size of it?"

218

The old man reddened as all eyes converged upon him, waiting for a response, any response.

"It could be our salvation, men." The fellow was trembling as he spoke. "I don't feel very certain," he stammered, "that any of us could manage to survive adrift on the Rio Madeira all the way down to Manaus."

The Moor was by now enraged with the servility of this bearded old man who had actually acted as intermediary for the company agents, scouring the docks of Hamburg for the unemployed and then coaxing them to try their luck in America. America! The old bastard had been a foreman on the docks but had lost his job for some obscure reason. So he spent his time ambling from bar to bar, boozing and chiseling, until the wave of unemployed grew into an army of the famished all too eager to sign up with the recruiting agents of the company. Gustav reappeared: well-dressed, sober, and smoking a cigar in the company of North Americans. He was swaggering now, and you nearly had to lick his boots to get him to put your name on the waiting list for departures. And here he was, palavering surrender, in spite of the fact that his patrons had not exactly been benevolent with the old weasel. No, they had put him to work right in with the others whom he had so humiliated, shoveling their way through the Abunã. Our Günter had a mind to jump the old man and tear him to shreds.

The old man, however, thought that Günter was finally relenting; and though he calculated wrongly he had already mustered too much confidence to be able to measure the effect of his words.

"I do not wish to place the blame on anyone," he began, "but we are all beginning to wonder if our flight was really the best solution. Yes, the ease with which we escaped the camp was extremely encouraging. But now we can understand precisely why security was never perfect back there. With this impenetrable wall of jungle all around, there was no need for policing—we were virtual prisoners in any case but were simply ignorant of the fact."

The old man turned now to Günter, as if to gauge the sheer power of what he was about to say.

"Our companion Günter," he continued with a rhetorical nod, "has told us that to be afraid does not make us cowards.

And neither would it be cowardice, in the light of present circumstances, to give up our flight and return to camp."

There was a brief pause as the men listened in silence and Günter grew tense as a steel spring at breaking point.

"We could never hope to reach Manaus on a raft of floating kegs. There are simply too many of us—the weight of five men to each cask, think of it! In addition to which, none of us knows how to navigate down those rivers. On our way here, if you remember, we traveled up the Rio Madeira and you saw what a labyrinth this whole jungle can be. This is no valley of the Rhine—it's a murderous place filled with unforeseen dangers for which we are totally unprepared. Nothing is familiar to us here. It is a journey full of darkness and we're playing it with our lives."

"But we only have to make it past Santo Antônio," the blond lad interjected. "Once we're there we'll find other boats to take us—there are lots of small craft navigating the river from there. Surely someone would help us to get to Manaus."

"It's possible," the old man conceded. "We could be lucky enough to just manage it. But you have to remember that most of the larger boats trafficking on the river belong to the company. The smaller craft used by the natives are only good for three or four people. We would have to commandeer some twenty boats like that in order to carry all of us—that's already begging for too much luck. The most probable thing is for us to be picked up by a ship of the company line and handed back to the English engineer. We still owe three months' work to our bosses. Don't forget, it cost them money to bring us over in the first place."

The arguments of the old man were having their effect. Even the blond lad was nodding his head in agreement, and the rest of the fugitives seemed relieved. The idea of any further trek through the jungle had considerably dampened whatever small self-esteem they might have still possessed. The Moor could barely contain himself, so strong was his hatred for that presumptuous old fool who had more than once betrayed them in the past. If anything, he had grown to behave more and more like a lackey for the bosses. Günter could not get over how he seemed to have purposely fostered the disarray of their frustrated strike, then restrained the men from staging a protest during the Sunday showers and refusing a change of clothing.

220

Only Günter himself had had the courage to spurn clean clothes and return to the basket of filthy discards for a usable set of rags. With every attempt at organization, old Gustav would terrorize his companions over the possible repercussions and thus discourage any nascent revolt on the part of the more belligerent workers. And in any case, Günter's plan had been to flee alone—not to include any of the others.

"If we do go back, what do you think will happen?" the lad asked no one in particular.

The Moor, however, his solitude broken, countered bitterly from where he sat: "Probably nothing to a little yellowbelly ... maybe they'll just pat your bum-bum and powder your armpits."

Furious, the lad made a lunge for the Moor but was restrained by his companions. Günter had not moved.

"We're talking serious matters!" the lad cried out.

"So am I," Günter responded wearily.

Old Gustav was shaking his head disapprovingly at the attitude of the Moor, attempting thereby to gain the confidence of the others. Tension had been growing and there already existed sharp division among the fugitives: some supporting the old man; others, albeit indecisively—because the Moor appeared so uninterested in defending himself—wanting to forge on ahead regardless of how insane the project seemed. The blond lad, in the meantime, had calmed down and Gustav felt he had the decision in hand.

Then Günter spoke: "You, Gustav, have got to be the shrewdest old weasel I ever met...."

The old man did not answer him.

"But I think you have already gotten us into enough muddles. We still have not forgotten the promises you painted when we were back home, looking for work. I never collected commissions from the company for every man they hired. No one here collected such commissions—only you did, Gustav."

"That was different," protested the old man weakly. "Now we are all in the same boat."

"I'm not so sure," Günter smiled.

"Of course we are! After all, I'm here, I came with all of you, I did not stay in the Abunã."

"And who can convince me that this was not exactly what the company desired? Who can prove to me that you did not

221

tell them our plan, that they did not simply close their eyes, saying, 'Let them escape! Leave it to old Gustav to pacify the animals and lead them back like sheep. Then we pay them half of what they were getting because they tried running off and deserve to be punished.'"

The old-timer paled and slammed his fist on his knee.

"This is a lie! They don't know anything! I told them nothing! I was also tricked—all the promises they made me were never kept!"

"But even with that you haven't stopped betraying us—isn't it true!"

"You want to lead us all to our doom, Günter."

"Don't try to change the subject, you old weasel. I asked no one to follow me, I planned my escape alone, I never tried to convince anyone."

The old Gustav's bearded face was aflame with confusion, to which the flickering lanterns added a bilious complexion. His lips began to tremble.

"You always were a troublemaker, Moor. You always set a bad example for the others. . . ."

Günter shrugged his shoulders and leaned back on his elbows, but he was boiling like a teakettle.

". . . I only want you to tell us how we're supposed to navigate along the Rio Madeira squatting in tubs of lard! Perhaps you can guarantee to us that we will arrive at Manaus in possession of our lives."

"What makes you think I'm here to guarantee anything? We are all grown-up enough to take care of ourselves, I hope!"

"This is hardly what I expected from you, Günter. You obviously haven't got a clue how to get out of here—you're gambling in the dark but you want us all to follow your madness."

Günter got up and started pacing among the fugitives, staring at each one in turn. "I want each of you to answer me for yourselves," he began. "Tell me . . . did I invite any of you to follow me? Did I?"

A few of them shook their heads no; the rest of them simply looked down or away.

"*Did I!* . . . well, then I certainly don't need to guarantee anything. I still don't care what any of you have in mind. What I have in mind is to get some sleep and proceed tomorrow

222

morning to the Rio Madeira. Whatever the rest of you do is your own concern. Go back to the fucking camp if you want with this old snake!"

"Stop talking about me as if I were one of your ilk, Moor," the old-timer shouted in a frenzy. "You should have kept your mouth shut from the very beginning! This kind of imbecility could only have originated with a vermin like you."

"Do you smell the stink of him?" Günter asked, turning to the others. "The old ass-licker suddenly has to shoulder the consequences and he starts shitting in his pants. Go on, old man, take everybody back to camp and wag your tail, that's what they're waiting for, isn't it?"

The old man's face contracted into a terrible expression: the furrows of his brow deepened and his lips paled as he clenched his teeth. Günter eyed him with scorn.

"You're worthless," growled the old-timer. "You're not worth the food you eat. The little runt who crawled around the piers digging for scraps out of garbage cans—not even good enough to pimp for prostitutes. The punk with the cheap shots! Never talk to me that way again, you hear me?"

The old-timer paused, turning to the others.

"You all remember Jenny, don't you? That whore close to her nineties? Now she is the only thing junior, here, ever managed to squeeze a little money out of . . . and do you know why? She's his mother! The one and only, Scummy Jenny—"

"I'm going to smash your skull, Gustav—"

The Moor sank a fist into the old man's stomach and Gustav doubled up from the impact and proceeded to vomit yellow bile with a hoarse cough. The other men jumped to their feet and opened a circle around the fight—in a sense, this was the argument they had been waiting for to decide once and for all what they were going to do. The old-timer had agility—close to fifty, he was still sinewy from all the hard work out of doors. But the Moor was powerful and cunning like a cat—he had practically weaned himself on fistfights with other boys, then with grown men. Whatever he lacked in height against Gustav, he made up for in astuteness, landing the greater number of blows and confusing the old fellow with dodges and feints.

Yet the fight did not confine itself to the principal opponents; immediately, others also began trading punches. There was no particular explanation for the rapid generalization of the conflict—unless the impetus to battle arose from the sheer desperation of all concerned before the fact that none of the options made much sense. If they went back to the camp, they knew that, as fugitives, they would face severe retribution; but should they push on through the jungle, the imponderables themselves might very well annihilate them. In the meantime they went at one another with a curious stoicism, pantomiming blows with a lack of the very energy they so desperately wished to awaken. The noises of broken branches and human voices finally coagulated into a homogenous din. With no weapons, the fugitives were obliged to kill each other with their bare hands.

From her hogshead Consuelo Campero eavesdropped in trepidation as the discussion rapidly degenerated into physical combat. Not understanding German, she could not make head or tail of what the fugitives were saying. As the fighting broke out, the pack mule had begun to get jittery, pawing the ground and threatening to bolt. Consuelo grew more and more apprehensive about just such a possibility, since the animal appeared to have been abandoned without the precaution of being tied to a tree. Paradoxically, what she feared the most at this moment was that the beast might run off and disappear into the jungle. Although a prisoner, she still preferred to risk herself in the company of the Germans with whom she suspected she might at least have a chance of survival. How could it happen that twice in so short a period fate had literally hurled her life into danger. She felt like a pawn, suspended like a stone on the edge of the abyss. Her position in the hogshead did not help matters any; every time the animal stirred, her own body bounced and rolled like a greasy medicine ball. Her hair was matted like paste and as stiff as a helmet. Her wrists were bloody; the tips of her fingers and toes, swollen from the ceaseless drubbing against the wooden staves of her tub.

After all that she had been through, it was with irony that she recollected now, for some reason or other, her father's constant admonition. Whenever she became annoyed at anything, the first words out of her father's mouth were inevitably to the effect that she shouldn't complain—that she was very lucky for a Bolivian. At first she had not understood what her father really meant by that, and supposed that he was referring her comfortable life at home, as an only child who provided the focus of all the family's attentions. It was only after she had grown up that Consuelo had finally realized the political connotation of her father's contention, and that she had been born in a period of rare institutional stability in Bolivia—an epoch when presidents assumed office and completed their terms without calamities or revolutions.

Consuelo had been born on February 12, 1881, in the city of Sucre, Bolivia. Her mother, Isabel Lopez Maldonado, a mid peasant woman who mixed Indian beliefs with a Catholicism already heavily tainted by spiritualism, would postulate repeatedly that—born under the sign of Aquarius—her little girl was predestined to fulfill great humanitarian ends. Thus, Consuelo passed her infancy hearing her mother sketch out the profile that she must inevitably assume to conform to the specifications of her zodiacal sign. For Dõna Isabel the broad outlines were sufficiently clear and her daughter should undoubtedly grow into a congenial, devoted young lady, kind-hearted and loving of the truth. For Consuelo, however, this was obviously not the case because each attribute her mother invoked could be variously interpreted. When her mother suggested that she would turn out to be a congenial young lady, this meant that Consuelo should participate in endless civic and religious gatherings that Dõna Isabel herself attended as the wife of a university professor—solicitous and smiling: the exact opposite of what Consuelo considered *congenial*. She detested everything from the tea they drank at such gatherings to the topics of conversation—local gossip about unfaithful husbands and duplicitous servants. To be congenial, for Consuelo, was more a matter of knowing how to talk with more interesting people than those at civic or religious functions—students from the university, for example—a point of view her mother would classify as reproachable in a young marriageable girl. As a result, mother and daughter could never come to terms and every attribute of her zodiacal profile was a source of endless quarrel between them. For what her mother failed to perceive in all this was that Consuelo's personality incorporated the most profoundly Aquarian trait of them all, which was a fierce sense of idealism that incapacitated her for practical matters. This trait was sometimes so strong in Consuelo that she lost all common sense.

225

The child, nevertheless, did eventually turn into a beautiful woman: devoted, congenial, kindhearted, and loving of the truth. She showed great devotion to her father, the laconic Professor Mariano Figueroa Maldonado, forever absorbed in some classic of the language. Certainly Alonso, her husband, had never complained of a lack of devotion in his wife; and had not Consuelo bathed with affection the Indian with the severed hands? Such affection was part of her kindheartedness. It was not a matter of going about distributing alms to the poor as her mother did, and thus imagining herself to be kindhearted. Consuelo was kindhearted because she had the capacity to understand other people—above all, the dreamers, the young men at the conservatory with their passionate love of music, struggling to become great performers. And her zeal for the truth would often cause more problems than it solved, particularly when conjoined with her lack of appetite for things of a practical nature. While, for her mother, to love the truth was to know how to simulate the truth; for Consuelo, that would have been contrary to her nature: she never checked herself when she felt the need to express an opinion or make a comment upon some matter.

Mariano Figueroa Maldonado, however, although he rarely offered an opinion that was not a literary one, lived contented with his daughter. She took after his side of the family, people of artistic temperament who despised common sense as much as they adored adventure. The great-grandfather of Consuelo had written poetry, played the violin, and died at forty of a brawl in a brothel. Her grandfather—like her father a university professor, as well as an amateur astronomer who spent his nights gazing at comets and constellations—had met his death in front of a firing squad back in the time of Melgarejo for refusing to accept the post of astrologist to the dictator. Melgarejo thought that an astronomer was a sort of wizard who could read a man's fate and foretell the future in the stars, and had therefore requested the services of the famous Maldonado. What should have been taken as a mark of distinction, however, was seen by the old man as an insult; and he preferred to be executed as a proof of his love of truth. Consuelo's father had countless stories in his head from the time of Melgarejo, and whenever he chose to tell one he found an enchanted listener in his daughter.

226

Sucre was more than two and a half thousand meters above sea level, but its altitude proved no obstacle for dictators. Although Consuelo's childhood had coincided with a period of unusual political calm, in 1896, when President Severo Alonso came to power, elected by the people, a rebellion broke out in Sucre. Alonso had decided to declare Sucre the perpetual capital of the country, a measure which displeased the politicians in La Paz but which could not be revoked because the citizens of Sucre had already taken up arms to insure its implementation. The streets of the city were turned into barricades, while troops loyal to president and the people of Sucre resisted for an entire week. Alonso was finally deposed, however, and Bolivia returned to normal—that is, to the coups and countercoups endemic to the military. The fall of President Alonso had brought to power the hapless General Pando, over whom the people of Sucre experienced a partial victory inasmuch as the decree designating the city as capital was not finally revoked, although the entire apparatus of federal administration became concentrated in La Paz.

It was with the rebellion of Sucre that Consuelo Campero had begun to understand the words of her father, a man scarred by the insecurities of successive dictatorial regimes and who took refuge, therefore, in the pages of Gongora and *Lazarillo*. The elderly Maldonado felt a mixture of repulsion and fascination for the dictator Melgarejo; he was one of the professor's favorite subjects, perhaps because the life of José Mariano Melgarejo had the same somber, chiaroscuro coloration as the picaresque literature of Spain which he was so passionately fond of reading. Melgarejo somehow incarnated the entire turbulent succession of military dictators that made Bolivia known throughout the world. Even more, Melgarejo seemed the very caricature of all dictators from Latin America, although this particular aspect of history merited no special pride on the part of Bolivians. By the time Consuelo was a year old, Melgarejo had already become an inveterate alcoholic exiled in Peru. The favorite diversion of the ex-dictator during this period seemed to have been that of slapping around his mistress Juana, until one day, when he tried to break down the door of her bedroom to give her another beating, he was struck down by bullets fired from a pistol by her brother.

The event, however, that Consuelo's father was particularly

227

fond of recalling was one that he himself had lived throug
during the dictatorship of that same Melgarejo. Mariano Fi
gueroa Maldonado was already professor in Spanish Classica
Literature of the Golden Age, at the university, when he wa
invited to lecture in the regal salon of the Faculty of Letters
The purpose of the event was to commemorate the indepen
dence of Bolivia, and due to arrive in Sucre—to participat
in all the solemnities—was the *caudillo* himself. Professo
Maldonado was not impressed, however, and proceeded t
prepare a paper of admirable erudition and eloquence postu
lating the thesis that, at least in the field of literature, Bolivi
still found itself inextricably bound by the strongest ties to th
former colonial metropolis. The lecture itself transpired withou
incident in an auditorium full of bored and somnolent face
which did not diminish the enthusiasm of the professor for hi
venerable classics. Only afterward, as he was leaving the salon
did the contingent of military police finally prevent his egres
and take him into custody. Although married only recently, h
managed to confront his plight with nobility, which might no
have been a possibility had his daughter already been born. T
the despair of his wife, Doña Isabel—at the time, a youn
woman of pink complexion and a voice that seemed foreve
on the verge of tears—Maldonado was detained for a perio
of two weeks, after which he was set free as inexplicably a
he had been arrested in the first place. His inquisitors told hin
very little and gave him a veritable grilling on Cervantes. Onl
some years later would Maldonado discover the true reason
for his perplexing incarceration. In the course of his famou
lecture, he had, as was to be expected, waxed eloquent i
praise of the author of *Don Quixote*, to the point of affirmin,
that he considered Cervantes to be a figure of unparallele
humanity. Melgarejo, recognizedly illiterate and therefor
wholly ignorant of the true identity of the author, felt certai
that such praises were being heaped upon his personal enemy—
General Lopez de Cervantes, at the time exiled in Peru bu
once in command of the most active group of conspirator
against the *caudillo!* He could barely contain himself until th
lecture was over and thereupon ordered the immediate impris
onment of the impertinent professor who had dared to exto
his worst enemy right to his own face! Not content with th
professor's arrest, Melgarejo ordered the detention of the di

rector of the Faculty of Letters and the organizers of the commemorative festivities. The *caudillo* wanted nothing less for those high-and-mighty intellectuals than to have them shot, but their lives were saved at the last minute thanks to the merciful intervention of Melgarejo's mistress, a good-natured woman and rather more well informed than the dictator. Juana had followed the investigation because she had also attended the commemorative lecture; she had never read Cervantes but felt that intellectuals were usually right in such matters. And since she was afraid, above all, of ridicule, she managed to finally dissuade her lover from executing the twenty-five intellectuals incarcerated in Sucre. Eventually, after weeks of pressure, Juana was able to obtain pardons for the intellectuals by convincing Melgarejo that he might obtain the definitive respect of his idol—Napoleon Bonaparte—were he only to do as she suggested. The Corsican had already been dead for several years at this point in time, but the *caudillo* supposed him to be still reigning triumphantly in France—mistaking Napoleon III for the great general long ago defeated at Waterloo. All the prisoners were now set free, including Consuelo's father, but it was required of each of them to write a letter to Napoleon himself, informing the emperor of Melgarejo's friendship for the arts and his love of culture. Professor Maldonado wrote his letter and, like the others, was obliged to travel to La Paz where all were to be met by the *caudillo*. As each of them read his letter aloud, Melgarejo passed out drams of *pulque* and smiled approvingly. The envelopes, duly sealed, were handed over to the French ambassador who had arrived at the palace to attend personally to the matter. Ridiculous as it all was, the French ambassador appeared deeply moved and assured Melgarejo that the "Emperor" Napoleon would no doubt feel extremely honored once he received the missives of such a gathering of illustrious men of letters. The ambassador knew, as did every diplomat in La Paz, that it was not healthy to antagonize a man like Melgarejo. The English ambassador had paid dearly for his audacity in once challenging the *caudillo*. He had censored the wanton murder of two English citizens, for which he was summarily whipped in public, obliged to swallow *pulque*, and subsequently forced to parade three times around the principal plaza of La Paz with a monkey tied to his back. When the news of this wanton outrage reached the attention of Queen Victoria, she summoned her most senior officers in the admiralty and ordered the immediate invasion of Bolivia. The invasion, however, was never destined to take place because, as her illustrious seawolves informed Her Majesty, Bolivia was unassailable by the most powerful, feared, and respected war flotilla in the world: the Royal Navy. The queen was asked to turn her attention to a terrestrial globe upon which one of her ministers might indicate the position of the diminutive Andes nation. The queen stood poised for a few seconds with the tip of her own index finger on the globe; then, taking out a pen, she drew an *X* across Bolivia and proclaimed: "The place has ceased to exist!"

Yet not all the stories Consuelo's father told her were so delightful; there were others of assassination, of political opposition smothered by imprisonment and torture, of old friends of her father who had suddenly disappeared and were never heard of again by family or friends. Whenever he addressed himself to the nightmares of the dictatorship under Melgarejo, his language became strangely coarse and he would abuse the *caudillo* with the vilest epithets: *cholo* bastard! Son of an Indian undoubtedly defiled by a Spanish cutthroat! Probably syphilitic and depraved since childhood! In short, a figure as close to brutishness as any villain in the Manichean adventures of the Spanish picaresques. Consuelo's mother, however, shunned such depraved conversations, and the two of them, father and daughter, were left alone in a study full of books and piles of paper that no doubt comprised the uncorrected homework or examinations of his university students. And while, in front of his wife, Maldonado was usually curtly polite, once left in the company of his darling daughter, he would turn positively effusive—perhaps because, in Consuelo, he recognized himself at last. Old Maldonado would confess to a little girl how life had become a prison, why he no longer cherished any illusions, that he could only find solace in the pages of the *Poema de mio Cid* or in the permutations of some *comedia* by Tirso de Molina.

As opposed to her mother, who did not like the idea of a daughter performing at the piano, Maldonado encouraged Consuelo's studies at the conservatory. He would buy musical scores for her and surprise her with tickets to concerts by the traveling opera and operetta troops that occasionally made their way to

230

Sucre. And when the inevitable had occurred and Consuelo became engaged, he was clearly piqued—an understandable reaction, she knew, since with her marriage he would lose the companion he no longer found in his wife.

Meanwhile, Consuelo Campero had more and more acceded to the role accorded to her by her father: the lucky girl who had arrived on earth at exactly the perfect moment. As he himself had predicted, however, Bolivia would never again enjoy a period of internal peace such as that which had coincided with the childhood of his daughter. General Pando had assumed power with considerable arrogance—an ominous portent that only served to increase in Maldonado the sensation of emptiness and confinement. True to form, as the new century arrived the new *caudillo* dragged the country into another imbecilic war, this time with Brazil. Brazilians had long been surreptitiously penetrating into Bolivian territories positioned in the heart of the Amazon jungle. No Bolivian president, heretofore, had ever interested himself in actually resolving the problem by peaceful negotiation; instead, they limited themselves to drafting hyperbolic protests against the Brazilian government. In 1902, when a Brazilian rebellion broke out far off in the jungle, the health of the old professor had already deteriorated to such a point that his daughter feared for his life. In the meantime, General Pando barely managed not to fall prisoner to the Brazilian rebels, and the war ended as wars always ended for Bolivia, with a piece of the country missing on the map. Maldonado finally retired from the university and withdrew completely. He almost never left the house, absorbed in writing a monumental study on the Spanish theater of the Golden Age. Consuelo and her husband would occasionally come over to invite him out to concerts or the theater, but he would invariably refuse. He was still living in Sucre, still amassing his erudition in a florid script that had already covered over a thousand pages of manuscript. His wife, during his illness, had suddenly converted to a spiritist sect and stopped drinking coffee. She claimed that her husband was being persecuted by two warring spirits who refused to accept the fact of their demise. One of the spirits was a Dominican friar who had moiled for the Inquisition and now suspected the professor of heresy—whence the wrenching aches in old Maldonado's spine. The other spirit, the more pernicious of the two—according to the arcane premonitions of Doña Isabel—had shamelessly driven her husband to waste hours and hours editing that useless fiasco of papers, scelerous and obscene, on the Renaissance theater.

Consuelo Campero could still clearly resurrect the countenance of her father, indifferent to the mutterings of his fanatical wife, engrossed in the reading of *comedias, farsas, entremeses,* and dramas of the Golden Age. Was not she herself now like one of those characters thrust about by destiny, sacrificed to impotence before the hands of the fates, listening to the shouts of the men fighting, jounced about inside of a hogshead every time the mule was suddenly startled in the darkness? Her father had obviously been only partially right about her luck! Her personal life, so placid to begin with, had during the last months of her marriage entered a vertiginous phase where life was being lived, if not to the fullest, to the extreme. Consuelo was burning with fatigue, as if the last ounce of strength had been sucked from her body.

A harder jerk than usual from the mule caused Richard Finnegan to slide about violently and bang his head against the inside of the hogshead. He heard a dull thud at the same instant that a bolt of pain reverberated against his eardrums. He could not scream because the gag was so tight, lacerating the corners of his mouth and bruising his lips. There was no means of escape and this bald fact made him desperate. Curses of various calibers of intensity ran through his head each time he tried to change positions or twist off the ropes. He had lost track of time, was thirsty, and had no idea what the intentions of the fugitives might be with respect to his person. Throughout their flight from the camp, no one had thought to offer him anything in the way of food or water, nor even to check his condition out of simple curiosity. It was as if they had forgotten that they had even brought prisoners along, and that may have actually been the case for a period of time. The severity of their flight through the jungle, coupled with their ignorance of the terrain, had totally occupied the minds of the fugitives. Finnegan considered himself completely abandoned and could not hope to resist for much longer so dismal and vexing a situation. The lack of circulation in his limbs, the asphyxiating gag, would complete the work of killing him far more quickly than his

232

captors might imagine. Worst of all, however, was to feel subject to the caprices of a handful of lunatics now assaulting and possibly even killing one another. What the physician could hardly have realized is that the Germans were continuing to wrestle with one another although they had already forgotten the reasons that had provoked them in the first place. They no longer even had the strength to maintain themselves on their feet, and the consequent din was making the pack animals uneasy—so much so that they had begun to shift about from one side of the path to the other, flickering their ears and attempting to huddle together, instinctively searching for protection. On the jungle floor, the men traded punches and rolled into the humid carpet of dead leaves. The ground was so moist that when the kerosene lamps fell and broke open, the flames were instantly snuffed, drowned by the mush of wet humus. Finnegan heard the braying of a mule. It had become thoroughly terrified and was kicking at the air while the men crawled about like worms, but so fatigued that they no longer managed even to coil about each other. The poor beast to which Finnegan and Consuelo had been tied appeared to receive a kick and bolted like a shot in a blind run along the track that had been cut through the forest, disappearing into the blackness.

"The mules!" someone finally shouted, "The mules are running off—"

The flight of the animal was a martyrdom for the physician and Consuelo. They slid violently from one side to the other, bruising themselves painfully with each additional impact against the staves of their containers. The darkness of the night was truly terrifying. Finnegan experienced blinding visions that cut through space like swift falling stars. The stampeding seemed endless and the excruciating pain of successive blows against the side of his tub finally caused him to lose consciousness. The Bolivian girl had already fainted some time ago, almost from the moment the mule had started. Both unconscious, they did not sense when the hapless animal began to slow its pace, becoming less and less afraid. Three pack mules had managed to escape together, and now they trotted along unhurriedly, as if in search of a safe shelter where they might sleep. The beasts sniffed the air and advanced through the tunnel of chopped and twisted branches, when suddenly a bolt of lightning whitened the jungle and sent them reeling once again into flight. A storm was approaching, the thunder grew louder, and a fine rain began to patter. In fact, the storm was intense, but the dense barrier of jungle only permitted a small portion of the rain to sift through the foliage overhead. Still, it was sufficient to soak the two oblivious passengers and to begin to fill the barrels, mixing the contents into a horrendous, putrid stew.

The physician opened his eyes and the light of day dawning upon him brought a renewed sense of hope. His clothes were sopped and his body seemed incredibly light and insentient. He glanced at his hand and saw a voluminous, ashen fishlike shape that nearly caused him to vomit. His tongue pressed the gag and he discovered it had loosened; the rain had soaked and stretched the cloth and he could now try to free himself of it slowly by pushing with his tongue and grinding it with his jaws. The fact that the mule continued to jog along made the operation more complicated. Eventually, however, his efforts paid off and the gag fell down upon his chin. Finnegan could open his mouth! With an additional shrug, he felt the knot slip down his neck and the gag dropped off his chin. He continued wriggling his jaw and running his tongue over his lips until he remembered Consuelo.

"Consuelo!" he cried.

Silence: only the chomping of the mule's hooves into the carpet of dead leaves—a steady staccato.

"Consuelo?"

He felt unable to catch his breath and certain that he was about to faint again; he felt an enormous emptiness in the pit of his stomach, similar to the giddiness that had always struck him whenever he tried to fast for communion on Sundays in the days he went to church. He did not faint and began to hear a quiet moaning, coming from the other side. It was the Bolivian girl. She had not managed to free herself from her gag and appeared to be struggling frantically.

"Calm down, calm down," Finnegan demanded. "Try not to get too desperate."

It so happened that there finally was no reason for desperation, not anymore, because the mules, by following the trails laid out for them, had brought them back to the camp. A couple of Barbadians had already spotted the animals and were running to secure them. In familiar surroundings, the animals were no longer afraid and let themselves be reined in. The English engineer, hearing the commotion of the Barbadians, peered out of his tent to observe three mules being led along by their bridles. The Negroes were smiling, patting the beasts as affectionately as if they had been reunited with loved ones. Richard Finnegan felt a final convulsion in his stomach and passed out.

13

It must have been no later than two in the afternoon when J. J. Seabra's mistress finally left the house. To avoid any surprises, J.J. had stationed a man in his confidence to watch carefully over every movement in and out of the place. The sun was still high above when the man saw her open the door and emerge in a dazzling dress of green silk, coiffed and toileted, to go strolling down the street. Were it not for the elegance of her attire, the man might have surmised a simple desire for a quiet walk, perhaps to relax from the tribulations she had so recently undergone. Yet the hour, the heat, and the sun were not propitious for leisurely perambulation along the sidewalks of São Cristóvão. Thus, he decided to follow her discreetly. He did so with no difficulty, since the girl walked along unconcernedly, as if it had never occurred to her that she might be being watched or followed.

The man paused as an unexpected gust of wind almost blew off her hat at the corner. She secured it with the palm of her hand, then continued on her way, disappearing around the corner. The man did not hurry his steps, even when an auto—a convertible with the black canvas top up—crossed the same intersection, rumbling along by the curb in low gear. By the time he realized the situation, upon reaching the intersection where the girl and then the auto had turned, she had vanished. The only sign of the vehicle was the cloud of dust in its wake as it sped away. The man could not even hazard whether she had actually gotten into the auto or simply entered one of the nearby houses. The street was deserted and the man leaned against a lamp post, astonished and perturbed, with no idea of what he was to tell his chief regarding what had transpired. He was busy mulling over excuses, with half a mind to invent a lie, when another car—the top of this one also drawn up—suddenly loomed up out of nowhere and slowly came to a stop nearly at his feet. Caught unawares, he instinctively reached for the revolver holstered under his jacket, just as the driver stuck his head out and shouted:

"Take it easy, my friend. No foolishness, now."

He stood frozen, blinking his eyes at the driver, who continued to stare at him from behind the windshield of the automobile.

"Get in," ordered the driver, leaning over and opening the door of the car.

The man complied without resistance and sat beside the driver. No one else was in the car. The vehicle lurched forward, raising dust, and followed what seemed to be a preestablished route. Yet the man could hardly be certain, since everything seemed to be happening unexpectedly. They drove along in silence for some time, until finally the man summoned his courage and turned to the driver.

"Where are we headed?"

The driver stared at him coldly, then let out a wrinkled smile. He was powerfully built, and his face of parched, wrinkled flesh seemed to belong to a professional boxer, an image heightened by his broken, twisted nose.

"You'll find out soon enough," said the driver.

The man, however, was growing recklessly angry.

"What the devil's going on? Who are you?"

The driver held the steering post with one hand while with the other he took out a sheet of paper from his jacket pocket. He held the sheet out to the man.

"I don't know how to read," Seabra's henchman humbly confessed.

"It's a document."

"I can see that. So what?"

"I'm an officer in the army. A pity you can't read."

The man shrugged his shoulders, apparently unimpressed by the fact that the driver was actually an officer.

"Don't you want to know what I'm here for?"

"What do I care? Maybe you're taking me in. . . ."

"Why would I want to do that? Aren't you in the employ of Minister Seabra?"

The man was obviously taken aback by the question.

"Well! . . . that is . . ."

"Are you or aren't you?" asked the army officer.

"Well, I'm a sort of friend of the minister's."

237

"And you were keeping an eye on the girl, isn't that right?"

The other made no answer and seemed embarrassed by the question.

"Beautiful job you were doing," the officer reproached him sarcastically. "You were supposed to be keeping tabs on her but you let her slip through your fingers."

"She took off so suddenly, I wasn't expecting it," the man blurted out. "By the time I made it around the corner, she was gone!"

"She got into that automobile."

"That's what I thought. . . ."

"And you stood there leaning on the lamp post like an old mutt."

The man did not enjoy the comparison and scowled.

"Anyway," he grumbled, "what exactly have you got to do with this?"

The army officer turned the vehicle down another sidestreet without slowing down. They were approaching the center of the city. Traffic was a lot heavier but it did not dampen the pace of the officer behind the wheel, who managed to maintain his speed.

"I'm also assigned to keeping a watch on that girl," the officer explained, "but I have no interest in whether she is faithful to her minister."

The other man coughed because the traffic was raising so much dust that it irritated his throat.

"She *is* a honey, though, isn't she," he continued.

The other man stared at the officer, but now with hatred in his eyes.

"It's not a matter for me to consider whether the woman of my friend is beautiful or ugly."

"You're not from here in Rio, am I right, friend?"

"No, sir . . . I'm from up in the state of Pernambuco."

"You people up there have rather strong ideas on the whole subject of honor, don't you?"

"Any man with self-respect ought to have a fair amount of ideas on the subject."

The army officer began to downshift because they were entering Avenida Central, where the traffic was congested.

"This business of honor, my friend, isn't exactly high on the list, here in the capital. Everyone prevaricates and to be

238

honorable seems to be nothing more around here than the height of prevarication."

Seabra's hoodlum scarcely fathomed what the officer was talking about.

The wide, busy thoroughfare basked in the breeze blowing off the oceanside, refreshing the elegant ladies and smiling damsels crossing in front of the automobile. Hats dominated sidewalks and windows. The vehicle slowly turned into Rua 7 de Setembro, weaving in and out among the pushcarts loaded with crates, and headed toward the Praça Tiradentes.

They pulled up in front of what appeared to the man to be a luxury hotel. The army officer leaned over and opened the door.

"You can get out here, friend."

"Why?"

"See that hotel? She's in there. Do your job but go in cautiously, preferably around the back entrance. . . ."

The officer gave several more directions, outlining precisely how and where he should proceed to find her. The man left the car and entered through a narrow alleyway full of garbage cans. As he disappeared from sight, the army officer drew the car door closed and drove the vehicle slowly off.

The man had by now reached the back of the hotel and ascertained the two doors through which he might enter. One door, from what he could see, led to the kitchen of the restaurant that operated on the ground floor, while the other took one down a corridor to the reception desk of the hotel and the stairs which led to the basement and the upper floors. He could have taken the elevator, but he did not like such modern contraptions and opted for the stairwell. He tried to follow the instructions of the officer from the army. It was all he could really do, given the strange circumstances of his adventure. He had lost sight of the woman he was told to keep an eye on, and then a stranger had popped out of nowhere with a desire to lend him a hand. He was unsure of the stranger's intentions in all this; so he kept his hand, even now, on his revolver, in case he were walking into a trap. He did not know how to read—he had never learned to decipher those cursed signs on the damn piece of paper— but something told him to take the purported document, shown to him by the other man, seriously. Being a simple man,

239

moreover, he was prone in any case to take the armed forces seriously. Even so, however, he gripped his weapon with a sweating hand and continued to follow the other's directions—quite easily, in fact, because the officer had been fairly detailed with them. At the end of the corridor, exactly on the floor indicated, he pushed lightly on the door still ajar (sufficiently to open a small crack through which he could safely observe whatever might be going on). There was no light turned on inside the room, but the sun was still strong enough to illuminate the interior, even with the curtains drawn.

Later on, in the presence of Seabra—with an air of professional triumph, because he had prudently omitted all reference to the assistance he had had from the armed forces—the man related what he had seen.

"She was not entirely undressed, Senhor Seabra. She had only stepped out of her dress, a green one. She was still wearing her . . . underthings, but was starting to remove the silk stockings."

While he talked thus, he did not take his eyes off his chief; he knew he might draw his wrath were he too explicit. Yet he could not erase the image from his mind of that woman with her breathlessly attractive body tucked in those white lacy underclothes, taking off her stockings as if she were peeling the skin off a fruit. Such white garments excited him—intimate feminine apparel barred to the eyes of men. Just as his own mother before her, the woman with whom he now raised his family would never put such clothes out to dry, after washing them, until he had left the house for the day—to bar them from his sight. But that girl had no such scruples; she showed them to her lover with a perilous innocence. Seabra was shaking his head with an expression somewhere between contrition, a posture meant to maintain his authority before one of his hirelings, and rage, an attitude far more appropriate to the substance of what he had just heard.

"She had obviously just arrived," the man continued. "They were talking—her more than him. She was saying something about the risk she was running in order to meet him that way."

"And you saw clearly what the blackguard looked like?"

240

"Clear as day. He was standing up, watching the lady get undressed, just in front of the door that I was looking in through. By his accent, I'm dead certain he's a gringo."

"He's not very tall?"

"That's right, he doesn't even look like a gringo, with the dark hair and all, but the speech is definitely gringo, yes, sir."

"Then it's him: Percival Farquhar, the son of a bitch!"

"Who is he, Your Excellency?"

"It doesn't matter."

"I was only thinking that you might like me to finish the job. Give a lesson to that gringo, a few taps with a pair of brass knuckles. . . ."

"Don't be a fool, man! You really have no idea who that son of a bitch is, do you?"

"To me he's a blackguard just like any other. Just because he's a gringo doesn't hold any water with me."

"But this one is different; he's powerful."

"Powerful? Then how was it I got so close to him? How could I watch his every move that way without any problem?"

"That's exactly what I find so strange."

"He was all alone with her. There was no one else: no hoods no bodyguard, nothing."

"I guess that's just a part of his style. He likes to think no one would have the guts to touch him."

"If you want, Your Excellency, I can pay him a visit and settle accounts."

"No, I already know all I need to know. The only thing that has to be done now is to get that little tramp out of circulation. I've no taste for whores!"

The man gaped in astonishment at Seabra's uncommon outburst.

"She's quite the little whore, in fact," J.J. confirmed to himself. "If we don't take the proper steps, she could actually compromise me."

He got up from his chair and slapped the man affably on the back. "You did a fine job, my compadre."

The man smiled. "She had no idea I was there."

"I would have liked to have seen the whole thing."

"She left the house without taking the slightest precautions—as if she were queen of the May. Never even looked behind."

"That's exactly what she thinks: that she's queen of the May—damned slut!"

"She is a very beautiful girl, Your Excellency," the man added thoughtfully.

Seabra appreciated the compliment. "Damned beautiful, but dangerous, as well."

The following morning, Minister Seabra walked into Catete Palace for one of his routine audiences with the president. There was not a great deal to discuss: two minor ventures planned for the state of Rio Grande do Sul and additional details regarding the projected presidential visit to the state of Bahia.

Marshal Hermes da Fonseca received him with his habitual cordiality, yet there was something strained in his demeanor. Near the entrance to his antechamber, Seabra spotted Colonel Agostinho animatedly conversing with a group of politicians from the state of São Paulo. On noticing Seabra, the colonel left the group and came over to receive the minister with a feigned smile. J.J. more and more disliked that petulant soldier with his waxed mustache and European swagger. The starched uniform he wore also irritated Seabra, inasmuch as it emphasized his skinniness. How J.J. despised skinny men! And yet Colonel Agostinho was apparently cynical enough to continue to ignore the minister's increasing animosity.

"Good day, minister," said the colonel, offering a hand to Seabra.

The minister did not reciprocate and the colonel remained with his hand in the air, without ceasing to smile.

"Your Excellency is annoyed at something?"

"It's not on your account, colonel. Personal problems . . .'

"Please forgive me. I did not mean to—"

"Listen, don't start your diddling around with me, Agostinho."

The colonel stopped smiling. The minister had gone too far.

"Minister Seabra, the president gave me direct orders, yesterday, to investigate a purported conspiracy involving your person."

"Conspiracy?"

"That is what the president has been told."

J.J. stared at the colonel as if he were about to leap at his throat.

242

"I wouldn't poke around where you're not welcome, Agostinho."

"I have my orders from the president, Minister Seabra. I appeal to Your Excellency to cooperate and try to be understanding."

"And I simply tell you the following: keep your nose out of other people's business, or I'll see that you wind up with your necktie up your ass!"

"You have no call to raise your voice with me or to use that kind of language, minister. I address you as a gentleman and I expect the same treatment."

"What precisely is going on, colonel? Have your boys decided to change their tactics? Or are they running scared?"

"I don't know what you can possibly be talking about."

J.J. suddenly let out such a harsh guffaw that everyone in the corridor turned to observe the two of them bickering at the door to the president's antechamber.

"You don't know? And am I the one to know? Well then, let me give you a few leads for your investigation. There is an economic group of North American provenience that threw its support in favor of the opposition during the last elections, but lost. Do you follow me? This same group now wants to go back to exerting its influence upon the federal government and has even attempted to penetrate the present administration through my own ministry—which, it so happens, regulates the major portion of the interests of this same group. Still following me?"

The colonel nodded his head, although it irritated him to have to listen to all this.

"Well then," J.J. proceeded, "this group has suddenly struck very hard at me, but my tempering is a bit too hard, even for them, and I didn't snap so easily. They came off rather badly, in fact, although they have managed to place one of their lackeys quite close to the president."

Colonel Agostinho was startled.

"Close to the president?" he managed, incredulously.

"Exactly. One of their toadies is at the president's door. You should investigate the matter thoroughly, colonel, to find out who it is. I believe that you will have no great difficulty in ascertaining the identity of the rascal."

The colonel stroked his soft whiskers.

243

"Minister, I would like to ask you one question."

"Then do it quickly. I have to speak with the president."

"Do you consider the interests of this economic group of North Americans to be prejudicial to those of the nation?"

"Would you like to hear the cruel truth, Colonel Agostinho? I don't give one solemn shit whether their interests are prejudicial to what you call national interests. All I care about was that your gringos were petulant enough to attempt to pull a fast one with me—inspired by I know exactly whom!"

"Whom, then? Would you care to spell out his name, Your Excellency?"

"Of course! Who else but that syphilitic dwarf Ruy Barbosa!"

Colonel Agostinho smiled, with relief.

"Minister, the president awaits you," he concluded with a polite nod.

Hardly had Seabra entered the president's office when the colonel scampered back to his own office and asked for an outside telephone line. The telephone system was rather precarious, full of noises and interferences, and the colonel did not relish using it because it obligated him to speak in such a loud voice, almost shouting. Yet, at that moment it was certainly the most efficient thing to do and it could be a rapid call. He was soon connected. . . .

"Percy, hello! Yes, it's me! I just spoke to him! The cat's about to jump into the bag!"

He hung up the receiver and stretched back in his chair.

In the presidential office, there had already accumulated a considerable pile of expedited documents, and two official clerks were busy rummaging through the mountain of papers. The marshal normally began his office hours extremely early and seldom missed the chance to add his own two cents to any legislation that might come to his attention. Seabra picked up the unusual atmosphere the moment he had entered. The marshal had not looked up and did not smile—he looked grave. He had not spoken as yet and had limited his gestures to pointing with a finger to where Seabra should find a seat.

"A lot of work today, Mr. President?" he finally interjected.

"As always, minister."

The marshal rarely called J.J. by the title of minister.

They continued to sit in ominous silence a few moments

244

longer, while the president examined a voluminous-looking piece of legislation. He swiftly made his determination and handed the file to an official clerk. Finally, the office was empty except for themselves.

"I am already well aware of what has been going on, my dear Minister Seabra."

The marshal's choice of words immediately sparked his attention. "Aware of what, Mr. President?"

"I've had a meeting this morning with Colonel Agostinho, who informed me of everything."

Seabra exploded.

"Mr. President! I find it strange that Your Excellency would confide in the likes of Colonel Agostinho!"

"I don't understand, Seabra? He's an honest man."

"Like some character out of vaudeville."

The marshal looked annoyed.

"Colonel Agostinho is, I can assure you, a thoroughly honest man. He is here, serving in my cabinet, at great financial sacrifice. He could be in the private sector, right now, making a fortune."

"Working for the Americans . . ."

"Exactly! And I see no crime in that. Yet he left his position to come work here, with me, earning what he earns."

"You're the one to know, Mr. President."

"What I cannot manage to fathom is this animosity you nurture in relation to the colonel. If you were still a general, I could understand, perhaps."

Seabra remained silent.

"Besides which, he has done you a great service."

"Me! A great service?"

There was now a vast tired sadness to the expression of the president, and it served as a warning to Seabra. He might be mistaken, but it seemed to him that the Americans' machinations had taken a turn toward renewed subtlety, like a dance in the dark; but he was still a man to turn the tables.

"I cannot believe that," he muttered finally, his face flushed by the blood rushing to his head like a typhoon of anger.

"He has looked after you, I can assure you," the president insisted.

"And I can assure you that that's hardly likely to have been the case."

245

The president shook his head in a sign that he did not intend to spend the entire morning playing yes-and-no games with J. J. Seabra.

"Does Your Excellency have any idea what Colonel Agostinho did down in Paraná?"

"Toward the end of the last administration—due to certain incompatibilities with some high-ranking officers of the army—the colonel was retired from active duty and began working for private enterprise."

"Do you know which *private enterprise*, Your Excellency?"

"Obviously I cannot recall the specific name of the company...."

"Let me refresh your memory, Your Excellency—"

"Stop calling me *your excellency!*"

"You are the president, sir."

"For that very reason! The manner in which you say it seems an insult."

"I beg your pardon, marshal."

"And don't call me *marshal* either!"

"You are a marshal: Marshal Hermes da Fonseca."

"I know! And I don't like the way you say it, understand?"

"What shall I call Your Excellency?"

"Anything you like—except your excellency or marshal. Is that clear, minister?"

"Then stop calling me *minister!*"

"You are my minister, you bastard, you!"

"I know, and it's not necessary to keep reminding me every minute."

"Very well, Mr. Seabra, continue...."

"Don't call me *mister* either—I don't like it."

"Oh, go fuck yourself, you northeastern shithead!"

"Go to hell, you military fart, you!"

The two fell silent for a few seconds, then broke into convulsive laughter. Seabra soon regained his composure because he had managed to win a round. The president yanked a handkerchief from his back pocket and wiped his forehead.

"To continue, sir..." Seabra hunted for a qualifier more to the president's liking.

"Address me the way you're accustomed to," da Fonseca suggested.

Seabra started laughing again.

246

"What's so funny, now?"

"You want me to say it?"

"Say what?"

"You asked for it: *blockhead!*"

"So that's what you call me."

"That's what everybody calls you: the blockhead of Catete Palace."

"And you, you think you don't have a nickname around here, smart aleck?"

J.J. turned icy. He knew most of the infamous nicknames that attended his person and he hated them all.

"Minister Ten Percent!"

"I didn't know about that one."

"Minister Ten Percent," the marshal repeated with redoubled delight.

"Marshal Hemorrhoid da Fonseca, tight-of-ass and bandy-legged."

"That's an old one, J.J. It's followed me around since my military academy days. Besides, the *ass*onance is lousy, even though I've always felt it lent me a certain Britannical air. Anyway, it hardly offends me anymore."

The president was now observing his minister with a half-smile of satisfaction.

"Not to mention," he added with a wink, "I actually am rather a tight-ass, as anyone could tell just by looking at me, right, J.J?"

"You're right about the assonance."

"I studied rhetoric with Ruy Barbosa, don't forget."

Seabra flushed. He could not camouflage the hatred he felt at the mere mention of that Bahian barrister.

"At any rate, O Fat-of-Ass, do you or do you not want to hear what I have to say about Colonel Agostinho?"

"Not fat, tight—do you hear? Tight-of-ass . . ."

"You're in a good mood today."

"No I'm not, I'm furious, J.J. Those politicians in São Paulo are after my balls."

"You have your alliance in the north."

"Which means I have shit . . ."

"It's that bad, eh?"

Seabra was now himself apprehensive: da Fonseca's trip to

247

Bahia might have to be set aside, which would come as a very personal defeat.

"By the look of it you haven't been paying much attention to the problems of this administration," the president chided.

"That's all I've been doing twenty-four hours a day."

"Then suppose you tell me what you've done concretely up to now to deal with São Paulo."

"Well, I've released all the pending budgets in my ministry which have a bearing on that sector."

"You've released all of them?"

"Would you like me to enumerate the projects?"

"That won't be necessary, J.J."

Da Fonseca remained silent for a few minutes.

"What precisely do you think the bosses in São Paulo are after?"

"They want to nail you by the balls," Seabra replied.

"Well, they won't succeed! Before they can get near enough I'll hang each and every one of them by the scrotum! You mean to tell me you released all the budgets for that sector?"

"All of them."

"A lot of money?"

"It runs into the thousands. . . ."

"And all the ministries have done the same thing? I think that's a mistake!"

"A mistake?"

"We've already released thousands but they keep on agitating. . . . Will you have some coffee, J.J.?"

"An excellent idea," he answered, smiling.

"It's pure Colombian," said the president, slapping the bell on his desk.

The officer of the day entered and the president requested coffee for two. When the officer withdrew, Hermes da Fonseca promptly opened a cabinet and removed a manila envelope— sealed and stamped SECRET front and back. J.J. surmised that probably half of Rio de Janeiro already knew the contents of that envelope.

"What was it you were talking to me about, J.J.?"

"Oh, nothing. You're very forgetful today, sir."

"Sorry, J.J. Do tell me what you have to say."

"It's about your Colonel Agostinho."

"The colonel again! It's incredible how no one likes that fellow around here."

"He's a son of a bitch."

"That explains nothing at all: there are enough sons of bitches in this country not to have any particular one draw so much attention."

"Just hear me out. He's a sly little fox! Just because he learned in France how to play with tin soldiers, he's got your full confidence."

"He happens to be versed in the techniques of modern warfare, which is frankly more than I can say about this troop of military numbskulls we have around here. The majority of our generals still believe they can win wars by studying Julius Caesar! The rest have it in their heads to repeat, here in Brazil, what Louis Napoleon did in France."

"Everybody agrees that the armed forces need to catch up to the times. They are backward and lack discipline. Your own term of office in the Ministry of War demonstrated just that, and things began to change for the better. But the so-called 'maneuvers' inspired by Colonel Agostinho wasted more money than the entire budget of the federal capital!"

"A modern army is expensive."

"But I'm not arguing with you about the modernization of the army! At the moment, the only thing about the armed forces that interests me is Colonel Agostinho."

"Always him—what an obsession you have!"

"Marshal! . . . excuse me, *sir*. Colonel Agostinho was down in Paraná working as director and president of the Southern Brazil Lumber & Colonization Company. Do you know who owns that company? The Farquhar Syndicate."

The president remained unimpressed, as if his thoughts were already on some other horizon.

"Colonel Agostinho is nothing less than Farquhar's man— the same Farquhar who aided the opposition and lost. Now he's attempting to infiltrate the government, to continue to plunder—"

"Sorry, J.J.?" the president interrupted, startled at hearing the word *plunder*.

"I'm trying to tell you that the enemy is right here in our midst, infiltrating Catete, at your doorstep!"

"The enemy?"

249

"Agostinho—he's one of them! He collects from the coffers of Percival Farquhar."

"The gentleman you refer to, Percival Farquhar, represents very large economic interests, J.J. He cannot afford to be left with the opposition."

"Obviously, he depends on our government, on our concessions."

"This administration does not make concessions!" affirmed the president with perverse pride in each syllable.

"We're tough, I know. . . ."

"Have you read what that journalistic Alberto Torres wrote the other day? He attacked the mortgage banks, saying that not even Turkey would have made so many concessions."

"We're not in Turkey."

"Precisely. But intellectuals are the same the world over. They never know when to keep their nose out."

A servant entered the office carrying a tray with cups and a pot of coffee. He served them both with the ambivalent solicitude that Seabra was aware came from years of life in the barracks. The servant must have been some corporal stationed at Catete in order to serve the marshal. Military all over the damn place, J.J. thought to himself.

"Excuse me for what I am about to tell you," said the president while sipping from a steaming cup of coffee. "Everything that you have told me concerning the colonel is already familiar to me. I'm not such a fool as you people seem to imagine. It's your interpretation of the facts, however, that's mistaken."

"Mistaken?" J.J. sighed.

"Precisely. The Farquhar Syndicate, at present, is one of the most important economic groups in the country. They bring capital from North America—a very promising nation by the way: modern, you see, without these impudent airs that characterize the old aristocracies and all the rusty privilege that goes with them. Their detractors characterize the Americans as barbarians. But barbarous, to me, is a favorable term. The Germans are also, in a certain sense, barbarous."

"They also have their aristocrats in Germany."

"True, demoralized aristocrats, with neither power nor charm. You're certainly aware of how much I know about the history of Germany. Well, in that country the aristocracy has lost its

250

shirt." Hermes da Fonseca broke into a smile. "Imagine: in a country like Germany, to have a nobleman come to the fore the likes of a Ludwig of Bavaria!"

"A madman, wasn't he?"

"Worse: he was a pederast! And while he was busy entertaining himself with his royal guard, the capitalists took over his country for him. Today, Germany is the one modern country in all of Europe. Just like the United States..."

The president took another sip of his coffee and proceeded.

"I confess that initially I felt a desire for revenge against the Farquhar syndicate. After all, hadn't they favored the opposition? But is it a crime to support the opposition? No, it isn't a crime, J.J. They were poorly advised, swept along by the rhetoric of Ruy Barbosa. You have to admit there are very few who manage to escape his infectious rhetoric. I've often allowed myself to be hoodwinked by his crafty little conceits. At any rate, I've come to take a different view as to how to handle the Farquhar syndicate—"

"Advised, no doubt, by the colonel."

"Yes, it was precisely Agostinho who opened my eyes. You know yourself that Barbosa never gives up a fight; and he's been courting a powerful ally. The Americans, barbarous to the hilt, wield a sharp blade when it comes to cutting the political pie." Hermes da Fonseca reached for the envelope now and opened it. He removed a few pages, scrawled in an almost illegible hand, although J.J. felt certain that most of Rio—minus himself, of course—had been given the opportunity to decipher it. "And this was going to give them their edge."

The minister waited: the decisive moment had arrived.

"You, my dear J.J., are the only man of iron in my ministry. No one is about to bend you very easily, I must say."

Seabra let his own vanity overtake him with a smile.

"The hatred you feel for Barbosa, however, has unfortunately encouraged a simultaneous distaste for the Farquhar syndicate. Barbosa was quick to grasp the opportunity there to create a ministerial crisis, just as we were about to face off with our enemies in São Paulo. Were you to have persisted in your animosity toward the Farquhar syndicate, there might have been more serious consequences, possibly ending with the necessity of your stepping down from the ministry."

Seabra watched his own vanity go up in smoke.

"But your simple departure from the ministry would not have been sufficient; not for Ruy Barbosa. You were to have left in disgrace, publicly smeared. No, the mind of that little fellow is no laughing matter! Just have a look at what he was plotting," said the president, thumbing through the dossier. "He'd spread the story that you were keeping a mistress, house and all, over in São Cristóvão. When I heard of it, naturally, I was rather piqued since, as you yourself know, I do not permit such goings-on in my administration. I can allow for almost anything—except conjugal infidelity! Nevertheless, Colonel Agostinho, whom you detest and he knows it, despite it all, felt more loyal to my administration than to whatever antipathy he might have nurtured against you, J.J. He led the investigation personally. He went directly to the address of the supposed mistress you were purportedly harboring in São Cristóvão. Take a look at his report."

The marshal, with a final flip through the pages of the dossier, handed them over to his minister.

Seabra snatched them roughly and began to read. He could not believe what was written there. The report reached the conclusion that the entire story was nothing but slander. At the address cited were found an upright Brazilian family, composed of eight members, the father of which—an invalid named Fabiano Lobato—had once worked for the Seabras in Pernambuco State. He had moved to Rio in 1901, with his wife Anastácia and their six young children. Sustaining an injury while apprenticed to a stone mason during the construction of Avenida Central, he found himself permanently disabled and in growing financial difficulties, at which point he had sought out J. J. Seabra, godfather to one of his children, to plead for some assistance. The minister, at the time still a congressman from the state of Bahia, had found him a little house in São Cristóvão and was helping the man and his family with a modest monthly stipend—a species of workman's compensation—enabling them to survive.

"Colonel Agostinho was quite moved, J.J. He had never imagined you to be a charitable fellow."

"I'm not a charitable fellow!" Seabra remarked with perplexity.

"Then what the hell was it you did for that poor family?"

"Charity, sir!"

14

For more than two days now, Richard Finnegan had been sleeping in his bed at Candelária Hospital, a deep sleep, interrupted only long enough to occasionally swallow some nourishment—a sweetish gruel the flavor of stale oatmeal. Gradually, however, the heat and the daylight began to force him to attempt to find new positions in his bed. The hours of sleep seemed to have already made up for the exhaustion and shock of the entire traumatizing adventure at the bottom of that fetid, empty lard vat. Our physician could no longer manage to fall back asleep really; he was simply keeping his eyes shut and letting his body twist about in bed, sweating up the sheets, motivated by the fear of finally getting up and being sent back into the inferno of the Abunã. The smell of rancid lard continued to plague him—it seemed to have penetrated his very flesh, lodged forever inside his nostrils, permanently corrupting his palate. Yet at least he no longer felt the nausea; most of his discomfort had left him, in sleep. Finnegan felt actually renewed; so much so, in fact, that during the two days he was asleep he had maintained a constant erection, to the considerable amusement of the medics on the staff. And now the heat wet his back and caused his pajamas to stick to his skin. And the light penetrated his closed eyelids, imposing a uniform, reddish field upon the retinae, and raising doubts in his mind as to how long he might persist in such a fashion. Finally, the light and the heat were triumphant: Finnegan opened his eyes.

"Welcome to the land of the living," said a painfully familiar voice, somewhere at his side.

The physician turned his head and saw the figure of the English engineer, also in pajamas, seated with his back against the headboard of an adjacent bed, holding an open magazine in his hands. It was Collier all right, even though the mosquito netting draped about Finnegan's bed lent to the world a malign imprecision.

254

"And Consuelo?" Finnegan asked, pulling aside the mosquito net and sitting up on the edge of the bed.

"What?"

"Consuelo!" Finnegan almost shouted.

"Not so loud, doctor, we're in a hospital."

"I'm not yelling."

"If you start raving, they're bound to think that your illness is getting worse and start to apply medication."

"Illness?"

"Of course! If you weren't looking so bloody well, I'd say your condition was beastly."

Finnegan rubbed a hand over his sweated face and looked around him. The ward was almost empty, save for two additional beds occupied by patients who seemed to be waiting to die.

"This is the company VIP wing," Collier informed him.

"I want to know about Consuelo. Do you think you can give me an answer?"

"Now that I understand," the engineer replied, reveling in a smile.

"Understand what?"

"The question. Didn't you just ask me about the girl, Consuelo Campero?"

The physician was irked. "Exactly, her!"

"Don't flare up—remember we're in a hospital."

"I'm not flaring up!"

"You're shouting," the engineer observed dryly.

A male nurse appeared in the doorway of the ward but Collier indicated with a dismissive gesture that everything was fine.

"There you are," Collier warned. "If you don't stop raving, they're bound to come and administer a sedative."

"Who's raving? I just want to know where Consuelo is. You're the one who sits there spouting one kind of nonsense after another."

"Like what, for example?"

"Whatever you understood, or didn't—how the hell do I know what it was!"

"Ah, well, obviously I only understood things once you asked me about her."

"Understood *what* things?"

"Not to be priggish, lad, but . . ."

Finnegan shot a menacing glance at the engineer.

"All right, all right, don't get steamed up again. It's merely that you've spent the last two days with a hard-on, and then the moment you wake up you inquire about Miss Campero. What else was there to understand?"

"A hard-on, you say?"

"Exactly, my lad, a veritable Mont Blanc. The nurses were quite amused; they dubbed you Dr. Matterhorn."

Finnegan instinctively ran his hand between his legs but his member was for the moment relaxed and well-behaved. Collier laughed. The doctor could not remember any dream, anything at all. The two days drifted through his memory as diffusely as the scarlet color of the light on his retinae.

"Your Bolivian girl is doing splendidly, my boy," the engineer assured him. "She's a woman and then some! They've put her in special quarters, since there's no facilities for women in here. She also never lets go of that Indian you saved."

"He's here too?"

"I brought him in with the two of you. Lovelace tells me you've performed quite a miracle on him."

Finnegan, however, was not impressed.

"How long are we to remain here?" he asked.

"As long as we like."

"Is that true?"

"Yes, as long as we keep pretending we're still sick."

"Have you been sick, sir?" Finnegan asked, resuming formalities.

"As sick as you are."

"Am I sick?"

"I wouldn't know. I'm not a physician."

"I don't feel ill at all. I don't think anything's wrong with me that sleep hasn't cured."

"Well, just keep your mouth shut anyway, stretch out on the bed there and let out an occasional moan."

"I need to see Consuelo."

"Why? She's remarkably well, I tell you, and taking care of her Indian. I suspect she's being naughty with her friend."

"With whom?"

"With that Indian you cured. Just because he's lost his hands

256

doesn't mean he still can't put the rest of his organs to good use."

"That's a sordid thing to say, Collier."

"I see nothing sordid about it. She's a healthy girl who simply can't keep her hands off a very astute Indian."

The physician felt that the heat bearing down on him, there in the ward, was about to drive him to commit some act of folly.

"Consuelo is of a generous nature," he said coldly, checking himself.

"Naturally . . . what else but her generosity would lead her to copulate with a poor Indian amputee?"

"I have no wish to continue this conversation!"

Finnegan lay down in a huff, stretching his body out on the length of the bed and clasping his hands under his head. He stared up at the white enamel ceiling that glimmered in the daylight. Collier went back to paging through his magazine.

"Were you dreaming about her?" he asked presently, tossing aside his reading.

"I can't remember anything."

The engineer let out with a long whistle.

"I tell you, doc, you needed to have seen how you were to believe it."

"It's perfectly natural—at *my* age," Finnegan suggested maliciously.

"Touché," Collier admitted ruefully.

The male nurse on duty peeked through the doorway again, but this time the engineer made a sign for him to enter. The medic, a young North American with a freckled face and his hair cropped short in soldierly fashion, came waddling in without a sound.

"He's not doing so well," Collier suggested, pointing his thumb at Finnegan.

"There's nothing the matter with me," Finnegan rejoined in the most convincingly amiable voice he could muster at the moment.

"Sshh! You're in a hospital," the medic scolded him with a whisper, popping a thermometer into his mouth.

"Christ," said Finnegan, practically chewing the instrument.

"Calm yourself, doctor, you'll soon be feeling better," the nurse tried to assure him.

Presently, Finnegan himself removed the thermometer to examine it. The nurse swept it from his hand.

"You have a touch of fever," he warned the physician.

"Fever? Don't be ridiculous, nurse. Since when is thirty-six a fever?"

The medic looked astonished: "Thirty-six is not a fever?"

"At least not among humans," Finnegan chided.

"This is exactly why we have orders not to furnish medical information to our patients. You should be ashamed of yourself, grabbing the thermometer like that—strictly against regulations."

The engineer motioned the medic to withdraw. The fellow first shook his thermometer down and slipped it back into the pocket of his immaculately clean and starched dressing gown, before waddling back out the way he had come. At the door, however, he stopped to turn around and announce, "I'm ordering an antipyretic to be administered to you, sir."

"Perfectly sound idea . . ."

The medic smiled.

". . . we could use a fan in here."

Collier rolled over the bed with laughter, while the nurse dropped his jaw disconcertedly.

"It's against regulations, doctor. We do not furnish that type of medication."

"A pity," the physician answered him, "that's the only antipyretic that would do me any good at the moment."

Just then, the two other patients in the ward began to writhe in their beds. Finnegan got up and walked over to eye them clinically, his hands set in the pockets of his pajamas.

"They're dying," Finnegan announced. "Call a doctor."

The nurse gave no sign that Finnegan's observation had registered in his mind. The two patients continued to toss about, in unison, then one after the other their bodies stiffened. They were dead.

"They're dead," Finnegan confirmed.

"They're really dead?" Collier queried uncertainly, hesitating to believe it.

"Positively," Finnegan warranted, examining a chart by one of the beds. "Acute avitaminosis!"

"Acute what?"

"'Herrera, Servulo. Administrative assistant. Nationality:

Spanish. Age: forty-six. Marital status: widower.'" Finnegan took another step and picked up the other chart: "'Macaulay, Frank. Civil engineer. Nationality: American. Age: thirty-five. Marital status: single.'"

"Your two patients over there got screwed, lad," Collier commented to the nurse.

"A fairly common occurrence at a hospital, sir," the medic replied with a certain air of triumph and walked out.

Finnegan pulled the sheet up over the head of first the one corpse and then the other. The engineer sat back down on his bed and proceeded to unbutton the shirt of his pajamas, which was soaked in his sweat.

A minute later a group of industrious-looking medics entered the ward to remove the bodies. They screened off the beds with partitions and began to wrap them.

"Real professionals," Finnegan commented ironically.

"What are the screens for?" Collier whispered.

"Not to upset the other patients," Finnegan responded wryly.

"But there are no other patients in this ward."

"*We* are the other patients," Finnegan explained wearily. "They don't want to upset *us*."

At one point the medic who had been with them earlier stepped away from the group, now actively at work behind the screens, and approached the two of them.

"Enough of you and your thermometer," Collier warned him.

The nurse smiled. "No, sir. It's just that I forgot to tell you before that the two of you have been invited to breakfast with Dr. Lovelace. Breakfast is served at ten forty-five in the hospital cantina.

"Neither of us has a watch," Collier reminded him.

"I'll go and check the time for you."

Consuelo Campero had slept very little but even so did not feel tired. Arriving at the hospital, despite their recommendation that she stay in bed, she did so only for one night, dressed in a nightgown and feigning a sleepiness she did not possess. The next morning, Consuelo got up and took a shower—something she had not done for an eternity. They had not interned her in any ward or pavilion of the hospital. She had been placed instead in one of the lodgings for company staff, where for the first time in her long odyssey she could enjoy the company of other women. Once she had finished her shower—a long, hot shower—she stepped out and found herself standing face to face with a short, chubby woman with a pink face and eyes like blue beads, holding a tray of continental coffee and smiling at her. They instantly became friends, perhaps because she was the first female whom Consuelo had met in almost a month.

The woman was Harriet Lowey, an American who spoke fluent Spanish with a decidedly Cuban accent—this because she was married to Doctor Eddy Azancoth, a Sephardic Jew born in Seville who had settled with her in Cuba, years ago, until he accepted a contract to come and practice in Porto Velho. Harriet herself had no connection whatsoever with the Madeira-Mamoré Railway Company—other than conjugal, through Dr. Azancoth—and she filled her time with malicious observations regarding the private lives of Porto Velho's inhabitants. Even so, there was little she could come up with of any importance, since the town was nothing more than an overgrown village with few women with whom she could share her observations. To complete matters, the fact of her being married to a Jew prevented any relationship at all with a number of those women. Harriet had also managed to incur the particular hostility of Marilyn John Kirkpatrick, the head nurse and a fanatical Methodist, who was the mistress of "King" John, the managing director of the company. All of which clearly facilitated a readiness to accept the friendship of Consuelo Campero.

On that very first morning, Consuelo had gone to visit the Indian, now interned in the indigents ward. Although clean enough, it was usually filled with workers in varying states of physical or mental collapse. Thus, it was not an especially comforting atmosphere for her Caripuna friend, but he never seemed to really notice: he kept on smiling with affection, lighting cigarettes with matches he would strike with his feet to the considerable delight of the nurses and those of the patients in less deplorable states.

Harriet Lowey Azancoth did not fail to notice Consuelo's strong interest in the Indian with no hands. She found the idea particularly repellent of an incomplete man, with two stumps of arms sticking out of his pajama shirt and a face marked by

260

ritual scars. Yet the devil of a savage had a smile of white teeth that was truly captivating—this she could not deny.

"You like him?" Harriet finally blurted out.

"Very much," Consuelo confessed.

"It must be disconcerting."

"Disconcerting?"

"Yes, I mean the fact of his having no hands."

"It is not in that particular sense that I like him, Señora Azancoth."

"Harriet, my dear. Call me Harriet."

"I feel sorry for him, Harriet, that's all."

"I thought perhaps something else was going on between you two," Harriet suggested insinuatingly. "To think of it *wickedly,* the fact of his not having any hands might not be so terrible. It might be even better than my husband."

Consuelo laughed, obviously misled by the words of Harriet Azancoth.

"It's not what you think, daughter. He's a very fine husband; I've nothing to complain of—if not for the fact of his knowing how to cook."

"He cooks?"

"Azancoth is a great chef. For me, on the other hand, it has always been a source of humiliation to prepare a meal in a kitchen. I simply don't have the gift for preparing victuals— I never learned; though, God knows, my mother tried to teach me. But Azancoth is *superb.* At times he really *annoys* me. We've had countless spats over the matter and have been separated because of it."

"You left him?"

"That's right, my dear, a long time ago, we were still quite young at the time. I had prepared some matzo balls—a Jewish dish, do you know it?—and he despised them. He got up from the table and *flew* into the kitchen, just to annoy me. Azancoth prepared the most delicious matzo balls I have ever tasted, to this day. Of course, I became absolutely furious and lost my head. I went and tore up his whole stamp collection."

"Good lord!"

"We made up a week later, when he consented to eat my own version of the dish, despite how bad it was."

Harriet could see that Consuelo's attention was focused elsewhere. . . .

"I would like to see Richard Finnegan," Consuelo finally confided with a special brightness twinkling in her eyes.

"He's a doctor, isn't he?" Harriet commented without failing to appreciate the urgency of Consuelo's demeanor. "A handsome young man, I know him by sight. He'd hardly spent a moment in Porto Velho before he was shipped off to the Abunã."

"He's back again, now, señora. Do you know what happened to us?"

"A terrible thing! You could have been killed—you were lucky. I still feel just *terrible* for the both of you."

"Dr. Finnegan has been very good to me."

"You'll find him in the ward set aside for company professionals."

"Where would that be? I'd like to pay him a visit."

"You would need a pass. Besides which, it's dangerous for a woman to go there."

"Dangerous? Why?"

"Of course, daughter, with all those men about . . ."

"The ward where they have Joe Caripuna interned is filled with men, too. It's hardly dangerous, for all that."

"The Indian is in the indigents wing, where most people are too sick to go about molesting women."

"But isn't Dr. Finnegan's ward also for the sick?"

"The company professionals are hardly ever that sick."

But the Bolivian girl was determined to find Finnegan, and since she was in no mood to solicit authorization from anyone, she quickly changed the subject.

"Harriet, why did you say that Joe's not having hands might actually be a good thing, or better than your husband?"

Harriet Azancoth smiled. "Were my husband without hands, he wouldn't have the power to *humiliate* me constantly by cooking the way he does."

Since breakfast had been scheduled for 10:45, Finnegan and Collier actually arrived an hour late at hospital commons—only to bump into Lovelace at the entrance. He had reserved a table for the three of them. He was wearing a white suit and entered with an entourage of young medics who immediately drifted off to other tables. The dining hall was a small one and must not have contained more than ten tables for four persons

262

each. A waiter and two waitresses, all dressed in white uniforms with blue aprons, were busy serving at tables.

Lovelace embraced Collier with a droll expression and then extended his hand warmly to Finnegan. Richard Finnegan no longer admired his Lovelace in quite the same fashion, but the latter hardly seemed to notice, so taken was he with his own omnipotent aura.

"My dear Richard," Lovelace began, "you're extraordinary! How did you manage to survive the odor of that barrel?"

Finnegan limited his response to a curt smile as they took their seats. Lovelace prattled on, addressing himself to Collier.

"This lad here at our side was actually dumped inside a tub of fat for cooking fritters. A nauseating brand of lard that our company imports from Italy, to be utilized here in our kitchen, but that the Italians actually manufacture to lubricate animal carts."

"He's a tough Irishman," Collier nodded.

"He must have the stomach of an ox!"

"I got sick just thinking of Finnegan, here, smearing his nose around in that putrescent barrel," Collier conceded. "Honestly, in his place I might have funked it."

"So the Germans simply vanished," Lovelace remarked more seriously now.

"The last information we have is what he and the Bolivian girl have told us: that they were at each other's throats."

"Over the girl?" Lovelace presumed.

Finnegan became suddenly agitated.

"They didn't even bother about Consuelo," he corrected. "They were fighting with each other over who was to lead them. At least that's what I could make of it."

"Fools! A girl like that is a much better thing to fight about, to my way of thinking."

"She's a woman and then some," the engineer agreed. "Even with her eccentricities—she would appear to have a taste for copulating with savages."

"That's not true!" protested Finnegan.

The engineer and the doctor eyed each other and laughed. Finnegan flushed in embarrassment; he had lost whatever appetite he might have had up to that moment, even though the food they began to serve looked rather appealing.

"You seem quite well, Lovelace," Collier observed. "A

health proportionate to your fanaticism, man. Those cheeks of yours are rosy as a child's buttocks."

Lovelace pinched his own cheeks coyly.

"You're in good spirits yourself, Stephan. It makes me happy just to see it!"

"I'm not in good spirits, Lovelace. In fact, I ought to be downright desperate, were I any kind of engineer. Our beloved Mad Maria should already have crossed the straits of the Abunã several weeks ago."

"Then you're the best-natured failure I know, Stephan Collier."

"Precisely!"

The engineer looked around the dining hall, paying particular attention to the many nurses who were seated at the tables, all of them young, male, and the majority apparently North American.

"No women here, Lovelace?"

"Women?"

"Females—nurses . . ."

"Of course, my dear Stephan, but only a few, given the fact that the majority of our patients are decidedly male."

"And why haven't you sent one of them—preferably with succulent breasts and an equivocal smile—to nurture Finnegan and myself over in our pavilion?"

"Because neither of you is sufficiently ill to merit such radical treatment."

"Then at least one with the kind of smile certain women cultivate—you know: somewhere between maternal and libidinal."

"If you were both fatally ill and this were your last request, I might consider it. . . ."

"What did you send us? Some waddling buffoon of a male nurse who can barely manage to wield his thermometer!"

"That must have been young Barth."

"Barth, eh?"

"Before his arrival here, he practiced metallurgy in Cleveland, where he controlled the temperature of smelting furnaces. Poor Barth still manages to confuse things terribly, I dare say."

There followed several moments during which no one spoke as they ate enthusiastically, with the exception of Richard Finnegan, who had lost his appetite over Consuelo's purported

264

affection for that pestilential Indian. The dining hall was grad-ually emptying of people.

"When are we to be discharged from the hospital?" Collier asked Lovelace, while wiping his mouth with a napkin.

"That remains to be seen," the doctor answered with smug satisfaction etched into his smile.

"What are you talking about?"

"It depends, my dear fellow, on when you return to your health."

"But neither one of us is sick, Lovelace."

"Then what on earth are you doing in my pavilion?"

Consuelo Campero had waited for everybody in the com-pany staff lodgings to be asleep, including Harriet Azancoth, who had sat knitting until her husband fell asleep in the chair where he always sat, fondling an old philatelic catalog of im-printed stamps before going to bed. Eventually, Consuelo was able to make her way without incident to the VIP pavilion. The nurses on the night shift were too busy snoring to notice a woman in a nightgown tiptoeing through the corridors washed in the half-light of dim electric lamps.

Only two of the beds in the ward were occupied and Con-suelo soon identified Richard Finnegan, secluded from his sur-roundings by a mosquito net which draped from the ceiling like the canopy of a bed from the Middle Ages. In the bed adjacent to Richard's, in defiance of regulations, Stephen Col-lier snored facedown with no pajama top and the mosquito netting drawn back behind the headboard.

Consuelo lifted Richard's netting and Richard, who was sleeping lightly, immediately opened his eyes. It was not a dream, because an odor of suspense and carnality drifted from her and began to eclipse his own will. Consuelo immediately placed her index finger across her fleshy lips, pleading silence as Richard got up cautiously and took her by the hand. She looked around her and noticed the screens. As she pulled Rich-ard in the direction of one of the beds hidden behind the par-titions, Consuelo felt surprised at his clear hesitation.

"Don't be silly," she whispered in his ear.

The image of a pair of dying patients floundering on those mattresses now hidden behind the screens, however, was still uppermost in the physician's mind, stifling in him any other conceivable fixation. Nonetheless, our Richard let himself be led to wherever the Bolivian girl wished to take him. Hardly had the two of them disappeared behind partitions when Collier rolled over and opened his eyes, letting out a smile before drifting back to sleep again.

Consuelo had to practically force poor Richard to sit on one of the beds from which the nurses had earlier removed all the sheets, leaving only the bare, gray mattresses.

"A man died here, today," Richard said to her but so softly that she misunderstood him entirely.

"I've been dying to see you, too, Richard," she whispered hotly. "When I was inside that barrel I discovered something."

"He croaked right here on this bed," Richard continued in the same inaudible voice.

"You were cloaked in the same discovery?" Consuelo was radiant. "Oh, Richard, how I thought about you that whole time . . . about how kind you'd been to me, the tender patience you showed me throughout my tribulations."

"The fellow agonized with convulsions just before he passed away," Richard volunteered feebly.

"I didn't realize you felt the same confusion about me."

Indeed, she herself still felt conflicting sensations—though not altogether disagreeable ones. Richard's reluctance, which she attributed to timidity, became a further proof of his fine character and thus fanned the species of fire that was already consuming Consuelo Campero. The more the morbid ambience perturbed the physician, the more the Bolivian girl had to admire what she thought to be his atypically masculine comportment. Until, on an impulse, she began to slip off her nightgown over her head, revealing in the half-light a pale fleshiness of luminescent intensity. The smell of her, of her sex, hit Richard Finnegan like a fist in the groin, and he reached out aching to embrace his revelation, bruising Consuelo's lips with a long-forgotten frenzy. He paused long enough to tear off his pajamas and wrap her in a naked embrace. Soon they were throbbing, one upon the other, frantically pumping to their climax.

Toward morning, Collier and Finnegan were awakened by the unusual commotion in the ward. The Bolivian girl had departed immediately after their midnight encounter, sending

266

Finnegan back to his bed. Now, the nurses were wheeling in three victims of beriberi. All three patients—topographers, rather young, recently returned from the region of Guajará-Mirim—were in deplorable states.

The engineer immediately sat up in his bed to observe with obvious displeasure the whole sad parade. He glanced over at Finnegan with a look of irritation, while the medics proceeded to transfer two of the patients into exactly the same beds where the two men had died on the previous day and where the physician had lately discovered the charms of the Bolivian. A third patient, less debilitated, was installed at the far end of the ward, directly beneath the tall open window.

Finnegan, who was still lying down, fully shared the engineer's displeasure.

"You know, you ought to take a bath," Collier said sarcastically to vent his annoyance.

"Not so loud, please," admonished one of the male nurses carrying an enameled chamber pot, "show some courtesy to the other patients."

"Fuck you," Collier growled facetiously.

"Why the hell should I take a bath?" Finnegan wanted to know.

"Because you have a smell."

"What smell?"

"The smell of low tide—do I make myself clear?" Collier smiled sarcastically.

The physician did not bother to answer. Instead, he got up, grabbed a towel, and headed toward the bathroom, feeling quite contented with the smell of seashells emanating from his loins. When he returned from his shower, he found the engineer already dressed, slipping on his boots. Two of the sick patients, hands clutching the headboards of their beds, were trembling throughout the length of their bodies in a strange dance that they themselves followed with stoic forbearance.

"Well, my lad," Collier asked him, "have you a mind to keep hanging around this pesthole?"

"What else? We still haven't been discharged, have we?"

The engineer stood up, trying out his boots, then turned a superior eye on the physician.

"You and I have just been awarded a discharge, my boy."

"By whom?"

"By me! You're a doctor—how long do you estimate those poor saps will last in such a condition?"

Finnegan glanced obliquely at the three patients, and a knot of pity welled up within him for the poor wretches who were now barely on their feet over by the window, dancing about in a ridiculous manner.

"About two days, no more. They're a lost cause, I'm afraid."

"Well, then: discharged for two days!"

"What will we do for two days?"

"Get well, man!"

"You're not planning anything foolhardy, now, are you, sir?"

"I thought you'd finally given up addressing me as *sir*."

"Sorry, Collier."

"That's better. Every time you call me *sir*, I get the feeling I've become one of those old, retired sergeants sitting out his days in some military home for the aged."

Finnegan smiled, combing his wet hair.

"Get some clothes on, man. And be quick about it!"

"Where are we going?"

"Anyplace, as long as it's not here. I've had enough of that dancing—I don't like the choreography. Folk dances have never appealed to me."

"Yes, it's hardly enjoyable," Finnegan said, casting another glance at the three.

"Let's bash off, then, before we really get morbid."

Although the engineer was in a jolly hurry, it was no easy matter to slip away from the ward. With the presence of three new patients, vigilance was redoubled and hordes of medics seemed to be constantly entering and exiting through the main receiving room, as well as sauntering along the corridors all throughout the pavilion. The two fugitives were summarily apprehended several times and forcefully returned to their beds. Collier, of course, blamed Finnegan for their repeated failures and spent the rest of the day muttering not entirely inaudible insults. Only toward the end of the afternoon, while dinner was being served, did they manage to escape—this time by jumping out of the window and walking inconspicuously as possible away from the hospital grounds, down to the bank of the river, where they found a canoe tied to a floating dock.

They were soon embarked and Collier indicated to Finnegan the direction they were to follow. The afternoon was dying and the yellow waters of the river commenced to turn a brownish gray, reflecting the ribbons of pink and violet clouds. The engineer was whistling an old English ditty and occasionally broke into singing a stanza here and there:

"The young swells in Rotten Row
All cut it mighty fine,
And quiz the fair sex, you know,
And swear it is divine.
The pretty little horsebreakers
Are breaking hearts for fun,
For in Rotten Row they all must go
The whole hog or none.

The two were rowing animatedly, though without haste, drinking in the night air that scudded along the surface of the waters. When the darkness became impenetrable, Collier lit a kerosene lamp that had been hung in the bow. Two or three dots of light appeared immediately ahead, while behind them a constellation of luminous points signaled their distance from the Candelária Hospital. The sky above was dark and satiny. Ahead was Porto Santo Antônio, the most important harbor city along that whole stretch of the Rio Madeira. It was there that the engineer was headed with his physician friend.

Finnegan, however, could not shake his nervousness at having committed an infraction of company regulations. Almost two hours later—a length of time that, to him, seemed an eternity—their canoe glided in silence, out of the jungle and the river's darkness, up to the docks that fronted the city of Santo Antônio.

Collier jumped out of the canoe, without ceasing to whistle his song, balancing himself along the precarious gangway that rocked upon the water's edge. The city seemed deserted. Without the concert of buzzing insects, there would have been no sign of life of any kind, let alone human. Collier tied up the canoe and took out the lantern. Finnegan remained where he sat, feeling chilled and repenting of having come along in the first place—his anxious eyes scanning the nearly invisible line of the city just above the riverbank.

"You plan to sit there all night?"

"Where are we, Collier?"

"Nowhere in particular. This is Porto Santo Antônio, one of the worst spots on earth."

The physician felt the urge to untie the canoe and row back, such was the degree of desperation which now took hold of him. Little did it matter to him that the city might turn out to be one of the worst places on earth; the serious thing was that they were off limits here: there were strict company prohibitions against any employees, regardless of rank, leaving company territory without explicit orders to that effect.

"Jump out, man! What's the matter?"

"We're off limits."

"That's what's interesting about it."

The breeze carried a stench of excrement and decayed meat. It was the first gutterings of Santo Antônio.

"Besides which, this town stinks," Finnegan added.

"Courage, my boy. Upwards and onwards—it's a repellent populace, I'll grant you, but you're about to get an education."

Finnegan stood up and nearly lost his balance.

"Careful," Collier warned him.

The physician leaped onto the wharf of old planks, steadied himself, and slipped his hands into his pockets.

"I don't think I'm going to like this," he complained forlornly.

"I just remembered," Collier said, looking strangely afflicted.

"What?" Finnegan asked, suddenly alarmed.

"I forgot to tell you something. You remember that Barbadian, Jonathan?"

"The one who broke into the infirmary that night? Of course, he tried to throw in with the Germans!"

"Well, he hung himself in his cell."

"Hung himself?"

"He confessed everything. We took him to Porto Velho and they threw him in the local quod. It seems he knotted a sheet and hung himself from the window bars."

"You were friends, weren't you, Collier."

"We worked together for a bit, but we weren't friends. Old Jonathan had high moral principles."

"That's probably why he killed himself; he wouldn't have endured prison."

"He killed himself because he had no moral principle—I

270

detest suicides! And in a place like this it's entirely superfluous. No one comes here, except to commit suicide!"

"But you just told me that Jonathan was a man of high moral principles!"

"And he was—I never met anyone with greater moral sense than that Barbadian."

Stephan Collier raised the lantern, illuminating a steep wooden stairway that ascended the side of the bank but had been partially rotted out by the flood tides.

"Be careful," he warned the physician. "This stairway is a bloody rat trap!"

The two of them began to climb carefully, checking each creaky step. The physician grew more and more irritated because the ascent was so precarious, and he was certain that in the end none of it would prove to have been worth the risk they were taking. Life bared its broken teeth with a vengeance, however, as both men fumbled their way up the bank toward the dingy lights of Santo Antônio.

15

Percival Farquhar had just finished ogling the display windows full of sweets at Colombo's while savoring the taste of his latest victory. Typically, he had not purchased any sweetmeats, for he would not dare to break the charm of it and allowed his gluttony to evaporate only through frustration.

Born among the Quakers—was he still one of them? Most assuredly! He could even hear the voice of his own father, muttering drunkenly that only with God must he ever settle accounts. And to Percival, God was none other than the Great Auditor, the Man-of-Business incarnate. He was still a Quaker because he could feel the stirring of inner voices, at every moment, the tremor of the Divine Word. Upon awakening each day, he forever found himself amidst the living silence of God. He was certainly an unequivocal man; he had the peculiar talent of being able to appear to be bargaining while insisting on his price. And this talent was sometimes exercized so swiftly that Farquhar himself might have actually doubted whether God in His Wisdom had managed to follow his steps, were it not an impiety to have wondered. In any case, since all his days were sanctified, our Farquhar clung to cultivating a solemnity befitting such a man of business.

Farquhar had always experienced these indescribable respites that would follow each victory, a pleasurable suspense—perhaps it was a tic gradually picked up and eventually engraved upon his poor farm boy's heart. With each deal shuffled in the darkness, there was the reassurance of the feigned compromise, the planned evasion, since a Quaker knew enough never to give his word. Indeed, the deals were felled into place with the adroitness of a champion pugilist. (Exactly so! Farquhar exulted.) The violence had been contained; its traces, erased. Ahead of him lay only the trajectory of his political predilections. He had imperceptibly climbed another step upward; he had outgrown his apprenticeship and few had even noticed the fact, only God and himself. Percival preferred it that way: the precise dissimulation of the prestidigitator, which was sometimes confused with sanctity itself.

Reflected in the shop window of Colombo's were the faces of the secretaries and ministers of state—including the especially dumbfounded face of J. J. Seabra—and his own clean-shaven face, healthy looking in the morning sunlight. This was a day to smile and to pursue fresh compromises. Once he had turned his back and began to walk briskly to his office, Percival could not help but remember (with a touch of nostalgia!) the body of the woman he had had to renounce. Immediately, however, the image disolved as his inner voice reassured him that none of that mattered anymore—Rio was full of women and the doors of Catete would never again slam in his face!

Farquhar was still a bit piqued at having allowed himself to have been drawn in by the typically Latin American arrogance of Colonel Agostinho. (How could I have been such a damned ding-a-ling! Though the fellow obviously disguised his fatuousness behind all the mumblety-peg of European manners and *raffine* gestures egregious for their punctuation of pinkies in the air. . . .) He cut across Avenida Central through the congestion of sputtering vehicles and cloppeting horses, nettled by his deficient appraisal of the colonel, yet bolstered by his own Quaker spirit.

Only he knew how much he loved the life he was leading, with no remorse, persistently nourishing his desire to profit by every moment, even the most exceptional. And he did nothing especial by this because even the unhappiest of men would act, he felt certain, in similar fashion. The wretched evidenced no great differences from himself. In their abject existences they dissipated life identically as he, with the one disparity: they demonstrated that he was on the right path. (Through God's will, he thought to himself, I am a positive being. By the act of God am I thus and, like the wretched, I also love life.)

It was a radiant morning along Avenida Central: the carts of peddlers, the carriages with powerful horses, the automobiles at twenty miles per hour, the orchestra of acrobats and violins advertising a haberdashery shop, jackets and ties. In the triumph and the scamper, in the strident and strange song of wooden wheels and rubber tires rolling along on the cobbled street, Percival found what he loved: money, life, the Farquhar syndicate, the heat, this morsel of life in summer. A glad highbinder, tickled with the easygoing tide of the national temperament!

Once, Percival had admitted that he loved wealth because wealth was like simplicity itself in the eyes of the people. Few persons understood what he had meant at the time. But wealth *was* nothing short of utter simplicity and in its faculty approached an attribute of the divine: that of the ease of being in many places at the same time. Wealth was ubiquitously there in the commotion of Avenida Central, among the vagabonds and Bohemians, in the voraciousness of the length and breadth of that tropical city, on the very sidewalks where gypsies turned up tarot cards to read the fortunes of passersby. Without sarcasm, wealth could even be found in the heart of the common idler.

Later, at his office, while sifting through the piles of correspondence, Percival had a talk with Colonel Agostinho. He had long expected such a visit, although he had not received any prior communication as to its fact. The morning proved to be particularly mild and the colonel seemed euphoric. Farquhar continued to browse through his mail—his manner of keeping at arm's length the ebullience of the colonel. He was also contemptuous of the degraded solidarity of this ambitious man who, with a report full of lies had so moved the marshal and disconcerted Seabra—that is, if J. J. Seabra were truly a man to let himself be disconcerted.

"The woman has been neutralized," Agostinho announced proudly. "At this moment she must be on her way to Lisbon."

"Why Lisbon?"

"One of the syndicate ships was embarking for Lisbon; so we decided to save the price of a passage. She took her mother with her, and a younger brother."

Farquhar, despite his attention to what the colonel was saying, did not lift his eyes from the mail on his desk, like a polished "overworked" impressario.

"And don't you worry about Seabra," Agostinho assured him. "He himself saw to the exit papers for her embarkation."

"Splendid!"

The colonel smiled.

"It was my idea. I called one of the hoods in Seabra's pocket and slipped him a few *milreis*. So the fellow agreed to deliver a message to the woman, *suggesting* she might want to take a

274

voyage. She was terrified, of course, and apparently begged Seabra to allow her to go. It seems the idea had already crossed Seabra's mind as well, so there were no objections. It was as if the thing were part of his own plans!"

"Splendid," Farquhar repeated, although his demeanor was a touch ambiguous because it was still concentrated upon the letter he pretended to read.

The colonel, however, refused to perceive the ambiguity.

"I made sure they arived directly in Seabra's hands, the tickets, I mean. On the pretext of amends for troubles caused. In your name, of course. Seabra accepted the offer without a wince. He must have wanted to be free of the girl as quickly as possible."

"So the house is empty?"

"No, obviously! You know how the marshal is. He might decide at any moment to check up on my informants."

"Then he doesn't have complete confidence in you?" Farquhar chided lightly.

"Of course he does—absolutely! The marshal has nothing but the greatest respect for me. But in these cases of promiscuity he can be extremely finicky. Besides which, there's always an unpredictable side to him. But there won't be any problem: for the moment I have a family living over there in São Cristóvão which corresponds exactly to the one in my report."

"So Seabra actually agreed to cough up the 'charity'?"

"Not on your life! Nor did I even consider asking him to pay. The family are in my confidence. After two or three months, when everything has blown over, they'll be evicted."

"That's the way it goes," said Farquhar.

"Yes, that's life," the colonel hastened to agree.

Farquhar set aside the letters on his desk and for the first time looked up to observe Colonel Agostinho.

"From now on, Agostinho, you stick to politics."

"I understand nothing of politics. My strength lies elsewhere, Percival. I'm a strategist."

"And what is strategy, if not politics, man?"

The colonel spent a moment or two pondering the words of the American.

"That's why I tell you, colonel—from now on, it's politics

for you. You will help to encourage Seabra's candidacy for the governorship of Bahia. You'll obtain it for him."

"I'm not the type to play ward boss, Percival."

Farquhar smiled.

"I don't want a ward boss. You're not going to stage rallies or run around shaking hands with the electorate."

"Thank God for that," the colonel sighed, relieved. "So what type of politics are you contemplating for me?"

"Palace strategy, something I know you're good at, Agostinho."

The colonel clasped his hands together in his lap. They felt curiously cold and sweated.

"The governorship of Bahia: that's what Seabra covets the most, right now, am I right?"

"Everything points in that direction, Percival."

"J. J. Seabra is no pushover—he's a tough man."

"But he's ours, now."

"I wouldn't be too sure, if I were you," Farquhar warned, with a growing irritation at the colonel's lack of strategic insight.

"Oh, I'm quite certain," the colonel reiterated, proving a lack of tactical sense as well.

Farquhar meditated a moment on the quality of his associates: crap!

"Seabra must go to Bahia."

"What advantages will accrue with Seabra's election?"

"With his election? None."

"Then why help him? Let him fall on his own face, bending over to drink at our coffers."

"I don't want Seabra drinking at *my* coffer."

"But isn't that what we're after, Percival?"

"If he goes to Bahia, what will happen, Agostinho?"

"He'll leave the ministry."

"Which will give *us* a ministry."

"Which *would* give us a ministry, that's what you mean, isn't it?"

"I believe that you still maintain sufficient prestige to indicate the next minister? Am I correct in that assumption, my strategist colonel?"

The colonel blushed; Farquhar was addressing him in that

same ironic manner as the many generals who so envied his military schooling in France.

"We will select the new minister, have no fear of that!"

"Splendid," Farquhar remarked dryly, returning to his perusal of a letter written on extremely delicate rice paper.

"I give Seabra no more than six months in the ministry," the colonel said with a wave of the fingers.

"A reasonable amount of time for all of us, I should think. During this time, however," Farquhar added as an afterthought, "we shall maintain, let us say, cordial relations."

"I will do everything to encourage his candidacy, Percival."

"Once he's in Bahia, there will be so much for him to do he will forget all about us. And, as we have no interests tied into Bahia . . . he will arrange himself another delicious mistress and Hermes da Fonseca will be none the wiser."

"You liked that woman, didn't you?" the colonel offered tentatively.

Farquhar did not choose to respond; he remained pensive for a while longer as Colonel Agostinho stared at the letter of thin, perfumed sheets of rice paper and judged that perhaps it was in the handwriting of that very same woman.

"It's a letter from her," Percival finally admitted, holding up three sheets of the delicate paper. "A farewell."

"Can you believe I never got to meet her? But they tell me she's quite a beauty. Seabra took her out of the gutter, turned her into a jewel, and shared it all with you!"

"It's a thing of the past," Farquhar concluded curtly, folding the delicate sheets of rustling paper.

The colonel nodded his head sympathetically. Farquhar slipped the letter into an inside pocket of his jacket and once more turned his attention to Agostinho.

"Seabra telephoned yesterday."

"And what did he say?" the colonel asked a little apprehensively.

"He wanted to confirm the meeting that was marked on his calendar, with myself, this afternoon at five o'clock."

"Did you really have such a meeting scheduled between you?"

"I verified the fact on my own agenda. Adams had written it down for me, but the meeting was actually for last week at this time—exactly on the day you ordered the girl to be kidnapped. . . ."

Agostinho's face reddened. "You still think it was an error?"

"What's the point of worrying about that now. What's done is done and there's no turning back."

"It was not a very good tactical maneuver, I realize that," confessed the colonel.

"An unpardonable strategic blunder," Farquhar corrected plainly.

The meeting between the head of the Farquhar syndicate and the minister of transportation and public works took place at six o'clock that afternoon, precisely because it had been planned for an hour earlier. J. J. Seabra received the American with his glacial backlander's courtesy. Percival Farquhar presented himself, there in the cabinet of the ministry, with all the polite affability of his Quaker mountebankery. They would soon reach their understanding, however, because each knew how to keep the distance that had always separated them.

It was already after office hours in the ministry and the corridors were nearly empty of employees. Seabra's office was stuffy and ponderous beneath the prismatic glitter of the crystal chandelier suspended from the ceiling.

"Please sit down," Seabra began, pointing to an easy chair and stepping out from behind his narrow desk.

Farquhar accommodated himself in one of the three armchairs that faced a longish sofa in a mediocre assemblage of dark blue velvet with fugitive pretensions to Second Empire. It was here that J.J. received his visitors when objectives were less than clear.

"Quite a pleasant day out today," Farquhar suggested.

"The weather doesn't interest me," Seabra replied. "It's a subject fit for those who have nothing on their minds."

Percival bowed his head, saluting the astuteness of the minister's observation.

"You're quite right: the weather doesn't matter at all," he conceded.

"But today has turned out to be a beautiful day. The heat's not oppressive and I'd like to be at the beach, frankly."

"I've never been one for the beach," Farquhar responded. "I don't have any patience for the sand or the ocean."

"Some day only the beaches will be left in this city . . . and the summer!"

"I'm rather fond of Rio de Janeiro."

"So you like Rio? Curious . . . I presumed you would find it too exotic a city."

Percival smiled. "I like the exotic—it's very lucrative, the exotic."

"Lucrative?" J.J.'s eyebrows lifted imperiously.

"It's difficult to explain, Your Excellency. Yet I find there's a strict connection between the exotic and my income."

"So I've heard," J.J. reflected.

"I'm rather pained whenever I'm obliged, for some reason, to leave Rio."

"Don't you like New York?"

"Has Your Excellency ever visited New York?"

"Of course, I've been there several times. It's a repellent city and filled with drunks."

"I come from a different part of the States, quite the opposite of New York—I'm from the country."

"I also come from the country—I grew up there."

"I hate the country," Farquhar remarked, recalling the drinking bouts of his father on those far-off weekends of his childhood.

"I have no special sentiments with regard to the country. I barely think of it since I left. A long time ago," J.J. explained.

"But you like it here in Rio, of course, don't you?"

"Rio is an abomination."

Seabra got up and went back to his desk, where he picked up a portfolio full of documents. He leafed through the papers as he came back to sit in the armchair closest to Farquhar's.

"How did you meet her?" he began in earnest.

"Who?"

"Her!"

"The girl?"

J.J. assented, nodding his head.

"She'd always go to Colombo's Confectionary in the mornings. Buying herself lots of sweets, she was charming."

"Now she will carry off her charms to the Portuguese," J.J. reflected a bit dejectedly. "A pity, she was the kind of product we should never have to export."

"Now we're faced with a *capital* loss, all right."

J.J. laughed, holding onto his file of papers.

"She had wonderful hair," Percival mused.

"It wasn't so much her hair I liked," J.J. interjected. "It was that birthmark on the inside of her right thigh that always excited me."

Farquhar tried to remember it.

"Funny, I never noticed. She would never let me turn on the light while we were together."

"I worshiped that birthmark, let me tell you. It looked like a juicy plum."

"And not her hair? You really didn't like her exquisite hair?"

"A little oily and coarse for my taste," Seabra mulled pensively. "But she had enough that was extraordinary."

"The eyes!" exclaimed Percival. "What eyes!"

"The breasts! Such pink nipples..."

"Her lips! Those teeth..."

"And such an incredibly honeyed whisper when she talked," J.J. sighed to himself.

"And her skin, perpetually warm, wherever you touched..."

"And smelling of oysters," J.J. echoed, recollecting.

"Oysters?" Percival was surprised by the description. "I thought it was more the smell of rain."

"What's the difference, as long as you never saw the birthmark like a plum that she had on her thigh."

"A pity I missed it."

"You see, I had some profit after all," Seabra concluded. "The birthmark at least was mine alone!"

Farquhar concurred with a nod, remembering to himself how many times he had run his tongue over that birthmark, imagining it was a tender plum.

"Well, she's gone to the Portuguese now. May they profit by her."

"Maybe we'll forget her, if it's possible...."

"I've already forgotten her," Seabra grumbled, opening the folder of documents. "Now, Senhor Percival, about your concessions in Paraná. You seem to be having problems with the Indians in the area, and the policy of the marshal is to protect the indigenous populations."

"Have you visited the area, Your Excellency?"

"Never."

"Well, I've been there any number of times and never came across any Indians to justify such concern."

"But there *are* Indians in that region!"

"Who gave you this information?"

"I don't even remember," Seabra confessed.

"Your Excellency, let me assure you that there are no Indians down there."

"Then your problems are over for Brazil Lumber."

"Thank you, Your Excellency, but there's one other small matter I'd like to discuss. It concerns the São Paulo-Rio Grande Railway."

"What about it?"

"It's one of my other companies. The plan is to cut a railway south."

Seabra leafed his way through the folder to the papers in question.

"But the territories have already been expropriated and handed over to your company. I don't see the problem."

"Some of the small farmers have been grumbling about the eviction. They may create a scandal. There's even some fanatic inciting them to rebellion."

"The Indians want to rebel there?"

"No Indians . . . they don't exist in that region. The peasants, for lack of a better word . . ."

"I'll see to that, I promise you! And the Madeira-Mamoré?"

"Moving along as scheduled. No peasants, there . . . just Indians."

"Thank God for that!" J.J. closed the portfolio, coughed, and stared up at the glittering crystal prisms of his chandelier. "It would have been a lot better . . ."

". . . if there were just Indians in Paraná as well?"

"No, no . . . if we hadn't lost her."

BOOK IV

If You Can't Escape, Relax and Enjoy It

16

Stephan Collier had already witnessed a great deal in his life, perhaps more than any one man should see. At Bull Run, while routing Union troops with Stonewall Jackson, he had scrutinized the perfect round hole, drilled into the forehead of an army friend, eighteen years old just like himself. At Chancellorsville, Virginia, during five days of running fire in May of 1863, he had watched Jackson himself agonize, mortally wounded, despite the victory of his army. In the following year during the bombardment of Atlanta by Sherman's troops, he had witnessed the brutal deaths of his mother and father and the sacking of their colonnaded mansion. At the surrender of Richmond, he barely escaped a firing squad—accused of being an English spy. Decidedly, Collier had already seen a great deal in his life. Yet, even with all that, he could never get over his astonishment—no matter how many times he came back to Santo Antônio—at the macabre array of leftover locomotives and abandoned tracks swallowed up by the boscage encrouching the wharf.

The night was limpidly clear and its white moon blenched a cluster of houses, just as Collier and the physician reached the crest of the bank, stepping gingerly and panting heavily because the wooden stairway was nearly rotted out and the slimy turf was cratered with puddles.

"I want to show you something, Finnegan," Collier said impulsively, dragging him off into the thicket.

The engineer swept aside the bracken and leaves, then held out the lantern to cast light upon a metallic, rusted shape half-buried in the mud. Procumbent among the tall weeds and yawning ferns was an old steam locomotive whose forlornness, Collier persisted in telling himself, had not diminished the dignity of its composure.

"That's the predecessor to Mad Maria," he explained.

"It looks like she didn't have quite the same luck," Finnegan commented indifferently.

"There she lies, abandoned like a stray bitch."

The engineer was clearly moved, but also disturbed at the doctor's indifference.

"This isn't the way to bury a queen," the Englishman in him insisted.

"Who left her here?"

"Colonel George Church; ever heard of him?"

"Never."

Collier lifted the lantern to the level of the doctor's face.

"Well, anyway, long before we came along there were other idiots who tried to put a railroad through here."

"Were they English?"

"No, Americans. Colonel Church brought his men down here in about 1870, before you were born, lad, with the same demented notion of building a railroad."

"Demented?"

"Without a doubt!"

The engineer lowered the lantern and said nothing more. He let go of the ferns and leaves he had pushed aside, and they once again enclosed the locomotive in its foliated tomb of verdure and silt. Collier walked back to the edge of the riverbank and, lantern swaying, abandoned the physician to the darkness. At the water's edge his thoughts drifted back to a point in time which for him epitomized the absurdity of it all. It was a winter night in Richmond, Virginia, in the year 1909, and he considered himself retired. He was asking Percival Farquhar why the devil he had decided to build a railway that left from nothing and went nowhere. And he could still recall how vexed he felt to even bother with such a question. He also felt rather old, although he was trim, athletic, even vigorous for his age. His vexation mounted each time he would return Farquhar's gaze. The Quaker was a stubby fellow, with a fortyish appearance and the mannerisms of a con artist that not even his expensive suit could conceal—however much he might otherwise pretend. They were seated at a table inside a tavern in Richmond, Virginia. It was the middle of winter. And he could remember how his irritation—or might it have been, who knows? blatant fury!—was actually provoked by that acute sensation of contumelious disorder which Farquhar unfailingly seemed to engender, no matter where he turned up. Collier recollected how long it had taken that same mountebank

286

to give his answer, lackadaisically procuring some superlative response, while he himself, the retired pensioner, sat accumulating in his mind's ear a succession of solemn swearwords that redoubled in ferocity the moment the Quaker uttered his response, annexing Collier's very question to his answer in the confounded process! Why construct a railway from nothing to nowhere? Why? I'll tell you why! Because it just might prove to be as lucrative as an act of the Divine. . . . And the Englishman had exploded with an oath: *Bloody hell!* And a second curse had strangulated in his dry throat: *Son of a Bitch!* Right you are, bloody hell! Why not sign your swinish contract! And then Farquhar proceeded to lament the way the engineer was forever flying off the handle at every connivance of his peerless mountebankery. I never understand you, Collier! If you're not having a conniption at me you're blowing a gasket. . . . You're the most total son of a bitch I know, Percival Farquhar! It's as simple as that. . . . Only a mule like Stephan Collier had the courage to put such things to Farquhar's face, and he was quite certain that this scoundrel of a Quaker had already chicaned more than himself—probably half the government, if not the entire nation! You're just the out-of-work construction engineer I've been looking for, Farquhar had chided jokingly. But Collier was not "out of work" nor in need of money. I'm retired, Farquhar, he had told him, so you can just count me out. . . . But that persistent Quaker son of a bitch had refused to give in: Retired? Don't make me laugh, Stephan Collier. . . . And Farquhar had laughed, spilling more bourbon over the engineer's shot glass, since he himself never touched anything alcoholic. And the engineer had tossed it down with a jerk of his head, never taking his eyes off the Quaker, who sat quietly massaging the tip of his nose. Just my Lady Luck, Collier concluded to himself, to always have to throw in with sons of bitches, the likes of Percival Farquhar!

Richard Finnegan commenced to walk alone in the darkness and promptly fell into a mud puddle, rousing the engineer from his reverie.

"You going to hang around at the edge of that bank all night?" Finnegan complained, more than ever repentant at having come to such a place.

Collier approached the physician and lifted the lantern. The moon had turned sallowish, and the cloud formations, rushing by, bleared its yellow eye. He and his companion now set out in the direction of the darkening cluster of houses. As they shambled along across the blighted stretch of sward, the odor of steaming rot intensified.

"Who exactly was this Colonel Church?" the physician inquired, more to break the silence than anything else.

"One hell of a soldier, to be sure—that much he managed to prove on the Potomac. But down here he needed something more than military prowess. To advance just two miles of track, he lost close to two hundred men! Can you imagine something like that?"

The physician was finding it difficult to pay attention to the engineer, afraid as he was of slipping again and tumbling into the putrid sump.

"A hundred men per mile!" Collier exclaimed.

"It would have taken most of humanity to finish the job at that rate," Finnegan ventured between the pools pocked into the slime.

"One hundred lives to the mile, just to get his silly train to go from one end to the other, hauling rubber."

"Sounds more like a slaughterhouse than a railroad. . . ."

"That's what Church must of thought, too, when he was obliged to bury over half of his work force."

"As a good officer he should have known the right moment to pull back his forces."

"A good officer maybe, but an inferior chess player."

"Chess player?"

"He lost his queen back there in the bushes," Collier said drolly.

They resumed walking along in silence—a silence that actually roared all around them, as thousands of frogs and millions of insects filled the night with sound.

"Poor George Church," the physician mused.

"Poor us, you mean—we're not of the same breed as Colonel Church. Cannon fodder is what we are. . . ."

"I guess you're right, Collier. We're probably fucked down here."

The engineer paused and turned to observe his colleague, shocked by such an admission.

"Have you lost your enthusiasm, lad?"

"I told you not to call me *lad*," Finnegan complained sourly.

"It's nothing personal, my lad."

"Fuck you!"

"You see, we *are* savages, Finnegan, savages who can't even down an occasional pint. We're chaste as little virgins."

Finnegan smiled embarrassedly.

"That's right, I forgot that you screwed that Bolivian girl," Collier chided.

The doctor stopped laughing in his tracks and scowled at his companion.

"It's no good denying it—I saw the whole show. In the same bed as one of our recently departed! Have you no respect, man?"

"Look here, Collier, I understand a man like you. That is, I try to. I can imagine how difficult it must be to spend years and years outside of your own country, the harrowing episodes, from one shithole to another. I imagine that's what it takes to be a true pioneer."

The Englishman looked up at Finnegan and bored his way into the physician's eyes, then gave vent to his frustration with stinging irony.

"Such a portrait of me positively warms my cockles, you little humbug!"

"Not at all, old fellow."

"Old is the bitch that bore you, Finnegan!"

"All right, Collier, all right..."

"You have talent, Finnegan, you really do. I think you're a perfect candidate for pioneering."

"No thank you, Collier, the pioneering days are over."

The engineer nodded, laughing. A stronger, chillier breeze was coming off the river, dissipating the smell of rot, rippling the pools of water that stippled the earth in the moonlight.

"It's you, the Americans, who have put an end to pioneering," Collier continued. "To be a pioneer, nowadays, is to be an Indian fighter or a gunslinger playing Puritan."

"Well, the world could use some order," Finnegan suggested with irony.

"Bravo, my boy! The old mania for greatness, so dear to the British Empire, will no longer do. There has to be a bit of order to the plunder."

"Who said anything about plunder?"

"Why else are we building the wheels of dominion?"

"Cut the crap, Collier. We're here to do a job."

"A job, is it? Give up the farce, Finnegan. I did."

"Is that why you pulled out your revolver on the Germans?"

"I happen to be a professional, that's all, and would gladly put a hole in the first one to start any foolishness."

"You're supposed to be an engineer, Collier, not a police officer."

"Down here, it all amounts to the same thing."

"I disagree. You and I are here to work for progress."

"Sheer rubbish! You want to know what progress is? A pack of thieves in politician's clothes humbugging an entire nation: Burma, India, Africa, Australia—those are the targets."

"So, we're leaving our mark on the world!"

"Yes, we make our little contributions. Next to the brick jail is the wooden schoolhouse to train native bureaucrats in subservience. And don't forget to teach the young babus a little soccer. And when they get older, to drink whiskey—especially to drink whiskey. Meanwhile, in the clubs of the *pukkasahibs*, year after year, we drag out the same impervious conversations about black swabs and inferior half-castes. All this, while we fill our faces and grow rich! While we infect the world with our own vices, destroying everything!"

Collier could see that Finnegan regarded him disapprovingly.

"Don't pretend you Americans are any different—things haven't changed at all. The only difference is that you won't have to stand up to the natives. We've left them so corrupted they will assume to be quite natural any supremacy on your part."

"What you're saying isn't worth a pile of manure."

"Quite right, ol' boy, manure it is!"

They moved on a few more paces. The physician was still confused, however. Not so much by what Collier had told him, but from the fact of their having tried to build a railroad that truly seemed to lead absolutely nowhere.

"Do you have any idea what the reason is for this crazy railroad?" he finally asked.

Collier responded without breaking his stride: "Just a matter of a tiny war they were waging, a quick little war to assist Brazil in biting a nice chunk of territory out of Bolivia's hip."

"This area used to be part of Bolivia?"

"Not quite where you're standing—a little farther up northwest of here." Collier observed the surprise on the physician's face. "You didn't know? Wipe that expression of shock off your face, doctor. I seem to remember your having done the same thing to Mexico. . . ."

"But what does that war have to do with building a railroad?"

"After the war, Brazil decided to *facilitate* Bolivian access to the Atlantic. That's the least they could do, and that's where we came in—or rather, first, our villainous Farquhar. Given that our tiny stretch of railroad has turned out to be the focal point of this altruistic Brazilian venture, Percival—our boss, to you—decided to lend to Brazil a little of your good old American know-how in exchange for some hard cash, preferably in large denominations."

"And did Bolivia need access to the ocean?"

"That's beside the point. Anyway, who is Bolivia to need anything?"

"I don't understand any of it!"

"Neither do I, lad; it's not for either of us to understand."

"Well, somebody ought to be able to make things clear!"

"They're already clear—clear as a bell."

"Then how is it neither of us understands?"

"Because I'm not Baron de Rothschild and you're not Percival Farquhar. It's as simple as that."

The two of them were already close to the rectangle of houses that surrounded a kind of plaza. A church stood out, though nearly in ruins, above the silhouettes of unlit shacks. The plaza, too, was a desolate landscape, pocked with pools of water gleaming in the moonlight and studded with mounds of garbage rising up like dunes, some of which even served to prop up the makeshift hovels. Collier and Finnegan were the only two shadows prowling the night. The engineer loped cautiously. The physician, from time to time, mired himself in the pools of mud that polka-dotted the ground like craters from some ancient bombardment. Each time that Finnegan sank up to his ankle, Collier could not contain his laughter. And this irritated the doctor so, that he began to walk ahead of the engineer, beyond the web of light flickering from the lantern— which only multiplied his blunders and slides. Eventually, he was some distance from the engineer and already walking up to the apparently uninhabited houses.

291

"Would the *gentleman* please *inform* me *which dump* we're *headed* for?" Collier yelled after him.

The doctor stopped walking and turned around to wait for the Englishman. He really did not have the vaguest idea what he was doing there, or where he was going.

Harriet Azancoth entered Consuelo's room and found the Bolivian girl in tears. Ever since she had found out that Richard had vanished from the hospital, together with the English engineer, Consuelo was desperate. Without Richard, her world began to spin again and she feared another loss of equilibrium, inasmuch as the doctor had so suddenly become her single passionate point of reference. She did not like the engineer Collier, and she knew that Richard had no liking for him either—which was all the more reason to be frightened about his disappearance. At the company's administrative offices, the manager dismissed her concern and treated her laconically. What information she had gathered was contradictory and she suffered from the fact. A few of the nurses had assured her that both of them were somewhere nearby, in town, at the casino, seeing a motion picture, strolling aimlessly about because naturally they were tired of remaining cooped up in a hospital bed. But one security guard, a Bolivian like herself, confided to her that the two had fled the hospital and by now were likely to be over in Santo Antônio, a city that was off limits to the company, for which they would probably be punished the minute they were found. This last bit of information filled her with terror. Richard might not even be permitted to return and she would never see him again. It was too much to bear in so fragile a state.

Harriet was carrying a tray with tea and cake.

"Señora Azancoth, he's disappeared!"

"Consuelo, my poor dear!"

"He's nowhere in the hospital! He's gone!"

"Nonsense, no one disappears into thin air, my dear. The Indian must be somewhere about...."

"I'm not talking about Joe...."

Harriet looked perplexed.

"Then whom are you talking about—who disappeared?"

"Richard!"

"The doctor?"

292

"He's left the hospital and no one will tell me anything. . . ."

"Doctors don't vanish from hospitals, my child. After all, it's their habitat."

"But he's gone, I tell you. I went to visit him, just after dinner, and he's disappeared. Not even the nurses on duty realized the fact."

"What an unheard-of phenomenon: doctors who disappear from hospitals—I'm sure there's some mistake."

Harriet placed the tray upon a small table against the window.

"Take some tea, it will help," she suggested while pouring the tea and passing a cup to Consuelo. "Come, come now, daughter—it's not the end of the world."

Consuelo wiped her eyes with the backs of her hands and took the steamy cup from her friend.

"Care for a piece of cake? It's orange cake, it's good."

"No, thank you."

"Come now, just a slice. My husband made it so now you know it's delicious."

Consuelo Campero smiled for the first time—imagining Dr. Azancoth dressed in his apron, beating the batter, placing the pan in the oven, following the entire ritual of the proverbial baker, his brown eyes poised on the recipe and his gray whiskers contrasting to the ingredients.

"You are laughing at my husband, aren't you!"

"I'm sorry, Harriet. I wasn't laughing out of maliciousness; I was just feeling a bit of tenderness, picturing Dr. Azancoth in the kitchen busy preparing a cake for the woman he loves."

"Don't fool yourself. He doesn't prepare anything for me— it's for himself, and to *humiliate* me. I don't know *how* to make desserts. . . ."

"Don't you think you're being a little harsh on him, Harriet?"

"Well, the cake *is* delicious. *That*, no one can deny!"

Consuelo sat sipping her tea and savoring the orange cake but was unable to rid her mind of the fact that the physician had disappeared, that her whole life seemed about to suffer another twist of fate.

"Don't be worried, child," Harriet tried to reassure her. "He'll show up. He wouldn't just evaporate for no rhyme or reason."

"But no one will tell me the truth."

"Do you really like him that much?"

"He's the only person in my life now."

"And you mean to say that he was there in the hospital and then he vanished?"

"He spent the morning there—he breakfasted with the director, Dr. Lovelace. He must have disappeared around dinner time, from what I can gather, He left with a man named Collier, an engineer."

"I know who Stephan Collier is; he's an amiable old goat."

"Collier? Really? Do you think so, señora?"

"It doesn't really matter *what* I think. I know it's not the first time that engineer has disappeared. And to tell you the honest truth, my own husband Eddy has occasionally done it as well. Twice, in fact."

"Twice!"

"I was appalled, too, the first time it happened. But it's nothing serious—they apparently run off to Santo Antônio and get it out of their system."

"That's what one of the security guards told me. Then I was even more frightened when he told me that the city was off limits and that there were stiff regulations against company employees setting foot in that place!"

"Those regulations apply only to the lower echelons of the staff, not to people like Richard or Stephan Collier. No, no, dear me, no . . ."

Consuelo Campero quickly swallowed the rest of her tea, unable to believe what Harriet was telling her.

"You mean he won't be punished?"

"Of course not, silly girl. He's a doctor, a professional."

"But what will they be doing in Santo Antônio?"

"Oh, nothing."

"Nothing?" she asked, incredulously.

"There's nothing to do in Santo Antônio: it's a dead city."

But Consuelo had already heard the facts of Santo Antônio—a fetid heap of garbage and a few hundred beggars.

"Santo Antônio is hardly dead, Harriet, though it may be dying."

"No, well, it's all the same, isn't it?"

The two remained at odds as to the true nature of Santo Antônio. Whatever its nature, it was there that the men were accustomed to go, and to Consuelo Campero this seemed incomprehensible. Harriet began to gather cups and saucers onto the tray; it was getting late.

"The only thing I don't understand is why they go to Santo Antônio in the first place," she confessed after a pause.

"Who goes?"

"The men . . . Collier, your husband . . . when they run off."

"Men are like that, my child. They need to escape from time to time. They get to feel imprisoned, here. Santo Antônio is the closest town, it's only natural. . . ."

"Do you feel imprisoned here, too, Harriet?"

"Imprisoned? Fiddlesticks! Of course not."

Harriet Azancoth was wiping one of her saucers and dabbing up crumbs of cake from a corner of the tray. She was trying to figure out if the quick response she had uttered was really correct. It was; she did not feel a prisoner.

"I think we women would find it difficult to feel imprisoned," she concluded.

Consuelo thought otherwise. Of late, her life had seemed to her nothing so much as imprisoned in some complicated labyrinth where each turn was a surprise, a shock that led to nothing, if not to further anguish as to her ultimate fate.

"Do you love him, my dear?" Harriet asked tenderly.

"Richard? I don't know . . . I believe I do love him, Harriet. Whatever it is, it's something very special I feel for him. We hardly know each other at all. We've barely said a few words to each other. He's very shy."

"You're not one to be shy, from what I have seen. . . ."

Consuelo blushed. She preferred to be taken for a timid woman. But Harriet's comment had not been meant to offend her. Like all people who ostensibly live only to observe others, Harriet Lowey Azancoth had totally lost her sense of discretion. And if our Bolivian girl still considered herself timid, though she did not appear to be thus on the surface, this was surely because she had changed all too quickly into the insecure, continually desperate figure the jungle had made her.

The patients in ward three—that is to say those patients in any condition to pay attention to what might be happening around their beds, called him Joe—Joe Caripuna, the Indian. To that atmosphere of extinction Joe brought an almost disconcerting good cheer. Day after day he would roam through the ward, dancing to the rhythms of a harmonica played by a convalescing Italian, performing additional prodigies with his toes, and chatting in a tongue that seemed to be the synthesis of all the languages spoken in Porto Velho.

His only true friend, Consuelo Campero, came once a day to pay him a short visit, escorted all the while by two male nurses. They kept her visits to a minimum and it always saddened him when the moment came—so quickly!—for her departure. Yet even such sadness dissipated swiftly, and Joe Caripuna, the Indian, would recover the playful spirit that had already made him the most popular figure in all of Candelária Hospital. And his days there were proving instructive to him, insofar as they allowed him to begin to penetrate and finally comprehend the various unfamiliar mechanisms of the world of the whites—a world that, day by day, revealed itself to be bewildering in its complexity.

His first important lesson in the infirmary was to acquire a sense of property. According to this lesson, property was ownership and possessions did not arise out of nowhere.

By the third day of his internment, already a popular figure, Joe Caripuna had earned his first salary—without wholly comprehending what had transpired. To begin with, he imagined the whites were giving him presents; only afterward did he begin to understand that, upon receipt of something from them, he had actually compromised himself with whoever awarded him thus to do whatever was asked of him in return. Under the genre of clever entertainment, the Indian had awakened the curiosity of nearly everyone and was constantly solicited to perform his tricks. Some patients were insistent and, when he would occasionally refuse with a smile, they interpreted his still amiable demeanor as a polite manner of soliciting payment for what they were asking of him. Thus, when at one point Joe had refused to light a certain patient's cigarette with his feet, the man—after much insisting, to no avail—presented Joe with a shirt. The Indian accepted graciously—he had admired the shirt—and returned to his cot, thereby infuriating the patient. The man got up and strode over to Joe's bed.

"Listen here, Indian, aren't you going to light my cigarette now?" he demanded.

Joe Caripuna smiled at him and shook his head no.

"Not now, my friend, Joe very *cansado*."

The man took his reply as an insult.

"Then give me back my shirt!"

"*Esta* shirt *não es mas usted*, my friend, you give to Joe," he said calmly.

"If you want to keep that shirt, you're going to have to light this cigarette. . . ."

"But Joe *não* feel like it, just now, okay?"

"No, not okay. I paid for you to light my cigarette—don't mess around with me, Indian, or I'll break your skull!"

"You *não* talk to Joe, *esta manei'a, por favor*."

"Damn right I do! I paid for what I'm asking. . . ."

"*Pagado?*"

"Right, Indian, *pagado*—with that shirt I gave you. It cost me half a *libra* in the company store. That's a lot of money just to light a cigarette."

"*Não* present?"

"I already told you, I don't like people crapping around with me. Either I get the shirt back or you light me a match, got it?"

Joe Caripuna took off the shirt he had put on over his pajamas and examined it carefully. It was a good shirt and he liked it. The man was waiting tensely, his skin welted with lesions from insect bites and his few rotting teeth bared in an otherwise empty mouth.

"*Tud' bem,* friend, Joe keep shirt."

And he lit the patient's cigarette.

After this lesson, Joe was no less cheerful but he had stopped showing his talents gratuitously. If he lit a cigarette or danced a polka, it was only because somebody offered him something to do it. In addition to the shirt, he was accumulating many more possessions and continued to marvel at this custom of the whites. At the same time he began to feel uneasy: the whites had cured his arms, restored his health, and he had nothing to give them in exchange for such value. One day this debt would have to be paid, and when the time arrived, what would Joe Caripuna have to offer to fulfill the ceremony of the whites? All the gifts he had amassed up to now, or might in future, were insufficient to satisfy the doctor who had given him back his life! Even in the imaginary hierarchy of prices that he was gradually piecing together to himself, the cost of

Dr. Finnegan's trick fled his comprehension. And Joe knew the whites well enough to realize that payment would be required and that, sooner or later, he would have to produce it, even if it meant lighting the cigarettes of every white man on earth.

His eyes scanned a heavily whitewashed wooden wall whose yellow humid stains, imbedded with nameless filth, seemed to epitomize its surroundings, dizzyingly illuminated by three candelabras hanging by their rusty nails. On that same wall were tacked and pasted a variety of prints—from devotional images of the Immaculate Conception to pinups in bathing suits, from Brazilian politicians to international movie stars. Against this tawdry backdrop of old, grimy pictures torn from illustrated magazines, his gaze lit upon the heads of two female Indians. The two, he knew, were prostitutes. Their faces still conserved their painted designs and their nasal septums were perforated according to custom, though they no longer exhibited the ornamental yellow feathers from tiny parrots that had the deceptive appearance of dyed mustaches. Finnegan, the observer, had often seen photographs of such Indians, but not for the life of him could he equate the specimens before him with the ones in the photographs. These were thoroughly decrepit and altogether jaded. The younger of the two shifted her eyes anxiously, while the older one stood stock-still like the statue of a nightmare sculpted by depravity. The younger woman suddenly opened her toothless mouth in a repulsive smile.

The physician and the engineer were seated on a crude wooden bench, in the anteroom of the best and only bordello in all of Porto Santo Antônio. They were observing and observed by the only two prostitutes available for the moment. Finnegan felt cornered by the stares of the prostitutes, by the odor of excrement infecting his surroundings, and for this reason began to ring his hands, while Stephan Collier indifferently ran the tip of his fingers over a button of his shirt. Unable to fathom what position he should assume on the hard bench, the physician finally opted for crossing this legs. As he lifted a foot to do so, he stopped, appalled—his boot was totally encrusted with mud, and blood. The engineer's boots were in the same deplorable state. Finnegan slowly lowered his leg again and attempted to conceal his boots under the bench, away from e eyes of the prostitutes—an odd propriety under the cirumstance. The younger Indian girl held the same hideous mile imprisoned on her dark lips. The physician retreated from er imagined scrutiny by gazing alternately at the floor or urtively at the row of bloodstained boots.

"Our boots," he finally whispered into the engineer's ear. Have you taken a look at our boots? They're smeared with lood!"

Collier took a casual glance at his feet and nodded to confirm he truth of the remark. The engineer's mild reaction was more hocking to Finnegan than even the smile of the prostitute.

"Quite right, ol' boy, looks as if we've had our stroll through he local blood bank."

Finnegan shook his head in disgust.

"You're the living proof, Collier, that English humor—like Queen Victoria—is a thing of the past."

"Calm yourself, lad. It's only blood and it's neither yours or mine."

"But it is blood!"

"Indian blood."

"What?"

"It's probably Indian blood. Some sort of fight must have roken out somewhere around here and the blood has renained."

"I don't think it was a fight—it must have been more like slaughter."

The physician raised his leg to examine the blood again.

"It can't be human blood," he concluded. "It's not possible."

"There's no reason for you to become obsessed about it. t's not our blood—that's the important thing." The engineer ooked up, as if inspired, and pointed to the prostitutes. "Maybe t's their blood . . . who knows?"

"Theirs?"

"That's right, maybe they menstruated, ol' boy."

"One more foul remark like that and I won't be able to esist slamming you in the teeth!"

Stephan Collier sensed that his companion was finally speaking seriously.

"All right, all right—let's see what we can do to get a little service around here. Hey, you, senhorita!"

299

The Indians remained aloof, and the smile of the younger girl took on the appearance of plain spite.

"I say! Senhoritas! Would one of you find us something to clean our boots . . . ?"

There was no response, not even the outline of a gesture.

"Damn!" he grumbled, banging the bench with his fist. "Damn! They don't understand English. Senhoritas! *Falam portugues? Por favor,* a cloth, *um pano para limpar aqui as nossas botas.* Our boots, see? *Por favor . . . botas . . . limpar!*"

There was no reaction; they stood there statically against the wall like a pair of dolls mutilated by a sadist.

"Damn!" Collier repeated, "No Portuguese either."

"Let's get the hell out of here, Collier."

Finnegan attempted to stand up but the engineer immediately pulled him back down onto the bench.

"Look at them, doctor. Are they the first native women you've ever laid eyes on in the flesh?"

"Let's go, Collier," Finnegan answered, an uneasiness burning in his throat like sour vomit.

"Look at them, doctor," the Englishman insisted, tightly gripping Finnegan's forearm.

The women did nothing, and the one continued to wear her smile as if it might last forever.

"They're repellent, so what?" the doctor replied, almost puking his response.

"Would you be able to fuck one of them, doctor?"

"Collier, you absolute son of a *bitch*—"

"Sit!" the engineer ordered with Finnegan's arm in his iron grip. "Sit, you callow turd—look at them, you swaggering bastard!"

Finnegan resigned himself to sitting there, like a spoiled, impotent child being punished by his daddy.

"They speak the same language as your patient. They are Caripuna. They might even be related to Joe, who knows? Perhaps his mother and sister."

"Are they really Caripunas?"

"I imagine so, but it hardly matters. Whatever they are, these harridans have been completely fucked."

"How could they have gotten to such a state of degradation?"

"We've educated them to it; we even have a language in

common for any required communication. Would you like to see?"

The physician watched Collier pull a crumpled Brazilian banknote out of his pocket and raise the bill to the level of his eyes. Immediately, the expression on the faces of the two women changed, as if the lethargic spell they were under had suddenly been broken. The engineer waved the money from left to right and the movement was followed by two avaricious stares.

"You see, lad? They still show signs of life."

"Let's get out of here, Collier, I'm not feeling too good," Finnegan beseeched him.

"Observe, doctor. What monstrous expressions, eh? And to think we taught it all to them . . ."

"The hell we did! What have I got to do with their ending up like this?"

"And can you believe there are still people capable of screwing with something like that? Of sticking their rods up a disgusting hole like that?"

"Stop it, Collier. Let's go."

"But it *was* us, Finnegan—we landed them here. It's what we're good at—turning native women into whores."

"Will you get off the podium? Enough pronouncements for today."

"Pronouncements? Those are two Caripuna—they still have a trace of the legendary beauty of Caripuna women, though you can barely see it."

"They're not my type—besides which, I don't find anything beautiful about native women."

"It's a question of taste, I agree, but that's no reason for us to be prostituting them."

"I fail to see how we're prostituting them. They do it themselves."

"You're wet behind the ears, Finnegan, and you're also full of shit. You know as well as I do they were living here without any need of the likes of us, but now they're fucked. Do you know what it is to be fucked? Completely? They were healthy once and probably quite beautiful. They've progressed considerably, haven't they? They no doubt have syphilis, and tuberculosis most likely—pardon my poking into your field, doctor."

"They're not tubercular, I can tell you."

"How can you know?"

"I know. They're not. They're merely suffering from undernourishment."

"Starving, you mean?"

"Malnutrition—they eat badly. . . ."

"When they eat at all."

"I've had enough, Collier," the physician announced, freeing his arm from the grip of the engineer and rising from the bench. "If you want to stay here it's none of my concern. I'm leaving!"

The Englishman let out a great guffaw as the physician headed for the door. The two professionals, however, were not so easily disposed to losing their two white, *gringo* customers who had miraculously materialized with so much money in their pockets. Demonstrating an agility impossible to have been foreseen, they leaped upon the physician: running their hands through his hair, muttering incomprehensible phrases, and forcibly leading him off to another annex of the house. Initially, Finnegan did not react, dominated by his own surprise, as well as by the now redoubled laughter of the English engineer. In addition to which, he did not have a clue as to how he should react, if not to say to them politely that while he appreciated their solicitude it was urgent for him to depart and they must allow him to be on his way.

"Hold on, lad, I'm coming to the rescue!" Collier shouted, pulling some money from his pocket again and holding it in the air without moving from the bench.

The two women immediately lost interest in Finnegan and feasted their eyes upon the hand held above the engineer's head, as if hypnotized by the crumpled old sheet of currency. The disheveled physician had no idea whether to make his escape or remain in his place and watch whatever might happen next.

"Collier, enough!" Finnegan exclaimed breathlessly, gathering his courage. "You've already played your games."

The engineer got up from the bench, and that single gesture so alleviated the physician that he decided to pardon Stephan Collier for everything dreadful that had happened so far that night together. Still, the women would not take their eyes off the money, and Collier finally crumpled the note in his hand and threw it to the other end of the establishment. The two ndians flew at it, grappling with each other over its ultimate possession. The engineer, with a laugh, calmly took his leave followed by a stupefied Finnegan, but they never even made t to the door. Suddenly, there were the strums of an approaching guitar which temporarily brought a truce to the women's altercation. The door to the brothel was flung open with such force that it caused the entire house to tremble and groan. A group of armed desperadoes—dirty, bearded, and swarthy ooking—stormed in, laughing and shouting to one another, with one of them playing the guitar. Collier and Finnegan backed off instinctively, and for the first time the engineer also felt afraid. The new arrivals, however, immediately noted the presence of the two strangers and stopped talking—only the guitar, fingered with great dexterity, continued its sad melody.

One of the men, physically dried up but apparently the leader, ordered with a brusque gesture that the music cease. The fellow's face was leathered by the sun, with lively brown eyes and a thick mustache drooping over his lips. The Negroid head of hair, bushy and uneven, was of a strange, faded auburn tint. He exhibited an expression of good will that in no way reassured either Collier or Finnegan.

"Americans?" he asked in Portuguese, smiling.

The physician, unable to understand even a word of Portuguese, looked pleadingly at Collier.

"I'm English," the engineer answered in the same language, his voice evincing the tone of authority with which he was always accustomed to command. "He's American."

"Amounts to the same," said the man dismissively, "both gringo."

"We were just leaving," Collier announced, prudently moderating his authoritarian demeanor.

"What do you mean, leaving? Aren't you looking for a good time?"

"We've already had our fun."

Finnegan, with no sense of what was going on, felt more and more helpless to predict the outcome.

"You people from the Madeira-Mamoré?" the man asked. Collier nodded.

"Well, let's have some fun together," he insisted rather menacingly. "You are my guests. My name is Lourival da Cunha. . . ."

303

He offered his hand in a gesture that was reciprocated immediately by the engineer.

"Stephan Collier, I'm a construction engineer. This is my friend Richard Finnegan. He's a doctor."

Collier made a sign for Finnegan to shake the other's hand.

"*Prazer*. I own a rubber plantation out near Guajará-Mirim and we're taking the harvest down to Manaus. I'd like to have you two join our celebration tonight."

"It would be a great pleasure, Senhor da Cunha."

The *seringalista* had anticipated his reply and was already crossing the room. On his way, he briefly eyed the two Indian whores and then disappeared through one of the doorways immersed in total darkness.

"Where is the owner of this flophouse," da Cunha began to shout once he had vanished into the interior of the establishment. "Hey, Macedo! What, are you hiding?"

The proprietor of the house, however, was nowhere to be found—perhaps he was dead—and the *seringalista* decided that that made him master of the establishment. The physician, who already feared a total ruckus, watched the others break out some bottles of White Horse, knife out the corks, and begin their drinking. The guitar had resumed playing the same plaintive melody and, surprisingly, no one spoke any further. Instead, they drank in silence, including Finnegan and Collier, each of whom had been presented the gift of a bottle. Two of the others had walked off with the whores to some other part of the house.

From the taciturn drinking they soon slid into a state of total inebriation, and finally: sleep. The physician had begun to slump after the third swig, the first to go down without burning his throat. The engineer resisted, for he was accustomed to heavy drinking; but on this night, for some reason, his consciousness also refused to quit him regardless of how much whiskey he drank. Yet it was not a matter of his being on his guard. Hardly had he introduced himself to the *seringalista*, than he seemed to have completely lost any fear of those rugged but modest men. The drinks went down caressingly and he no longer felt the cold of the midnight hours nor noticed the stench of the establishment.

He began to reflect on how hot tempered he had been for most of the night; he always got himself into a temper whenever

304

he came to Porto Santo Antônio. On this particular trip, however, the immaturity of his companion had exacerbated the sentiment. Not that he had any complaint against Finnegan—on the contrary, he even nourished a certain paternal caring, mixed with cruelty, toward the lad. It was just that the engineer was a man too old and too experienced to put up with naiveties. Besides which, had he not lost all faith in the human species once he had found his family butchered among the ruins of their house in Richmond, Virginia? Anyway, virtually ruined himself after the Civil War, when a pardon suddenly released him from prison, he had decided to return to England—only to arrive in London, in the spring of '66, and feel a stranger in his own country. Not even the affection of his Uncle Edmond Dalton—his mother's brother, a small industrialist who manufactured railway equipment—could make him recover his belief in human beings. And Edmund was a good man, a confirmed bachelor highly respected by those who knew him. He had received his relative like a son and before the first year was out had found a place for him as manager in a shop he owned in Manchester, where Stephan also began studies at the Polytechnic Institute of Owens College.

After receiving his degree in 1870, Collier seemed to have grown even more aloof and irritable than when he had first arrived with his ruined prospects on the heels of the disastrous American Civil War. A graduate, almost arrogantly proud, without ever having accepted charity from his uncle, Stephan Collier went to work as a topographical engineer for the London and Northeastern Railway. In that same year he had met Elizabeth Arnold, teacher in a Cambridge public school, a timid girl with an oval face and dark hair that flowed like silk from under one or another of her perennially flowery bonnets. The following year, in 1871, he married Elizabeth and moved to Cambridge, but his marriage to her did not signal any change in his staunchly unsociable behavior. Elizabeth, a provincial girl, would never manage to break through the crust of bitterness that forever encased Stephan Collier. The marriage would exist in merely a formal sense, and Elizabeth, for the first two years, would prove to be a discreet wife, continuing to live in her own private world—a convenient enough arrangement for Collier. Their tribulations commenced only in 1873, when, Stephan having resigned from the Northeastern Railway, the

305

two of them moved to Philadelphia and he went to work for the Pennsylvania Railroad. Elizabeth found it too difficult to adapt to the United States, and after attempting every means to convince her husband to return to England, she isolated herself in their house and began drinking heavily, becoming steadily more somber and sickly.

In 1874, Viola was born and, from complications at delivery, Elizabeth's health degenerated. Collier looked after the child while his wife went back to England, to spend a few months at the home of her parents, in Cambridge. When she returned to Pennsylvania, her incapacity to adapt to the States had evolved into a hatred of America and of her little girl Viola. At this point Stephan had met Ginnie Cloyd, a secretary at the railroad office and the only daughter of a fundamentalist preacher, the founder of his own sect: the Church of Corpus Christi, which taught the Scriptures in the light of a curious sensualism. Ginnie was not exactly a follower of her father's preachings, but there was something about her that strangely attracted Collier and for a time revived him. The two became lovers and met openly. Elizabeth, feeling wronged, sought out Ginnie and publicly assaulted her, without further consequences; but Collier, fearing another, more serious scandal, had Elizabeth interned in a private clinic for the mentally ill. Ginnie, troubled by all the repercussions, quit her lover and moved from Philadelphia to New York, where she would eventually marry a jazz musician.

The real crisis came in 1877, when Collier mistakenly believed that his wife had completely recovered. Elizabeth totally neglected her daughter and Viola died of dehydration. Collier divorced her after the funeral and she returned to England, walking out of his life forever and reinforcing his conviction that humanity was no better than a pit full of talking vermin whose excretions amounted to a pile of manure. Seated now in the only bordello in Santo Antônio, savoring one peg after another, Collier was even more convinced than ever that humanity was hardly worth a dog's vomit. When sleep finally overcame him, he was the only one still muttering incomprehensible phrases while the tourniquet of alcohol that compressed his consciousness gradually reduced his brain to a liquefied wax that slowly burned until it went out altogether, like the candelabras that were hanging from the wall and emitting their black, extinguished smoke.

306

By early morning a strong light had already penetrated the house and was glinting off the bottles of whiskey. The bottles lay empty. The men were still asleep, stretched out everywhere upon the floor. Finnegan was snugly ensconced underneath the bench, his mouth open and his head cradled in his arms. In another corner of the room, Collier was snoring from an almost fetal position, curled up like a snail. The whores were gone.

The physician stirred, banging his head against the underside of the bench. The blow awakened him rudely and he opened his eyes with pain; the world was already spinning in his head. He was still appreciably drunk, however, and tried to assume a new position in which to sleep. But sleep refused to return, for he was already in that stage of inebriation when drunkenness still remains to be overcome but one is not sufficiently drunk anymore to remain unconscious, nor sufficiently sober to pretend to be lucid. He pushed the bench aside and sat up, his eyes burning and his arms asleep, while a poor circulation provoked pins and needles. At his side there still rested a bottle of White Horse with a little whiskey left. Tremulously, he lifted the bottle to his mouth and sipped at the contents, then hurled the bottle on the floor and spit out the mouthful of liquor with an expression of distaste. It was then that he noticed the engineer, huddled against the wall.

"Collier! Collier," he attempted to shout, but what emerged was a pasty echo that hardly seemed to come from his own throat.

The engineer was sound asleep.

"Collier!" he tried to shout again.

The engineer shuddered slightly and then muttered something incomprehensible. His first sensation was that of his own sticky tongue wallowing between his dry lips. Little by little, Collier began to open his eyes as well, with a certain perverse pleasure in the pain of it.

"Tell them I'm not here," he muttered. "Tell them I left and I'm not coming back."

"Collier, it's already daybreak."

"Daybreak be damned!"

"I think my head is about to crack open like the shell of an egg," the physician complained.

"Then make an omelette."

Finnegan felt stabbing pains around his eyes and a lacerating emptiness in his stomach.

"We have to get going, Collier."

"To where? I'm fine here."

"If we leave now, we can still arrive at the hospital before lunch."

"Don't talk to me about food."

"We have to get back to the hospital, Collier."

"The hospital be damned!" the engineer shouted, finally awakening.

"We still haven't been released officially. Dr. Lovelace—"

"You and your devotion to Lovelace . . ."

"*Bull*shit, devotion."

"It's devotion, all right," Collier insisted. "None of my business, of course, but I still can't imagine the purpose of such devotion to a bastard like Lovelace."

The physician shook his aching head negatively and attempted to get up but immediately failed.

"You're *drunk*, Collier."

"*In vino veritas!*"

"What?"

"In wine, truth—imbecile! I will not tolerate talking with illiterates."

"You want to know something, Collier? I'm *fed* up with your insults."

The engineer laughed, stretching his arms and legs.

"Insults, eh?"

Finnegan felt he had no energy to even argue.

"I'm also *drunk* . . . my head is splitting."

The physician leaned his head back against the wall, staring at the straw ceiling darkened with soot.

"Lovelace is a grand son of a bitch, Finnegan. You cannot trust the fellow—I even have my doubts about whether Lovelace is a real doctor."

Finnegan looked horrified.

"*Doctor* Lovelace happens to be one of the most eminent parasitologists in the world. What you're telling me is nonsense."

"Lovelace is a loathsome parasite."

"Collier! He was the one who established sanitary conditions

308

down here for the construction of your railroad. He brought us all the scientific know-how he'd acquired in Panama."

"It wasn't *he*, Finnegan. It was Oswaldo Cruz!"

"Who?"

"That's what I said: Oswaldo Cruz, a *Brazilian* doctor. He visited here in 1909 and published a report the following year presenting his conclusions and offering various suggestions. Some of those suggestions were actually accepted by the company and did make for better sanitary conditions around here. At least in Porto Velho, because on the actual work sites conditions have remained more or less static. But your beloved Lovelace had nothing to do with the improvement."

"You don't like anything about him, do you?"

"Oh, I adore the ol' chap, positively bosom buddies!"

"Then why detract from his accomplishments?"

"You misunderstand me, lad. I find Lovelace positively enthralling—only an exquisite scoundrel like him could manage to steal credit for the work of some poor Brazilian doctor in such brilliant fashion."

"I refuse to believe such lies."

"Think as you like, lad. When we get back to Porto Velho, I'm going to see if I can get ahold of a copy of Dr. Cruz's report, so I can rub it in your face."

Finnegan ceased to argue, leaning his head against the wall and shutting his eyes. His temples were throbbing horribly and the emptiness of his stomach was growing as if a balloon were being pumped up in his abdomen.

"There are certain things that I simply don't understand about you, Collier," the physician confessed with a sigh. "I really don't understand them. . . ."

"Why, I'm clear as crystal, lad."

"You are the unclearest creature I ever came across. You spend your life criticizing others, pointing out errors and defects, but you don't walk away from them yourself—you continue to work for people whom you consider to be crooks and scoundrels. You spend your life reviling the scum of the earth but, even so, you like them!"

"That's because I'm just as much a scoundrel myself. Just as base as the rest of them."

"It's not true, although at the moment I'd like to be able to agree with you."

309

"That's because I'm also a sort of doctor myself. . . ."

The physician smiled: "A doctor!"

"That's right—of a certain kind."

"You must have a rather low opinion of doctors, Collier."

"I have a bloody low opinion of everything. But I really am a sort of physician: I can diagnose the infection—knavishness or corruption. On the other hand, I see no reason to cease to admire the body thus contaminated. I'm a true clinician, Finnegan."

"You're a moralist, that's what you are."

"Who's to say? A moralist, perhaps, with no morals whatsoever."

"A cynic."

"A practitioner of the only religion I profess: medical engineering."

"Medical engineering?"

"A childish old bloke whose youth was filled with romantic ideals which fucked him in the end."

"I'm certainly not a romantic, that's for sure."

"Who said you were? Don't be so pretentious, lad. You're an American; impossible for you to be a romantic."

"What's so terrible about being an American?"

"Nothing at all, my boy, you have only the advantages."

"We're a people like any other."

"You'd like to believe that, wouldn't you, Finnegan?"

The physician opened his eyes again and felt the light of morning pulsing cruelly against his aching retinae.

"You want to know why I came down to the Amazon?"

Collier shrugged. "If it makes you feel good, then tell me about it, but I'll wager you're nothing more than a charlatan like the rest of us."

"I really am a physician, diploma and all."

"I know lots of scoundrels with diplomas; they tend to be the most sinister variety."

"Let me finish, will you?" Finnegan complained, repenting immediately because the pains in his temples intensified to an unbearable degree.

"Jolly good," the engineer crowed, "not another word from me, I promise you."

"My family is extremely rich, Collier."

"Hullo! then what the devil are you doing down here?"

310

"You promised to listen!"

"My apologies, doctor..."

"I'm a wealthy fellow, Collier, I'm going to inherit a fortune calculated to be in the vicinity of ten million dollars."

"Damnation!"

"I went to the best school in the country to study medicine, in Baltimore."

"Nauseating city—they should burn it to the ground and salt the ashes."

"Collier!" Finnegan shouted once more in exasperation, and like the last time the pounding in his head was thoroughly excruciating.

"Sorry, infamous of me, I know..."

"I was not a very brilliant student, but I wasn't mediocre. I was the only son of Irish parents privileged to attend such a school in those days. It's still extremely rare. In any case, I was feeling rather cornered."

"But you pegged your share of females, I'd be willing to wager...."

"Son of a bitch! You never shut up, Collier, do you?"

"Well, a man—"

"Will you let me speak, for God sakes!"

"Go ahead, lad, your move."

"By the end of my coursework I still had not decided upon my field of specialization. Yet my life was already totally mapped out for me. My family lives in Saint Louis and my father had already built a practice for me to take over, when I graduated, in the best part of town. Hell, it all began to irritate me—you can't just have your whole life mapped out that way."

"Life does get to be tedious."

"Tedious is right. Anyway, that was when Dr. Lovelace visited the campus and gave a lecture on medicine in the tropics—I was fascinated. I decided to travel a bit and accepted the job down here."

"That was all?"

"I also had a sweetheart in Baltimore. She, too, was very rich. Protestant. Her parents didn't want us to marry. I think that deep down I didn't want to either."

"You didn't love her? Or she didn't fuck well?"

"We never fucked at all; her family was extremely puritanical and watched us all the time."

"And you two just dying for a little toss in the hay."

"She was just as puritanical as they were; she even wanted me to give up my Catholicism."

"You were still a Catholic?"

"I was losing my faith . . . she wished me to keep faith in something."

"With that type of thing the only faith possible is the belief in the body of the woman you possess."

"I don't even know if she really interested me. We spent a lot of time together. There were also the nurses—they liked having a bit of fun."

"And you were ready to oblige them with their bit of fun, I can well imagine."

"Now and then, when the opportunity arose. In the meantime, my relationship with my fiancée was falling apart. Her parents, of course, although they didn't approve of our marrying on religious grounds, still could not forget that my father was an extremely wealthy man. It became tedious to have to put up with the hostility—cloaked in the utmost amicableness, to be sure—of the whole prejudiced lot of them. And they began to pressure me, that the marriage should take place immediately—everything very veiled, of course. They were a sad lot, that bunch, thinking I should be obligated to rescue their daughter from her state of potential spinsterhood."

"So you fled your conjugal duty! Naughty boy!"

"I fled everything: marriage, wealth . . ."

"I'm going to tell you something, doctor, that happens to be the one thing that nobody can flee."

"What? Marriage?"

"Wealth, my boy, wealth! It's something you'll never escape."

The physician felt a bitter taste rising in his crop, which brought him strangely to the edge of tears.

"But it's not so dour a fate, my boy," Collier comforted him. "Wealth will not debar you from glory. You can still make your mark by committing great extravagancies, holding tremendous orgies, succumbing to grand madnesses."

"But I'm not an extravagant person, Collier."

"But you're a rich one—which is already a good beginning."

Richard Finnegan could see the aging lips of his father,

jowled by years of heavy drinking and the long wakeful hours of work, counting money and then praying. The same quantitative attention to both: ordering masses to be celebrated for all his deceased relatives and hiring the church to say masses, for the next twenty years, on behalf of his soul, should the Lord decide to beckon him to a better world.

"Was she beautiful?" Collier asked.

"Yes, she was beautiful—perhaps too much so."

"More than Consuelo?"

The physician blushed, but at the same time he felt a sudden desire to be back in Porto Velho with the Bolivian girl.

"They're totally different women."

"And Consuelo, what's she like?"

"A mystery to me . . . I still have no idea why she gave herself to me that night."

"She's mad about you, Finnegan, that's all."

"I'm not so sure; it could just be gratitude."

"It's a lovely way to show gratitude, I'll warrant you that."

"And you, Collier, have you never loved a woman?"

The engineer watched the stern face of Elizabeth flicker across his mind, then the petulant smile of Ginnie Cloyd. He weighed the two on his imaginary balance to try to fathom the answer. The scales lacked clarity, and he decided that neither one of them represented anything to him.

"I loved one woman, obviously."

The physician stared at his companion, almost in surprise.

"But . . . she's long dead," the engineer concluded.

"I'm very sorry."

"That's all right, ol' boy. She never even met me."

"Never met you?" Finnegan was intrigued.

"It's true, she didn't even know I existed."

"You're pulling my leg again."

"There's no point in talking about it. She was a very busy woman."

"What did she do?"

"She was serious about a lot of things, very serious."

The physician felt certain that Collier was no doubt enjoying himself at his expense. Still, he could not resist the temptation.

"What was her name?" he finally asked, almost from inertia.

"Vicky . . ."

"A lovely name, quite British sounding, however."

"Oh, she was eminently British, I can assure you."

"Vickeh!" said the physician, trying to put forth a British accent.

"Queen Victoria, to be precise," Collier chortled triumphantly.

Finnegan accompanied him in his laughter as the crushed silk dresses of his fiancée rustled in his memory. Why had he lied to Collier, insisting that they had never made love? Was it the silliness of an Irish Catholic bent on protecting the reputation of his bride to be? It was fair to say that she did not resemble the Bolivian, however; although perhaps in certain ways she was preferable to Consuelo Campero. His single encounter with the Bolivian girl did not represent any great affair—true, there was the recollection of her warm skin and her hands gently caressing his shoulder blades. The girl from Baltimore was much more vulnerable than that. Her puritanism—genuine—incited Finnegan to commit certain excesses, losing all gentility and sometimes shoving his penis into her mouth, causing her to choke, which excited him terribly. With Consuelo, such impulses seemed inadequate. Her warm flesh asked to be scratched and bitten and her sex impregnated his fingers with a penetrating, telling odor.

"I swear to you I was enamoured of Queen Victoria!"

The physician shook his head, which felt as heavy as lead.

"Impossible to talk seriously about anything with you, Collier."

The engineer yawned and stretched his powerful arms.

"But I am speaking seriously," he pleaded. "I loved that woman; she epitomized for me a sort of feminine ideal. She was ugly, short, and extremely capable. She cared for the destiny of millions of human beings, and many times she played with those destinies, which made her even more enchanting. She was mother and stateswoman. She rode on horseback like a man, spoke with a masculine voice, and always wore dark clothes. When I was fourteen years old I was given a portrait of Queen Victoria mounted on a beautiful-looking thoroughbred. I adored that portrait, quite as much as I did the pubic hairs that were sprouting in my crotch. For me, she was the Venus incarnate. How many times I masturbated before that equestrian figure, imagining myself her prince consort."

314

"But Queen Victoria! Even the nurses back at school weren't that homely."

"You're no better than a degenerate, Finnegan. How could you sleep with women reeking of disinfectant, who've spent their whole day emptying urinals? My relationship at least was wholesome."

"Wholesome and onanistic."

"Onanistic but platonic."

"Platonic? It's a wonder you don't have more hair on the palms of your hands than the scalp of your head, Collier."

"She was worth the risk. Besides, it didn't infect anyone."

The already powerful heat and the fetidness seemed to have suddenly increased in their intensity. The physician felt the sweat begin to lick his armpits and his neck. His lungs were struggling for a breath of air and his head grew lighter and lighter. The drunkenness had passed, leaving, however, a taste of corncob in his mouth. Next to Finnegan, the engineer had closed his eyes and was panting heavily, his shirt entirely mopped in sweat. The other men continued their deep sleeping.

Stephan Collier was not about to drift back into sleep. He had shut his eyes because the memory of Ginnie had come upon him too strongly, disguised in the protestations of his supposed love for Queen Victoria. Ginnie was not ugly, but she was short and capable. Ginnie was now a widow; her jazz musician had died from the poisonous effects of so much opium; and she herself had turned matronly, converting finally to her father's sect, lacking imagination now and bordering on senility. Not by any stretch of the imagination could she be said to resemble the Ginnie Cloyd that he had held so often with his arms and lips, probing and caressing her small body, spreading her pale, plump thighs. What fucking twattle! Collier was thinking: all that fuss just to shoot two or three thick, milky spurts into Ginnie's moist interior, and hear her moan!

For the first time since awakening, the physician heard some voices, a human murmuring originating from somewhere outside and indicating the presence of a few actual inhabitants of the city. He was hungry, ravenously hungry—a sign that his drunkenness had finally subsided, which nearly sent him into a panic.

"Collier!" he shouted in agitation. "We better get back to the hospital right away."

315

"Why?"

"I think I'm over the worst of my hangover, that's why."

The engineer got himself up with one impulsive movement and stood there like a lamp post in a hurricane. He brought his hands to his head and pressed his temples.

"I think someone has ripped off my bloody scalp," he said making a face.

The physician observed his companion and for the first time perceived how old he really was, his reddish skin covered with dark blotches. There's a man who has lived, Finnegan thought to himself, with no self-pity or commiseration.

"Would you like to hear something, doctor. Pay close attention, now, and maybe you'll understand me: we are nothing but mechanisms of survival. That has always been my over-riding ambition: to survive!"

Finnegan found it altogether too depressing to think of passing his time on earth under the sad rubric of survivor. He preferred to take Collier's words as typically belligerent.

"Collier, you are the worst character I have ever encountered."

"Bravo, lad!"

The engineer pulled Finnegan by the arm, dragging him out of the house and into the sunlight. The central square of the little town was toasting in the morning heat, and the mud with its puddles of fetid water seemed ready to boil. There was an unexpected amount of traffic for a town that during the night had seemed virtually uninhabited. They crossed the square together and walked in the direction of the wharf. Passing the copse of jungle where the abandoned locomotive lay hidden behind the ferns, Finnegan spotted the smokestack in the form of a cone but deteriorated by the inclemencies of time and weather. Just behind a luxuriant cabbage palm sprouting its way toward heaven, a man was coming out of the clearing, buttoning his fly.

"Now she fulfills another purpose," Collier commented wryly. "Santo Antônio is the only town on the whole Madeira to possess a public lavatory imported from the U.S.A."

As they proceeded down the wooden stairway to the wharf, the physician could hardly believe that they had managed to reach the top the previous night without breaking their necks. The docks were also bustling with activity and several canoes

316

were circling around a small flatboat to which oval *pelas* of rubber were tied, forming an immense raft. But there was no sign of the canoe that they had used to come to Santo Antônio.

"Damn! I always forget," said Collier.

"Forget what?"

"To hide the bloody canoe!"

"Don't tell me that . . ."

"Exactly, my lad—we've been robbed. A canoe here is as precious as a thoroughbred horse."

Finnegan felt suddenly desperate.

"Why didn't you remember! How will we get back to the hospital?"

"Who knows? We'll just have to wait and see."

The engineer went over to sit on some empty crates that were piled on the edge of the bank. The physician, with no other choice, imitated his companion. What he wanted most was to have a bath, a change of clothes; to get out of his filthy boots, brush his teeth; and to get away from such a place as fast as possible.

"We could rent a canoe!" it suddenly occurred to him.

Collier did not respond, but Finnegan had already jumped up and hastened over to some canoes that were tied up at the wharf. Collier watched him attempt to convince their occupants, in vain, and then saunter back to his side, more depressed than ever.

"They all seem to work here for some rubber plantation. They say they can't leave the vicinity and are prohibited from docking at Porto Velho."

"I could have saved you the bother," Collier commented. "Percival Farquhar won't stand for his employees' coming into contact with one another. Those canoes are his property; they belong to the Guaporé Rubber Company plantations."

The physician had already lost interest in the matter. He was staring at the stinking city behind them and his attention had been distracted. In the square, a few head of cattle were being led along by a group of barely dressed individuals—no women among them. Suddenly they commenced to slaughter the cattle with blows of a machete, right there in the putrid mud, and then to strip the bloody carcasses in the midst of the filth. That finally explained the presence of so much blood in the pools of slime that dotted the streets, as if the town itself had been the object of a bloody massacre. As each steer was hacked to pieces and scattered into parts upon the bare earth, there would form about the remains a tiny crowd of passersby.

"My God," said Finnegan in disgust, "they're quartering cattle in the middle of that filthy street!"

The engineer was revolted only by the fact that the men were slaughtering the steers without the slightest notion of how to quarter the parts properly. The buyers selected the bloody sections with their bare hands.

"Do you have any notion of how much a kilo of that meat costs?" Collier asked the physician.

"I haven't the faintest idea," he replied with irritation.

"Six *milreis*—almost fifteen dollars a kilo. Only a half-dozen or so of the most privileged can afford to buy it. The rest must content themselves with manioc meal, a bit of fish, and nothing else."

"I can't believe how they manage to survive here. Just look at the garbage piled up around the houses. This place must be a hatchery for every disease in the region."

"You could make a small fortune here, doctor."

The engineer got up and walked toward the open warehouse. He was obviously troubled by other matters.

"I'm dying of thirst," he explained to his companion as the doctor came up behind him. "It must be this bloody hangover."

"You're not thinking of drinking the water around here?"

"With this heat I feel quite capable of taking a drink out of one of those puddles in the square."

Just then, Collier noticed the *seringalista* Lourival da Cunha and his men coming down the steps to the wharf.

"Our friends from last night," he announced to Finnegan.

The physician watched as Lourival da Cunha, at the head of his well-armed band, approached them with a wide smile. In the daylight the *seringalista* looked even dirtier in his shabby clothes.

Collier and he fell into animated conversation while, as usual, Finnegan stayed aloof because he could not understand a single word of Portuguese. Lourival and the engineer talked for some fifteen minutes, until he finally embraced Collier farewell and then did the same to Finnegan. The *seringalista* and his men proceeded to board the small flatboat to which

318

the *pelas* of rubber were tied and slowly weighed anchor, hoisting sail and heading downriver.

"Why didn't you have them give us a lift?" Finnegan asked, annoyed.

"They are likewise forbidden to dock at Porto Velho."

"Christ, after all that conversation. What the hell were you two talking about for so long?"

"Oh, this and that, lad, this and that. He wanted to know how we were this morning and I told him we were fine, just topping—we are topping, aren't we, lad?"

"Oh, we're *topping*, all right!" Finnegan exclaimed, lifting his hands to his head and running his fingers through his hair.

"I also told him how grateful we were for the night of revelry—just to show friendly, you see."

The physician was watching the small craft glide slowly out of Porto Santo Antônio.

"Heading for Manaus," Collier explained. "Jolly-looking craft, the *Gigante do Brasil* they call her."

"That's rubber they're hauling, isn't it?"

Collier nodded. "A very good harvest, they tell me. Claim to have extracted some four hundred tons of rubber."

"That'll bring in a lot of money, won't it?"

"I dare say the price of rubber on the market is falling. And Lourival tells me their debts are quite heavy. He complains that life is very expensive here in Brazil."

"At fifteen dollars a kilo for meat, it can't be cheap."

"The *coronel* tells me—"

"The what?"

"The colonel, Lourival..."

"Colonel?"

"It's a sign of respect, not a military rank. He's the local landowner. Lourival tells me he plans to spend some six months away from here."

"He sounds like a sensible man—that's what we should do."

"He intends to visit his children."

"His children live in Manaus?"

"No, in Paris."

"You don't mean to tell me that grubby little gunslinger is going to spend six months in Paris? France?"

"It's no more than he's accustomed to doing every now and

then. He has his children there, two sons. From what he told me, one is studying law and the other throws his money after women and drinking."

"Was the *colonel* born here in Santo Antônio?"

"Not at all, he was born a long way from here, over in the state of Ceará. No one is born in this squalid place, doctor. You can pad around the whole of Porto Santo Antônio, trying to find a native of the city and you'll come up empty-handed. The colonel came here in 1887."

"I suppose you're right. I haven't seen a single child any-place in town."

"Children can't exist here. They all die. There's no way to grow here and this is no place to be born."

In fact, Porto Santo Antônio could hardly be termed a city. It was more of an occasional retreat for between harvests. It had actually been abandoned for nearly a century, until rubber succeeded in attracting people once more to the region. Not even the Jesuits, it seemed, who had founded the city in the eighteenth century, had been able to hold out; they abandoned it twenty years later—an unheard-of-event at the time, because the Jesuits were known never voluntarily to abandon any of their missions. If they did so with Porto Santo Antônio, it was because the place was not even worth a martyrdom, as minor as it might have been.

The two had had their attention drawn to a metal craft now approaching the wharf.

"It's from the company," Collier commented. "They've come to look for us."

His companion felt more like a college student, caught in some mischief, than a physician at the moment. Collier perceived his anxiety.

"Don't worry, doctor, they're used to my escapades."

"They're going to fix our wagons," the doctor said fretfully.

"Clearly! We've deviated from the path of virtue."

The small, sleek craft used by the company for trips of short duration was now docking at the wharf. From the masthead fluttered an American flag and on the bow was painted: "Property of the Madeira-Mamoré Railway Company."

The engineer immediately recognized the tall man of about the same age who leaped onto the dock.

"Well, 'King' John himself, in the flesh. This is an honor."

320

The physician recognized the name of the notorious general manager of the company for Porto Velho.

"Now what are we going to do?" he lamented.

"Don't start sniveling, lad. We don't have to do anything." Collier went up to "King" John and warmly embraced him.

"Collier, you old buzzard! You might have let me know you were going to fly the coop. I could have stood for a bit of carousing myself!"

Richard Finnegan felt he no longer understood anything.

"It was no great shenanigans, John," the engineer complained dismissively, "but at least we ran into some Brazilians with some fine whiskey."

"King" John took in the panorama: the square, the encroaching jungle, the canoes tied up in the harbor, the throng of people cutting a line from the town to the docks.

"You didn't by any chance run into some of our former employees in the vicinity?"

"No, only the natives. Why, John?"

"Well, I confess you had me a mite worried, Collier, when I heard that you had come out here with the doctor."

"Worried? About what?"

"Yes, I was afraid that the Germans who ran off from the Abunã might be holding up here. We found out yesterday that they sacked a couple of houses belonging to some *seringueiros* over the past few days."

"Might have been entertaining, John. Especially as they're so fond of their Dr. Finnegan, over there."

17

The newspaper opened to page two on Percival Farquhar's desk was the *Correio da Manha*. The discreet headline—true to the spirit of this prestigious Carioca paper, the leading daily in the federal capital—read as follows: FEAT OF THE CENTURY OR AMALGAM OF CARNAGE AND SCANDAL? The article had been signed by Alberto Torres, a fervent nationalist and a man of impeccable reputation. The piece was intended as a response to the recent reportage regarding the construction of the Madeira-Mamoré as some sort of technological miracle, and its text comprised a series of vigorous denunciations, as was to be expected from a man like Alberto Torres.

Farquhar was clearly disturbed—the text was abusive and direct; and what was worse, the author was incorruptible. There in black and white, he contested once again the fairness of the public bidding in which the engineer Catambry had emerged victorious; and further down the page, the intromission of a man like Farquhar in such an undertaking. Torres had characterized the affair as one among many of the crimes of *lese patria* committed recently by corrupt politicians and cited Percival's dealings in Brazil as those of "an avid octopus whose tentacles reach everywhere, in an intricate stretch of hidden interests whose principal victims would always be the nation and its people." Also citing a report by Dr. Oswaldo Cruz, Torres ridiculed the company's claim that the high mortality rate among workers involved in the construction of the railroad was to be explained by the harshness of the Amazonian terrain. Elaborating with considerable intelligence upon the data of Cruz, Torres suggested that the real culprit was the "absurd and cruel system of forced labor which continues to proffer inhuman conditions for survival, where even a healthy man could credibly aspire, under such conditions, to no more than ninety days of life." In addition, he continued, that particular stretch of territory, recently the object of strenuous litigation, was now virtually monopolized by a powerful group of foreign

nterests who posed an evident threat to the national sover-
ignty. As for the government, Alberto Torres found it strangely
assive—given the campaign promises of Marshal Hermes da
onseca to clean up Catete Palace—and even provocative to
he extent that the marshal's own cabinet figures were linked
y pecuniary and personal interests to this dangerous North
American cartel.

These were ominous words to the ears of Percival Farquhar;
hey could unleash another avalanche of protests which might
rejudice his other projects—above all, that of his lumber
ompany, already faced with serious problems along the bor-
ers of Paraná and Santa Catarina states, in the form of near-
ebellions among the peasants dispossessed of lands by the
arquhar syndicate.

Although it was still quite early, big, burly Alexander Mac-
enzie arrived with another copy of the *Correio* tucked under
is arm. He was visibly infuriated because, toward the middle
of the article, Torres had referred to him in passing as a "water
at snouting his way through the public basements of an in-
ompetent and venal federal administration." The classification
of "water rat" for some reason struck him as more insulting
han the "bird of prey feeding upon the carrion that has gov-
rned us for the past several years," used to characterize his
Quaker boss.

Mackenzie sat down and immediately pulled a handkerchief
from his pocket to wipe the cold sweat dripping from his
forehead. It was not a particularly humid day and Farquhar's
office was well ventilated, but Mackenzie's grievance made
his blood boil.

"I already got hold of Agostinho," he informed Percival.
"He should be here any minute."

"Good."

"This is a serious attack. We could take legal action."

"On what grounds, Mac?"

"Slander! Loss of credit, I don't care."

The door to the office was again opened, this time to give
passage to Colonel Agostinho, who was also armed with his
own copy of the paper.

"At least you came out unscathed," Farquhar commented.

"No, I'm there between the lines," the colonel answered,

constrained at not being able to share fully in the category of victim of that virulent attack.

Farquhar indicated a place for the colonel to sit down.

"Have you decided upon a response," Agostinho quizzed them both.

"Mac, here, wants to sue."

"Sue Alberto Torres?" he gasped, as if Mackenzie's suggestion were to sue the Pope.

"For slander . . . for loss of credit," Mackenzie almost shouted.

Percival signaled with a hand for Alexander Mackenzie to calm down.

"Tell me something," he asked, addressing himself to the colonel, "has the president seen this?"

Agostinho shook his head: "No, not yet, in any case. Normally, he's not in the habit of reading the morning papers until after working hours. He's obsessed with the idea that all the newspapers are against his administration, and whenever he reads anything the slightest bit critical he loses the will to work."

"But he's certainly going to read it at some point," Farquhar insisted.

"Of course he is, sometime today, probably before dinner."

"And what do you think his reaction is going to be?" Mackenzie interjected.

"He will want to drink the blood of Alberto Torres, which will spoil his dinner. That's nothing new, of course . . . he hasn't had many dinners since he took office. He generally goes to bed angry and hungry."

Farquhar settled back in his chair and crossed his legs under the desk. His hands were roaming about the surface, searching for something to occupy them.

"I wouldn't give it a second thought—I tell you we should institute proceedings against the guy," Mackenzie repeated.

"I consider the idea of a court fight rather dangerous," the colonel reflected.

Mackenzie eyed him with clenched fists and was reciprocated with an expression of disdain.

"Why dangerous?" Percival inquired, pressing the tips of his fingers together.

"Alberto Torres is a very respected man in this country. You

324

bring a suit against him and you'll raise more of a scandal around yourself than all his accusations."

"Is it true he can't be bought?"

"Percival, I cannot imagine the price that would bring in Alberto Torres," the colonel replied, shaking his head. "Perhaps there is no such price. Alberto Torres is a man of principle."

"There's no such thing as a man of principle," Percival chided.

Agostinho smiled.

"Alberto Torres is the exception that proves the rule."

The colonel began to take out a rather thick file he was carrying inside his leather grip.

"What's this?" Percival asked as the colonel handed him the file.

"It's the secret service dossier on Alberto Torres."

Farquhar laid out the file on his desk and examined it meticulously. As he did so, the others fell silent and stared into space. Some twenty-five minutes later, Percival Farquhar closed the file and returned it to the colonel.

"The man is immaculate," he concluded laconically.

"Exactly," confirmed the colonel. "We can't buy him and we can't touch a hair on his head. If anything should happen to Alberto Torres, you'd have pandemonium and we would be sacrificed like rats."

Mackenzie nearly jumped out of his chair.

"What the *hell* did you say?"

"I said they'd sweep us out like rats."

"Don't you *dare* provoke me, you army shithead!"

Agostinho turned livid.

"Have you gone crazy, Mackenzie!"

"Just keep provoking me and you'll find out. . . ."

Percival Farquhar got up from his chair and walked to the window. The gesture attracted the attention of the others from their quarrel, because it was a telltale sign of the Quaker's preoccupation.

"I still think we ought to prosecute," Mackenzie insisted. "It's a perfectly normal reaction. Haul him into court to make him prove what he says."

Percival returned to his desk, where his eyes settled upon the figure of the colonel. The fixity of his stare made Agostinho uncomfortable, provoking an uneasy feeling that he was obliged to say something in return.

"Perhaps it may not be such a bad idea to prosecute him," the colonel ventured hesitantly. "It might be the most civilized thing to do, and it'll certainly make his life miserable for a while."

"Have you spoken to Seabra?" Farquhar interrupted.

"I talked to him just before coming to see you. He was a bit shocked, but his campaign for the governorship of Bahia is his chief concern, right now. He showed little interest in getting tangled up in this affair."

"Let's go to court, I tell you," Mackenzie snorted bullishly. "We'll hire ourselves the best lawyers, buy out all the judges, and throw the mother in jail."

Agostinho felt degraded by Mackenzie's outburst and stood up from his chair.

"Not everything's for sale in this country, Mackenzie!"

"Let's prosecute!" Mackenzie insisted, almost in a trance, the image of a water rat boring through his skull. "He's slandered us, the son of a bitch!"

"I suggest the two of you get your minds back on your own affairs," Farquhar avouched bluntly. "We don't have many options. I'll consider the idea of a suit."

After the colonel and Mackenzie had closed the door behind them, Percival returned to have a second look out the window. The President's reaction was unpredictable—it could as easily be a mild fit of anger as a decision to eliminate his concessions for the construction of the Madeira-Mamoré. Under such dubious circumstances, there could be nothing more sensible than a consultation with his lawyer friend Ruy Barbosa. Thus, Percival set out immediately to find him.

Ruy Barbosa was busy at work on an article intended to lambast the ineptitude of the policies of President da Fonseca. As he would admit of no interruptions while he was writing, the barrister unwittingly obliged his Quaker colleague to pace for nearly half an hour in the great hall that served as a vestibule, drinking coffee after cup of coffee served again and again by an elderly Negro maidservant. By the time he was allowed to enter Barbosa's study, he was so nauseated from the coffees that he wore a miserable expression on his face.

326

"So gloomy from a simple article by our old nemesis Torres?" the lawyer observed ironically.

Percival Farquhar attempted a smile.

"Just nauseated from the kind of coffee they brew in your kitchen!"

"It comes from São Paulo, alas," Barbosa remarked by way of apology. "Lately, everything that comes from São Paulo seems to cause the country indigestion."

But Farquhar failed to understand double entendre.

"Well, you already seem to know what brought me here. It was a vicious attack."

"And very well written. Alberto certainly knows how to wield the Portuguese language."

"Mackenzie wants to sue him."

"And you, Percy?"

"I'm also inclined to press charges."

"But you have no legal grounds," the lawyer informed him politely.

"We would prosecute him for slander."

"I would never accept such a case."

"Why not?"

"I would lose the case to any fourth-year law student."

Farquhar looked wholly perplexed.

"Of course I would lose, Percy. Don't you wish to prosecute Torres for slander?"

"That's what I said," Percival replied, as if Barbosa's attitude were absurd.

"We wouldn't stand a chance, even were you to purchase every judge in the country."

"Would you mind telling me why?"

"Because what he wrote is the truth, and you'd have to clean your Augean stables in public if it ever came to court. Old Torres would prove every word!"

"Yes, he did tell the truth, but the truth should never be told."

"The one thing you can never cover totally is the truth, my dear Percy."

"You say totally—never *totally* cover. . . ."

"I say it and I repeat it. You cannot totally cover the truth . . . but it is occasionally possible to cloud it to some degree."

Barbosa raised his eyebrows and Farquhar broke into a smile.

"I can only suggest to you that judicial proceedings would not be the best tack to jib the truth."

"And what would be the best course—nautically speaking?"

"Alberto Torres has never been to Porto Velho. He wrote that article by basing it upon information that had, in fact, been gathered by third parties."

"Especially by a certain Oswaldo Cruz."

"A good doctor, Oswaldo Cruz, but an execrable writer."

Percival Farquhar sat up on the edge of his seat, waiting, because he was certain now that his gnomelike friend had already devised the answer.

"But if we don't prosecute and simply do nothing," Percival pressed his enigmatic mentor, "we will be signing a confession at the bottom of that list of denunciations!"

"You needn't go that far, rest assured. Has the blockhead of Catete, our president, gotten around to reading this?"

"Not yet!"

"Well, it's of no importance. What ought to be done is fairly straightforward and should have been done long ago. You must invite Seabra and a delegation of deputies and senators for a visit to Porto Velho. Thus, you will have all the eyewitnesses you need to attest to the situation as you see it."

"A little Sunday excursion by train through the jungle— what a marvelous idea. I've got to hand it to you, Ruy."

"Thank you, Percy, but eyewitnesses who must only see what is convenient for them to see . . . and for you. When they return, they will deliver their speeches in Parliament. They will write articles. They will spread the gospel that your project is developing miraculously like some eighth wonder of the world. They won't be persons of the pedigree or stripe of our old Torres, but they will bear witness like a flock of sheep and belie the truth of his secondhand meddling."

On the following day, Farquhar's emissaries delivered the invitations. In a daring gesture the marshal himself was invited but declined, unable to set aside enough time for the long voyage. Seabra also said no, a bit distressed that he could not make the trip in person, but promised to send his vice-minister instead. J.J. found it impossible to forsake the federal capital while the governorship of Bahia was not yet in his pocket. In

328

general, however, the invitations were an overwhelming hit with Congress. A senator from Amazonas, two federal deputies from Minas Gerais, two from Paraíba, and another from Ceará had all accepted. The voyage was planned for ten days hence, and would last nearly two months from embarkation to return. Farquhar was even able to make use of a steamer arriving from India, with a new shipment of laborers, to transport the illustrious commission. The vessel was a comfortable one which normally navigated the Mediterranean sea, with summer crossings between Ceuta and Cadiz. To assure completely the success of the mission, Percival himself would accompany his guests, who with their wives, lovers, servants, and other dependents already numbered more than fifty passengers.

18

On the quay in Porto Velho stood a small committee of welcome for the engineer and the physician. Thomas Gallagher, the locomotive engineer; Harold Appleton, his stoker; and Consuelo Campero, the pianist, were anxiously awaiting the fugitives. The instant she saw Richard Finnegan on board, the Bolivian girl had to stifle the desire to throw herself upon him in a passionate embrace. Finally, the vessel was tied up at the wharf and the fugitives disembarked. Stephan Collier received affectionate welcomes from Gallagher and the stoker, while Finnegan was extended a timid hand from Consuelo, who inquired after his health.

"They've already heard their punishment," boasted "King" John. "They are prohibited from eating dessert for a week."

Collier gave a friendly slap on back to the boisterous company manager and everybody laughed.

"I cannot pass that last remark, John," Collier chided him. "I'll get Gallagher there to pay off the cook."

The group set out from the quay along a pier constructed of iron with a line of tracks for freight cars. A huge crane threw its shadow across the length of the pier, and the city of Porto Velho shimmered in the efflux of heat that was gradually evaporating the humidity. Richard and the Bolivian girl lingered apart from the conviviality which seemed to dominate the others. Old Thomas and his sidekick were explaining to the engineer that they would probably have to remain there in Porto Velho for at least another two months.

"Is that true, John?" Collier asked.

"Most likely. If you're to continue work on the Abunã, you will need additional men. We can only reckon for the moment on the fifteen Barbadians who were already employed. I received a telegram yesterday confirming the arrival of two hundred more laborers whom our agents have contracted in India. But they won't arrive here for another sixty days."

330

"That's a bloody lot of time to spend in a hospital," Collier complained, already anticipating his own boredom.

"Fear not, Stephan, Lovelace has released the both of you. I suspect he doesn't want a pair of lunatics fouling up his routine."

"Routine? That hospital is run like an elephant burial ground!"

"But a disciplined elephant burial ground."

Finnegan was also relieved to know that they would not have to remain interned at Candelária, but his happiness was short-lived. The manager informed him that Lovelace expected the physician to work in the ward until the laborers arrived.

The group headed for the casino, where they could gamble their paychecks, sip various fruit juices, but where no alcoholic beverages were served. The physician and Consuelo prudently allowed the others to go on ahead and enter the casino.

"And have you decided what you plan to do?" Finnegan asked her.

The Bolivian girl lowered her head and nearly broke into tears.

"I have no idea what to do," she replied shrilly, her eyes burning.

"Don't you have any relatives? Don't you have a home to return to?"

"I have no one anymore," Consuelo lied to him.

"Would you like to remain here in Porto Velho?"

"They won't permit it. There's not much time, I will soon have to go away."

"But where?"

"I don't know."

"You're a pianist, aren't you?"

"I play the piano. I've already told you: I used to give lessons on the piano. Didn't I tell you? But who would be interested in learning the piano here in Porto Velho."

"You could work in the hospital."

"I've already checked—there are no openings. There's very little use for women around here."

The physician began to feel uncomfortable because he knew what was coming. She was putting herself in his hands—totally in his hands. Yet he was no longer the same person and, whenever he would dare to look ahead (which was less and less), he could only see the darkest void. And this Bolivian

331

woman was handing her life over to *him?* Even now, when she could no longer manage to hold back the tears, she obviously desired the doctor to be her salvation and was prepared to cling to him tenaciously.

Finnegan watched the tears flow and was simultaneously clawed by conflicting sensations: pity for a woman as vulnerable as she, wholly without prospects for the future; anger at her having put herself in his path; discomfort that he was a shit without the least initiative; and insecurity before the burden of having his acknowledged lack of initiative be linked to a complete readiness on her part. The only thing of which he was sure was that he had become incapable, perhaps forever, of feeling anything that even resembled the sensation he had cataloged in his own mind as love. The world was too terribly fucked up and befouled a place for anyone to feel love. What he did not know, however, was that Consuelo Campero had also shed the last remnant of any illusions, and only for this reason was she offering herself to him.

"Calm down," the physician told her. "Everything will work out somehow."

Yet the sobbing grew more uncontrollable, because those were not the words of comfort that she had been hoping to hear.

"Don't worry about me," she finally managed to say. "I'm just a little stunned by your return. I was terrified that something might have happened to you."

Finnegan felt a knot of emptiness in his throat.

"It's hard to believe someone still worries about me."

"I worry about you, Richard."

At the sound of his Christian name in that tearful tone of voice, the doctor nearly melted.

"Enough of those tears, Consuelo. It's all in the past, I'm here," he offered in the most tender tone he could muster.

The Bolivian girl took a handkerchief from her pocket and blew her nose. Her reddened eyes were shining in the sunlight and the teardrops dried upon the dark, smooth skin of her face.

Several Barbadian workers crossing the street waved to the physician. He returned the greeting, then ran a hand through his hair, imagining how disheveled he must be from the strong wind that had buffeted the vessel during the entire voyage back to Porto Velho.

"You look exhausted, Richard."

"I slept very badly," he complained. "It was a dreadful night."

"You're not hungry?" she asked him.

The physician reflected that his stomach really did feel like an empty balloon and was still inflating.

"Actually I am rather hungry, now that you mention it. I haven't had a thing to eat since yesterday."

"Let's go to my quarters and I'll make you something to eat."

Consuelo took the physician's hand and the two ambled along in the direction of a series of decent-looking dwellings which served as lodgings for the company professionals. Richard Finnegan peered again at the Rio Madeira, which cut like a yellow scar through the greenish waste of jungle, and he thought he might very well faint. He did not feel the slightest bit grateful for Consuelo's shower of attentions. Yet he was resigned to the dismal notion that her future was at his side.

They entered the house where she was staying for the moment. It was a collective space, which she shared with three other girls who worked as nurses at Candelária. The Bolivian newcomer had little contact with the others, but since she generally spent the entire day at home, she had managed to make herself mistress of the house. She went into the kitchen, while Finnegan allowed himself to luxuriate on the clean bed, its sheets discreetly perfumed with the odor of Consuelo. But not before he had carefully removed his dirty boots, his socks reeking of sweat, and set them both out of the room. Exhaustion stifled any further proprieties and the doctor opened his shirt and collapsed into bed.

There the two of them remained for most of the day: Finnegan withdrawing whenever possible and Consuelo acting like a reprimanded child. Predictably, the inveterate, clichéd, human spark of young bodies rubbing together finally ignited them both, and the sparse vestiges of their mutual flights were compliantly subdued, because the weather was like a prolonged insomnia. And Finnegan—whose certainties lay in shreds, his mind overwrought with fatigue and confusion—no longer managed to understand anything because the rules of life had been shuffled to oblivion. Not to mention that before he could even attempt any sort of redefinition, there still remained the

333

additional year and a half to his contract with the company. For the moment, though he may have possessed her, Consuelo Campero represented a tantalizing antithesis to his own collapse as a human being. Yet a sadness was welling up from the walls of that impersonal boudoir; and Richard Finnegan, who now affected to see the world as an absurd comedy, had crushed to his chest and coiled around his thighs the body of a woman. And that was a hell of a situation!

BOOK V

The Delights of Primitive Accumulation

19

In 1911, the city of Porto Velho was perhaps a singular phenomenon in the whole of South America. It was an artificial city that principally served as the central offices for the firm building the railroad called Madeira-Mamoré.

It was a peculiar city for Brazil, where there were no carnival celebrations but Thanksgiving was duly commemorated. Where Independence Day had yet to be recalled on September 7, but the city inevitably decked out reds, whites, and blues come the Fourth of July. Where throughout the month of June, when the cold winds whistled down off the Andes, there were no signs of such traditional festivals as *bumba-meu-boi* or "Green Brandy," but toward the end of October most of the inhabitants would already be breaking out their Halloween costumes for the upcoming revelries, despite the fact that no children lived in the town.

Porto Velho had been wholly contrived, as artificial an invention as nearly everything else within the 36,600 square kilometers of territory granted to a cartel headed by Percival Farquhar. The official language was English, and even the most painstaking of surveys would have uncovered few persons who could speak any Portuguese. From its original collection of slapped-down tents, Porto Velho was gradually sprawling into the dimensions of a small village, inhabited entirely by employees of the Madeira-Mamoré Railway Company. As a result it lacked its commercial street; there were no bars, no cafes, no restaurants. In sum, it stood as an absolute embodiment of what has been called private initiative: everything in existence there was an extension of the monopoly of the Farquhar syndicate — including the law.

The most expressive monuments in Porto Velho were the prodigiously giant trees that surrounded the plaza and shaded several of the main streets. In keeping with the healthy spirit of any vigorous monopolist, the general store, the cleaners, the cinema, the casino, all public buildings and private dwellings, the hospital, the docks and depots—everything belonged to the Farquhar syndicate. Porto Velho, in 1911, did not have to reckon with the presence of any Brazilian authorities. Order was maintained by a private police force, and the Farquhar syndicate made a profit on everything down to the sale of each creamcracker that its modern cookie factory turned out unceasingly.

Yet, these were hardly the most evident of reasons why Porto Velho stood out as an exception on the continent. Its very architecture was fundamentally alien to all the other small cities dotting South America. There existed here no vestiges of Colonial times: no tiny Baroque church, no seignorial mansion, no rough-hewn ruin of an Iberian fortress. All the facades—aside from being new and judiciously glossed in oil-base paint—faithfully reduplicated the myriad wooden towns of western North America. The only differences lay in the ample, screened-in verandas and the addition of electricity, which many hamlets of the hemisphere had yet to dream of.

The houses were methodically aligned, producing perpendicular, tidy streets. At the entrance to the ultramodern quay stood the main plaza—a broad public square spitted by an imposing metal flagpole, from which there fluttered throughout the day, in the capricious winds that crisscrossed the Rio Madeira, an American flag. Surrounding the plaza were the vast warehouses and administrative buildings, in addition to the railway station, which replicated the innumerable railroad depots of small dimensions starkly bracketing the thousands of towns across the United States. No street was without its wooden sidewalks, the necessary safeguard to pedestrians during the rainy season that habitually transformed the dusty byways into muddy gruel. Few vehicles existed in the city and, clearly, those which did exist pertained to the Farquhar syndicate. Yet in the background, not very far from the blocks of warehouses and storage depots, the jungle stood like a muzzled wall of green, routed but still defiant.

On that morning toward the end of summer, the sun was particularly strong and a rampant blue sky hovered cloudlessly. The day seemed to have a special significance because the entire staff of the company was already lined up around the perimeter of the plaza and along the adjacent streets. The police force—a batallion of fifty men sporting navy blue uniforms,

338

smart kepis, and polished Winchesters—was stationed in a double row stretching the entire length of the quay. The city waited. The long-expected arrival of an official delegation, personally accompanied by the legendary Percival Farquhar, was about to be played out. This would be the first time that the Quaker had come to Porto Velho, and only two or three company officials in the city even knew the great impressario. For the vast majority, his was only a name to be feared or hated, depending upon the circumstances.

Immediately in front of the main administrative edifice of the company stood the highest officials from the upper echelons of Porto Velho. Among them were the physicians from Candelária, headed by Dr. Lovelace; the engineers and topographers like Stephan Collier; technicians and mechanics, in the midst of whom stood Old Thomas Gallagher; and the different-level bureaucrats fawning over "King" John himself, the living incarnation of the spirit of Percival Farquhar.

The most strained group gathered there seemed to be that of the bureaucrats, while the disciplinary ladder grew gradually more lax as it approached the craven disorder that appeared to reign among the engineers. Collier and Lovelace, who knew Farquhar from years back and expected nothing from all this official buffoonery, were standing together with expressions of total peevishness on their faces, especially for having allowed themselves to be relegated to their location, where the sun was beating down mercilessly. Lovelace was red as a beet and his eyes could barely take the glare of daylight. To Collier's even greater chagrin, the doctor had just pointed out to him what a better location the bureaucrats had assigned themselves, in the shade of one of the tallest trees in the plaza.

Dr. Lovelace was showing serious signs of not being able to cope much longer with the violent heat, which encouraged his gruff English companion to take the initiative. The engineer extricated himself from his fellow technocrats and led a waning Lovelace by the arm, across the plaza, pulling him into the shadows there in front of "King" John and his retinue of bureaucrats.

"This whole thing is plainly idiotic," Collier muttered into Lovelace's ear, himself on the edge of apoplexy.

"Christ, I was about to pass out."

"All this to await that scoundrel Farquhar as if he were the bloody queen!"

"Every crowd gets the queen it deserves, Stephan."

"You're right, Lovelace. Ours is a slut named Percival Farquhar."

The doctor, revived by the fresh breeze billowing through the shade, began to laugh.

"And he's bringing others, I understand, a veritable political harem."

"Exactly, doctor—a commission of Bolivian politicians and two hundred dacoit swabs his agents probably picked out of the gutter in Calcutta."

"I don't know about the allotment from India, but the politicians are Brazilian."

"They amount to the same pilfering rotters!"

"The worst, my dear Stephan, will be trying to endure that insufferable Percival citing the New Testament at the drop of a hat."

"And messing it up, every time! He's a fraud even when it comes to that."

"We must try to be patient with him, Collier—patience above all!"

The ship was already mooring at the dock. It was a huge vessel which, nevertheless, did not hide the ravages of time. Once the lines were secured, the wooden gangway was lowered in place by a contingent of bedraggled deckhands who looked more like a gang of pirates from out of the eighteenth century. On the deck in first class, a number of passengers scanned the town of Porto Velho with eager curiosity. They were well-dressed gentlemen with elegant ladies in jeweled brooches and plumed hats. First to be unloaded was the baggage belonging to the congressional delegation who were to be put up in lavish apartments especially prepared for the occasion. Next, Percival Farquhar appeared at the top of the gangway, followed by a stern-looking man, impeccably dressed in a suit of white linen with a panama hat on his grizzled head. It was the vice-minister and personal representative of J. J. Seabra, who would see very little during his stay in the city, suffering a dyspepsia at dinner and remaining bedridden until his departure, whereupon he would have only marvelous things to say about the Candelária Hospital, and above all about his nurses—all of them

340

lovely, luscious, accommodating females. The other major personality to disembark was the senator from Amazonas, a tall, dark gentleman of middle age and extraordinary polish. Then, finally, came the various federal deputies with their wives or lovers, maids, and dependents, all of them pointing at their surroundings and chattering loudly.

Percival was met by "King" John, though they did not embrace—perhaps because Farquhar was not habitually effusive; perhaps because "King" John was afraid of losing his wallet.

"It's a pleasure to see you here, Mr. Percival Farquhar," the manager contented himself by saying.

The two shook hands, and immediately Farquhar proceeded to make the customary introductions. A train composed of a locomotive and three coaches decorated by strips of red, white, and blue cloth, with wicker armchairs in each carriage was shunted over to the quay, and the guests were boarded while Farquhar slowly made his way toward the administrative building. The three coaches were slowly backtracked to the vicinity of the lodgings prepared for the members of the commission, where all debarked marveling and surprised. The guest quarters comprised one of the largest complexes in the town, which had been entirely redecorated with furniture shipped in from Manaus. The outside presented the same antiseptic facade as did most of the buildings, but the interior had been transformed into a luxury hotel with lavish red carpets, mirrors, candelabras, and assorted styles of furniture that ran the gamut from English medieval to contemporary Brazilian art nouveau.

Once the guests had been safely ensconced in such unexpected, dreamlike accommodations, the ship began to pour out its new lot of laborers. Still in their white loincloths, loaded down with their worldly possessions, a flock of young Hindus, nearly all of them barefoot, were padding along the scalding hot quay in the direction of the barracks set aside for screening and disinfecting. These indentured laborers inched along rather timidly, as if unaccustomed to walking, which irritated the Cuban overseers who tried to drive them along with insults, without success, since none of the Hindus understood any Spanish, and most of them very little English.

"King" John and Percival Farquhar paused to observe the

341

bumbling disembarkation, then moved on to "review" the company officials "on parade."

"It's the worst shipment we've ever received, Mr. Farquhar," the manager commented, shaking his head.

"It's the best we can do right now, John. Our agents are finding it impossible to work in Europe. Nearly all the governments have enacted laws there prohibiting such contracts."

"Well, now we're down to the dregs, I suppose."

But Farquhar had already walked on ahead and broke into a smile at the sight of Dr. Lovelace, wiping his face with a handkerchief sopping with sweat.

"Lovelace, it's been a long time."

"You look splendid, Percival, I must say. All those ladies you bed down with in Rio must be keeping you in shape."

"I've no time for such things, Lovelace. But you, you probably spend your time fornicating with your nurses all day."

"Ah, if you'd seen the nurses we have here, you wouldn't say such naughty things about me."

Farquhar suddenly discovered Stephan Collier sitting on the doorstep of the administrative building.

"Well, Collier, still surviving, I see."

The engineer made no effort to get up but simply tilted his head to stare at the Quaker.

"Still giving everybody a hard time?" Farquhar added.

"Only for the good of the company, Farquhar."

"King" John caught up with his boss at the very moment that the latter seemed to be peering into the sky with an expression of shock, then rage.

"What in tarnation have you got up there, John?" Farquhar yelled.

"What do you mean, boss?"

"Up there! On the flagpole."

His manager failed to understand, but heard the nettlesome voice of Collier intervene.

"Farquhar, are you blind? It's the American flag!"

"I *know*," the Quaker riposted violently.

"It's our flag," John repeated hesitantly.

"It shouldn't *be* there," Farquhar sighed.

Collier stood up and came over to the two of them.

"It's the Bolivian flag you ought to have up there," the engineer remarked, winking to "King" John.

342

The manager did not hesitate further and turned to one of his staff, bellowing out his orders.

"Go find me a Bolivian flag, and be quick about it! Bunch of cretins . . ."

"It's not the Bolivian flag I want, John," Farquhar corrected, coldly as a fanatical assassin.

"Aren't we in Bolivia, Mr. Farquhar?"

"Of course not, you idiot, they're all speaking Portuguese! What country do you *think* it is!"

"Brazil, I guess," he answered sheepishly, glaring at Collier.

"And who do you think these visitors are, whom I've brought here at such expense?"

"Bo-li-vi-an po-li-ti-cians," the engineer mouthed silently with his lips.

"Bolivian politicians, boss," the manager repeated, looking from Collier to Farquhar, then seeing his mistake reflected in the fiery eyes of the Quaker. "I mean Brazilian! Brazilian politicians, Mr. Farquhar—obviously, Brazilians."

"That's right, John, *Brazilians*."

"They're all the same malingering *babus!*"

"Collier, I warn you," Farquhar crowed with demonical fury, "another word and I'll serve you your head on a platter."

In the meantime, a flustered "King" John was savagely issuing orders—"A Brazilian flag, you fools, I said a *Brazilian* flag!"—provoking mayhem among his staff, while turning now and then to apologize to his boss: "But Farquhar . . . how was I supposed to know?"

"This is not American territory, you dummy. Not yet!"

"Don't trouble yourself, Farquhar," Collier tried to soothe him, "your guests didn't even notice the difference."

"They're a villainous bunch, I'll warrant you, but there's no reason to give them added ammunition with some flapdoodle over patriotism." The stocky Quaker was still breathing with difficulty from sheer impatience.

Two employees from the manager's staff came hurrying out of the administrative building and one of them carried a green bundle in his arms. The American flag was immediately lowered and "King" John himself hoisted the Brazilian flag as rapidly as possible in its place.

"There now," he said triumphantly.

Collier looked up and turned red in the face.

"Where did you get that flag?" he asked and burst out laughing.

"We had it made special," the manager explained, growing more perplexed.

"Where did you have it made?"

"Right here, by a woman who works as a seamstress. Why?"

"An American seamstress, am I right?"

"Right, Collier, so what?" the manager confirmed with growing exasperation.

"Son of a bitch!" Farquhar exclaimed, scratching his poll and turning away in frustration. "You explain, Collier."

"It may be the Brazilian flag, John, but it's hoisted upside down. And what's more, there on that white strip it's not 'Order and Progress' that should be written. It should have been *'Ordem e Progresso,'* in Portuguese!"

"Take down that flag this minute!" ordered Percival Farquhar, provoking a new flurry of pandemonium among his bureaucrats.

"Then, what are we going to put up there?" asked "King" John. "You can't have an empty flagpole."

"Do you know what we ought to put up there, John?"

"No, Mr. Farquhar."

"You, John, you! Hoisted by the neck like a dead cat!"

"Now, now, you don't want to go insulting your Brazilians," Collier cheerfully interjected. "At the sight of him hanging from that pole, Brazil might be driven to break diplomatic relations! . . . Of course, you might have him just sit up there for a little while."

The thought of "King" John seated upon the flagpole provoked an unexpected burst of laughter from Percival Farquhar, joined by the engineer. The rest of the staff greeted with an abundant show of smiles the welcome relief from all the tension. Only "King" John failed to share the merriment. He felt humiliated and eyed his staff to select which among them would be the perfect victim to alleviate his shame. He noticed a smiling office boy, still standing there with the American flag under his arm. He flew at the lad and grabbed him by the collar.

"What's that you've got there under your arm, you gaping imbecile?"

344

But before the terror-stricken lad had a chance to speak, Collier had intervened:

"That's Farquhar's greatcoat—a gift from his Uncle Sam!"

The manager snatched the flag and thrust the boy aside, glaring at the engineer. Then he stormed like a hurricane into the administrative building, crashing the door behind him.

"Fifty dollars to the first one to go in there and come out alive," Collier trumpeted.

No one laughed. Percival Farquhar had commenced to realize that this was the reality of Porto Velho. They were all plum *loco* down here—the denunciations in the newspapers back in the capital didn't come close to the half of it. The visit would have to be curtailed because you couldn't expect to control a bunch of crackpots indefinitely! Well, lunatic or not, certain insanities also had their practical (lucrative!) side. . . .

Consuelo Campero had not been present at the disembarkation of the visitors because she had had other duties to attend to. In point of fact, she was extremely busy because from one day to the next she had turned into one of the major factors in the programming to be offered the guests of Percival Farquhar.

In those two months during which the whole of Porto Velho had anticipated this day, Consuelo had suddenly found herself a job—the last thing she could have expected to do in such a town. She woke up to discover herself hired as a piano teacher. She was placed on the company payroll and given administrative status, with special privileges that included the right to her own lodgings and an entire year's holiday to be paid for by the company once her task had been completed. Certainly she was no ordinary piano teacher and had been forbidden to take in students—that is, she was restricted to a single student to whom she was to dedicate all her energies. Her pupil was also an employee of the company, although he had been alloted an inferior status. Her pupil was Joe Caripuna, the Indian.

The idea had originated with Richard Finnegan, almost as a joke. Consuelo had managed to salvage some of her musical scores, which Collier had discarded back at their camp in Abunã. She rarely opened the precious packet because it still brought back bitter memories. On the same week in which Richard had returned from his escapade in Santo Antônio, the Bolivian girl had discovered that there actually existed a piano

345

in Porto Velho. It was no grand piano such as the one she had set her heart on——and broken it!——but it was a piano, nevertheless, sitting there in the casino dismally out of tune, seldom if ever used because most of the music heard there came from the North American records played on the gramophone.

Consuelo discovered that the casino was scarcely frequented in the mornings; and even in the afternoons, if it was a weekday; it seemed that few men had the time to sit there several hours, drinking cider, playing poker, or smoking their cigars. So she began to visit the casino during such off-hours, making friends first with the two Chinese waiters and then with the manager of the place, a likable Italian-American fellow who loved to play, whenever the casino was empty, his beloved albums of Italian music.

For several days she spent her time retuning the piano until it was in reasonably good condition. By the end of that week, after having told Richard of her discovery and practiced a bit, she came up with the idea of asking "King" John for permission to give an audition to the customers at the casino. He saw nothing wrong with the idea and allowed her to proceed. Yet the audition was by no means a success because the men continued gambling the whole time, paying no attention and thereby demonstrating a wholesale insensibility to the sonatas of Beethoven and the nocturnes of Frederic Chopin. Still, their behavior did not dismay the Bolivian girl. She was obviously out of practice and had only to return with renewed vigor to rehearsing at the keyboard, with her newfound critic and companion Joe Caripuna. True, he likewise did not seem to be terribly moved by the harmonies of the great masters, but at least he demonstrated an eager curiosity with respect to the instrument from which tones enigmatically resounded whenever she pushed down on the white and black teeth that must have been taken from some mysterious dead animal or spirit.

Consuelo's painstaking practice, fatiguing and demanding for her, surprisingly did not produce the same impression in Joe. The Indian began to speculate that he could also do the same, although he could not count on hands to imitate the Bolivian girl. He had his toes, however, and with them he believed he could also make the black box sing. Thus, it occurred that one morning, when Consuelo Campero arrived at the casino, she confronted Joe Caripuna, seated upon a pile of empty crates which elevated him above the keyboard, agilely toeing the keys in a way that many of her past students might have envied. The music did not pass for more than aleatoric resonatings, but by the amazing dexterity of his big toes he had managed to strike each note distinctly, and perhaps with a little training he might one day be able to eke out a few simple melodies. The Bolivian girl felt both jubilant and astonished at such capacity for adapting to formidable circumstances as this Indian seemed to continually demonstrate. On that same morning, forgetting her own exercises, Consuelo amused herself with Joe by playing little melodies that he was able to imitate with a fair degree of success, to the amazement of the manager of the casino.

"Is in*cre*dible, dissa Joe," said the Italian-American, marveling at his accomplishment.

The Caripuna limited himself to smiling, while Consuelo helped him down from the pile of boxes.

"How can he have so mucha music in da toes!"

"Feet *não* just for walk," said Joe, still smiling.

Consuelo and the manager watched the Indian walk out of the casino, then turned to each other, almost at the same instant, struck by the identical notion.

"You tink data guy could really *play* somating?"

The Bolivian girl, who knew full well the power of Joe's resilience and determination, had no doubts as to the answer.

"I think he could play almost anything, if we keep it simple."

"Dat woulda be fantastic! You teacha him and leave da resta to me. I have him play right here in da casino."

"What a grand idea! Then Joe would have a profession, too."

Consuelo confided nothing to Richard Finnegan until Joe had had a chance to make some real progress. For two weeks, every morning, the Caripuna would seat himself on the pile of crates and Consuelo would give him instruction. At first she attempted to have Joe follow the standard method of learning piano, recognition of individual notes and reinforcement through constant drill. But she soon noticed that the method was inappropriate for Joe and, while it may have been efficient for whoever had hands, this particular pupil had to make do with his feet. Besides which, Joe had difficulty in assimilating the nature of music as Consuelo understood it, and this further

347

complicated matters. The Indian could follow the outlines of a melody but seemed to have no sense of timing and would vary the harmony from one note to the next. In fact, Joe Caripuna might have been recognized to be a born dodecaphonic musician, had the system been known to the South America of the year 1911.

In that first week her pupil had managed to toe several measures of "Happy Birthday to You," but his execution did not please Consuelo inasmuch as his timing eluded her and he would introduce a semitone at the most unexpected intervals. His inaptitude for proper timing and his propensity for semitones in the end caused his teacher to fear that perhaps, as an Indian, Joe might prove culturally incapable of assimilating the musicality of civilization. Still, he had a good ear; that much she could tell. And she soon discovered that, if she played the melody over and over, measure by measure (instead of persisting with the method), her pupil eventually managed to reproduce exactly the same piece, tone for tone! Indeed, by the end of the second week—an exceptionally short time by any standard—Joe Caripuna had mastered, with perfect ease and no mistakes, not only "Happy Birthday" but two other popular North American tunes.

On Sunday, when Richard had his day off, Consuelo invited him to come to the casino to hear an audition on the piano. The physician was certain that it was Consuelo who was going to try out her repertoire once again.

"This is incredible," Finnegan told her, listening to the Caripuna tinker with the piano from high on top of the pile of crates.

"I'm so happy, Richard," Consuelo said warmly. "Joe is no longer just an invalid but an example for humanity."

The physician's judgment did not go that far, but he was greatly impressed by the Indian's success.

"*Ella* teach me," Joe said, pointing to Consuelo with his perennial smile.

The manager of the casino came out from behind the counter to greet the physician.

"Datsa quita guy, anhh?" he said, squeezing Finnegan's hand and nodding at the Indian. "I gonna ask d'administration to booka dissa boy here at da casino."

To the surprise of Richard and Consuelo, the person who

proved to be most enthusiastic about Joe's ability would not
be "King" John. Actually, John was never one to get enthusiastic about anything, if it did not relate directly to himself.
It was Lovelace who turned out to be the one to twitter with
excitement after attending a command performance. Finnegan
could not imagine what had come over the doctor, but the
clever rogue had really appreciated the performance, though
his motives were not as artistic as Finnegan might have imagined.

"You're going to give him a contract, John, but not to waste
his time here in the casino."

The manager of the casino lost his temper.

"Listen to me, Dr. Lovalaces, dissa discovery, she'sa mine—
datsa to say, mine and da signorina's, Dona Consuelo."

"King" John remained indifferent. In truth, he found the
whole spectacle repellent. In principle, he hated Indians.

"I'll not deny the merit of whoever among you made this
discovery," Lovelace continued unperturbed, "but Joe Caripuna
needs to be put to better use by the company."

Hearing the name of the company invoked, its manager
became more interested.

"The company can make something from him?" he asked,
incredulous but at the same time attentive to whatever Lovelace
might have in mind.

"You sign him up now, John. But no wasting the Indian's
time playing here in the casino. He's still not ready, he needs
more drilling at the keyboard."

"But why should I put him under contract?"

"Because he's the perfect surprise," Lovelace went on, as
if lecturing to a child. "We'll make him the main attraction at
the reception for Farquhar's visiting commission. Don't you
see?"

But "King" John simply could not fathom how any Indian
could be an attraction to a group of visiting politicians.

"Just do as I say, John! You won't regret it."

Thus, Joe Caripuna, who played "Happy Birthday" with his
feet, was signed up by the Madeira-Mamoré Railway company
as a lower-echelon employee with rights to a salary of eight
milreis a month, or twenty dollars. Consuelo Campero, his
piano teacher, received the post of technical instructor, which

accorded her all the amenities of a senior official in the town of Porto Velho.

To the program for the benefit of Percival Farquhar's guests of honor, along with all the receptions and tours, there was enigmatically added a piano recital—scheduled to follow a visit by the commission to the ultramodern facilities of the Candelária Hospital.

20

The auditorium of the cinema was almost completely filled up. Not only the visitors to Porto Velho, but the engineers, doctors, and officials of the highest echelons of the company were in attendance. A long table, covered by a white linen tablecloth and urns of flowers, had been set in front of the screen hidden behind a curtain. At this table sat the senator from Amazonas, Percival Farquhar, Dr. Lovelace, "King" John, and one of the federal deputies. The vice-minister had been unable to put in an appearance because he was for the moment interned in the Candelária Hospital, under the "constant care" of at least two female nurses.

Percival was on his feet and discoursing with the soft, convincing voice of the professional huckster. The majority of the audience had not managed to follow anything he was saying—laced with approximate quotations from the Bible—and some had finally fallen asleep, including the senator from Amazonas, who had perfected his technique in the longer, more repetitive sessions of Parliament.

". . . We knew what lay ahead of us," the Quaker impresario was perorating. "There were nineteen perilous rapids—some with channels of nearly five hundred feet of lethal waters. And we were conscious of the fact that it was such accidents of nature which inhibited the transport of any raw materials, above all any significant quantity of rubber gathered with such heroism from this region. The time wasted fording these rapids became unforgivable, not to mention the losses which invariably ran as high as forty percent—unacceptable in the face of so many sacrifices. Now once we begin to operate this railway, with the Lord's help all such dangers will disappear, and, what is more important, losses will be virtually eliminated. Our vast undertaking, for this reason alone, more than justifies itself because any loss at all is like a crime against the virtues of profit and, therefore, a crime against nature. Even the Lord lamented the loss of a single lamb. And by avoiding this crime,

351

the Madeira-Mamoré will be enriching the lives of Brazilian peoples with upwards of millions of pounds-sterling in additional profits that until today have been sinfully adulterated in the waters of the Rio Madeira.

"We have reawakened a dream that stretches back to eighteen seventy, when the optimism of Brazil first demanded the impossible. And we have attempted to fulfill our purpose here with the diligence and fervor of true soldiers warring upon the curtailment of ever-increasing benefice. We have felled millennial trees. We have confronted and civilized tribes of savages living like slaves in the Stone Age. We have even accepted the risk of human lives—thus, the perseverance of American genius!

"For such intrepid workers, gathering from the four corners of the Earth, who have journeyed here with hope in their eyes and an unblemished desire to contribute to the greatness of Brazil, we offer the finest obtainable conditions in an otherwise inhospitable and totally barbarous terrain. A modern medical assistance program administered by the most competent and respected team of professionals we could find, headed by the eminent parasitologist from the United States—my personal friend and colleague—Dr. Seymour Lovelace, offered free of charge to all, reduces to an almost negligible statistic the incidence of disease. In order to augment the qualitative level of medical attention—a fundamental corollary to the success of an undertaking the magnitude of the construction of such a railway—we decided to build and equip the Candelária Hospital, with facilities to handle three hundred patients and, to date, one of the most advanced medical centers in the entire country.

"Beyond these benefits in the field of health care, we offer our employees a diet in keeping with the rigors of the climate and the nutrition required for a healthy day's work. All of our food, I might add, is imported directly by the company in accordance with the most rigorous standards of quality control. For their greater comfort, workers are quartered in model dormitories which our distinguished guests, ladies and gentlemen, will have the occasion to view personally. These dormitories have been erected with precisely the severe meteorological conditions of the tropics in mind and boast of treated water, full electricity, telephone service, automatic laundries, and other

352

modern conveniences. And the human necessity for cultural diversion has not been overlooked. Porto Velho, the mecca of our Cyclopean undertaking, offers—in addition to this moving picture theater—a newspaper and a casino. . . ."

The Quaker continued his peroration for the better part of half an hour, stumbling at times over his own phrases because the speech had been written up in Portuguese for him, a language he tended to manage rather poorly. When finally he finished—with a dramatic flourish that was lost upon the house—the auditorium rang out with relieved applause. Even the senator from Amazonas awoke and clapped with enthusiasm, shouting, "Well spoken, hear hear!" and "Very good, indeed!" perhaps thinking that he had just taken a nap in the midst of a parliamentary session.

"King" John stood up, motioning for the audience to cease their applause, and announced, "A word or two, now, from our illustrious congressman from Amazonas, Senator Montenegro."

The senator stood up unsteadily, staring for a few seconds at an equally somnolent auditorium, then mysteriously unlocked the gates of what could only be described as a verbal dam, which sluiced from his lips such a torrent of arcane vocabulary that no one could make head or tail of the resulting slough.

Stephan Collier could barely contain the urge to get up and leave the auditorium. Bad enough was the mockery of discourse delivered by Percival Farquhar, though at least that humbugger had an instinct for the burlesque! An irritated engineer leaned his head on one of his hands and promptly fell asleep. When he awoke a bit later, he saw the senator from Amazonas still discoursing, almost levitating from the stage in front of its red velvet curtain.

". . . all of which offers salient proof of the inexorable spirit of Modernity on the march. Watch as he forges ahead through the primeval stretches of isolated wilderness that have lain dormant for centuries, extending his lovingly civilizing embrace like some fulgurous spark from the ethereal conjunction of Latin and Anglo-Saxon genius. And to you, intrepid sons of that great nation to the North—O glorious American shores, symbol and profession of your eternal zeal for humanity's redemption through the fecundating progress of Culture and

353

Spirit—to you I intone the immortal words of Olavo Bilac, our prince of poets . . ."

The audience sighed and Collier shifted positions in his chair, staring in Finnegan's direction, two rows ahead, where he was seated beside the Bolivian girl. The physician was also aghast, unable to distinguish the quite incomprehensible tenor of the senator's Portuguese. Still, even to him, the senator seemed to have entirely lost his wits.

". . . Not always wilt thou endure thus,
You were shades of moral wretchedness!
Thou awaitest the dawn, O Patria! And she,
She will come, like other Eras, other Suns,
Other Creeds of other times, hither and anon!
The noble ambitions, strength and generosity,
Justice and Peace will one day greet these Zones
in their confused fusion of torrid dross.
Then, in her Divine majesty, let Amazonas,
Virgin, reawaken to the splendid cavalcade
of her sempiternal Pomp!"

The senator bowed deeply, but for a few seconds the audience sat in stunned silence. Then Farquhar suddenly applauded, clapping a little too hurriedly, seconded by his administrators and finally the rest of the auditorium. The painful phase of speechmaking had finally drawn to a close, and the company, to demonstrate that the theater was no mirage, turned to the projection of an actual film. Percival Farquhar and his table of dignitaries left the stage to take seats in the orchestra, the lights were dimmed, and the curtain began to rise, phosphorescently illuminated by the flickering image of a projection upon the screen entitled "Edwin S. Porter's THE GREAT TRAIN ROBBERY."

The tour of Candelária Hospital had been scheduled for that same afternoon. As Dr. Lovelace had foreseen, Joe Caripuna proved to be a sensational attraction. The politicians, after a brief visit to the vice-minister interned in a special suite with his pair of appetizing nurses, wandered through all the wings of the complex, impressed with the impeccable order, the fanatical standards that Lovelace seemed to uphold for company

354

hygienics. Afterward, assembled in the cafeteria where they drank refreshments, the guests were astonished to see an Indian with no hands enter in the company of a beautiful Bolivian girl. With her assistance he mounted an elevated bench set before a piano—in his bare feet! Dr. Lovelace came forward and, with a grave demeanor, cavalierly bid Consuelo Campero to take a seat.

"This lad who sits before you," he began, "whom everyone here knows as Joe, because he never had a Christian name, is an Indian from the great Caripuna nation. Victimized by his own brothers, by the members of his tribe who, in some aberrant ritual proper only to savages, are accustomed to hacking off the hands of a number of their young warriors, thus Joe was mutilated in a kind of pagan sacrifice to their barbarous gods. After such revolting savagery, for which the victim has been carefully chosen, he is customarily abandoned to his own fate until death overtakes him. Thus we discovered our dear Joe, nearly lifeless, without his hands, in the arms of death. Miraculously, our workers stumbled upon him, in the vicinity of the camp on the Abunã, and brought him in to the infirmary. There, he was treated with unparalleled expertise by Dr. Richard Finnegan, a young physician whom I have the honor of numbering among my staff. Now, happily recuperated, Joe is with us today to share his joy. He brings ample proof of how the company extends its thoughtful altruism to even the helpless natives—not only in the form of medical rehabilitation but, more importantly, in the tenor of spiritual regeneration. Joe is an eloquent example, an exceptional example, but proof nevertheless, of how much civilization can accomplish in its struggle against the forces of barbarism."

Lovelace received the applause that he was expecting and walked back to his seat beside Percival Farquhar. Joe looked to Consuelo Campero, who indicated with a smile that he should begin.

At the piano, with an amazing agility, Joe Caripuna executed a simplified version of the overture to the opera *O Guarani*. To the extent that it was a matter of a pianist who played with his feet, the performance was masterful, indeed. Joe brought the house down: politicians applauded, then hurried to be the first to embrace an astonished Farquhar and a proud Lovelace. The ladies were moved to tears, but Consuelo, blushing from the substance of what Lovelace had told his audience, remained in her seat—her legs and her heart lacking the strength to do otherwise. A delighted Joe, with a smile on his face, interrupted the tumult with a jazz rendition of his *pièce de résistance*, the unbeatable "Happy Birthday." He was a star!

After nearly everyone else had left the cafeteria, Percival pulled Lovelace over to the piano.

"What's the trick?" he asked the astonished doctor.

"Trick?"

"It's an electrical pianola, isn't it?"

Farquhar continued to peruse the piano but gradually came to the conclusion that in fact there was no gimmick. The mystery was wholly contained in that placid savage who could even strike a match with his feet to light a damned cigarette that Lovelace had just taken out to smoke.

"So he actually plays the thing," Farquhar mused aloud.

"Don't be so cynical, Percy," Lovelace scolded drolly. "Of course he plays. He uses his toes, you naughty boy."

"Crap! How did you manage it, Lovelace?"

"Merely the techniques of social rehabilitation," Lovelace informed him mischievously.

"Social rehabilitation, eh? Don't hand me that hogwash, or I'll—"

"Percival, please! There's a lady present!"

Farquhar looked around quickly and spotted Consuelo still seated in her chair, head bowed, almost in tears.

"Who's she?"

"She happens to be Joe's teacher—used to teach piano in Bolivia, I gather."

"How did you manage to bring her here?" Farquhar inquired, still staring at Consuelo.

"It's a long story, Percy."

"More hogwash!"

Farquhar began scrutinizing Joe as if he doubted that the Indian really existed, as if the Caripuna hardly passed for more than a marionette invented and somehow manipulated by the disordered mind of Seymour Lovelace.

"He *is* real," Consuelo observed.

"What, ma'am?" Farquhar said, taken by surprise.

"Ella say Joe *real,"* the Indian confirmed, smiling.

Farquhar stepped back prudently but kept staring at Joe.

356

"He doesn't bite," Lovelace chided.

"I've got to hand it to you," Farquhar conceded, "he pulled it off."

The Bolivian girl had quietly gathered her strength and managed to slip out of the cafeteria without drawing the attention of the other two. Only Joe followed his *maestra* with his eyes, but said nothing, waiting for Lovelace to give him a present.

Outside, Richard Finnegan awaited Consuelo, but she was so stunned and nauseated by Lovelace's performance that she passed him by and hurried out of the hospital. Finnegan pursued her.

"What happened?" he inquired.

She was staring out at the green wall of jungle, her eyes about to flow with tears. The physician abhorred her in that condition.

"Were you there?"

Finnegan nodded without the faintest notion of what could be on her mind, this time.

"Joe is no longer ours, Richard."

"What are you getting at?" he said impatiently.

"We've lost him—he belongs to them. . . ."

"Joe Caripuna was never ours."

Consuelo fell into his arms, sobbing, her head against his chest.

"Stop crying, for God's sake! The life of that crappy Indian has nothing to do with us!"

"Don't talk of Joe that way, Richard!"

"Okay, okay, but stop blubbering. It doesn't do any good."

"That *unspeakable* Dr. Lovelace—did you hear what he said? All lies, lies about Joe."

"Lovelace has always been a liar."

Consuelo shook her head negatively and Finnegan held her at arm's length for a moment to look into her eyes.

"Dr. Lovelace is not just a liar, he's a wretched fraud!"

Richard Finnegan felt the urge to smile at her discovery, but contained the impulse.

"It's very serious, Richard. Why, he's no better than a vulgar charlatan."

"We're all charlatans, Consuelo."

She disengaged herself from the doctor's arms. She was

357

truly scandalized, for her Latin temperament was still unable to endure such Anglo-Saxon cynicism.

"*You*, Richard, may be a charlatan but I'm not what you seem to think!"

Even in her shattered state, what she wanted most was to be loved as before. She desired nothing so much as for Finnegan to consider her a good person, a woman who was not tarnished and could not be despised. Torn violently from her former life, which had wholly absorbed her as if she were encapsulated in a precious stone, Consuelo Campero had suddenly lost her innocence but had not managed to acquire the terrible but necessary coldness to deal with such men. It was appalling to have to act like a shadow. Her physician lover at times would seem so timid, then at other times this very timidity revealed an ingrained egocentricity that she still attempted to deny in him.

"Don't you have anything to say, Richard?"

Our Finnegan restricted himself to a stare because he was such an ass with women, and had yet to find a way to dissemble the fact.

"Say something!" Consuelo demanded furiously.

"Calm down," he moaned gauchely.

"I already had my suspicions you were just like the others."

"Don't say stupid things . . . you're upset, that's all."

The Bolivian girl felt that she was unmasking every last illusion by which she had been living lately. And all the sordidness that she found within seemed to be breaking painfully out of her in the form of unquenchable sorrow.

"What have you decided after all these months, Richard?"

"Decided?"

"About me . . . about us."

"I'm in love with you. . . ."

"No, I hardly believe that you love me, Richard."

The Bolivian girl had dreamed that Richard Finnegan would take care of her future, that they would always be together. Harriet Azancoth, who made it her business to know something about everybody, had told her how rich the young doctor was. And Consuelo would find herself falling asleep each night dreaming of the day she would stand beside Richard, somewhere in the United States of America. Was it possible, then, that her interest in the doctor, the eagerness with which she had given herself to him, turned upon her own self interest? Beyond the fact of her really loving him? And if that were so? At times she would ask herself if this really was not the proper time to cultivate her own self-interest and, even so, to continue to be a good person.

"You've never spoken to me about yourself, Richard."

"I've already told you a thousand times—I have nothing to tell."

"You've never spoken about your family, about your home."

Finnegan, with his mouth galled, thought to himself: Oh, Christ! What's the purpose of this shit, now, out in the frying sun?

"You don't love me, Richard."

"If I didn't love you, Consuelo, why would I be standing here with you?"

"That means nothing and you know it. Maybe you're standing here with me because I'm available to sleep with. An easy lay! And for free!"

Finnegan was appalled. "Consuelo! That's cruel and unjust...."

He pronounced his words in a downcast tone of voice since he really was with her principally because she provided an easy lay; and for nothing—which did not, he conceded to himself, prevent him from liking her.

"That's exactly it, Richard. You don't have to pretend."

"I'm not pretending," he postured.

"I'm nothing but a good lay for you, Richard Finnegan, very comfortable for you, here, where women are so scarce."

The physician would have liked to feel rancor at Consuelo's remarks, but her words hit the mark. He had been cultivating the illusion that he was truly in love with her. And in point of fact, he loved her all right—that is, loved copulating with her—and not because women were scarce in Porto Velho. He would have loved her in any city in the world, and would always see her as a very special woman who knew how to give any man a wonderfully good lay.

"Don't you think you're judging me rather harshly, Consuelo. I would want you as I want you here in any place in the world."

"Even in the United States?"

"Anywhere... you would always be my Consuelo."

And Consuelo thought to herself: Then why have you never decided? You've never said a word about yourself to me, or what a rich man you happen to be. You complain that you still have to finish another year and a half on your contract with the company before you decide what the future holds . . . when you could kick everything aside and return to the United States whenever you wanted!

But Finnegan shunned any more entanglements. He knew, of course, from the moment their liaison had begun, the Bolivian girl had believed that they would marry. Only he had the knowledge of how preposterous it was—she, a Latin American woman; and he, a rich heir: they could never remain together for very long. The alchemy between them functioned only on the level of physical charm, or so he liked to imagine. Each night was a wonderful moment of bliss, despite the vertiginous misgivings. Yet all the bewitchment would have been lost under other circumstances. Only Finnegan also understood that Consuelo Campero would more than likely never manage to take reality for what it was, because she was a woman—and don't women tenaciously cling to even the falsest representation of a permanent commitment?

"Richard, you're a fake!"

Finnegan seized her by the wrists and crushed her to his chest. Consuelo let herself be pawed, as one of his hands moved up to caress her hair.

"Darling, let's go to your place," the physician wooed in a husky voice, pressed to her ear.

Consuelo broke away from him.

"Didn't I tell you, Richard? All you want is to fuck me!"

As they argued their way toward her lodgings, the two of them arrived at the conclusion that a truce was necessary. Finnegan forced himself to like her as a person and not only as a good lay. Consuelo, in turn, tried to adjust to the idea that she should also consider Richard a good lay, and not only a person. After all, she was lucky . . . he was handsome, young, and even though he might be terribly gauche, the bastard really could give a ravishing fuck!

At the principal entrance to the central administrative building, several wicker chairs had been set in front of the steps; and seated under the light of the lamp post were Percival

Farquhar, "King" John, and the engineer Collier. Night had fallen and Porto Velho cast its light upon the waters of the Madeira. The three had attended a boring dinner with the members of the commission, and now, while the guests were getting ready for bed, they had the opportunity to converse.

"Where did you dig up that senator?" Collier asked, amused.

Farquhar seemed to be lost in contemplation of the shimmering reflections of the city.

"He's a very rich man," he responded without turning from the river, "and a very great thief."

"He's a windbag," Collier responded. "I prefer to deal with even you, Farquhar. At least you're a thief who doesn't do so much talking."

"I slept through the whole damn dinner," "King" John confided.

"You're an old roughrider, Johnny, my friend. You'd go to sleep anywhere, including Theda Bara's lap," Collier observed, and the three of them laughed.

"How about those eucalyptus ties," Farquhar asked. "Are they going to do the trick?"

"I hope so," said the engineer.

"They better! I'm paying their weight in gold to have them shipped from Formosa."

"I suspect the termites don't like Chinese food."

A security guard approached deferentially. The manager, "King" John, turned a hostile stare on the fellow.

"What is it now! Can't I have a blasted minute without interruptions?"

The guard removed his kepi and came close to kneeling at the manager's feet.

"I fear, señor, that we have a serious problem."

"What? There'll be no problems while we have these Bolivian politicians here with us!"

"Paraguayan," Collier corrected.

"That's what I said, Paraguayans!" the manager crowed.

"But, señor, it's most serious. It concerns the German fugitives."

Collier leaped out of his chair.

"You're saying the Germans have come back?"

"In a way, señor," the guard said hesitantly.

"Well, man, where are they? Spit it out, man," "King" John berated him.

"In the harbor, señor. They were discovered by some of the sentinels from the north sector."

Farquhar remained in his seat, listening to what was being said and imagining the audacity of the Germans, to attempt such an escape.

"Well, they didn't get very far," he reflected at last.

"I wonder how the hell did they manage to cross those rapids?" the manager asked, almost to himself.

Finally, Percival Farquhar stood up from his chair.

"I think we'd better have a look for ourselves."

The three of them followed the guard across the well-lit plaza, in the direction of the wharf. The huge ship that had delivered the commission sat at anchor in the harbor, the decks completely illuminated, but with only a few sailors still awake at this hour.

"What made them run off that way, Collier?" the Quaker asked. "We make the effort to treat these people as best we can."

"Don't be cynical, Farquhar. As best we can, we grind the shit out of these workers."

"Exaggerating as always, Collier. You never change."

"Right you are . . . How about: 'They fled because they're too European and haven't managed the adjustment to the tropical clime.' How's that?"

Farquhar smiled because the explanation was ridiculous and convincing.

"Don't worry your head about it, my hyperbolic engineer," Farquhar warned the Englishman. "We don't intend to have any more European workers down here. We've begun recruiting laborers from India, as well as China."

"It's a relief to know that I'll only be working with people of inferior races from now on," Collier concluded maliciously.

But Farquhar was suddenly offended.

"Don't say a blasphemous thing like that again. There's no such thing as an inferior race, Collier. Each person is a distinctive attestation to God's handiwork."

"Touching, Farquhar . . . very touching, indeed."

Percival Farquhar stormed ahead, even more piqued by the insolence of the engineer.

362

They soon reached the pier, where they were met by a group of security guards. The men were holding ropes that fed out from the dock and threaded off downriver, into the darkness.

"They're right down there," the security chief informed them, pointing to a shadow undulating in the darkness close to the shore.

"Why haven't they been brought ashore?" Farquhar demanded, attempting to distinguish something from the darkness.

"They are all dead, señor."

"Dead!"

"Yes, señor, dead."

One of the guards, who was clinging to a rope and sweating profusely, turned to the three foreigners with an expression of fear.

"*Mais gente morta!*" he exclaimed. "*Que Deus tenha piedade!*"

Farquhar flashed a crushing look of disdain at the fellow.

The engineer signaled them to pull in the ropes. The men began to obey and there slowly surged out of the darkness a makeshift raft constructed from a series of hogsheads bound together.

"They tried to flee on that?" Farquhar remarked perplexedly.

The raft floated into view, rocking gently against the current and straining against the ropes. It appeared to be empty, until an additional pull on the ropes swung it around to reveal the truth. A man, in an advanced state of decomposition, studied the void with a dreadful grimace.

"Haul this thing over to the west end," ordered "King" John with disgust, "identify the corpses and bury them immediately."

The head of security listened to the orders with a handkerchief to his nose, because the stench of carrion was close to unbearable.

"Almost all of them have been decapitated, senhor," commented another of the sentinels to the engineer.

Collier noticed a fellow seated on a coil of rope, surrounded by additional guards.

"And that one, over there. Who is he?"

The guards forced the man to rise and brought him closer to the administrators.

363

"He is one of the peasants who brought the raft into port," explained the chief of security.

"You mean to tell me that this *thing* was actually brought *here*?" Farquhar asked incredulously.

The officer turned to "King" John to request permission to speak. The manager was more or less petrified himself and could barely take his eyes off the floating graveyard.

"You can speak, man," Collier ordered.

The officer stiffened his carriage and obeyed.

"These men, the German fugitives, invaded Santo Antônio just two days ago. They entered the town like madmen. They killed four inhabitants but were finally surrounded when they fled into one of the houses. Some of the townspeople eventually came up with the idea that the house should be burned to the ground with the Germans inside, but that notion was apparently disregarded and the Germans were simply overpowered and slaughtered. The majority of them were also beheaded. Afterwards, the peasants placed the bodies back on the raft and hauled it down here. It took five canoes to do the job, but we only managed to capture one of them—the one in which this fellow was rowing."

Collier looked at the prisoner: a short, stunted, skinny fellow in worn-out shoes and clothes. The shoes were molded from gum-elastic.

"Whom do you work for?" Collier asked him.

The man answered without looking up.

"Guaporé Rubber Company, senhor."

The engineer turned to Farquhar, with no special emotion on his face, only the simple stare itself, which was nevertheless disturbing for being precisely that: stripped of any moral judgment.

"Let him go," Farquhar ordered.

21

In order to vitiate the possibility of boredom on the part of the commission—given that Porto Velho, as had become increasingly clear, was a city for labor and not for diversions—the program was brought to a close, without any special event, on the morning of the third day. After an early lunch the visitors embarked, impressed by the efficiency of the entire operation, though hardly sad to leave the place—except, of course, for the vice-minister, who had fallen hopelessly under the spell of modern medical techniques as evinced by the treatment he was administered at Candelária Hospital.

During that same morning, Percival Farquhar saw to the departure of his indentured Hindu laborers for the Abunā sector of the railway. They were milling about with their bundles and rags in the Central Station, together with a new shipment of draft animals. These latter were no longer Arkansas mules, which died too easily in the heat of the tropics, but native Northeastern donkeys, already broken by the backlanders of that region and accustomed to supporting the high temperatures, and to living on an almost nonexistent diet, capable of eating stones if necessary.

The Hindu workers in their turbans and white ragged dress moved in patient, orderly fashion as they boarded two freight cars hitched behind a single passenger coach. At the head of the train puffed Mad Maria, spewing clouds of smoke. Between the passenger coach and the locomotive herself was a small coal tender, filled with black ore, which Harold was busy shoveling about while shouting to Old Thomas, there at his post, in the cab of Mad Maria.

From the combination telegraph office and traffic control room Farquhar, Collier, "King" John, and Finnegan watched the loading. Gallagher waved to them from the window of his cab, musing at how similar the station in Porto Velho was to the many stops along the Union Pacific, lost in the vast desert of the American West. He did not recall them with longing or, indeed, any sense of nostalgia—all he could think of was that he was about to return to the inferno of the Abunã.

The beasts of burden were now being loaded into the last freight car, into which a third of the Hindu laborers had also been herded. In contrast to the Germans, however, who from the very hour of embarkation to the sector of the Abunã were already angrily protesting, the Hindus had not reacted negatively at all and had acceded to any orders in complete silence. The fifteen Barbadian workmen, through rights acquired by their long years of service to the Farquhar syndicate, had already boarded the passenger coach. But the contrast between the docility of these new Hindus and the aggressivity of the previous Germans had not escaped Percival Farquhar's notice.

"I think that we have finally hit upon the ideal type of laborer," he reflected, going up to the window of the traffic control room.

His manager, who to a certain extent would have preferred the familiar roughness of the Germans, was still dubious as to the capacity for work of that beardless, gaunt-looking people.

"You think they'll be able to take it out there?"

Collier, who had had a bellyful of India and seen, firsthand, what that humiliated people were capable of doing to manage something to eat, had a ready answer.

"Johnny, if we'd had the likes of them to begin with, your railway would have been already built a long time ago."

"I'll go along with that," said Farquhar. "They are submissive, but they're tough as well."

"They are from the lowest caste, I presume," the engineer stated dryly.

Farquhar smiled. "All pariahs. Here they will lead a far more respectable life than was possible in India."

"Respectable?" "King" John repeated, unable to determine if what his boss was saying was actually the truth, or just more of his Quaker bombast. "What was their life like in India?"

"The kind of thing you cannot imagine, John," Percival exhorted. "Bestial jobs, no opportunities. . . ."

"Here, of course, they'll be treated like human beings," added the engineer with a detached tone of voice that left the manager even more disconcerted.

The slatted doors of the freight cars were rolled shut and the Hindus disappeared from sight. The Barbadians peered out

366

at the city through the windows of the passenger coach, as if anxious to get back to the Abunã.

"Untouchables! The ideal subjects for Mad Maria," Collier exclaimed.

Farquhar, who had been distractedly observing the Negroes in the coach, turned to face the engineer.

"What was that you said?"

The engineeer shrugged. "Oh, nothing. They look like the ideal workers."

"Precisely what I was saying, and they'll give you no trouble."

"Let's hope so, Farquhar," he muttered dubiously, picking up the leather suitcase on the floor beside him, in which he carried his possessions. "Every time you contract new laborers for me, you act like I'm getting the eighth wonder of the world."

"Well, what in tarnation do you expect, Collier, His Majesty's grenadiers!"

"Grenadiers would never accept the seventy shillings a day that you pay."

"They would never earn what I'm paying here if they went on working in India."

The engineer waved good-bye to put an end to the matter and started to walk out the door. Looking over his shoulder one last time, he noticed a somber Dr. Finnegan leaning against the wall at the back of the room.

"I say, doctor, aren't you coming along?"

Richard Finnegan grabbed his valise and followed the engineer out the door, with a farewell nod to the others. Gallagher climbed down simian-fashion from the cab of Mad Maria.

"What do you say, Thomas, did you have a good holiday?"

The old locomotive operator nodded his head and spit some tobacco, pumping Collier's hand.

"Mar' er less, mar' er less . . . it's a tedious town, yer Parto Velio. I prefer the Aboona."

"What you need is a leisurely retirement," Collier quipped, but Gallagher dismissed the idea, even as a joke.

"Ye'd only get me lavin' me job when I'm lyin' horizontal."

A cloud of steam enveloped both engineers. The doctor boarded the passenger coach and went to sit by a window. Collier emerged from the cloud of steam to also get aboard, with a final wave to those who had remained in the telegraph office.

Mad Maria began to jerk forward, then roll, while inside the passenger coach, balancing himself, Stephan Collier took one look at the Barbadians and the doctor—enough for him to decide not to remain there any longer. He opened the coach door that gave access to the coal tender, climbed up and over the mound of ore and descended into the cab, where he was greeted with a friendly nod from Gallagher. Smoke inundated the station as the train slowly crossed a vast deforested expanse and then vanished through a chink in the steep wall of jungle cleft by the railroad tracks.

Once the train had disappeared, Percival Farquhar gave "King" John a final slap on the shoulder, and the two of them walked out of the station, cutting across the tracks.

The station stood empty against the landscape, and from afar it seemed to undulate beneath the waves of evaporating humidity.

Thomas Gallagher was entirely absorbed with the task of operating the locomotive and maintaining its speed. His fireman was seated on a small wooden bench, while Collier watched the steam engine lap up the tracks that tore through the jungle like whiplashes across the back of Nature herself. The Englishman tilted his head out the window of the cab to peer at the monotonous landscape of dense vegetation. Powerful though it may have been, the great green barrier had been forced back by the toil of hundreds of desperate men. Harold Appleton was already nodding off, his head rocking to the rhythm of the locomotive, and his somnolence proved more curious to ponder than the routine green of jungle, at least to the mind of the Englishman. Harold's sleep, it seemed to him as Mad Maria thundered down the tracks, was charged with a kind of pathos; for surely it anticipated the future succession of identical days when the railway was fully operative and his own task would have been completed. The oblivious attitude of the stoker, in peculiar fashion, complemented the earnest professionalism of his mentor Thomas Gallagher.

In the passenger coach Richard Finnegan was hugging his valise to his chest while observing with no particular interest the uniform landscape of green waste, persistent and opaque, as it flew by his window. The bench on which he sat, of raw

368

wood, was otherwise empty; for the Barbadians were gathered at the back of the coach, conversing inaudibly. The doctor set his valise down beside him to stare back at those familiar black faces; one of which, he remembered, had held the gleaming machete on the night the two Negroes had surreptitiously invaded the infirmary—futilely attempting to impede an autopsy that had already taken place, on the corpses of their "brothers." Although familiar to him, they remained strangers, steeped in an imperviousness that bordered on insolence. Yet he knew the truth of it was that they were men for whom it little mattered whether they were there or somewhere else; and the knowledge devastated him because it meant they were no different than he—Finnegan himself cared not at all whether he were in St. Louis, Missouri, or in the jungle. He turned back to his window just as they were rolling across a beautiful iron bridge suspended over a thread of reddish water that streamed some twenty meters below. Their train clickety-clacked, discharging great helixes of black smoke like the clouds of a miniature tempest brooding overhead, while the fanned jaw of a Cyclopean Mad Maria feasted on the twin metallic rails.

Harold Appleton continued to doze with his total faith in Old Thomas Gallagher, because that veteran Irish engineer knew his trade and could stand there forever, if necessary, splitting his gaze between the instruments before him and the tracks up ahead. So it would have come as no surprise, had he been awake, to see Gallagher suddenly jump to attention and pull the brakes, making the driving wheels groan and the connecting rods strain, cleaving the train's momentum even as her very inertia struggled to hurl her ahead—and her passengers with her—until the locked trucks should finally squeal to a halt. The stoker woke up with a plop, just in time to see an astonished Collier be flung forward, his hands resisting the weight of his body in a desperate effort to cling to the window frame of the cab. A great sigh of steam issued from Mad Maria and then there was silence, quickly engulfed by the odorous solemnity of a jungle redolent of decay and the flagrant stillness of cracked reddish earth, composing the railway bed, toasting in the sunlight.

Hardly had Mad Maria screeched to a halt than Gallagher, Appleton, and Collier scrambled down the ladder and leaped to the ground. From the windows of the passenger coach Finnegan and the Barbadians squinted into the daylight in varying states of confusion and shock. There up ahead, crushing the tracks, were two gigantic fallen trees with trunks of more than ten meters in diameter.

The three figures timidly approached the mammoth obstruction which dwarfed them to insignificance.

"Only fer sheer luck I didn't plow right into 'em," Thomas admitted, his heart still pounding. "With this blasted sunlight they blended right into yer shadows there, as we come round the curve."

Collier examined the mangled rails.

"Each one of these bloody trunks must weigh a couple of tons. We'll have to replace some fifteen meters of track. Dammit!"

The doors to the freight cars rolled open and the guards climbed down. Finnegan also sauntered over, gradually taking in the magnitude of the wreckage.

"Imagine if something like that ever plunked on Mad Maria," Harold commented, massaging his head and whistling at the size of the trunks.

"Shut yer gob, Harold," Gallagher howled, "afore I break one o' them trunks o'er yer poll!"

Collier stalked back to the security guards milling in front of the freight cars.

"Break out the men," the engineer shouted. "We have to clear these tracks right away or we'll end up spending the night here!"

The workers began to disgorge from the cars and Collier, taking a second glance at the fallen trees, felt certain they really would spend the bloody night there!

By nightfall the twin giants, hacked into sections with axes and machetes, had already been hauled off the railway bed, exposing the tangle of crushed tracks. Yet the workers were exhausted and Collier decided to call a temporary halt. He ordered a meal for his men, with the idea of getting back to the task of re-laying the tracks as soon as they'd had some dinner.

The meal consisted of coffee and some crusts of bread. Since the passenger coach was empty, the engineer decided to invite Gallagher and his fireman to join him there for coffee.

370

Finnegan was already back in his seat, munching bread and perusing a newspaper.

"Damn an' blast it, I swear we won't be outa here fer another ten hours," Gallagher complained, as if he were positively aching to get to the Abunã.

The doctor finally decided to break his own silence.

"That was quite a scare you gave us, Thomas. It was a hell of a way to put on the brakes!"

"Lemme tell ye somethin', sonny, 'twas precisely the right way, God help us!"

No one disagreed with that, to be sure.

"Still, when you pulled those brakes and we went flying, I'll tell you one thing," Collier added good-naturedly, "I thought for sure that Harold here was going to wind up in the boiler."

Harold flushed to recollect his being asleep at the instant that Thomas had to reach for the brakes.

"No chance o' that, Collier," Gallagher assured him, "Mad Maria has too fine a palate."

"I still got the lump on my damn head," said Harold reproachfully, rubbing the side of his forehead.

"Scared the hell out of me," Finnegan repeated.

Thomas took another sip of coffee and scowled into his cup.

"Ain't it just like life—I mane this here iron road: all of it happens 'tween one station an' another."

Between one station and another, all right, thought Collier to himself, sensing the futility of things—even of Mad Maria, seemingly so powerful, but proving as fragile as the rest of them. Still, he was sure there would always be a few eccentrics like himself, capable of feigning anything to get to face a few surprises, lying in wait between one station and another.

"Me rheumatism's achin'," Gallagher announced, "we're in fer some rain, Collier."

"Damn your rheumatism, Thomas Gallagher," the engineer exploded. "All we need is rain on top of everything else— we'll have six months on our hands before we get back to Abunã!"

Between one station and another, thought Richard Finnegan to himself, not giving a good goddamn if it actually took six months to reach the Abunã. At that hour, the Bolivian girl was far down the Rio Madeira and probably more deluded than ever, imagining herself already adjusted to the life ahead of

371

her. Their last encounter had been disastrous, with him playing the role, as always, of the fool.

He had finished his shift at the hospital and gone to look for her at her lodgings, but discovered the place was empty. The little baggage belonging to her had vanished, and the bed was stripped of its linens, ready to receive the next lodger. On his way out, perplexed, he ran into Mrs. Azancoth.

"She's moved out," Harriet informed him.

"Where have they got her living now?"

The woman smiled, delighted to be the first to impart the news.

"She took her bags to the ship—didn't you know Consuelo was leaving?"

"Leaving?"

"She and her Indian friend . . . off to Rio de Janeiro with all expenses paid by the company. Isn't it *wonderful?*"

"She didn't tell me anything!"

"There just hasn't been *time* to—she was summoned early this morning by the administration. Mr. Farquhar has invited her to accompany the Indian. That devil of a native will actually do a series of concerts in the *capital!*"

The doctor could scarcely believe it. Yet, at the same time he could only too well imagine: it was exactly what he should have expected following the enthusiasm of the commission at Joe's presentation in the dining hall of Candelária. What he hadn't counted on was Consuelo's becoming involved in the sideshow.

"If you still want to catch her, try looking for her on board. I understand they've given her a *wonderful* cabin."

"Thank you, Mrs. Azancoth."

Consuelo Campero had, indeed, been installed in a luxurious compartment. It would be quite a voyage! He found her alone. She was readying herself for bed, stunningly outfitted in a lacy peignoir that Percival Farquhar had presented to her as a little gift. She hardly resembled the sedulous piano teacher and had more the demeanor of the rising vaudeville starlet—a Latin version, of course—far from depraved, but not too far. The doctor, even if he should deny it, enjoyed seeing Consuelo in that camisole, her hair flowing loose and long, her heart bent upon her revenge. Yet as an actress, she was still the ingenue, managing the role of avenger with decided ups and downs.

372

Once she had admitted the doctor to her cabin, she stood close to the pale light of a bedside lamp with its garish shade of greenish tinted glass. Her peignoir scarcely concealed the ravishing silhouette of a body that would long leave Richard Finnegan aching with more than nostalgia.

"Who gave you that thing?" the doctor asked her, running his eyes over the length of her body.

The Bolivian girl was distressed to see that he was neither furious or wounded, nor even deeply disturbed by the fact of her having abandoned him so abruptly.

"Isn't it marvelous what's happening, Richard?"

Finnegan shrugged his shoulders.

"I don't want you to think badly of me," she said, her voice barely concealing her chagrin.

He shook his head. "I'm not going to think badly of you. . . ."

"I'll always think well of you, Richard."

He thanked her awkwardly: "I'm grateful."

"And you," she asked, "will you always think of me?"

He responded: "I'll think of you always. . . ."

"As a person?"

"I'll think of my Consuelo," he said, thinking of her body and of the perfect lays she had repeatedly given him with such evident emotion.

"I'll write you, Richard. I promise!"

He thanked her with an inaudible grunt which she took as a sign of disbelief.

"I *will* write, you'll see."

For a moment—the only one—Richard loved Consuelo for what she was: a woman, a person, not simply a body to sleep with. Which was a pity because she failed to even perceive it, and so did he.

"You aren't going to end up thinking I'm a slut?"

She asked the question suddenly, eyeing him with coldness, or perhaps it was only the pale, greenish light of the cabin lamp that made this impression.

"Don't be silly, Consuelo," he said, thinking that, matter of fact, she was nothing less than a slut.

"I had no other way out. . . ."

"You don't owe me explanations, Consuelo."

Her chestnut eyes sparkled and she grew sentimental.

"I want to explain to you why I accepted. I want you to try to understand."

Finnegan did not respond—he knew it would not have helped to respond: she had reached the point where she must have her melodrama from which to derive some savor of victory.

"You were never going to marry me, Richard."

He was still doubtful he needed to respond.

"Not that I was expecting to marry *you*, but at least in the beginning I felt you loved me," she said, thinking that what she really had expected was to be married to him. "But you never loved me, Richard. Did you?"

"Why do you want to know that now?"

Finnegan was playing but she did not seem to realize—she still could not imagine that he might be given to playacting himself. Instead, she took a few steps around the room, but the limited space of the cabin reduced the effect of her improvisation.

"You're right, Richard. What does anything matter now."

"You're going to be happy, Consuelo, that's what matters."

She began to cry. What crap, thought Finnegan, now she'll plead with me in that whining voice of hers and I'm a son of a bitching goner.

"Richard . . ." she said with a tearful voice.

"Please, Consuelo . . ."

Finnegan sighed and she continued sobbing.

"Richard . . ."

The pathetic tone of his first name began to envelop him. He would soon play the fool if he did not take his stand.

"You're going to enjoy your new life, Consuelo," he said, imagining how rich Percival Farquhar must be, much richer than he was, though Percival Farquhar would never marry her either. "You're going to like Mr. Farquhar."

"Mr. Farquhar's a charming man," she insisted, still crying.

"Then why are you crying?"

"Oh, Richard!"

The doctor felt an irresistible urge to ask for her hand in marriage and simultaneously the impulse to throw her down on the narrow bed and fuck her there instead. Consuelo prevented him from committing either indiscretion by slapping him in the face.

374

"Why did you do that?" Finnegan asked in astonishment, his face stinging.

"So that you don't end up thinking I'm a slut!"

At least she had stopped crying.

"I'm not going to end up thinking you're a slut, for God's sake," he complained, with the deepest sense of conviction that she was just that.

"Even if you were to find out that I was sleeping with Joe?"

"What!"

"That I was going to bed with Joe."

"Why are you telling me this now?"

"Because I'm sincere with you, Richard, because I hate lies," she said with fervor, certain that to reveal her intimacy with the Indian now was to avoid that later on, after she was gone, the doctor might learn from Harriet that she had discovered her with Joe.

"Christ, enough of this, Consuelo," Finnegan groaned, unable to muster more of a response to what had just been revealed to him.

"It's *true*, Finnegan!"

He felt relieved at hearing her use his last name and at seeing she wasn't about to break into tears all over again. Yet, what a female she was! So brimming with natural sensuality that he could well imagine the difficulty of committing all that body to a single sexual partner.

On an impulse, Finnegan grabbed her by the hair and pulled her to him. Consuelo surrendered without resistance, enfolding him in a furious embrace. He could smell the fragrance of low tide that was always with her. He began lifting her camisole to paw her flesh and at the same time strip her naked. The camisole quickly ended up on the floor of the cabin and the two of them in the bed. He spread her thighs and kissed her there, probing deeply, moving slowly up, solemnly exploring her until he lay completely upon her and she felt the pressure of his penis as it bobbed between her legs. She fed it into herself with a passionate urgency to feel penetrated by its thrust. They panted together with the greenish light washing over his back . . . until finally . . . spent, he halted, pulling out of her, then got up from the bed, put on his clothes and left the stateroom—like a fool, as always—without saying a word, without breaking his stride, without any good-byes whatsoever.

375

She lay there naked, sweated, still panting, with an enormous desire for him not to perceive her as a slut.

A slap on his shoulder brought him back to reality. It was Collier, holding a tin cup in his hand.

"I thought maybe you were dead," the engineer smiled.

Finnegan laughed.

"Thinking of her, lad?"

"What?"

"Of her, Consuelo!"

"I was," he confessed.

"Forget it, Dick, she was just a slut."

The Barbadians had all returned to the coach and there was a strange noise on the roof. Finnegan peered into the darkness of the night.

"Is it raining?"

Collier nodded. "Old Thomas's rheumatism is never wrong."

"Christ! We're going to spend the next century here!"

It was hardly that, but the trip was delayed far beyond the reckonings of even the engineer. The rain lasted the entire night and by daybreak showed no signs of letting up. The replacement of the damaged tracks had to be carried out in the downpour, making the task far more difficult and less than perfectly accomplished. Furthermore, the engineer did not relish sitting like ducks along the iron road when such storms were underway. He knew that the trees, though gigantic in size, had small roots and more or less supported one another against keeling over. Once that equilibrium was disturbed, such as along the vegetal gorge of the railway bed, the larger trees were likely to tumble in the least bit of wind.

Five days later, still under a persistent downpour, they were back at work along the sector of the Abunã. The bridge was receiving the final touches, having surprisingly withstood the overflow of the river. Mad Maria could now cross the Rio Abunã and the men were already busy on the far side of the river: the Hindus now carrying out the task of leveling the terrain and the Barbadians, as always, setting down the tracks.

Lunch was served in the rain. Donkeys with huge pots strapped across them transported the meals to where the workers would assemble. At the sound of the whistle, every laborer dropped what he was doing and lined up to receive his ration of darkish vittles that had the look of fried meat. Each man's

376

ration got immediately soaked but no one complained. Dr. Finnegan, who had finally forsaken his anti-mosquito garb, administered the daily dose of quinine, dressed in a poncho and sided by armed guards. His medical staff was replenished by five new arrivals, eager lads who had just recently arrived from the United States. It's true, they were a bit careless, but our Finnegan had grown less meticulous of late.

Eventually, when no one in that humid broth had any hope that the sun still existed anywhere above the Rio Abunã, the day dawned clear with the heat evaporating the atmosphere of slime as in the Devonian period. But the days and days of rain had left their special revenge. The infirmary was filled with patients whose poor diet, coupled with the pervasive dampness, had sapped their lungs, provoking an epidemic of influenza, high fever, and fatal pneumonia.

Stephan Collier hardly left the infirmary. He had lost so many men in such a few days that he was truly worried.

"How many do you think will recover?"

"I have no idea," Finnegan answered him candidly.

The engineer felt deeply discouraged—he had to finish those last ten miles of track still left to be laid.

"Do you know what I've discovered, Steve?" Finnegan remarked almost casually, interrupting Collier's train of thought. "Nearly all your workers from India have leprosy."

"Leprosy?"

"Exactly. You must have known they have the highest incidence of leprosy in world there."

Collier hardly knew *what* to say; it was obviously Farquhar's agents who were to blame, neglecting the beastly physicals in order to increase their own profits!

"Well, that's the jolly limit! Wouldn't you say so, doctor?"

"I think they can keep working," Finnegan replied. "I've ordered an isolation ward readied for the ones who are stricken. I'll have to have your cooperation."

"How?"

"By keeping the infected men apart from the healthy ones— that is, if there are any healthy ones left in the lot."

Collier accepted the idea with a wave of the hand. "Go ahead, Dick."

A Hindu youth, stretched prone on the floor with a blanket under him, cried out with an ungodly moan, then was silent.

The physician went over to him, stooped down, and took hold of his wrist. After a moment he dropped the skeletal arm, brown as a cigar, and covered the body with a sheet.

"He didn't make it, I'm afraid," he concluded indifferently.

"Leprosy?"

"Not that one," he said smiling at the engineer's ignorance. "Pneumonia."

All had become peaceful in the inferno. Gallagher and the stoker played pinochle every night. Finnegan no longer bothered to perform autopsies on the cadavers, leaving himself even more time with which to do nothing. Collier, in his tent, enjoyed tracing with the tip of his finger the route of the railway indicated on the map that he would invariably have spread open on his camp table.

Nearly every night the doctor took a walk over to the engineer's tent, where they would pass the hours in idle conversation. One night, however, when they had received another shipment of supplies from Porto Velho, along with personal correspondence and other items conveyed by the weekly coach, a packet of newspapers also turned up. It was an edition of the paper printed in Porto Velho, the company periodical entitled *The Marconigram,* another of Farquhar's ingenious ideas meant to impress the Brazilian commission—even though it had not a single word written in Portuguese.

Finnegan had brought a copy to Collier's tent and the engineer had already spent a good deal of time ridiculing him for the fact.

"I don't know how you can waste your time on a putrid rag like that," he chided. "Hardly fit to wipe your crupper!"

The paper, besides being dreadful, wove a blatant tissue of lies. Although the facts of the upcoming American elections were alluded to in passing, the whole thrust of the paper's pious editorializing was demagogically slanted in favor of the Democratic Party, presenting Woodrow Wilson as a species of political messiah. There was also an article on the gratitude of workers who had fled starvation in India, and another attributing a different flight—that of the German contractees—to the impossibility of Europeans' adapting themselves to the rigors of the tropics.

"Did you read this article?" Finnegan asked.

"I already told you I wouldn't waste my time."

"I know, Steve, but you should have a look at this one article just for laughs—about the speech by that Brazilian senator we had here. You must remember—you understand Portuguese and you were sitting right there."

"So what?"

"Well, I didn't understand a word he said, but I had the sense that toward the end there he was reciting some kind of poem."

"That he did, lad, that he did—and what a ballbuster that was!"

"Well, here it claims the poem was by a famous Brazilian poet and they give a translation. It's unbelievable! And the guy still exists! Look, they give his biography."

Finnegan leaned over to show it to the engineer.

"Olavo Bilac," Collier read out loud.

"So that's how you pronounce it," Finnegan mused.

"Don't tell me you like his stuff?"

Finnegan laughed. "Hardly, it's a ridiculous poem. But when the senator began to declaim it, with that look of ecstasy on his face, I thought he might have been inventing it on the spot—Latin hyperbole, you know?"

"By the sound of you, Dick, I should think you were about to discover another tropical disease: poetry!"

The physician went back to his reading. "Christ, he really does exist. . . ."

"My personal belief is all your poets are alike: one's as balmy as the next."

The physician, however, who prided himself on treasuring the sonnets of Shakespeare, Keats, and Elizabeth Barrett Browning, refused to take Collier's grumblings at their face value, and kept his nose in the newspaper.

"You know what you ought to do, doctor," the engineer finally recommended.

"No, what should I do?" he said in resignation.

"In homage to that Brazilian poet of yours . . ."

"Who would want to pay homage to a cretin like that?"

"You, damn you! The way you sit there drooling over his biography."

Finnegan finally laughed and the engineer accompanied him with malicious pleasure lighting his eyes.

"I've got an idea for you, doctor. Why don't you come up with some new disease and baptize it in the name of your poet—something like, let's see: Bilac syndrome, or Olavus lung?"

"Olavus lung, not bad!" the doctor conceded.

"I prefer Bilac syndrome—it has a touch of class. And since you're hardly on the verge of discovering any new disease, you might consider trying it out on something more familiar—like terminal cases of beriberi."

"Terminal beriberi," the physician shook his head, "only someone with your jaded imagination."

"It's the perfect metaphor, lad. As the limbs tremble, so the flowering of poetic imagination—and both are equally fatal!"

To the relief of the physician, there did not occur for the rest of that season a single outbreak of "Bilac's syndrome." But the numerous fatalities brought on by pneumonia nearly prompted him to reconsider the idea of "Olavo's lung."

22

Richard Finnegan had begun to dream of scorpions again, preferring them to the thought of Consuelo or any other woman. But the scorpions had disappeared and the infirmary only seemed to be visited now by the red ants with their stinging bites and virtual indestructibility. The doctor was stretched out on his bed, naked from the waist up, eyes shut, listening to the comings and goings of the medics who were finishing up their duties before going to bed themselves. Although he could no longer be said to be the avid physician he once was, he kept his infirmary perfectly clean, the sheets always washed and the reports cogently organized and well written, even if entirely falacious.

The absence of the Germans had not brought total peace to the Abuná. The Barbadians, though small in number, had grown more and more aggressive of late and would not forbear the presence of the Hindus. Practically every day another Hindu laborer was delivered to the infirmary, either dead or badly wounded. The physician had no idea of the reasons for such hatred but was too preoccupied with doing nothing to trouble himself about possible motives. Neither would Collier know how to explain—of that he was certain. The engineer liked his Barbadians and failed to appreciate the Hindus for their virtues. It was a deeply ingrained repulsion, from the time when he had himself lived in India and grown accustomed to see in the Hindus a mass of wretched indigents who would rather lie on their bed of nails waiting for hunger to wipe them off the face of the earth, while letting half a dozen maharajas and their babu bureaucrats feather their nests with the wealth of a subcontinent, inhabiting magnificent palaces full of elephant dung, gorging on concubines fetid with incense and tobacco, counting their precious stones wrapped in old newspaper. For such reasons and more, Stephan Collier could only be availed to break up the inevitable

381

fights between Negro and pariah, from which some Hindu or another invariably emerged the worse for it.

On this particular night, the physician opened his sleep-filled eyes to the sound of three gunshots. He leaped out of bed, grabbed his pistol—because he, too, had learned to go about armed—and rushed out of the infirmary without even bothering to put on a shirt. There was the crashing of many footsteps in the direction of Collier's tent. Finnegan recoiled at the thought that something awful might have befallen that cussed engineer. He raced to the tent and elbowed his way through a throng of security guards. Collier still had his re-volver drawn and on the ground at his feet lay the body of a man—naked, dirty, and burbling blood through three perfectly round holes in the chest.

The engineer seemed relieved at the arrival of the doctor.

"He was prowling around my tent," Collier explained, still clearly excited.

The physician succeeded in pushing him over to his bunk bed, to calm him down, though the engineer resisted.

"I don't need any of your bedside mumbo jumbo, Dick, I'm fine!"

Finnegan sat down beside the engineer.

"I was studying my map when I heard a noise," Collier continued. "I had a feeling something was prowling around outside the tent, so I got out of the chair very slowly and reached for the revolver I keep right here above the bed."

"Who is he?"

"That's just it, I have no idea."

The chief security guard, with his bushy mustache, peered in to inform them:

"He does not work for the company, señor."

Finnegan went out and knelt beside the body. The bullets had entered the thorax and certainly penetrated the heart and lungs. Death must have been nearly instantaneous.

"I saw that something was pressing against one wall of the tent," the engineer went on, coming out of the tent as well. "I knew it was a man. With my revolver drawn, I decided to step out of the tent. That's when he appeared in the doorway and I fired instantly. He looked like one of our Hindu friends and I suspected that he might have gone off the deep end."

382

"At first glance, he really does seem like one of them," the physician confirmed.

"It's a Caripuna Indian," Collier flatly concluded.

"He wasn't armed," Finnegan remarked indifferently.

Indeed, the engineer heard no trace of recrimination in the doctor's words, but the fact that the savage was unarmed still left him rather uncomfortable.

"Right, lad, nothing on him, but he drew lead just the same. The world is hardly ready for another Indian piano player."

Amid protests from the Brazilian Positivist Church and despite the refusal of the celebrated mestizo Marshal Rondon to attend the event, Joe Caripuna gave his first and only concert in Rio de Janeiro.

Percival Farquhar had actually planned to have three concerts in the federal capital: one at Catete Palace, and two others at the Rio headquarters of the Brazilian Chamber of Commerce. The concert at Catete—given the hostility of Rondon—had to be canceled; and the schedule for the Chamber of Commerce, curtailed to a single performance—to be attended by a still impressive audience of congressmen, ministers, leading journalists, renowned intellectuals, and President Hermes da Fonseca himself.

The reaction of the Positivists was violently negative and left Farquhar feeling irritated. As a good American, he enjoyed novelties; he fondly recollected the impression made upon him when—still a young boy—the Siamese twins, Chang and Eng, were presented at Platt's New Music Hall, in California. But Brazilians seemed oddly disinclined to indulge themselves in this type of phenomenon. In an open letter, released in all the major newspapers, the Positivists accused the American of ridiculing the "authentic patrimony of Brazil, by transforming a helpless Caripuna Indian into nothing more than a circus animal." What piqued our Quaker the most, however, was the idea that he might for the first time in his long career as a quintessential bamboozler suffer a loss in a deal: the boat passage for the Indian and his instructress (true, she was a tasty little heifer) and the cost of their accommodations here in the capital (hers especially) were adding up to quite a sum of money.

In the end, the concert at the Chamber of Commerce was

383

poorly attended, passing virtually unnoticed because the main Carioca "show biz" attraction continued to be the recent arrival of Victoria Perez, with the Vaudville Company of Lisbon, warbling maxixis and declaiming lascivious verses of a strongly symbolist bent. In the handbill that Percival Farquhar had printed at his own expense, to be distributed before the performance, was reproduced, nearly word for word, the original discourse delivered by Dr. Lovelace when he had first presented Joe back in Porto Velho; but not even that mawkish brew seemed to move the Brazilians! Following the concert, the president acted rather weary of the whole thing and observed only that the Indian had dropped several bars from the overture to *O Guarani*. A columnist who hid behind the pseudonym of "Pepper Malagueta" wrote a couplet for his daily, commemorating the disaster by dubbing the Indian:

The clumsy pianist whom only a gringo could not see
Was using both feet where his hands ought to be.

Yet Farquhar would soon recover from the frustrating event. Ten days after the concert fiasco he was sought out by an appreciative fellow patriot, Mr. Lawrence Halle, a New York shipper who wanted to put forth a business proposition. Halle was a personal friend to the manager of Barnum's American Museum, the renowned creation of Phineas T. Barnum which specialized in extravaganzas featuring freaks and curiosities. Since Halle was accustomed to making regular trips to far-flung countries around the globe, Barnum's manager asked him to be sure and bring back anything he might run across in the course of his travels that he thought would fit the museum's bill. Halle was certain that Farquhar's Indian pianist was just the thing.

The Quaker and the shipper hit it off from the very start, and together sweetly reminisced over the many marvels already presented at Barnum's American Museum. In the end, Joe Caripuna and his teacher, Consuelo Campero, were turned over to the merchant, under contract, whereby Percival Farquhar would enjoy thirty percent of all revenues to be earned by the act, in addition to a tidy remuneration for all his expenses in bringing the two thus far from the Amazon.

The Bolivian girl and the Caripuna were shipped to the

384

United States and arrived in New York harbor sometime in December of 1911. It was particularly cold in that bustling metropolis and the sidewalks of New York were blanketed by falling snow. Joe took ill almost immediately and had to be hospitalized for the next two months. When he was finally released in February, he went back into intensive training, making his debut in the spring of 1912, with a thoroughly appealing performance. In addition to toeing the American national anthem, he managed to finish—to the delight of his enchanted audience—the "Minute Waltz" by Frederic Chopin, in thirty seconds. Miss Campero first walked on stage and executed the piece in accordance with the timing originally suggested by the composer. Then Joe appeared, and an immense stop-clock was lowered onto the stage, whereupon he toed the same piece to the ticks of the giant chronometer and the rowdy cheers of a delighted auditorium.

Joe Caripuna died of syphilis in 1927.

On the seventh of September 1912, without the knowledge or approval of the Brazilian government, the Madeira-Mamoré Railroad was finally inaugurated.

By 1912, Amazonian rubber had already lost its international monopoly to the English plantations in Asia.

By 1912, the Madeira-Mamoré Railroad had, in effect, ceased to have any purpose for its existence.

In 1916, the Brazilian government paid the Farquhar group the sum of *(reis)* 62.194:374$366, although the intrepid entrepreneurs were actually asking a total of *(reis)* 100.223:281$372 for their trouble.

By the original contract the Brazilian government had committed itself to paying—in accordance with the group's own economic projections—the sum of *(reis)* 47.682:058$402.

In the court action initiated by the Farquhar syndicate against the Brazilian government that year, the following Brazilian jurists decided in favor of the Farquhar group: Ruy Barbosa, Clóvis Bevilácqua, Sanchos de Barros Pimentel, and Inglês de Sousa.

In 1966, at the decision of Juares Távora, minister of transportation, the Madeira-Mamoré Railroad was closed down and sold for scrap to a businessman from São Paulo. It is not known what sum of money was paid.

On the eleventh of July 1927, a poet wearing a hat, a dark jacket, a shirt with cuff links and a tie, white pants and nondescript socks and shoes, sat on a rail of the Madeira-Mamoré and smiled. In the photograph the poet is still smiling. It's a rather gray photograph with little contrast. The sky is an ashen pulp and the jungle a horizontal stain. The poet was smiling because he had every reason for doing so—he was a happy man. Actually, only part of his face is clearly visible in that worn-out photograph: just the tip of the nose and the mouth opened to a smile. He has on a hat with a soft brim—probably to protect his head from the midday sun—and he's smiling. The photograph was taken, there in Porto Velho, at exactly twelve-thirty. It's for that reason that the shadows blend into the objects around him, and it's probably why the poet is seated with only one buttock on the track. By noon, the metal rail must have been rather hot—burning up, as a matter of fact. Yet the poet smiled, because two yellow butterflies had entered the frame of the picture and were fluttering about him just as it was taken. But the speed of the film was rather low, which transformed the butterflies into whitish blurs: one on the shoulder of the poet and the other covering his right hand, which he had just placed firmly on the rail, probably to raise his buttocks a few centimeters above the heat of that shining metal.

In 1927, the Madeira-Mamoré Railroad was in perfect running order. Yet its locale was not one to attract many visitors, much less poets. In the photograph there are two white stains in the corner of the image. Who knows? They may well have been yellow butterflies. But only the poet could answer such a question. Unhappily, he is dead. The poet was named Mário de Andrade.

There are hundreds of photographs of the Madeira-Mamoré Railroad, many photographs taken by fine professionals. Much better than the photograph where Mário de Andrade is still smiling.

The following day, in 1927, Mário de Andrade walked along the railroad tracks as far as Guajará-Mirim. He made some interesting discoveries along the way. A Pacaá-Novo who dreamed of being a telegraph operator, so he could marry a white woman and become civilized. Reaching the town of Guajará-Mirim, he went into a latrine, where he noticed a

386

curious text instructing the *seringueiros,* or rubber gatherers from the region, in the civilized use of that particular sanctuary. Around there, they seemed to take the word CIVILIZED very seriously. The latrine was the property of the GUAPORÉ RUBBER CORPORATION. Later, the poet had the chance to watch the Barbadian women in their colorfully flowered bonnets filing up and down the streets of the village. That same night, he did not wish to attend the ball with Dona Olívia Penteado, the coffee baroness, and the other ladies. Instead, he went out into the moonlight.

Today, it is difficult to surmise what the poet must have felt in the moonlight of Guajará-Mirim. Perhaps the poet was overwhelmed by contradictory feelings, wary of those discreetly romantic situations that the moonlight seemed to invite. Who knows whether he didn't actually feel something pitiless and cruel in his surroundings, especially since only a man of great sensibilities, such as he, could have found himself in Guajará-Mirim, on that night in 1927, filled with doubts and contradictions. Later, the poet would ask in his diary:

> Why did I come here!... What's the point of all the international casualties, drowned in the din of the locomotive, who show up here in the guise of Chinese, Portuguese, Bolivians, Barbadians, Italians, Arabs, or Greeks, trading their lives for a few pounds-sterling. Every conceivable shape of the nose and color of the skin has walked down these streets, gone to bed with a slight fever one night and awakened the next morning in the nevermore.

"Awakened the next morning in the nevermore" is one hell of an expression, O My Poet!

So much foolishness. Life's way, perhaps.

Ah, what a beautiful land is our Brazil, where an author who writes in a neo-Latin tongue can compose an entire novel filled with Anglo-Saxon names. And where there once was a locomotive called Mad Mary, Marie Folle, María Loca, Maria Louca, Mad Maria, Mad Maria, MAD MARIA!

A Hindu laborer was hammering a rail to a eucalyptus tie with a vigorous but mechanical motion. He was a man of

387

repulsive aspect because his nose was deformed and his fingers eaten by leprosy. Further up the line, Barbadians were laying additional rails that were being brought to them by teams of ten men each. Whenever the Barbadians approached the vicinity of the Hindu, the latter would stop working and move out of the way to give a wide birth to the Negroes. It was almost routine: the Hindus making sure they kept their distance from the Barbadians, often dropping their tasks and trotting off diffidently, to avoid any confrontation until the Negroes had passed.

The group of ten Barbadians happened to amble past a gathering of Hindu workers who, as usual, reacted fearfully. The Barbadians were also being provocative, hurling insults that were more or less understood by the pariahs, since they all now spoke a bit of English.

From the front of the tender loaded with pit-coal, Harold Appleton was eyeing the behavior of the Barbadians but without spotting any guard in the vicinity. He knew that that alone was enough to cause a fresh row. The locomotive, stationed on the other side of the bridge over the Abuná, puffed her dark clouds of heavy smoke imperviously into the air.

All along the railway bed that extended beyond the bridge, activity was feverish as Hindus worked to finish securing tracks to sleepers with flat, cadent hammer strokes. Still farther ahead, the Barbadians continued to lay the rails in place.

Richard Finnegan walked along the line of construction with his team of medics. His shirt was already grimy with sweat, opened down the front to reveal a chest reddened by the sun. He walked slowly—he might have been out for a stroll— observing without interest all that was happening around him. He consulted his watch from time to time, to see if he could yet minister the daily ration of quinine. He was no longer accompanied by security guards, for the medics were now armed with Winchesters, along with the small bottles of pills packed in the wire balings. The time refused to pass, but our Finnegan was in no great hurry. It mattered little to him that the Barbadians continued to provoke the Hindus, forcing the latter to interrupt their work at every turn. Still, even the patience of the Hindus had its limits, if only to be proved by the number of daily fatalities.

One Hindu worker on this particular day, perhaps more

emboldened than his brethren, refused finally to interrupt his labors or step aside at the approach of the Barbadians. Still, they passed him by, carrying a rail, practically trampling him in the process. The fellow was kicked and struck across the arm, but the doctor had not noticed because he continued to study his watch. Seeing the injury to their companion, several of the Hindus, however, waited for the Barbadians to lay down the rail and went over to them. They exchanged a few words, which were met with laughter from some of the Barbadians. One skinny Negro, crusted with mud, stepped up to a Hindu and punched him. Immediately, the altercation generalized and the physician, awakening from his reverie, began to shout for the medics. They arrived on the run at the site of the commotion, but their presence was not perceived by any of the men involved in the fighting. They were too busy rolling on the ground, kicking up the dust, and murdering one another. The physician attempted to intervene but was shoved about and even took a random punch from one of the Barbadians, which momentarily landed him on his back. His face was aching and a homicidal rage took hold of him. He scrambled to his feet and drew his pistol.

"Stop fighting, I tell you!" he screamed.

The fight, however, grew more and more ferocious.

"Stop it you sons of bitches! Stop it! I warn you, you'll pay dearly!"

Finnegan knew that they would not listen to his haranguing. He gripped his pistol tighter and flared up at the medics standing behind him, holding onto their Winchesters.

"Look at you!" he shouted at them. "What are you doing? Just standing around?"

The medics watched him, astonished.

"Enough of this," he screamed, turning back to the melee.

He began to shoot his pistol into the air while letting fly with an occasional kick at the men rolling at his feet as he reloaded. Still, none of brawlers responded to either the shots or the blows— they were numb with hatred, the identical hatred that had just possessed the physician in its irrational way.

"Open fire!" Finnegan ordered, turning once again to his medics.

The youths pointed their weapons at the free-for-all, but with no great conviction behind the gesture.

"I tell you shoot the sons of bitches!"

"You mean fire on them, sir?" one of them asked, unable to believe such an order.

"Exactly, you idiot! Fire! Shoot! Pour some lead into these sons of bitches!" Richard Finnegan continued to scream, his chin still stinging with pain.

The lads looked at one another in terror, aimed their rifles and opened fire at point-blank range. Barbadians and Hindus, hit indiscriminately, began to fall like dolls. The carnage was brief. Immediately the men stopped fighting, got up on their feet—wounded, scratched, bruised, and tattered—and placed their hands upon the back of their heads.

The physician, still wielding his pistol, stalked around the group of terrified men, shouting insensately:

"I could finish off the lot of you, sons of bitches!"

Finally, the engineer appeared and grabbed hold of Finnegan, who was still waving the gun menacingly. The maddened physician tried to wrench free of his grip but Collier twisted his arm and managed to knock the weapon out of his hand, then shook him by his shirt lapels.

"Good gracious, man, have you taken leave of your senses! At this rate you'll liquidate my entire labor force!"

Three men were still writhing on the ground, seriously injured. Six were already dead from the volley of the Winchesters. Their blood eddied through the dust, seeping into the earth and disappearing under the railroad ties. Finnegan rubbed his hand on his aching chin, staring at the engineer. The Englishman shook his head, and our Finnegan read in the gesture a tinge of irony. He couldn't care less: the ironies, the taunts, the impudence of Stephan Collier no longer reached him, which was a pity.

He picked up his pistol, wiped the dust off and replaced it in his holster. The sweat bathed his sunburned chest. Finnegan felt tired. The most he was capable of feeling now was tired, profoundly tired, since only fools could bother with anything beyond the art of staying alive.

Manaus, 1977–1980

AVON BARD DISTINGUISHED LATIN AMERICAN FICTION

AUNT JULIA AND THE SCRIPTWRITER Mario Vargas Llosa	63727-8/$3.95
CANEK: HISTORY AND LEGEND OF A MAYA HERO Ermilio Abreu Gómes	61937-7/$2.50
THE CELEBRATION Ivan Ângelo	78808-X/$2.95
THE DEAD GIRLS Jorge Ibargüengoitia	81612-1/$2.95
DON CASMURRO Machado De Assis	49668-2/$2.95
DORA, DORALINA Rachel de Queiroz	84822-8/$4.50
EL CENTRAL Reinaldo Arenas	86934-9/$3.50
THE EMPEROR OF THE AMAZON Marcio Souza	76240-4/$2.95
THE EX-MAGICIAN AND OTHER STORIES Murilo Rubião	69146-9/$2.95
THE EYE OF THE HEART Barbara Howes, Ed.	00163-2/$4.95 US/ $5.95 CAN
THE FAMILY OF PASCUAL DUARTE Camilio Jose	01175-1/$2.95
THE GIRL IN THE PHOTOGRAPH Lygia Fagundes Telles	80176-0/$3.95
HOPSCOTCH Julio Cortazar	00372-4/$4.95
THE LOST STEPS Alejo Carpentier	46177-3/$2.50
MACHO CAMACHO'S BEAT Luis Rafael Sanchez	58008-X/$3.50
MULATA Miguel Angel Asturias	58552-9/$3.50
P'S THREE WOMEN Paulo Emilio Salleo Gomes	86256-6/$3.50
PHILOSOPHER OR DOG! Machado De Assis	58982-6/$3.95
SERGEANT GETULIO Joao Ubaldo Ribeiro	67082-8/$2.95
SEVEN SERPENTS AND SEVEN MOONS Demetrio Aguilena-Malta	54767-8/$3.50
ZERO Ignacio de Loyola Brandao	84533-5/$3.95
62: A MODEL KIT Julio Cortazar	57562-0/$3.50